I0710372

TEMPEST HALL

BOOK TWO OF THE LANIS CHRONICLES

V. BRICKER

K. NOBLES

BRICKER
NOBLES

To strong drinks, summer nights, and good friends

CONTENTS

Acknowledgments

Where to begin?

We had a few beta readers this time around. Their comments made this book that much better... and closed a few plot holes. So, to Brock, Kit, Nicole, Rhett, Robin, and Simona, thank you for your feedback.

Shelley—our amazing editor—has made a huge difference in getting Tempest Hall finished. I know it wasn't easy to deal with the opinions of two different authors during the editing process, but you made it look easy. Thank you for all your hard work on getting Tempest Hall ready to publish.

And finally, we offer our sincerest thanks to our ever-patient readers. Writing this book was not a fast process and many of you have eagerly awaited its release. Your support makes it all worth it.

PROLOGUE

The Sword and Scimitar, a bar that Khalil frequented in Markaza, the capital city of Alkhazai, was not as busy as it normally was. On most nights, the place would be flooded with patrons, but either it was still too early for such a crowd, or the coming monsoons had the city's people working extra hours to make up for the time lost during the rains. Settling himself at his usual table, Khalil watched a few people drift in and out of the front door. He caught the bartender's eye, and the older man promptly poured a tankard of ale for him and sent it over with one of the serving women. Her long black curls bounced as she approached, and she set the drink on the table in front of him, white foam spilling over the side. The woman gave him a wink and turned away, sauntering back to the bar. Khalil grinned as he watched her leave, enjoying the sway of her hips, before picking up the tankard and taking a long drink. It was cool and brisk on his parched throat.

Loud giggling drew his attention to another table near him. A man with a face identical to his sat between a woman dressed in tight clothing that accentuated her curves and a man, who looked like he'd crawled up from the city's underbelly, with a narrow face and dark eyes that constantly darted around the room. The woman fawned over his twin brother, Jamal, leaning in to whisper in his ear and making him chuckle. He looked up and his eyes met Khalil's, which were the same golden amber color as his. Jamal grinned at him and turned his head to whisper something back to the woman, making her blush.

Khalil raised his eyebrows, amazed at the ease with which his brother operated. Jamal had no difficulty accepting his lot in life and enjoyed himself thoroughly. He and Jamal had grown up together, and while they looked alike, Khalil felt that they had radically different personalities. Jamal seemed to revel in what they did, but Khalil... Well, he knew what they were doing wasn't right. Sometimes, he felt so disgusted with himself that no amount of drink or soft flesh could wash the feeling away.

But what could he do about it? Maybe it wasn't what he wanted in life, but he didn't have the power to change it. This was what the gods had given him.

Khalil felt a prickling sensation on the back of his neck. It was the feeling of being watched. He lifted the tankard to his lips again and glanced around the room. There were a couple of the usual girls, who were leering and whispering to each other, as well as patrons that he'd seen before. Two older men with long graying beards played chess in the corner, another larger man in his thirties sat at the bar, and a local merchant and his son worked on their ledgers at another table in between drinks. There was Jamal, of course, but he seemed too occupied with his companion to pay him any mind.

The only person he didn't recognize was the bard

playing softly on a sitar at the back of the room, but that wasn't odd. Performers constantly flowed through the area. This woman was not from Alkhazai or the surrounding countries, with her fair skin and hazel eyes. She was older than him by a few years and was dressed in the styles he'd seen coming out of the west, with their layers of clothing that covered most of their bodies. It was unfortunate for her that she wouldn't make much coin with such a sparse crowd.

He glanced at the leering girls and caught the eye of the pretty dark-haired one dressed in red. Lowering her eyelashes seductively, she grinned at Khalil, then wove her way toward him. She added an extra sway to her step, making her hips that much more pronounced. Setting his drink on the table, Khalil returned her grin, and the feeling of being watched passed. The woman slid into the chair next to him and placed one manicured hand on his arm as the bard struck up a more stirring tune. He downed the rest of his ale in one long pull and waved to the barkeep for another. With a glance down at her bosom, he leaned into her, the heady scent of poppies flooding his senses. Khalil let himself be carried away in the melody and in the wandering hands and exposed flesh of the woman attending him.

Several ales later, the dark-haired woman had moved to sit in his lap, and another woman with large eyes and skin the color of charcoal had joined them. It was getting late, and he should probably have started making his way back to his quarters, but he was enjoying himself too much. Maybe he would stay the night. Places like this always had rooms available for private entertainment, for a price.

Khalil stood, the two women still hanging off him. They grinned, and his dark-haired companion started tugging his arm while the other urged him along from behind. They pulled him toward the stairs that led to the bedrooms on the upper floor. He didn't resist.

It wasn't uncommon that he found himself in this position after a mission, after a kill. After such an assignment, he wanted to feel alive, to feel anything. He wanted to drown out the voice that nagged at the back of his mind, telling him that he could be more than the prince's dog.

The bard's eyes met Khalil's as he surveyed the room one last time. The greenish-brown gaze seemed to pierce through him, and he was certain that she had been the cause of the feeling he'd had earlier. She frowned slightly before turning away, giving a placating smile to a man who leered drunkenly at her.

Khalil felt another gentle tug on his shirt and push on his back. He grinned at his companions and let himself be led up the stairs, to the pleasures that awaited. If the bard was a threat, he could deal with her

later. He was an assassin, after all.

Khalil stood amid a crowded, dusty square. It looked like a market in Markaza, a place he could have walked through over a hundred times and never taken notice. As he considered his location, the rooftops and buildings he knew so well materialized out of the darkness beyond the square, matching his thoughts of the city beyond the little market. The wind kicked up the sand lining the street and flung it into the air, tinting his vision with a goldish-brown cloud and obstructing the view of the city again.

Through the haze, he spotted a man and a woman watching him. The man was tall and muscular with an angular face and hair like the sun. The woman was slender and pale with long black hair. Their eyes met his for a moment, and Khalil felt as if he was being crushed under the weight of those gazes. It was hard to breathe. His instincts screamed to either fall to his knees before them or run, but he stood rooted to the spot, unable to move. Then, as abruptly as it came, the feeling was gone. The woman placed a hand on the man's shoulder and gave a small shake of her head, then the two figures turned and faded once more into the dust.

What is going on? What am I doing here? Khalil's thoughts seemed to hang in the air around him.

Looking at all the people crowding the market, he felt the hairs on the back of his neck stand up. Something was very, very wrong. The people didn't seem to be going anywhere or doing anything. Normally, a place like this would be filled with colorful stalls selling anything the heart could desire and shouts of haggling men and women loud enough for the gods to hear. These people didn't seem to have any purpose to their movements, and the only sound he could hear was his own heavy breathing as sweat gathered in his palms. They were silent in their vigil, as silent as the dead.

They stopped milling about the square and all turned to stare at him at the same time, ashen-skinned under the fine coating of sand and grit.

"Who are you?" Khalil asked, and his voice echoed like he was in a long hallway. But that wasn't right. He was outside, wasn't he?

A heavyset man stood in front of him; dried clumps of dirt flecked his dark beard. Blood soaked the front of the man's tunic from a small hole in his chest right above his heart. With a chill, Khalil recognized him as a merchant who had failed to pay the prince's tax. The man had been one of his first kills.

Khalil jumped back from the merchant, but his back hit the stone wall of the building. With a sinking feeling in the pit of his stomach, he looked more closely at the people surrounding him—men, women, and even a few children— each bearing the marks of the mortal wounds he had dealt them. They did not speak. They did not move. They only stood and stared at him with dull, lifeless eyes and blood-less faces.

Panic began to creep in on him, closing his throat with an unfamiliar sense of suffocation, even more intense than what he'd felt under the gaze of the mysterious man and woman. He reached for his sword, but it was gone. Even the dagger he kept tucked up his sleeve was missing. Khalil balled his hands into fists, ready to strike. What else could he do? Everywhere he turned were the ghosts of those he'd murdered.

"Khalil," a small voice whispered from behind him.

He whirled around and came face to face with a woman, a woman who was only a distant memory. She had long, silken, dark-brown hair and darkly bronzed skin that was exactly like his own. She looked up at him, the golden eyes he remembered in his dreams swimming with sadness. He didn't remember her being shorter than him, but he hadn't seen her since he was young. The woman was beautiful, as beautiful as she had been in life.

Khalil's arms dropped to his side, and he felt tears welling up in his eyes. This couldn't be real. "Mama..." he said softly.

She reached out her arms, and suddenly he was a child again, enveloped in the safety of his mother's embrace, all panic forgotten. The fear and shame he'd felt moments ago melted away until all that remained was a great sadness within him. "Mama…" he said again, sobbing into her shoulder as she embraced him. She patted his hair as they sank to the ground, holding one another.

Khalil's mother was dead. She'd been dead for nine years. She couldn't be here, but he found it hard to grasp logic when she was there, holding him, comforting him. He could feel the warmth of her body as he pressed himself against her. "I've missed you," she said, kissing the top of his head, and her voice sounded pained.

He had to get her away from here, away from the ghosts that had come for him. With great effort, he pushed himself away from her, but still grasped her arms. Khalil glanced around them, looking for an escape from the market, but he needn't have bothered. The square had disappeared along with the remnants of the lives he'd destroyed. They were in a small, dark room that was covered in dust and furnished plainly with only a bed and wardrobe. He knew this place too. It was the room in which his father had kept his mother prisoner.

She stared at his face, examining every line and contour as if she were committing it to memory. "Khalil, I've come to give you a second chance."

"A second chance?" he asked, voice hoarse.

"Redemption," she clarified. "Another chance to live."

"What are you talking about? How are you here? I thought you died. Did Father hide you from us?" There were so many questions he wanted to ask her, but she just shook her head and smiled sadly.

Leaning in to kiss his forehead, Anakah's lips were soft and warm against his skin. "Seek the monks at Ta'Shela. Earn your redemption, my son." She pulled back from him, a single tear sliding down her cheek. Then she reached out her hands, gently covering both of his eyes, the world around him slowly going dark.

"I'm sorry, Khalil..."

Khalil awoke with a start. The room was pitch black, so dark that he couldn't see the barest hint of his surroundings. He shook his head and groaned. It felt like thousands of tiny sprites were hammering away at his skull. Rolling over, he felt soft, warm skin brush against his arm. Memories of the night before came flooding back to him as the woman let out a quiet "Mmmm..."

He reached over her to the bedside table that he was sure had been there earlier, feeling for something to use as a light. He remembered seeing an oil lamp. Was it still the middle of the night? Why was it so dark? His hand bumped something cold and hard, knocking it over. The item tumbled to the ground, the sound of breaking glass banishing the remaining drowsiness he felt. That must have been the lamp.

The woman gasped and knocked his arm back as she moved away from him. There was the sound of a door opening and quick footsteps coming toward them.

"Levana! Are you all right?" came another voice that he recognized, the dark-skinned woman that had shared his bed. He still could not see anything. Shouldn't the hallway have been lit? Why hadn't she brought a light with her? It was hard to imagine either of his companions moving around so deftly in the dark.

"Yes," said the woman called Levana from very close to Khalil. "It just startled me. Are you all right, my..." she trailed off with a squeak. He felt the blankets flail around him and a loud thump as she moved. Khalil patted the bed around him, but she had gone.

"What? What is it?!" He reached out for her but only grasped at air.

"Your eyes!" she shrieked, her voice piercing into his skull.

Khalil winced, recoiling from the sudden flare of pain in his head, as the sound of their feet hitting the floor echoed through the darkened room and then faded moments later as they ran from him.

He felt his face. Nothing felt different, yet he still couldn't see anything. Not even the barest hint or indication of the bed or blankets that surrounded him. A cold feeling settled itself at the bottom of his stomach as his heart rate sped up. How had the women been able to see well enough to leave the room so quickly when he was still enveloped in this blackness?

Khalil heard the light thumping of booted feet and then a softly whispered curse. The door creaked as it swung closed, and a small clinking sound told him that the door latch had been slid into place. He reached around for his sword and dagger, but like in his dream, they were gone. The sigh of released breath and the subtle creak of leather told him that he was not alone. Soft footfalls began to approach him.

He leaped out of bed in an instant, hands up, ready to defend himself from this new assailant. Unarmed combat was not his specialty, but even without his weapons, he could still prove deadly.

The footsteps halted and the intruder let out a scoff. "Oh, stop that," came a strangely accented woman's voice, sounding impatient. There was another rustle of cloth before something light hit Khalil's hands. He batted it aside and resumed his defensive stance, listening for approaching footsteps. None came. Only another creak of leather and an exasperated huff.

"You have an undeniably fine physique, but considering the circumstances, it might be best if you clothe it." The voice was amused, but Khalil didn't drop his guard.

Her statement broke through his confusion. Could this woman see him? A cold panic began to crawl up Khalil's spine as he remembered the words spoken before. *Your eyes…*

"Who are you?" he asked, resisting the panic as best he could and trying to appear calm. He was met with only silence. Khalil was about to repeat the question when he heard the thumps of heavy footsteps out in the hall. A knock sounded at the door. The woman's boots crossed the room quickly, the latch lifting with another click and the slight creaking of the door.

"What's going on up here?!" an outraged male voice demanded, the innkeeper who'd been serving him drinks the night before. "Levana was in hysterics when she woke me!"

"What do you think is going on up here?" the female voice said back coolly, the strange accent she had earlier was now gone. "Surely, you're used to the sounds of a good tumble 'round here," she spat. "It's not my problem if your whore is too stupid to know the difference between the sounds of flaying and rutting. Now, get the hell out of my face before I find you something to scream about!" The door slammed shut.

There was silence in the hallway. After what felt like an eternity to Khalil, the heavy footsteps retreated, and the woman let out a relieved sigh.

"Well," she said, accent back. "Perhaps you'll consider

getting dressed now?" The boots slowly approached again. Her voice took on a soothing tone. The same tone that he'd heard used to calm a frightened animal. "It's all right. I'm here to help you."

Khalil dropped his fists and blinked rapidly, still unable to see. He was beginning to understand what was wrong. He was... he was blind. There wasn't any other explanation for why the world was still dark when it wasn't for this woman or the others. How had this happened to him? Why had this happened to him?

"Who are you?" he whispered with a tremor in his voice as she guided him back to the bed to sit and handed him his clothes. As she helped him dress, he struggled to fight down the panic that threatened to overwhelm him.

"You can call me Rhyn. I was playing down in the tavern last night." She was the bard he'd seen watching him. Rhyn moved away and, moments later, handed Khalil a long strip of leather that was his belt and weapons. He could feel his heart pounding heavily in his chest as she helped him dress, the anxiety making his hands shake violently.

Once he was fully clothed, Khalil asked the question that his mind had been screaming at him the entire time.

"What's happened to me, Rhyn?"

Wisps of clouds scurried across the face of Thaera, briefly dimming the moon's radiance. The Phoenix glanced up at the silver-tinged sky as she crept along the high stone wall, wishing this could have been a darker night. Still, the moon's position beyond the stronghold's wall offered a deep shadow for her to follow, and for that, she was grateful.

Her bare fingertips dragged lightly over the familiar grit of the rough-hewn stones, and she was careful not to let her close-fitting dark clothes snag on their jagged edges as she slowly moved forward. Even though it had been over ten years since she'd last set eyes on Tempest Hall, long before joining the Nightingales of Morigael, very little had changed about the place. The surrounding farmsteads and villages had seen better seasons, but the guards that patrolled the walls kept in the same patterns and numbers as they always had.

She and her apprentice, Winna, had discovered as much when they surveyed the place a few weeks ago. Technically, it was Winna's responsibility as this was the girl's final mission before becoming a "sparrow," an initiate of the Nightingales. Still, the Phoenix had checked the burgeoning agent's work. With stakes this high, what good mentor wouldn't?

A scrape of metal on stone came from above, and the Phoenix froze in her tracks. Moving only her eyes, she double-checked her position to see that she was still fully concealed in the wall's shadow. The moonlight on the frosty meadow in front of her cast the shifting guard in relief. He had both arms extended overhead. The man fell back into his former stance with a loud sigh and another scrape and clatter of metal armor. A few heartbeats and slow breaths later, assured that the guard had only been stretching, the Phoenix resumed her course.

Once she was at a relatively safe distance from the restless guard, she fell back into her mental review of the situation. She and her apprentice had been sent to gather information on the recent political maneuverings of Lord Darian Castellus, head of one of the most influential Tanalinian families. There had been rumblings that the Tanalin lord was forming an alliance with another, but nothing that could be confirmed yet. The Tanalin Empire had become less powerful over the last century. Although Morigael and Tanalin had a respectful, if grudging, peace treaty, it was always wise to keep an eye on the stability of neighboring countries, especially with Castellus lands being so close to Morigael's borders.

Winna had found that Lord Castellus was currently in residence at Tempest Hall, the ancestral home of House Castellus and one of the northernmost holdings in the Empire. Eager to complete her final mission as an apprentice, Winna had set out immediately with the Phoenix acting only as a silent observer. However, after a couple of weeks of reconnaissance, it became apparent even to the casual passer-by that Lord Castellus was planning something. He was building up his supply stores and hiring more servants, which gave Winna the perfect opportunity to infiltrate Tempest Hall by posing as a maid.

Nine days had passed since the Phoenix had watched her apprentice disappear beyond the broad wooden gates. Two days ago, Winna missed her scheduled check-in. She was supposed to have left the castle after receiving her weekly pay under the pretense of taking money to her family. Servants flowed freely enough in and out of the keep, but the Phoenix knew all too well that sometimes plans needed to change.

This evening, when Winna still hadn't emerged from the castle nor sent a message with any of the other servants who lived in the village, the Phoenix had known something was wrong. It was tempting to speculate *what* had gone wrong, but the bottom line was that Winna was still an apprentice, and the Phoenix was still responsible for her. She could have left her apprentice to her fate, but she knew what Lord Castellus would do to the young woman to get her to talk, and she couldn't allow that to happen to Winna.

Her only mission now was to get Winna out safely. Fortunately, the Phoenix needed no ruse to enter Tempest Hall. As with many ancient Tanalinian castles, Tempest Hall had a secret escape tunnel that the family could use if the walls were ever penetrated and the keep overrun. Not many of the castle staff would know about it, so, with any luck, it wouldn't be heavily guarded.

Rounding the base of a turret, she spotted the slight depression in the earth and the shadow that marked the end of the passage. It was tempting to make a dash for it, but to reach the shelter of the tunnel, she would have to cross several paces of well-illuminated ground. There were no shadows cast from the parapets, and she knew that the roaming guards would pass by this area at some point. Forcing her limbs to relax, she leaned back against the cold stone of the wall.

As she waited, it was difficult to keep her mind from wandering. The last time she was here had been a long time ago, during a harsh winter, one with much more snowfall than this one. It would have been impossible to use the tunnel without someone finding her tracks in the deep snow, but this winter had been unusually dry, and the Phoenix had no fear of traversing that way. She wondered idly when the passage might have been used last. It was possible that it was no longer passable, but if it was, it was the best chance to get into the keep unnoticed with what little information she had of Winna's disappearance. If it wasn't, she'd have to retreat and come up with something else.

She was jarred from her thoughts by the faint crunch and rustle of the roaming guards above approaching her position. She forced herself to remain relaxed and wait for them to pass.

Once she could no longer hear their footsteps, she turned to face the wall and slowly walked backward a few steps until she could see just over the merlons. As expected, no helmets or spears could be seen. She took another step back, then another, and another until she was confident that no one could see her. Then, turning, she hurried to the mouth of the passage and, with one final glance at the empty wall, ducked inside it.

The Phoenix paused to allow her breathing to slow and her eyes to adjust to the darker environment. Soon, she could see the faint features of an iron door that stood a few feet farther down the tunnel.

She knew the door would be locked, but she tried it anyway, pressing gently against it at first and then with the weight of her whole body. As she had expected, the door didn't budge. With a resigned sigh, she pulled a vial of oil out of a pouch on her belt and crouched so that the keyhole was at eye level. She peered into the hole but was not surprised to see nothing in the darkness. Fishing into the same pouch, she pulled out a syringe and, after pulling the cork out of the vial with her teeth, poured the oil into the metal tube. Inserting the tip into the hole and slowly depressing the plunger, she dribbled a few drops of oil into the keyhole. It would work its way into the mechanism and make it easier to manipulate with her tools, having the added benefit of keeping the tumblers quiet. With a lock that probably hadn't been opened in ages, it was better not to take chances.

After replacing the cork and returning the vial and syringe to their pouch, she pulled back her hood and fished a couple of slim lockpicks from within her long dark braid before setting to work on the keyhole. She knew that no one outside the tunnel could hear her, let alone any guards on the wall, but the click-clack of the picks sounded as loud as falling trees to her. Fortunately, either the oil had done its job, or the lock was in better repair than she had feared, and the tumblers fell into place after a few moments.

Returning the picks to their place in her hair, she stood and drew in a deep breath. She stepped forward to press against the door again, as gingerly as possible this time. After a few moments, the hinges protested with a low groan, and the door began to open. The Phoenix continued her steady pressure until the opening was just wide enough for her to slip through.

Once inside, she removed the vial of oil and syringe from the pouch again, this time dribbling a generous amount on the door's hinges. She took an extra moment to smear the oil into the joints of each. When she cautiously pushed against the door to close it, she grinned as the door swung silently.

Turning her back to the entrance, she faced the yawning darkness of the tunnel. The air was cool, musty, and slightly damp, as disused underground structures often were. The only sound was her own shallow breath. Satisfied that she was alone, she considered her next steps.

She had contemplated how to navigate the passage as she had been planning her rescue mission but had not decided on a course of action. In her experience, even the best-laid schemes often went awry, and since she did not know what she would find within the keep, she would have to rely on her well-honed instincts to adjust to whatever situation awaited her. She could have brought a lamp or candle with her but had thought better of bringing any tools or equipment that were not strictly necessary. Extra things always risked being dropped or jangled about when one was trying to move stealthily, and a guard could've heard the strike of flint and steel to produce a flame.

That left her with two options. One was to traverse the tunnel with no light. That, however, would be slow-going, and if someone had been safeguarding the passage against intruders, she would be blind to any deterrents that might be in place.

The other option was magic. She was no mage and couldn't produce a flame, but she knew a few tricks that helped her in her work from time to time. The Phoenix couldn't sense the more subtle spells the way a trained wizard would be able to, but the few charms she was capable of she could do well. The magic needed here would be minute in scale, unlikely to draw the notice of whatever court magician was currently in residence. Still, it would require almost all her attention and could leave her vulnerable to anything not readily visible. Either way, some of her senses would be limited.

She stretched out a hand to one side until her fingertips contacted a grimy stone. Then, as though the wall would give her the answer, the Phoenix stood there for a long moment before giving her head a small shake and allowing her arm to fall.

Resolved, she opened another pouch at her waist and retrieved a tiny canister no larger than her thumbnail. She pried the lid off, being careful not to drop it. With the open canister pressed firmly between her hands, she rotated them until she felt the powder inside it dust her left palm. Rotating her hands again, she lifted her left hand away from the canister, careful not to disturb the fine layer of dust that now coated a small circle on her palm.

In the blackness of the tunnel, she raised her dusted palm near her face and closed her eyes. Concentrating, she pictured the radiance of Thaera. Then she envisioned that same glow in her hand, as if she were holding one of the twin moons, before opening her eyes again. The thin film of dust on her hand started to glow with a soft silver light. Pleased, she turned her palm to face down the length of the tunnel and began to move forward, careful to keep the image of Thaera in her mind's eye the whole time.

Now that she had light, she could see that the tunnel was constructed of bricks that arched overhead and disappeared into the earth on either side near her feet, just as she remembered. It was too narrow for two men to walk abreast, and a tall person would risk scraping their head on the bricks above. The light only illuminated a few paces before her, but the tunnel sloped slightly upward from where she began.

Unexpectedly, she faced no obstacles as she made her way down the tunnel. Cobwebs coated the ceiling and there was no indication that anyone had traversed this area for a long time. The Phoenix scowled to herself. As meticulous as the Lord Castellus she knew was, she was surprised he'd let such an important asset fall into disrepair. But then, she doubted anyone but the most loyal of guards knew about this egress from the castle, and he certainly wasn't going to maintain it himself, so it shouldn't have been surprising it was in such a state.

After several minutes of steady progress, she began to make out a rectangular shape ahead of her, another door. This one, she recalled, would lead into one of the castle's storerooms just off the kitchen. With a grateful thought to Thaera for sharing her light, she let go of the mental image she had been holding and let the passage fall back into blackness. Reaching out to touch the brick wall with her fingers, she made her way to the door in the darkness.

When her hand brushed the cold metal of the iron door, she quietly crouched again to peer through the keyhole. Flickering light illuminated the room beyond in a soft yellow glow and cast long shadows behind barrels, crates, and bags of supplies. Though it appeared that the area immediately in front of the door was clear, a stack of crates blocked her view of the rest of the room, including the source of the light.

Pulling away, she turned her ear toward the lock. She could hear the intermittent crackling of a torch. She also heard what she thought sounded like faint snoring. After listening for a full minute, she heard no new sounds and was sure there was at least one person sleeping in the storeroom. Though having at least one guard posted at this tunnel was to be expected, it complicated things but was nothing she couldn't manage.

There was one other problem. If the court wizard under Castellus's employ were to place a magical ward on a door to alert his lord to intruders, it would be this one. The Phoenix didn't sense anything, but that didn't rule it out. But she had already made her decision before she had come here. She *would* rescue her apprentice. Even if this door was warded, if she could find Winna quickly, they could escape before anyone was the wiser, or if her intrusion was discovered, they could hide in the confusion and find another opportunity for escape. With all the new faces coming in and out of the castle, she hoped no one would think her presence odd.

Standing, she reached for her vial again and dressed the hinges and lock in the same way she had the outer door. This time, she moved slowly and carefully to minimize the clicks and rumbles of the locking mechanism as she picked it. It took a little more time but proved no more complicated than the first lock had. After a few minutes, the door swung open soundlessly with only a light tug on the ring above the keyhole.

Once she was in the room, with the door closed firmly behind her, the Phoenix crept forward, peering around the closest stack of crates. There, on some sacks of grain near the entrance to the kitchen, lounged a sleeping guard. His helmet was pushed forward, obscuring his eyes, and a small dribble of drool at the corner of his mouth caught the light from the nearby torch.

Despite the comical tableau, the Phoenix's expression was grim as she surveyed the rest of the storeroom. The Lord Castellus she'd known would never have suffered such dereliction in his staff, but he couldn't keep eyes on them all the time. She, for one, was glad. While she had no problem disposing of any guards who got in her way tonight, she did not relish the thought. Leaving no trace of her passing would be impossible if the bodies of guards were found in the morning. And these men were paid to serve the ruling lord. They were not her enemy.

She made her way across the room, careful to keep supplies between her and the sleeping guard in case he awoke. If he did wake, she would have to hide so he wouldn't see her or silence him before he made a sound. The man twitched a few times, but he seemed to be in a deep sleep and didn't stir at all as she crept along. When she reached the door, she kept her eyes on the guard as she lifted the latch with both hands. The door began to open, and she tore her gaze from the man to survey the kitchen.

A bright glow illuminated the room from the banked fireplace that dominated the empty kitchen. With a backward glance at the slumbering man, the Phoenix crossed into the kitchen on silent feet and closed the door softly behind her.

From there, there would be only two places that Winna would likely be: the servants' quarters or the dungeon. Had the girl been in the servants' quarters, meaning she'd not been discovered, she would have been able to get word to her mentor at the appointed time. Those same quarters would also be full to the brim with all the extra help that Lord Castellus had hired. More eyes and ears to take note of a darkly clad figure wandering the halls. No, it was more likely that Winna had been found out and imprisoned.

Believing that to be the case, the Phoenix headed to the dungeon.

As she made her way out of the kitchen and through the familiar corridors, she remembered the last time she had walked these halls. As with the castle's exterior, little inside Tempest Hall had changed over the years. The servants' passages were still as dark and frigid as she remembered. The same smells permeated the air, the same tapestries hung on the walls, and the guards she dodged—three sets of them—seemed to roam the halls in the same patterns and intervals.

Not everything was the same, though. *She* was not the same.

Realizing she had stopped short in reflection, the Phoenix shook her head as if to shake off the tendrils of memories that threatened to intrude on her consciousness. Such thoughts in the middle of a mission were dangerous, but as much as she told herself that this was just another job, like the countless ones before it, this place still affected her emotions in a way that facing down certain death never had. It made her feel small and worthless again, though it had been a long time since either of those things was true. Leaning on her years of training to steel her resolve, she continued toward her destination, brushing off the remnants of memories that threatened to overwhelm her.

The heavy door that led to the dungeon stood at the end of a dark hallway. She examined the torch in the sconce next to it and could tell by the remnants of warmth that it had burned out or been put out sometime recently. There are a multitude of reasons that the source of light could have been allowed to die, but she decided that it was to her advantage as she oiled the door and picked the lock. If anyone decided to glance down this corridor, she would not immediately be recognized as an intruder.

Opening the dungeon door, she was greeted with the foul odor of blood, unwashed bodies, and human excrement that characterized such places. She could just make out the steps leading down to the cells. Moonlight filtered through the few grates that were set high in the dungeon walls. Knowing that any additional light she used now would be visible outside through those same grates, she closed the dungeon door and carefully picked her way down the stairs and toward the soft glow of torchlight below. This was a part of the castle that she had not visited before, so she was careful as she descended into the unfamiliar space. Hand hovering over the hilt of her dagger, she neared a bend in the stairwell and held her breath as she listened.

There was a heavy breath and a sigh from someone below, most likely the jailor on shift. That meant there was at least one prisoner below, but was it Winna? The Phoenix reached into another pouch on her belt, pulling out a small, three-inch mirror. As she crouched low on the last step, she slowly pushed the mirror around the bend.

There were two men in heavy armor sitting at a small table. The jailor's head was turned away from the stairwell, with his chin resting on his palm as he looked at the playing cards held in his other hand. The man sitting across from him was dressed in the same armor, examining his own cards closely. He pulled a card from his hand and set it on the table, causing the other guard to swear loudly.

The Phoenix slowly pulled her mirror back, trying not to draw attention to the movement. She took a deep breath and shut her eyes, clearing her mind and reaching deep within herself for the power to fuel the spell she wanted. It took a full minute to gather the energy she needed. Eyes snapping open, she began to hum a few notes of a soft melody, using her magic to carry the tune to the ears of the guards. The lullaby beckoned them to sleep, pulling at the tiredness they were surely feeling at the late hour.

She focused on the guards, feeling their eyelids droop as the magic took hold, their heads slumping as they drifted off to sleep. The haunting tune reverberated off the stone walls, causing a ghostly echo to fill the dungeon.

Two thuds broke into her consciousness, and she risked a peek around the corner. Both men were asleep, bodies splayed over their playing cards. The spell wouldn't last long, but it should be long enough to free Winna and get back to the tunnel.

Rising to her feet, the Phoenix carefully stepped out of the stairwell, watching to see if either man stirred. Neither did.

The Phoenix immediately began inspecting the cells that stood in a long row opposite the keep's outer wall. As she had surmised, Thaera was beaming her pale light through the barred grates. That and the torchlight by the table the guards were sleeping at allowed her to see clearly in the dank and shadowy dungeon. The first several cells were empty, save what looked like a tattered blanket in one and buckets in a couple of others. As she approached the end of the row, the Phoenix wondered if she had been wrong to dismiss the servants' quarters so quickly.

A new smell reached her then, sour and putrid. It was enough to make her gag. She hadn't suffered many injuries in her twenty-seven years, but she'd seen enough to know the stench of an infected wound. At the same time, she spotted a shadowy mound lying on the floor of the last cell.

The Phoenix rushed over and immediately set to work on the lock, all stealth abandoned.

Fingers shaking, she forced herself to take a few steadying breaths and spring the lock. As she worked, she glanced at the form lying motionless on the floor. The figure was covered in tattered rags that must have once been a blanket and a servant's uniform, stained with dirt and filth to the point that it looked black in the dim light. It was impossible to make out any features of the poor soul, but every instinct she had cried out that it was Winna.

When the door finally swung open with the grinding of rusty metal, the Phoenix rushed in and fell to her knees next to the prone figure. Carefully, she lifted the blanket and brushed aside locks of dark hair to reveal Winna's broken and swollen face.

"*Winna*," the Phoenix choked out.

The girl opened her one good eye in the dimness and struggled to focus. Lips cracked and bleeding, her mouth moved as if to speak, but no sound came forth.

The Phoenix quickly assessed her apprentice's injuries. Aside from her battered face, she had suffered lacerations on her arms and legs. Every inch of skin that was visible was either a mottled yellow and purple or an angry red. Greenish puss oozed out of the open cuts, being the source of the smell. It was clear from the swelling and discharge that those wounds were being allowed to putrefy. Winna gasped twice as her mentor passed her hands over the girl's body, revealing at the very least a broken leg and cracked ribs on her right side.

Fresh hate burned in the Phoenix's chest as she moved to lift the younger woman. Delicately, she managed to get an arm under her apprentice's and behind her shoulders.

Winna was still trying to speak, so she leaned closer to hear.

"Trap," the girl rasped.

As the Phoenix drew back, she felt her limbs lock in place, and, a moment later, a light bloomed overhead so brightly that it temporarily blinded her. She struggled to escape whatever magic held her. She could feel it wrapped around her so tightly, it was suffocating. Winna slipped out of her arms and fell back to the ground with a groan of pain.

Suddenly, in the dungeon that had been silent moments before, came the painfully loud clatter of several heavy footfalls coming to a stop behind her. Unable to move, she dropped to her knees next to the crumpled form of Winna, her back to the door.

"Korynne," said a man's harsh voice.

Terror shot through her heart like an arrow, and if she hadn't been held in place magically, that one word would have immobilized her. Her hate became a cold thing that sent ice flowing through every vein in her body.

"Father."

CHAPTER

TWO

*V*aran's Refuge wasn't the nicest establishment that Turin had ever stayed in. Not even close. But Varan, the inn's namesake, had a reputation for discretion, and discretion was necessary in Turin's line of work.

It was one of only three inns in Mattina, and probably the cheapest among them if he had to judge by the well-worn and poorly cared for furnishings. The small port town was known to cater to sailors on their way to grander destinations, men who didn't care where they spent their coin. Mattina was located in Tanalin on the coast of the Silver Sea, so the locals welcomed men and women sailing from the eastern continent from places like Omer and Alkhazai. It was a long journey but one that was made often enough to keep the town in relative profit, even considering its distance from Tanalin's capital farther to the south.

Turin liked Mattina. It was quiet and peaceful, aside from the occasional drunken brawl. He'd traveled here a few times before, but this journey brought him here almost a month ago to await travelers that still had not arrived.

They were supposed to have been here by now, but sea travel could be unpredictable sometimes, so Turin had paid for another two weeks' stay at *Varan's Refuge*.

At the moment, his limbs flowed through a series of stretches to pass the time, sweat trickling down his neck as he transitioned into the next form. Yin'dar was a martial art that the monks in Omer practiced, focusing mostly on power stances and grabs. While Turin preferred to fight with a sword and shield, he found going through the forms helped to clear his mind. Plus, it was good exercise.

With any luck, today would be the day he would meet the small group of people he was supposed to guide to Morigael at the docks. From what he knew prior to his arrival in the port town, they'd been sailing across the Silver Sea and required an escort to Griffin's Bluff, a fortress nestled in the mountains that surrounded Morigael. Khalil, a man he had worked with previously, had sent his order a message a few months ago, and they had sent Turin out to meet the travelers. Apparently, there was someone of interest that Khalil had stolen out of the clutches of the wizards in Zo'rahn. The blind man never ceased to impress him, but that was quite a feat.

Turin belonged to the Knights of the Realm, an order of knights based in Morigael. Among their many duties, they assisted those seeking sanctuary from other places in Lanis. Mostly, these people were refugees and escaped slaves from the southern and eastern countries, but, sometimes, they included politicians and nobles running from collapse and ruin. Maybe this was one of those cases.

There had been quite a commotion when his order had first been contacted by the monks, but he hadn't been privy to the details. It was likely then that whoever this person was, he or she was not his typical charge.

A sharp tapping brought Turin out of his thoughts. Slowly, he straightened, wiping the sweat out of his eyes, and looked over at the window.

A handsome black hawk was sitting on the windowsill, staring at him through the glass, waiting to be let in. It ruffled its feathers, and Turin caught sight of the long leather tube strapped to its back.

Turin blinked, silently praying to Aganor that he was not seeing what he thought he saw. That could only be a messenger hawk. There were few people who knew he was staying here, just the Lord High Commander and a handful of other knights. No one else knew where he was or how to reach him and getting a letter from the Commander in the middle of a mission was never good.

The bird cocked its head to one side and tapped on the glass again with its beak.

"I'm coming, I'm coming," Turin muttered, and he strode across the room and pulled the window open, the cold air outside hitting him in the face and chilling his sweat-slicked skin. "Dammit, what now?"

With a great flap of its wings, the hawk hopped in through the window and landed on the table against the wall. It eyed Turin as if it were going to fly at him with its sharp beak and talons. Then, after a look from the winged beast that he assumed meant the bird had decided he didn't look tasty enough for the trouble, Turin stepped over to the table.

After a moment's hesitation, Turin reached over the bird, pulling a rolled-up piece of parchment from the tube on its back. He really didn't like these messenger hawks, and the scar he had on his left forearm was a constant reminder of that fact, but it was how his order sent and received messages, so they were unavoidable. He turned the parchment over in his hand and spotted the dark-red wax seal that held the scroll together. The image of a compass with tiny birds replacing the letters for north, east, south, and west was pressed into the wax. The birds were so small that if the receiver didn't know to look for them, they would never have noticed that difference.

Turin raised one eyebrow as he broke the seal. This message had come from the Emissary, not the Lord High Commander. The Commander must have informed him where Turin was.

On the surface, the Emissary oversaw foreign affairs in Morigael and was a member of the King's Council. The council consisted of four men whom the king trusted to help him run the country. The Emissary met with foreign dignitaries and wrote the laws concerning trade with Morigael's neighboring countries.

But in the shadows, the Emissary played another part. Turin wasn't quite sure what exactly it was, but he knew that the organization called the Nightingales reported to the man.

Getting a message from him directly could only mean something had gone terribly wrong.

The hawk flapped its wings irritably at Turin. It probably wanted food and water after the long journey, but he ignored it as he hurriedly unrolled the small scroll, his eyes flashing over the words as they were revealed.

Lightbringer,

The Phoenix has gone missing at the House of the Storm. Your new priority is to investigate this disappearance and take flight if needed. Proceed with caution. The night is not your friend.

—E

He read through the message two more times before

setting the paper on the table and sighing. Then he poured water from a jug into a bowl and unwrapped a partially eaten loaf of bread for the bird.

The Phoenix, he considered as he watched the bird eat. Turin thought he knew who that was referring to. The Nightingales, a network of contacts out of Morigael, worked alongside his order from time to time, presumably all for the betterment of their country. Whatever that meant. They were spies, envoys, investigators, and anything else the Emissary needed them to be. The Nightingales were spread all across Lanis, providing information about what other countries were doing. If he remembered correctly, each of the high-level operatives was named after a bird, so the Phoenix must be one of them. He didn't know much else about the Nightingales, but he'd helped them before.

The House of the Storm had to be Tempest Hall, an old castle in northwestern Tanalin. It was at least a week's ride from here, but it was late in the winter months, which in this area usually brought excessive snow and rain. "Take flight" meant that the Emissary assumed that extraction would be needed, and the last part told him that it would be dangerous. The Emissary loved speaking in code, and if someone had intercepted this message, they would gain little knowledge from it.

As he thought, he pulled a light linen tunic over his head. It was time to head over to the harbor, to see if his charges had finally arrived. This additional mission sounded like it would need to be handled discreetly, which was not one of his strengths. Turin would not shy away from this task, but he wasn't an idiot.

No, he was going to need help with this, and he knew exactly who to ask.

THREE

The deck of the *Westwind* was alive with activity, men and women rushing about, shouting orders at each other as they made the small sailing ship ready to enter the port in the Tanalin town of Mattina. The caravel had been moored just outside the channel of the small but busy port all morning. Everyone aboard was restless, and there was a sense of relief rising from the sailors when the harbormaster finally granted them permission to make berth. After months at sea, the last few hours had felt like an eternity when their destination was in sight.

Squinting in the afternoon sun, Sophie imagined she could see the people of Mattina going about their business—men readying ships, loading and unloading cargo, people running errands on the streets, and young children sprinting in every direction. She imagined the firm ground beneath her feet, experiencing something, anything, other than the constant rocking and bobbing that came with being on a boat for so long. The *Westwind* was a nice ship, but she had been trapped on it for ages and was more than ready to be on solid land once again.

It shouldn't have taken as long as it had to sail to the western continent, but the main mast had been broken by a bolt of lightning as they'd left the shores of Omer. The ship had been attacked by a wizard who wanted to take her back to her family, and they had barely managed to get away. The journey leading up to that grand escape had been just as fraught with danger, and if she counted the days correctly, she had now been gone from her old home for almost four months.

Sophie tilted her head back and closed her eyes, breathing in the salty sea air, the sunlight warm and inviting on her skin. She'd climbed up onto a large pile of crates so that she could get an unobstructed view as they approached the town. From her perch, she listened to the bustle around her as a cold breeze lifted tendrils of her red hair away from her face. After her last sunburn, she knew she shouldn't sit out there for too long, but she preferred the feeling of the wind in her hair and the sun on her face to the musty darkness belowdecks.

Not long ago, she had been a favored apprentice to one of the seven Viziers, the ruling council of a country called Zo'rahn, and a member of one of the most powerful magical families there. She had been a mage in the "Land of Mages," as some people called her home country, and had spent the better part of her eighteen years of life training to be a wizard in a society that revered magic users. Forsaking everything that had been bestowed upon her—her family, the training, the privileges—Sophie had run away from it all, fearing how she'd be asked to use her abilities.

Some five months ago, Sophie had stumbled across a very dangerous artifact in the Vizier's possession that responded to her touch when it had not for any other. The first time she'd held it, another apprentice had died. Vizier

Lau'ren, a man she had trusted as the head of her family to care for and protect her, had been determined to test her abilities with other similar items, regardless of who was hurt because of it. That was when she'd decided to leave.

If the time spent sailing across the Silver Sea felt long, the day that she'd fled Tanzar, the capital city of Zo'rahn and her home, seemed like a lifetime ago. She'd walked for miles and miles through the plains, trekked through forests and mountains to an ancient monastery, and fled across an endless desert. Her friends said her choice to leave was an act of bravery, but Sophie didn't know if she believed that.

So many had suffered for her, and that guilt wouldn't allow her to think the actions she'd taken were anything but cowardice.

"Sophie! Are you listening?" demanded a voice from the deck below her.

Sophie jumped and almost lost her balance. Grabbing the edge of the crate on which she sat, she steadied herself and looked down at a young woman with long auburn hair, an angular face, and delicately pointed ears. By appearance, one would guess her to be about the same age as Sophie, but her people aged more slowly than humans. The Anai had her fists on her slender hips, and a pout marred her tanned face. She was dressed in her armor, something Sophie hadn't seen her wear since they'd been at sea, and her sword was in its sheath strapped to her back, with the hilt peeking out over her right shoulder. Eolisti was a skilled swordswoman and the first friend she'd made since she left her home. She'd appointed herself as Sophie's *Vendarii*, her protector, when Sophie had sought aid at the Anaiian city of Elasariin. Eolisti had been an invaluable friend and ally.

"Sorry," Sophie said, unsure how long the Anai had

been standing there. "I was lost in thought. What were you saying?"

Eolisti huffed with more exasperation than Sophie suspected she actually felt and hauled herself up the pile of crates, sitting next to the mage. She leaned over and nudged Sophie with her shoulder, making her smile. "I was *saying* we need to find some real food when we finally get to the docks. If I have to eat one more butter bean, I'm going to throw that cook overboard."

Sophie gasped in mock outrage as Eolisti launched into a rant about the ship's limited fare, using words like "boring" and "bland" so often that it reminded her of when she'd first met the Anai back in Elasariin. Eolisti had been curious about the outside world and desperate to see it for herself—so desperate that she'd decided to accompany Sophie without the permission of her people.

The Anaiian woman was everything Sophie was not. She was bold, confident, and not at all shy about speaking her mind. If there was something Eolisti wanted, she pursued it until it was hers... or until she got bored.

As they were talking, a male Anai emerged from belowdecks, the sunlight glinting off his white-gold hair. Elindiir, the ambassador from the Anaiian country of Nemethy, had caught Eolisti's attention with his elegant mannerisms and striking features as soon as she'd laid eyes on him back in Omer. Sophie and Eolisti had met him at an inn before they'd set sail, and, as luck would have it, he, too, was traveling through Tanalin on his way home. Eolisti had spent much of their time at sea close to Elindiir, asking him questions about all the places he'd been. She was infatuated with Elindiir, and Sophie thought it was adorable how she followed him around like a duckling.

Eolisti trailed off as she eyed the ambassador with a speculative look. Today, he was dressed in a flattering shade of blue. "We should ask him to join us on the road," she said as she watched him. "He told me that he usually travels through Morigael on his way back home." She turned big green eyes on Sophie, and it took all of the mage's willpower not to laugh. The Anai looked like a child asking her mother for a new puppy.

They'd talked about—and with—Elindiir many times in their days aboard the *Westwind*, and Sophie had been a part of the conversation that Eolisti was referring to. What Elindiir had actually said was that he'd been to Morigael on his way to Nemethy before, but he usually just hired a ship to take him straight there. Recalling a map she'd seen of the western continent on which they were about to make landfall, she suspected the most direct path for Elindiir was nowhere near the route they were taking. Their destination was Morigael, and it lay to the north while Nemethy was farther west.

"That could be fun," Sophie responded with the same answer she'd given the last time Eolisti suggested this. "But we should probably check with Khalil first."

Eolisti snorted derisively but didn't object. Khalil, their mysterious guide, had been assigned to be their escort by the monks at the monastery of Ta'Shela, high in the mountains between Omer and Zo'rahn. The Anai had been suspicious of the man from the moment they'd met. It was hard to blame her. Sophie herself had been suspicious. Khalil spoke little, and when he did speak, he managed to somehow be both direct and infuriatingly cryptic at the same time. The first time she'd met him, she'd sensed something different about him that she couldn't quite put her finger on. She could use her magic to sharpen her sense of the metaphysical, and there was something about Khalil's condition that was unnatural.

Her cheeks flushed at the memory of the night when her suspicions had gotten the better of her, culminating in her pulling back the hood of Khalil's cloak, revealing eyes clouded over with a milky, golden hue. He was blind, but that fact didn't seem to hamper him much. There was some sort of magic at work in him that allowed him to better use his other senses, she could sense as much, but for all her studies, she had no idea what it was.

Sophie scanned the deck of the *Westwind* until she spotted Khalil. His hood was thrown back now, as it had been since they boarded the ship, and his usually serious demeanor was gone. He had changed some in the time since they'd met. Now that they were out of the east, Khalil seemed more relaxed and friendly. At least to Sophie. He and Eolisti were still cold to each other, but he was more forthcoming than he had been in Omer.

As she watched him, Khalil laughed at something Captain Alvar said, and it occurred to Sophie that under his gruff exterior, he was quite good-looking with his almost-black hair and bronzed skin.

She flushed even harder. Where had that thought come from?

Sophie shook her head just as Eolisti said softly, "I wish Joel were still here."

That immediately sobered Sophie. Unbidden, memories of Joel flooded her mind—his easy smile, his laugh, his willingness just to listen and comfort. Joel had worked for the monks of Ta'Shela, just as Khalil did. He hadn't really wanted to join them on the journey from the monastery to the port in Omer, but Eolisti had insisted that they have someone they trusted with them in case Khalil "tried anything funny."

But Joel had betrayed Sophie. He'd sold her to a man named the Spider. The thought of the cruel mercenary made her blood run cold even now.

In the end, Joel had a change of heart and helped Eolisti and Khalil free her from the Spider's clutches, sacrificing himself in the process.

A thick wooden shaft with black fletching stuck out of his side. Blood stained his clothes from where the bolt had hit him and trickled down his tunic to drip onto the dock. "Take care of them, Khalil."

The image of his last fight brought tears to her eyes. No matter what had happened before, in the end, he really had been her friend. May the gods have mercy on him.

Sophie leaned her head on Eolisti's shoulder. "I miss him too," she murmured.

The ship lurched forward, and the crates they were on swayed dangerously. One of the sails had been unfurled and was swiftly carrying them toward the channel into the port. As they climbed down, sailors bustled to their various stations, and the blond-haired Captain Alvar began barking orders.

The crew seemed to move with renewed purpose and speed, while those not on duty lurked in out-of-the-way corners of the deck. All eyes were drawn to the rapidly approaching coastline with apparent longing. Sophie could relate. She was as impatient to be off the *Westwind* as she'd been when she'd first boarded it.

They leaned over the taffrail, and the anticipation was palpable in the air as land drew ever closer. A few sailors stood ready with the mooring lines and others moved the gangplank into position. Finally, with a bump that shook the entire deck, the ship came to a stop, and with the expediency born of months at sea, the men set the gangplank in place, securing the ship.

Sophie jogged back down to her cabin below to grab her things, all fitting neatly into a pack that had been enchanted to hold more than it should, and hurried back. Eolisti and Khalil were waiting for her when she returned, Eolisti with her shield and a large bag of supplies slung over her shoulder. Under his cloak, Khalil wore the same dark-red half robe with its closely fitted sleeves and gold sash that he'd worn when she'd met him. He pulled the hood of his cloak low so that all that was visible of his face was from the tip of his nose down. Sophie knew this was to hide the fact that he was blind, but when she'd first seen him, it had reminded her of a Soulless—an undead monster that she had thought was a myth. Now looking at him, all she saw was the man that had helped and protected her.

One side of his mouth tilted up in a lopsided smile as she approached. "Ready?" he asked, the deep rumble of his voice making her return his grin, though he couldn't see it.

"Yes," she said, looking at Eolisti, who nodded back to her. Dodging the sailors that carried barrels and crates off the ship, they walked down the gangplank and onto the docks. Sophie resisted the urge to skip and twirl once her feet left the *Westwind*. Barely.

She looked around. The port city of Mattina must not have been all that large. There was only room for four ships to dock at a time. All the docks were full, and people milled about, unloading crates and barrels from the ships while men with ledger books took inventory. As her eyes scanned the town and the men and women going about their various tasks, Captain Alvar stepped up beside her.

"If you are going to be traveling through here, you

should know that Tanalin isn't in great shape right now," he said with a sigh. "There was a blight earlier this year, and the government isn't doing much to help its people. They're having to bring in food from other countries." He gestured back toward the ship where his men were bringing large crates onto the deck while others offloaded them. "Most of our cargo is crops and dried meats from Omer. Some crews are gouging the citizens of Tanalin with exorbitant prices." He scowled as if the thought left a bad taste in his mouth. "But there just isn't enough food to go around, so some people resort to theft. Be careful."

"Doesn't Tanalin have wizards that can cure the blight or otherwise help provide for the people?" Sophie asked. Why weren't they using their magic to help the people? Back in Zo'rahn, a crisis like this would have been a priority for the Viziers.

Alvar smiled bitterly. "This place is far from the capital. The emperor doesn't care much about folk like this. All his mages are making sure that he and his family are comfortable and that the capital is thriving." He sighed again. "It's been a problem for a while now, but there's nothing we can do about it."

"It's dangerous to stay here for too long," Khalil said from right behind Sophie, startling her. She hadn't noticed him approach. "Alvar's told me all about what's happening here."

"And we came here anyway?" Eolisti asked coolly. The Anai was more tolerant and trusting of Khalil than she had been back in Omer, but she still didn't seem to like him. "Why didn't we sail straight to Morigael if it's so dangerous?"

Khalil's mouth pressed into that familiar thin line that it did when he was dealing with Eolisti.

The captain answered her. "Because this was where I was sailing to." He raised an eyebrow at Eolisti, daring her to challenge him. "I wasn't going to change course just because it would have been more convenient for you."

With that, Alvar turned back to the ship and ascended the gangplank, directing his crew in offloading their cargo.

Elindiir moved past the captain as he left the ship, a travel pack slung over his shoulder. "This is where we part, then." He smiled first at Eolisti, then at Sophie. "I have a horse waiting for me here, and it's a long ride to the next city." Eolisti frowned and looked down. Elindiir's smile faded, and he looked out over the town, then back at the younger Anai. "I'm sure our paths will cross again." His tone was gentle, and the look he gave her was full of a tenderness that almost seemed too intimate for Sophie to witness.

Eolisti's cheeks flushed, but she refused to look up into his face. "Yeah, I guess." From the sound of it, she must have talked to him already about coming with them. By his words, Sophie guessed he had declined.

He opened his mouth as if to say more, but shook his head instead. "I need to leave before nightfall." Elindiir leaned over and pressed his lips to the top of Eolisti's head. "Azorah willing, I will see you again. Morigael is not so far from Nemethy. Perhaps you can visit once your business is concluded."

Eolisti grumbled something inaudible and Elindiir sighed. He pulled a long gold chain that had been tucked inside his tunic over his head and placed it around Eolisti's neck. There was a pendant at the end of the chain—three interlocking circles, the symbol of Azorah, goddess of fate. Then he walked past them and into the crowd at the docks, disappearing among the people waiting beyond.

Sophie wrapped an arm around Eolisti and squeezed. "It will be okay," she said soothingly. "We'll meet him again."

The Anai glanced at her, cheeks still pink, then away again, but she did not pull out of Sophie's embrace.

"Khalil!" a voice called out over the bustle around them, making the two women look up.

A man was approaching them, waving one arm above his head with a big grin on his face. Sunlight glittered in his shiny black hair, eyes the color of the greenest spring grass focused on their hooded companion. He wore a belted leather tunic and traveling cloak, but judging from his size, he was well-muscled underneath the heavy clothes. A longsword hung from his belt, as well as a variety of pouches, but he seemed friendly.

"Khalil!" the stranger shouted over the heads of the people around him again. "You're late!"

Sophie glanced over at Khalil. A frown that mimicked the look he sometimes had when dealing with Eolisti flashed across his face, then he smoothed his features.

"It's all right," he whispered and folded his arms across his chest.

"Who are you?" Eolisti demanded as her hand drifted to the hilt of her own sword now resting in its sheath on her side. Either she'd not heard Khalil or was ignoring him. Judging by how she'd treated him in the past, Sophie guessed it was the latter.

As he approached, the stranger fixed the Anai with a grin that lit up his already attractive features. He had the squarest jaw Sophie had ever seen and was very tall. "My name is Turin," he said, dipping into a courtly bow once he was a few paces away. The man didn't seem intimidated by Eolisti's attitude. He straightened and gave her a playful wink, then turned his attention back to Khalil. "It's been a while, Khalil."

Khalil's lips pressed into a thin line before he said, "Not long enough," which caused the other man to burst out laughing. Khalil looked even more petulant as Turin's rich laughter echoed all around them.

Sophie and Eolisti exchanged a look. What was going on?

"Excuse me," Sophie said as Turin's laughter died down. "But I'm a little confused. How—?"

"Who are you and how do you know each other?" Eolisti said over her.

The tall man smiled down at Eolisti, not seeming to take offense at her tone. "Khalil and I have known each other for a long time. But I'm here because I'm your guide to Morigael," he said, then surveyed the two women. "You must be the one who escaped from Zo'rahn," he said to Sophie. "Interesting. You don't look Zo'rahni. Are you some sort of ambassador? What country do you come from?"

Sophie felt heat rush to her cheeks. "I *am* Zo'rahni," she said indignantly. She'd dealt with people thinking she was not from Zo'rahn all her life. Sophie had inherited her mother's bright red hair, gray eyes, and lighter skin, a look so different from the tanned complexion and black hair of her peers. She couldn't help the way she looked, but she'd been born and raised in Zo'rahn, and her father had been a member of one of the richest merchant families there. As a child, she'd been taken from her parents and adopted into one of the ruling magical families. It was traditional for children showing the aptitude to be adopted into a family that could properly train them, and she'd learned magic from the best wizards in the world. If that didn't make her Zo'rahni, she didn't know what would.

"All right, all right," Turin said, holding his hands up in surrender. "I meant no offense. What is your name?"

"Sophie," she grumbled, still irked by his earlier remark.

Turin bowed with a flourish and held his hand out to her. It took Sophie a moment of staring at it to realize what he wanted. She hesitantly put her hand in his, and he leaned forward to kiss her knuckles. "A pleasure, Lady Sophie."

"Okay. That's enough, pretty boy," Eolisti growled as Turin straightened.

Sophie glanced over at her companion. Despite her tone, Eolisti looked amused. She probably thought he was interesting.

Turin grinned at the Anai. He seemed to be genuinely enjoying himself. "And who are you, my lovely Anaiian friend? I'm afraid I wasn't given a lot of information about who exactly I was meeting." He glanced at Khalil. "The message was vague."

"My name is Eolisti, and I am Sophie's Vendarii." Eolisti raised her chin proudly. "I will protect her until she reaches her destination."

"A Vendarii!" Turin exclaimed, his eyes wide. "I've never met one of you before. Usually, by the time the assets get to this side of the Silver Sea, the Vendarii is long gone."

"Keep your voice down," Khalil hissed. He was scowling at Turin in a way that Sophie had never seen before. "We may be far away from those pursuing her, but there is still danger before us. We should get out of the open."

"Right you are, Khalil," the other man said, unfazed by their hooded companion's tone. "I've reserved a few rooms for us at an inn nearby." Turin winked at Sophie before turning away from them. "Follow me."

CHAPTER

FOUR

As the group made their way to the inn where Turin had secured their lodging, Sophie's eyes were drawn to the people and structures they passed. Row upon row of buildings lined the main thoroughfare. Most appeared to be well maintained, but too many had boards nailed up over windows and doors. Only every third or fourth one showed any signs of use, with a line of laundry hanging out an upper window here, the distinct scent of cooking fish there, or a couple of laughing children running in and out of an open door in some game.

More disturbing than the half-abandoned look of the town was the sight of the other children they passed. Little faces could be seen lurking in the shadows of alleyways, their hungry eyes staring at those passing by. A handful of others sat along the street, their palms outstretched in a plea for food or coin. Not even the ghost of laughter remained on those forlorn faces. Sophie shivered, and it had little to do with the chill in the air.

Before she knew it, she was walking toward one of the begging children, with one hand reaching into her unslung pack in search of a spare morsel. The only thing she found to offer the little one was a hard heel of bread. Snatching it out of her hands, the boy's eyes grew wide a moment before he tore into it hungrily. A shuffle of movement in the shadow of the nearest side street drew her attention to a cluster of youngsters looking on with longing.

Unable to turn away, Sophie opened her pack up fully, searching inside for anything more she could share, but there was nothing. She looked at the group of children and gave a sad shake of her head. Realizing that no more would be forthcoming, the pack of children began to melt back into the recesses of the byway, their faces downturned.

A sharp breeze lifted her cloak and made her shiver again. As she shouldered her pack and drew her cloak tighter, she was struck by the awful realization that many of these children would probably not survive to see the spring. The harvest couldn't have been more than a few months earlier, and if things were already this dire, there was likely little hope of relief for these people.

With a sad sigh, she turned back to see that Turin and Eolisti had stopped a few paces up the street and were waiting while Khalil had remained close to her, but at a respectful distance. He nodded at her as she approached, and as she rejoined them and the group resumed their course, she caught the last of a query Eolisti had been directing at Turin.

"...like this everywhere?"

"Not everywhere," Turin answered, "but too many places here in Tanalin. Some are much worse."

The Anai seemed both puzzled and disgusted with that answer, and Sophie found herself agreeing with those sentiments. She wanted to help all these children, but all she had was magic, and magic could only go so far. The energy that fueled spells had to come from either some living thing around the mage or her own limited strength. She could condense moisture from plants, or even the air in some cases, into drinking water, but could not turn a stone into bread. She could heal blighted plants that could later be harvested or make a fire to cook with, but she couldn't form those materials out of thin air. A base of sorts was needed to work her magic, and Sophie had nothing she could use to make food for these people. Even if she had enough food to fill every child's belly right now, there was nothing she could do for them in the long term.

It made her feel useless. What good was all this power if she couldn't use it to help those who needed it?

There should have been aid provided to these people. Tanalin had wizards. If she remembered correctly from her readings, it was home to a mages college. So why wasn't anyone helping them? Pursing her lips, Sophie tried to remind herself that those born with the ability to use the art were much less common outside of Zo'rahn, which practiced selective breeding to produce more wizards than any other country. Even with what Captain Alvar had told her, perhaps there were just not enough mages in Tanalin to help everyone.

Nearing the edge of the town, Turin abruptly turned and led them toward an especially shabby-looking building. The only difference it had from the abandoned buildings they'd passed was that the windows were not boarded. A weathered sign hung above the door from two rusty chains. Any paint that might have once graced the wooden plaque had long since peeled away, but Sophie could make out a carved picture of two foaming mugs and lettering below them that read "Varan's Refuge."

The big man opened the door of the inn and entered

without breaking stride. They followed him to a large common room that was empty and nearly dark, the only light filtering in through dingy curtains that hung over a few windows. In the dimness, Sophie could see that though the place was clean, the furnishings and walls were in nearly as poor a condition as the sign above the door had been. The varnish had worn away on the edges of the tables and there were missing panels on the walls. Embers in the hearth must have been the source of the acrid smell that hung in the air. They radiated a small glow, but not enough to illuminate more than the legs of the nearest chair.

At the sound of their entry, a middle-aged man emerged through a door behind the bar, his face lined with wrinkles and gray streaking his dark, scraggly hair. He held a lamp in one hand and a loaded crossbow in the other, his bushy whiskers twitching in irritation. Turin lifted a hand in greeting despite the obvious threat from the crossbow, still not bothering to pause or check to see that everyone was following. Seeing Turin, the older man relaxed his grip on the weapon. He watched as each person passed, and Sophie could feel his eyes until they were out of his line of sight.

It grew even harder to see as they walked halfway down a hall lined with doors, and up a set of stairs. Sophie spotted lamps hanging from sconces on the walls, but they were empty of any candles to light. She wondered if it was not just food that was scarce in Mattina.

A few rooms from the staircase, Turin paused to fish a key out of his pocket. He fumbled for a moment in the dimness, but soon swung the door open and gestured for them to enter.

Eolisti strode past Turin like she owned the place, dropped her pack at the foot of one of the room's two beds, and promptly plopped down beside it. Sophie followed but remained standing as she surveyed the room. It was clean but consistent with the rest of the inn. The curtain over the window looked to have been laundered recently but was covered in little holes. The unclaimed bed had lost a leg at some point and was now propped up on a fat log, but at least the sheets were neat, and the blankets looked warm. Maybe she could even get a bath. Cleaning herself hadn't been easy or convenient on the ship.

Turin cleared his throat from where he remained standing outside the door, drawing her attention away from her inspection.

"Ladies," he began as he set the room key on a little table just inside the door, "we'll leave you alone for a few minutes to get freshened up. I need Khalil's help…" Turin glanced at the hooded man in an awkward pause. "Getting horses! Yes, I need his help getting an extra horse. I hadn't realized we'd be a party of four, you see, so I didn't get us enough horses."

With that, he closed the door behind him. Sophie looked at Eolisti, who was swaying from side to side where she sat and staring at the wall across from her as if in a trance.

"That was odd," Sophie remarked.

Eolisti continued to stare but frowned a little. "Yeah, that *was* odd. You'd think with these people being professional rescuers and all, they'd be a little better informed."

Sophie snorted despite herself and went to sit next to Eolisti on the bed. "No, I mean it was odd that he wanted to talk to Khalil without us around. It makes me think that he's hiding something from us."

The swaying stopped, and Eolisti's gaze began to

sharpen until, at last, she turned and met Sophie's eyes. "Should we...?"

Sophie grinned, knowing what the Anai was about to suggest. "Yes, but we'll have to be smart about it. Here," she said, slipping out of her pack and rummaging through it for a moment before withdrawing a small bottle sloshing with a pink viscous liquid. When she opened it, a light scent of roses filled the air. With one finger over the opening, she turned the bottle quickly before righting it again, depositing a round drop of the oil on her fingertip. Her hands trembled with excitement as she tried not to spill the oil. Back in Omer, Sophie had not been able to use magic because the energy it left behind could have been used to track her. Even on the *Westwind*, she had kept the use of her abilities minimal on the off chance she was still being pursued. But here in Tanalin, she didn't have to fear the Vizier's men and could do magic as she pleased.

"I can use this to keep us from being heard, but we won't be able to hear each other since we'll both be under the spell."

Eolisti frowned at the drop before shrugging. "Shouldn't be a problem."

Realizing that the men already had a lead on them, Sophie wasted no more time. She wiped the tip of her finger across her lower lip, then used another drop to do the same to Eolisti. Once the bottle was secure, she focused on the sensation of the oil on her lip while looking at the shiny smear on Eolisti's mouth.

Technically speaking, she didn't need to use the oil to produce her desired magical effect, but it made things much easier. A wizard did not have to use items like this in their magic, but having a physical object to focus on took a small part of the strain of casting off her mind, and many other mages employed small tricks like this when they could.

Sophie imagined not being able to hear her breathing or that of her companion. She imagined that every step they took was a silent one and that even the rustling of cloth from their garments left no sound of their passing. Then she focused her power and willed her magic into the oil.

She could tell immediately that the spell was active, feeling the energy washing over her and sitting on her skin like a shawl, but Eolisti mouthed, "Did it work?" Or at least tried to ask it, but no sound escaped her lips. She broke into a wide grin. Spinning toward the entrance, the Anai grabbed the room key, and Sophie rose to follow her.

Once she locked the door behind them, Eolisti grabbed Sophie's hand and pulled her along down the stairs, that sharp Anaiian vision allowing her to see better than most humans probably could in the dim hallway. Sophie had used this spell a few times before to steal tarts out of the kitchen back at her family's estate, but, every time, it was disorienting to be moving but not hearing the sound of her own feet on the wooden planks. The other sounds around them seemed sharper. She could hear someone on the street calling out and the faint rustling of what she guessed was the innkeeper moving about in his backroom.

They emerged from the inn to fading daylight. A woman and a man walked down the street arm in arm, but otherwise, the road nearby was empty. Eolisti paused to look back and forth at the ground in front of her for a few moments before setting off at a jog. Sophie followed quickly at her heels as they rounded one corner of the inn, and then another to find themselves a few strides from a large barn. Mounds of dried grass could be seen through an upper window, and the young wizard heard a soft whicker through the large wooden doors that stood ajar.

Rather than approaching the front of the structure, the women circled around to the side and slipped between the rails of a small pen that connected to a smaller open door. Eolisti stopped just outside, her back to the wall, head cocked in concentration. Though the sounds around her were clearer with her own breath and heartbeat silenced, all Sophie could hear was the vague rumble of Turin's voice.

Sophie stooped low and began to move through the open door, but Eolisti's hand closed around her arm. She threw the Anai a questioning look, to which Eolisti responded with a shake of her head before dramatically drawing a foot back and kicking it out in front of her. Sophie just stared at her, still puzzled, until Eolisti pointed inside to where a horse stood with its back to them, placidly munching away at something. Right, the horse couldn't hear them either, so if she spooked it with her silent approach, not only would she alert the men to their presence, but she could also find herself with a hoof to her face.

Sophie shot a sheepishly grateful smile back at Eolisti and moved to flank the other side of the doorway. She concentrated harder this time, but still only heard the murmur of voices. Another glance at Eolisti told Sophie that her friend was clearly able to hear the conversation, but that gave her an idea.

As a young girl, one of the first spells she had learned was an eavesdropping spell. It was so simple, all she had to do was fuse her desire to hear what was being said with magic. On instinct, she focused on that power that lay inside her, waiting for her to call it forth.

"... will be glad to see you again."

"What's this really about, Turin?" Khalil asked impatiently.

There was a long pause before Turin let out a deep sigh. "I need your help."

"With what?"

Another period of silence followed before Turin responded, his tone reluctant. "Nightingale business."

"I'm already on Nightingale business." Khalil sounded annoyed. He seemed to hold Turin in a similar regard as he did Eolisti.

"I know, but this comes from the top. Someone important has gone missing, and I'm supposed to go find this person and bring whoever it is back if I can."

"That sounds like your problem, not mine."

A frustrated snort followed. "You don't understand. One of their most accomplished agents has disappeared, probably captured, and *I'm* supposed to sneak in and free them? Me? I'm great at a lot of things, but have you seen me 'sneak'?"

It was Khalil's turn to snort softly.

Turin chuckled before continuing in a more serious tone. "Look, I don't want to be asking you this either, but if someone like the Phoenix has somehow gotten into trouble, I'll *need* your help."

The two men fell silent. The seconds dragged by, and it was quiet for so long that Sophie decided to risk a peek. Standing on her toes to see past the resident horse's flanks, she spotted Turin with his back to her while Khalil stood facing the other man, his lips drawn into that firm line she'd come to recognize as deep thought, displeasure, or both.

"What am I supposed to do about my current charge?" he asked finally.

"We could figure something out," Turin said with a wave of his hand. "They could stay here until we get back, or maybe they could get to Griffin's Bluff on their own? The tall one looks like she knows her way around that sword."

Sophie glanced over at Eolisti. The wicked grin stretching across her face told Sophie that the Anai wanted to show the big man just how well she handled herself. Her own eyes crinkled in amusement before she realized what Turin's assessment of *her* must be. He'd barely said anything to her since they'd arrived in Mattina, but he must have thought that she wasn't able to take care of herself.

She glanced down at her small frame and delicate hands and couldn't help comparing herself to Eolisti for the hundredth time. It was true that the Anai was obviously the more powerful of the two of them physically. She was brash and confrontational, whereas Sophie was more cautious and thoughtful. But those were her strengths, she realized as she drew herself up in indignation.

Khalil's voice abruptly brought her attention back to the two men.

"I'll have to think about it."

"Great! We can figure out our next steps in the morning, after you've all gotten some rest. I'd like to be on the road as soon as possible so we can get this over with."

"I said I'll have to think about it," Khalil repeated, the irritation in his voice unmistakable.

"Of course, of course," Turin answered, his palms raised in surrender.

The men turned toward the open door, and with a start, Sophie waved to Eolisti that they should leave. Instead of going back the way they'd come, the two women sprinted around the opposite end of the inn, desperately trying to keep out of sight. Soundlessly they burst through the door and scrambled up the stairs. Eolisti herself fumbled with the key to their room, her lips moving in what, by the look on her face, Sophie assumed was swearing.

Once they were inside, Eolisti quickly swung the door closed, the sound reminding Sophie to undo the muffling spell. As soon as the spell dissipated, the room was filled with the sound of gasping as the two women caught their breath.

Eolisti grinned and leaned back against the door, clutching a stitch in her side as strands of her dark hair stuck to her sweat-slicked forehead. "I like this side of you."

Sophie smiled broadly in return and couldn't help but agree with her friend's remark. She was also surprised to realize that somewhere between the barn and the inn, she had decided. The Nightingale organization had arranged her escape from Zo'rahn, effectively saving her life as far as she was concerned. If Khalil had to choose between completing his duty to her or rescuing a Nightingale from some sort of imprisonment, the least she could do was offer them assistance in return.

Besides, she had one thing none of the rest of them had. Magic.

CHAPTER
FIVE

While they waited for Turin and Khalil to return, Sophie and Eolisti talked more about what they had overheard. Eolisti decided that it would be best if Sophie was the one to convince Khalil that they needed to go along with them on this mission for the Nightingales. Since the Anai did not get along well with their hooded companion, Sophie agreed. She still didn't know what she was going to say to him, but she would get him to listen.

This mission sounded important, and she did not want Khalil to have to choose between her and helping someone else. If this Phoenix person was imprisoned and Turin needed Khalil's help to free him—or her, he would have her assistance as well. It was as simple as that. For all their aid, Sophie owed the Nightingales a debt she didn't know if she could ever repay. There was no way that she would allow herself to be the reason that Khalil turned his back on them.

"Have fun with that," Eolisti said sarcastically as she laid back, having claimed the bed closest to the window.

She placed one hand on her stomach and grimaced. "It's weird not to be swaying anymore. It kind of feels like the room is spinning."

"You mean it feels great? I'm not sure I ever want to get on another ship again." As Sophie stretched her arms out above her, there was a knock at the door. "Come in," she called, a sudden nervousness making her wrap a lock of hair around her fingers and tug at it absently.

The door slowly swung open to reveal Khalil, his hood still pulled low over his face. "There's food downstairs," he said to them.

"Good," Eolisti said, jumping up. "I'm starving." Sophie frowned, the image of the hungry children from before coming to the front of her mind. The Anai strode past Khalil, who stepped aside for her. She glanced back at Sophie over her shoulder, her eyebrows raised, then left down the hall.

This was her chance. If she could convince Khalil that she and Eolisti could be useful in rescuing the Phoenix, he would be able to persuade Turin to take them on this mission.

"Khalil," Sophie said, gathering her courage and pushing ahead. "I'd like to speak with you."

He'd been turning to follow the Anai, but paused at the sound of her voice, then came into the room and shut the door behind him. He took a few steps toward Sophie and waited for her to speak. His face—what she could see of it —was expressionless. If he found her request odd, there was no indication of it.

Sophie had been agonizing over how to tell him what she knew about what Turin had asked of him, and how she knew it. He probably wouldn't be happy that they'd eavesdropped on them, but Sophie decided that he'd like it less if she lied to him. "That conversation you had earlier with Turin…" Her fingers fidgeted at the hems of her sleeves. The next words spilled out of her mouth before she could change her mind. "Eolisti and I followed you. We know what Turin asked you to do."

She waited for his reaction, muscles tense. Would he press his mouth into that disapproving line? Or would he just walk out of the room and leave her there?

Instead, one side of his mouth quirked in a lopsided smile. "Did you?" he asked wryly. "I didn't hear you."

"I used a muffling spell so you wouldn't be able to." Sophie was a little embarrassed at the confession but took a breath to steady her nerves. Based on how well he moved despite his lack of sight, she suspected that Khalil had a kind of supernatural hearing. Perhaps it was something to do with the magic she'd sensed from him when they'd first met back in Ta'Shela. There had to be something aiding his senses. "I think you need to help this Phoenix person. I know that you are supposed to take me to Morigael, but I can't ask you to forsake someone who needs your help. If Turin can't do it alone, you can assist him." She smiled up at him, even though he couldn't see it. "You've done so much for me already. The Nightingales have done so much for me already."

She bit her bottom lip, trying to think of how to phrase what she wanted to say next. "And Eolisti and I want to come along. We want to help."

He was silent, a small frown marring his features. She thought he would object, and, for a moment, he looked like he would but, instead, folded his arms across his chest. It was an action that she'd come to learn meant he was not pleased. "My priority is you, Sophie. I wouldn't even consider diverting from taking you to Morigael if it…" He sighed, and it sounded like he'd lived a thousand years in that one breath. "If it wasn't the Phoenix."

"Is this person important to you?" Sophie asked, but, based on his reaction, she suspected the answer to that was yes.

Khalil took a few steps and sat on the little single bed closest to the door, the one that Sophie had claimed as her own for the night. Running a hand over his chin, he exhaled through his nose. He looked tired, more so than she'd seen him during their entire journey.

Sophie hesitated, then sat across from him on the other bed.

"I've told you before that a long time ago, a woman helped me escape from those who wanted me dead after I was blinded. Do you remember?"

She nodded, then realizing that he could not see her said, "Yes, I do." It had been a cool desert night in Omer when he had given her a brief glimpse into his past.

"The woman who helped me is the Phoenix. I don't think she was called that at the time, but she saved my life." He turned his face aside, and his shoulders slumped in defeat, another reaction that Sophie had never seen from him before. "I want to go on this mission and do whatever I can, but I'm also obligated to you, and I won't let you and the Anai travel to Morigael alone."

Scooting to the edge of the bed, she leaned toward the man she'd grown to consider a friend. "Khalil, you shouldn't have to choose. You need to free her." She reached out and took one of his hands in hers, staring up at his face intently. "Please, let me help you. My magic would be useful. *I* can be useful." She heard the desperation in her voice at that last part but was determined not to let him refuse her. Her magic would be invaluable on this mission. It had to be. "Together we can help this woman."

They stayed like that for a while, Sophie gripping Khalil's hand as he sat there unmoving. She knew he was thinking, weighing his options, but Sophie was determined not to show weakness, so she did not try to move away from him. He had to believe that she was absolutely certain in her desire to assist them.

Eventually, Khalil sighed. "I have no right to tell you what you can or cannot do, but you need to know how dangerous this could be. Your magic *would* be a great benefit to us, but you may not be the only person there with those abilities. Something unexpected can always happen." He turned the hand she still held, then squeezed her fingers back and offered her a half-smile. "I would die before abandoning my duty to you, but with the risks, it could well be that I am killed or captured in this endeavor."

"Even more reason for me to go then," she said earnestly. "If nothing else, I can counter whatever another wizard can do." She'd done just that during their escape from Omer. It had been the first time Sophie had pitted her magic against another, more experienced wizard, but she had been able to outmaneuver him in the end, and she could do it again. Sophie had faith in her abilities and was certain that she was experienced enough to aid them.

"I do realize how dangerous this could be, Khalil. I could be throwing away my chance at freedom after everything we've just been through, but I can't leave someone else to that fate. It wouldn't be right."

A few moments passed before he answered her. "You're much braver than you give yourself credit for." He turned his face back to her, the lopsided smile still present. "All right, as long as you are aware of the risks, it is your decision, and I won't take that away from you." He stood, still holding her hand in his.

"Yes, I'm aware, and I still want to help," she said fervently, letting him pull her to her feet to join the others downstairs.

Even though rooms were plentiful at the inn, the lack of any activity or sounds gave Sophie the impression that there were no other patrons. The tavern had been empty when they'd arrived, but with every step, Sophie could almost feel an energy through the old wood, like a sad melody lamenting over what once was. The life and merriment within its walls had faded with the town's misfortune.

When they reached the bottom of the stairs, Sophie spotted Eolisti and Turin sitting at the table closest to the hearth, the only occupants in a room that could have seated dozens. A fire roared in the hearth, illuminating their corner of the room. The innkeeper was nowhere in sight, so she and Khalil made their way over to join them. Food was on the table in the form of steaming bowls of what looked like soup and a single loaf of bread.

Sophie slid into an empty chair and looked down at the bowl in front of her. The watery soup had green and orange vegetables floating here and there. It didn't look very appetizing, but with the food shortage in Tanalin, she was surprised that the inn had even a single morsel for them to eat, and she was grateful that they had anything to spare.

Eolisti, who had already finished her bowl said in a low voice, "It's not very good, but don't worry. I'll do some hunting once we get on the road." She leaned in closer. "How did it go?"

Sophie waved her away as Khalil stepped up beside her

and placed a hand on her shoulder. Eolisti's eyebrows raised but she didn't say anything.

Turin eyed first Sophie, then Khalil, suspicion making the corners of his mouth turn down.

"Turin," Khalil began. "These two are coming with us." Without another word, he took his seat and began to eat.

CHAPTER

SIX

One day in, and things were already not going according to plan. There wasn't much of a plan to begin with, but it was already changing far more than Turin liked. The knight had to admit to himself that he couldn't be too upset when he didn't really have a good idea of how to handle the whole "Phoenix" debacle. Still, he had a hard time believing that having two young civilians, *female* civilians, along would be anything but a hindrance.

When Khalil had told him the night before at dinner that Sophie and Eolisti would be joining them, even ignoring the fact that Khalil had shared the details of this sensitive mission with them in the first place, Turin had been at a loss for words. He had been prepared for Khalil to insist on taking them to their destination. Hells, he'd even planned out how he was going to talk the other man out of it.

It had never occurred to him that Khalil would want the women to come along with them. It was dangerous and reckless. For the silent and stern Khalil, it also seemed out of character. Why would he risk bringing them to a place that would put his charge in danger?

Turin had first met Khalil a few years earlier on another one of these escort missions. Turin had heard of him before that though—a young blind man from across the Silver Sea that helped those needing succor find their way to new, safer homes. At the time, he thought it was odd for a blind person to be leading people anywhere. Okay, he *may* have laughed at the idea.

When the two finally did cross paths at Griffin's Bluff, Turin hadn't been able to help himself. He *might* have teased the other man, and some might even say he provoked Khalil into a friendly sparring contest, which was no easy feat. He'd had to goad him for days, and the other man had only agreed to it to stop Turin's incessant pestering. Rarely had Turin met a more no-nonsense person than Khalil. The man was downright unflappable. Even more surprising was his skill. He was at least a few years younger than Turin, but his abilities surpassed many men ten years his senior.

After the defeat that Khalil had handed him that day, Turin had gained a measure of grudging respect for the blind man.

Turin shook his head to get the snow out of his raven black hair before glancing over his shoulder at the other three. Eolisti and Sophie were riding together, chatting softly, and Khalil followed as usual. As he turned to face forward again to gaze at the Tanalin countryside, Turin wondered for the hundredth time what could possibly have possessed Khalil to complicate their task this way. When Khalil had announced his decision at dinner, Turin's first thought was that Khalil was joking. He'd actually laughed for a moment before taking in the serious expressions on the two ladies' faces. He remembered the rest of their dinner as if he'd been watching himself from a distance. He'd smiled at them all, lifted his cup to them, and, ever the affable person, said, "Excellent!"

After dinner, he had caught up with Khalil to question the man, but all he would say was that it was all of them or none of them. *I'm Khalil, and I do what I want,* Turin thought to himself mockingly. They didn't get along very well, anyone could see that, but did the man have to override him so soundly? Granted, Turin had asked for his help, but the man wasn't being reasonable.

And how were those two supposed to help them? The Anai would probably be good in a fight, but the quiet little noble girl? Turin was sure that she was one of those high-value assets that he had assumed from the start of this mission, but she wasn't cut out for something like this. When things started to go awry, he needed people who could still work under pressure and keep their wits about them if everything went to hell. She seemed nice enough, but her demeanor would mean nothing when they were sneaking into Tempest Hall.

Pulling himself out of his dark thoughts, Turin looked up at the sky. Behind the clouds, he could see that the sun had begun to dip low on the horizon and was just touching the tops of the trees. It had been gray and cold for most of the afternoon, and he knew that it would only get colder the farther they went. Snow dusted the trees that dotted either side of the road and the hills before them were white with dead, yellow grass poking through powder. Winter was in full grip, and it would only make their journey more difficult. Turning in his saddle, he called to the others.

"We'll make camp a little farther up the road. There's a good place not far from here."

Turin rolled his shoulders to try to ease some of the tension he'd been carrying all day. He'd been over this in his head more times than he could count, but it all came down to one main objection. Untrained people on this mission would be worse than dead weight. If things got sticky, which in his experience they often did, not only could the women get hurt, but *he* could get hurt because he was distracted worrying about them. Curse Khalil, curse the Phoenix, and curse the bloody Emissary for saddling him with this task.

A hundred yards away, a clearing came into view off to one side of the road. Turin reined his horse toward it, expecting the others to follow. Near a large, felled tree, he pulled to a halt and dismounted, pleased to see that the others did the same.

"Just hold the reins for a moment," he said over his mare's withers as he hurried to secure her. He patted the animal's flank gently and kept his hand on the horse as he walked around behind her. He was grudgingly appreciative to see that Eolisti had already tied off her horse and was helping Sophie with hers. "Oh, good. Once you take the saddles and bridles off, don't forget to give the horses a good brushing. It'll help keep them from getting sores."

"We *have* done this before you know," the Anai retorted with a roll of her eyes, causing Sophie to cover her smile with a hand. The two women exchanged a look and the Anai frowned.

Turin just blinked for a moment before finally recovering. "Of course. Just let me know if you need any help." He could feel a slight heating of his cheeks. They weren't incompetent. He knew that, but he'd been so caught up in his brooding that he'd forgotten the fact that they had already traveled quite far and would be used to it.

Unconcerned with Khalil, he turned back to his own horse, removed the tack, and rubbed the beast down with practiced motions. As he worked, he made a mental note to check the other horses again later, just to make sure they were cared for properly. Maybe they did know what they were doing, but the last thing they'd need was to lose one to lameness or infection. Yet another complication to having more people along.

Finally, with his bedroll under one arm, he shouldered his saddlebags before stooping to pick up the saddle. With one last glance at the women, who seemed to be doing fine with their own mounts, he carried his things over to the well-used firepit near the center of the clearing. The last occupant of the campsite had left a small pile of twigs and bark along with a few slender branches, which Turin promptly scooped up and set to work building a fire.

By the time the others made their way over to him with their own belongings, tiny flames were licking at the dry tinder. Khalil silently began pitching a small tent, so Turin turned to Eolisti and Sophie and smiled.

"This won't last us very long," he said, gesturing to the fire. "Would one of you mind helping me gather some wood?"

"Are you sure you trust us with something so difficult?" Eolisti shot back.

Clearly, he'd offended the Anai with his comment about the horses. Turin was about to apologize for upsetting her when Sophie patted the other woman's arm in a placating gesture.

"I can help," said the small red-haired woman with a conciliatory smile.

"Great," he said with another glance at the sky. It was getting darker, and he guessed they had about thirty minutes or so before the sun fully set, though it was hard to tell with the clouds. Then he gave Sophie a smile. At least she knew how to soothe the Anai. "We should hurry before it gets much darker."

Together, he and the young woman headed for the tree line. A backward glance revealed an annoyed-looking Eolisti watching them go, fists on hips. Turin shot her a grin and a wave before disappearing around a tree. Despite how cross he was about his situation, he could never resist an opportunity to make a great exit.

Turin and Sophie scoured the forest floor in silence for several minutes before the woman spoke up.

"I think I owe you an apology," Sophie said, ducking her head a little before seeming to catch herself, her gray eyes meeting his.

Ah, Turin thought, *she thinks it's her fault*. Well, it was a little bit her fault since he suspected that it had been she who'd spoken with Khalil back at the inn, but, mostly, it was the blind man's. He wasn't upset with her or Eolisti, not really, but it probably didn't look that way from their perspective. Before he could give voice to any of these thoughts, Sophie continued.

"I'm not sure if Khalil told you, but Eolisti and I eavesdropped on your conversation in the barn." The fingers of one hand were messing with the hem of her sleeve in a way that betrayed the confidence she was attempting to present. At least she kept eye contact. "It was wrong of us to intrude when it was clear you wanted to speak in private. I'm sorry."

Turin stared at her before bursting out with a loud laugh. He couldn't help it. Sophie was startled by his reaction, eyebrows raised. "You mean Khalil didn't tell you about our mission? *You* were able to sneak up on *him*? I could probably count on one hand the number of people who could do that!"

Sophie looked both embarrassed and pleased at the admiration in his voice. Once he was able to contain his laughter, he said, "Thank you for telling me the truth. Apology accepted. It's almost a fair trade to know someone who can get the better of Khalil's bizarre sense of hearing." They both chuckled a little at that and continued the hunt for fuel until both of their arms were full. The tense air that had been hanging over them had cleared, and Turin felt much lighter than he had earlier. It occurred to him that maybe Khalil had let them eavesdrop and not said anything, but that didn't track with what he knew of the man. She'd found some way around his incredible hearing.

Eyes sliding over to her, he tried to assess Sophie in a new light. Perhaps he'd been too quick to judge the red-haired woman walking beside him. She looked far too young to have any skills that they would need, but maybe, just maybe, he should give her a chance to prove herself.

When they emerged once again into the clearing, the clouds had finally broken, and the sky had turned a dark orange as the sun dipped low behind the trees. Khalil and Eolisti were just finishing setting up a second larger tent. The tiny fire that Turin had started had nearly burned itself out. Turin turned to Sophie and took the heaviest chunk of wood from her arms, then leaned it up against the glowing embers. He set his pile of wood down a safe distance from the pit and motioned for her to do the same.

"I'm going hunting," Eolisti suddenly declared.

"I'm not sure that's a great idea," said Turin, looking over at the Anai. "I brought some food supplies, and it's nearly dark."

Letting out an indelicate snort at his comment, Eolisti

shouldered a quiver of arrows and snatched up the hunting bow she kept with her supplies. "I don't care about the darkness, and you're welcome to keep your *food supplies* if they're anything like what we ate last night." She made a disgusted face. "I can do better."

Frowning, Turin lifted his hands in surrender. "Have it your way. Just don't come crying to me when some troll decides to make an evening snack out of you."

"Let them try," she challenged, tossing her head and letting her hair whip out behind her. With that, she stalked off into the trees.

He turned to look to Khalil for support, or at least an explanation, but he, too, was nowhere to be seen. *Well, that's just great.* Turin squeezed his eyes shut and pinched the bridge of his nose, letting out a deep, frustrated breath. This whole thing was going to be a disaster. How were they going to pull this off when people were already wandering off on their own?

"She really will be fine." Sophie's voice shook him from his inner monologue.

He straightened to look at her, and she gave him a weak smile. With another deep sigh, he turned his attention to stoking the fire. There was probably no point in getting upset about this now. Khalil was going to do whatever the hell he wanted, and it was becoming clear that the Anai would be doing the same.

Despite that resolution, Turin continued to stew as he poked at the burning wood with a long stick, the lighter feeling he'd had before gone. As he listened to the pops and hisses, he tried to figure out how he could salvage this situation, but his head hurt from the long day. All Turin seemed able to do was dwell on the same sour thoughts he'd been going over since last night. Sophie laid a blanket over the snow-damp grass and sat near the flames, holding her hands out to warm them.

At some point, Khalil rejoined them at the fire, sitting near the young woman, but Turin only gave him a passing glance. It was fully dark by then, and the moonlight was beginning to illuminate the sky behind the trees on the opposite horizon. Turin wasn't sure how much time had passed, but Eolisti still had not returned.

He was about to stand to go look for her when Khalil jumped to his feet and pulled his sword in one smooth motion. Instinctively, Turin got to his feet and unsheathed his sword as well, straining to hear what Khalil already had.

He felt it before he heard it. The earth shook with a steady crashing and crunching of underbrush like someone was using the forest floor as their own personal war drums. Looking around frantically, he swore under his breath.

"What is it?" Sophie asked, also rising. Her eyes were wide as she looked out into the trees, taking an anxious step toward Khalil.

Turin gritted his teeth. There was only one thing it could be. "Trolls."

SEVEN

The rumbling and crunching grew louder as something enormous approached their camp. Turin rushed over to the horses, making sure they were tightly secured. Returning, he stood at Sophie's side and picked up his shield. He hunkered down behind it and glanced at her. "Sophie, get behind the horses and stay down! I'll keep it away from you. If one of us falls, cut them free, and get out of here. Ride back to Mattina and don't look back."

"But—"

"Now!" he shouted and moved forward, closer to where the trees were shaking.

Khalil stepped up on her other side. He held the slightly curved blade she'd seen him use before out in front of him, the metal glinting in the firelight.

"Are you ready?" Khalil asked, and Sophie knew what he meant.

Back in Omer, Khalil had told her that her power would be necessary to evade the people pursuing her. The fear that her energy signature would be tracked was a risk, but in the end, she'd had to use her spells to help them get away. Now that they were across the Silver Sea, she should be able to use her abilities without fear.

"Yes," she said as she took a step back, strengthening her resolve and clearing her mind as a giant mound of fur and teeth came crashing into their clearing.

The creature was large, as tall as two men, and its limbs were covered in dense muscle. It was wide, almost as wide as an ox and covered in white, mottled fur. Wicked-looking claws sharp as knives dug furrows into the ground. The beast stood on two legs, its long arms nearly touching the grass. Fangs protruded from its upper jaw, and black, beady eyes stared out of an almost lupine face, surveying the clearing.

A sharp, metal *clang* sounded as the knight hit his sword against his shield twice, drawing the creature's attention. Feral, yellow eyes locking on Turin, it let out a roar that Sophie could feel all the way down to her toes, then charged at him.

Sophie held her breath as Turin rolled out of the way, one claw scraping on his shield as his sword flashed, making the creature screech as it came away stained with blue-black blood. He feinted to the right, then darted left when the beast lunged after him.

As it snarled and tried to follow Turin, Khalil approached from behind, silent as a shadow. He drove his curved blade deep into the troll's shoulder, then jumped back as it shrieked in pain and turned to swipe at him. Khalil lured it away from Turin, dodging its claws and scoring shallow hits with his blade, allowing the other man to sneak up behind the monster as he had just done.

While it was distracted, Turin dashed forward, and, before it realized what he was doing, the large man was within reach. As it turned, he sliced across its barrel chest, drawing a long line of dark fluid, and then rolled between the beast's legs before it could snap its jaws at him. With the smooth movement that came from years of training, he landed another well-placed hit on the back of its thigh as he and Khalil darted away in opposite directions.

Enraged, the troll stumbled after Turin. He turned to face it, and the beast swiped a huge hand at him. Sidestepping the deadly blow, he brought his sword down on the arm, drawing another scream of pain from the creature. With a few quick steps, Turin was out of reach again as Khalil pounced, stabbing deep at the bloody fur on its leg, the same spot Turin had landed his blow.

Sophie watched the battle, her mind racing as the troll struggled with the two combatants. There were a couple of spells that would be useful, but the men would need to be far enough from the beast for her to use them. She didn't want to injure either of them by mistake.

While she thought, Turin had come up behind the troll again, steel flashing in the firelight as he went for the same strike as Khalil, trying to cripple it.

The beast, however, was not as mindless as it appeared, and this time it knew what they were doing. Quick as lightning, the troll spun and slapped Turin's sword aside with one giant hand. The Morigaelian lost his grip on the blade, and it clattered to the ground as he scrambled back to avoid the beast's claws. Lucky to not have also lost his shield, Turin swore loudly as it whipped around and rushed Khalil, who'd been attempting to attack again from behind, knocking him across the clearing with a kick. Khalil hit the ground and rolled but lost his own weapon in the process.

As Turin tried to snatch up his blade, one large foot landed where the sword had fallen, pressing it into the ground under the troll's weight. The creature backhanded him before he could dodge, and he landed on his back a few feet farther away. It took a slow step and loomed over him, leaning down and opening its jaws wide. Turin thrust his shield up to bash its face, but the troll caught the metal in its claws and ripped his only form of protection away from him. Having no other means of defending himself, Turin lifted an arm in front of his face to try to block the blow, but it was pointless. His arm would simply be the beast's appetizer.

As those jaws bore down on Turin, Sophie focused her mind and wove her hands in front of her, releasing the energy she'd gathered within herself in an instant. As the troll widened its maw to attack, it bounced off an invisible barrier a foot above Turin's prone body.

The beast hesitated for a moment in confusion, then lashed out again, hitting the barrier with an audible *thump*. Sophie's shield spell held. She allowed herself a small, satisfied smile. She'd deflected bolts of lightning with this spell before. The troll didn't have a chance of breaking it.

Turin stared up at the beast, every bit as puzzled as the monster was. With a start, he whipped his head to the side to stare at Sophie, the shock clear on his face, even in what little light there was. She smiled more. She'd tried to tell him, but in a situation like this, a demonstration was more meaningful.

The troll howled in rage and slammed a fist down on her spell, but with the same result as before. While it thrashed at the prone man, two arrows flew out of the darkness to Sophie's right, catching the beast in the shoulder. It screamed in agony and whirled away from Turin, allowing Khalil, who'd recovered his own weapon, to retrieve his comrade's sword and shield and rush to his side. Sophie followed the pair with her spell until they were well out of reach, then turned her focus back to the troll which was now chasing Eolisti.

The Anai danced out of the reach of the troll's claws with apparent ease as it swiped at her again and again. Sophie had seen Eolisti fight before, and, every time she saw it, the Anai reminded her of a dancer. She stepped and pivoted, turned and ducked gracefully, making the deadly attacks look like something rehearsed between the two combatants. She wasn't attacking the troll, just dodging. Eolisti's eyes met Sophie's, and the Anai started drawing the creature farther away from the mage, leaving its back wide open.

As Sophie reached for the power within herself, electricity crackled at her fingertips. She held out one hand, pointing it toward the creature's back, and sent a spark flying at it. In the moments it took to reach the troll, it swelled into a sphere of white-hot fire, bathing the clearing in blinding light as it collided with the creature and set the fur aflame.

The troll squealed in panic and agony, jumping away from the Anai, and rolling on the ground to put out the fire that had rapidly spread over the entirety of its back. Sophie carefully moved toward Eolisti and held herself ready, gathering more energy for another strike should the troll come at them. Together, they approached the beast.

Having smothered most of the flames, the troll staggered to its feet, snarling as the two women approached from one side while Khalil and Turin boxed it in from the other. The scent of burnt fur and singed flesh filled the night as the creature whipped its head back and forth between them, grunting and growling in pain and fear.

With a last snap of fangs, it turned from them and raced into the trees, disappearing in the darkness.

The trembling of the earth subsided as the creature fled, and, within a few minutes, the clearing was silent once more.

Sophie sighed, allowing her shoulders to slump, and as the feeling of excitement from the attack abated, her hands started shaking. Eolisti caught her by the arm and kept her from collapsing to the ground. "I'm fine," she said, waving the Anai off, and gave her a watery smile. "So, that's a troll. I've never seen anything like it before."

"It didn't seem that scary," Eolisti said, flipping some of her long auburn hair over her shoulder. She tossed Turin a triumphant grin. "It looked like you needed help. Was this your first time in a real fight?" she teased.

Turin sheathed his sword. Next to him, Khalil did the same, his mouth drawn into its familiar thin line. Sophie wondered if he didn't approve of the teasing or was anticipating an argument between the Anai and the black-haired man. She thought she and Eolisti had proven themselves capable, but perhaps he wouldn't see it that way.

Turin didn't seem upset by the jab, though. In fact, his eyes glittered with excitement, and a wide grin spread across his face.

"A wizard?!" His sudden exclamation made Sophie jump. "Why didn't you tell me she was a *wizard?*" It must have been a rhetorical question because he didn't wait for anyone to answer. He stepped up to Sophie, his eyes roving up and down her. She had the impression that this was the first time he was really seeing her as a woman who could take care of herself. It was a little irritating, but maybe now he would stop treating her like a burden. "A Zo'rahni wizard," he mused. "I've heard a lot about them. But you look so young. I thought all wizards were old. Have you finished your training?"

"I've been learning about magic since I was seven," she said, a little annoyed by his tone. True, she was young, but even her old master had said that she was advanced for her age. Most children started showing an aptitude for magic when they hit puberty, but she'd shown the signs years in advance. Still, as rare as her situation might have been in Zo'rahn, she was not unique in it. "I'm not ranked, so I'm technically still an apprentice," Sophie added after a few moments. Even though she was far from her old home and customs, it felt dishonest to let him think she was a fully-fledged wizard.

"I've never seen an apprentice fend off a troll before," he said, ignoring an indignant protest from Eolisti. "I can see why Khalil was sent out to retrieve you." He glanced over his shoulder at the other man. "Does the Lord High Commander know about this?"

Khalil just shrugged. "My orders don't come from him."

"What are you talking about?" Eolisti interjected hotly. She was clearly upset about her contributions to the fight being overlooked. "Who is this 'Lord High Commander'?"

Turin raised an eyebrow. "You're a Vendarii, right? You should know who that is." Eolisti just glared at him. "He's the leader of my order, the Knights of the Realm. He's who you were taking Sophie to meet with at Griffin's Bluff in Morigael. Well, at least that was the plan before this detour came up."

Eolisti scoffed. "Of course, I know who that is," she grumbled in a way that Sophie knew meant she did not. Sophie covered her smile with a hand, causing Eolisti to turn her glare on her before addressing Turin again. "I just needed to make sure Sophie knew that." She turned away from them, leaving an expression of utter confusion on the knight's face, and crossed the clearing to retrieve her bow, which she must have dropped when facing off with the troll.

Sophie glanced at Khalil, and she thought she saw the beginnings of a smile tugging at his lips.

"What just happened?" Turin asked. He looked first at Sophie, then at Khalil.

Sophie did laugh then. She leaned into Turin and whispered conspiratorially. "She gets that way sometimes. It's nothing to worry about."

"I heard that!" Eolisti growled as she held up two silver-furred rabbits by their hind legs. She must have caught them before the troll attacked. Eolisti placed her bow next to her bag and pulled a small dagger out of one of the pockets. "Just for that, I'm not sharing." She stomped over to the fire and threw on a few more logs, which caused the already-minuscule flames to sputter and die. "For the love of—"

Turin shook his head in surrender. "Women," he muttered so low that Sophie almost missed it. More loudly, he said, "I think we are going to have to move camp." He made a show of looking around the clearing. "It might not be a good idea to stay here with troll blood everywhere. It will attract other predators—or even another troll—to this area. We should get at least a mile farther down the road."

It was difficult to see in the dark, but blue-black blood was sprayed liberally in various areas in the grass. Dirt was upturned where the beast's claws had dug furrows into the ground, and there was a large patch of scorched earth where it had rolled around to put out the fire. The clearing was a mess, and they were lucky that the beast hadn't trampled through their supplies or tents, or even killed the horses.

"I can still smell its breath. Like dead, rotting flesh," Eolisti said with a grimace, poking at the coals with a stick and wrinkling her nose. She tossed the stick into the ashes and unsheathed the dagger. "Maybe we *should* move. I don't think I'll be able to sleep with this stench."

"We don't need to move," Sophie said, looking around, an idea forming in her mind. Inhaling deeply, she drew in just the barest bit of energy from the plant life surrounding them, letting it mix with her own power and shaping it to her will. She closed her eyes and focused, visualizing the clearing as it had been before the battle, whole and unmarred. It was harder to fix something than it was to destroy, but nature tended to set itself right again. She was only speeding along the process.

With a great sigh, Sophie released the spell. A breeze drifted through the clearing, and the ground knit itself back together where the troll's claws had disturbed it. The singed grass rippled and healed, black scorch marks fading to the green of new stalks. The dark blood sizzled and evaporated from where it had been spilled. With a last snap of her fingers, the campfire sparked to life, and the breeze died out, taking the scent of the troll with it.

"Impressive," Turin said, looking around for a moment before taking a seat by the fire. He pulled some of the food supplies he'd been talking about earlier from a sack, comprised of mostly bread and cheese. There was still a wide grin on his face, looking as if the dour mood he'd been in all day had finally lifted. "It's getting late, so you'd better get some sleep. I'll be taking the first watch."

"Not alone you aren't," Eolisti said with a growl. "I don't trust you."

Turin responded with a genial smile. "You're welcome to join me. I'd appreciate the company," he said with a wink. "We'll be leaving at sunrise, so don't stay up too late."

Eolisti scoffed, but her cheeks turned faintly pink. She continued skinning the rabbits in silence, the only sound the scraping of her dagger.

Seeming to have nothing to add to the conversation, Khalil turned and placed a hand on Sophie's shoulder. "Good job," he said so softly that only she could have heard it, then made his way over to the tents.

Watching the Anai, Sophie suddenly didn't feel hungry anymore. With the power that she'd just expended, both in the fight with the troll and on the cleaning of their campsite, she was more tired than expected. Sophie imagined she'd still be exhausted from the fight even if she hadn't spent the whole day riding. Even using the energy from what was around her, it was her focus and will that shaped the spells that she cast. The more magic she used, the more taxing it was.

Muttering that she was going to sleep, Sophie pulled a few blankets out of their pile of supplies and made her way over to the larger of the two tents that Khalil had pitched earlier. As Sophie crawled inside and settled down for the night, she smiled to herself. Turin's excitement about her abilities meant he thought she would be useful in rescuing the Phoenix, and that gave her even greater confidence in her decision to come along. She wouldn't disappoint him.

EIGHT

Sophie awoke early the following morning to the twittering of birds. Blinking, she rubbed the sleep out of her eyes and looked around the tent. In the rumpled bedroll next to her, Eolisti lay with her arms flung up over her head, still snoring softly. She smiled to herself as she gazed at her friend's peaceful face, wondering how long the Anai had been on watch last night.

Careful not to wake her, Sophie slowly extracted her limbs from within her own tangled blankets. Then, quietly picking up her pack, she gently lifted the tent's flap, squinting in the early morning light as she emerged and glanced around the campsite. Most of the area appeared just as they had found it the evening before, thanks to her little cleaning trick. However, nearer to the tree line, there were still a few depressions in the ground where the troll's blows, or perhaps its feet, had landed, and broken branches still hung from the trees.

Remembering the creature left a sick feeling in her stomach. Sophie had read about trolls before, but seeing them in a book and getting an up-close view of one was entirely different. There were no trolls in Zo'rahn. It had been so big and heavy that the ground had trembled beneath its feet. She shivered, hoping that was the last troll they saw on their journey.

Sophie heard movement from behind the tent, and she peeked around the side to find Khalil standing in a crouch, his arms raised, looking ready to attack some invisible assailant.

As she watched, his breath clouded in the chill morning air as he exhaled. He swept his hands down before advancing and crouching again, arms outstretched before him as he balanced on the balls of his feet. Seeing him move alone was like watching a feather swirling in the breeze. Sophie had seen him fight often enough now to know that his movements were nothing so innocuous. It was different from the way Eolisti moved. When she fought, it was more elegant, even peaceful somehow, like a dance. She was powerful and effective, but Khalil fought on an instinctual level that the Anai just didn't have. It was almost like when Sophie used her magic, a power that came to her with little more than a thought.

Without so much as a change of expression, Khalil straightened to his full height and turned to face Sophie. She smiled. It wasn't surprising that he'd heard her approach. She pushed away the awkward feeling that was tugging at her chest.

"Good morning," she said. "Please, don't let me interrupt."

A corner of Khalil's mouth quirked, and he waved a hand dismissively as he took a few steps in her direction. As he approached, she was struck again by how different the man before her was from the one she'd first met. It was surprising how so much could change in just a few short months. Or maybe it was just that her perception of him had changed.

"You're not interrupting. I've been thinking it might be good for you to know a few techniques that could be useful on this... adventure we find ourselves on." He ran a hand through his hair, brushing back the strands that had been sticking to his sweat-slicked forehead, then turned and gestured to the open area where he'd been training. "Would you like to learn?"

Sophie looked at the clearing and pictured herself going through the motions she'd just seen Khalil complete. They didn't seem overly complex. There was a flutter of excitement in her breast at the thought of being able to handle herself in a physical confrontation. She wasn't skilled in that way, but under Khalil's tutelage, perhaps she could learn.

"Yes, I'd like that."

The corners of those remarkable eyes crinkled as the quirk of his lips blossomed into an easy smile. "Good. Come."

He led the way to the center of the clearing and turned to face her again. The smile was gone now, replaced by a contemplative expression. At first, he didn't say anything, and the silence dragged on long enough that Sophie was nearly squirming under his scrutiny before he finally spoke.

"There won't be time to teach you much more than the basics, but the basics can be enough to get you out of a bad situation. Let's start with how to escape when someone grabs you." He approached her cautiously, one hand raised, palm facing her, before gently but firmly clamping his fingers around her wrist.

"Now, don't think too much. Just do what comes naturally and try to break free."

Sophie felt a rush of premature embarrassment as she worried she wouldn't be able to do as he said, but she fought it down. She made a fist and pulled her trapped arm toward herself, easily breaking his light grip.

"Yes," he said with a smile. "You did that just right. Always pull in the direction of the other person's thumb. If you try to break free in the other direction, four fingers are working against you instead of one. You could also make the fist but grab it with your free hand and pull so that all your strength is working against your opponent."

Khalil paused, his brows drawing down in a slight frown of contemplation. Finally, he said, "Let's try something a little harder. Turn and face away from me."

As she moved, he stepped closer, resting one palm on her shoulder, and explained, "If someone comes up and grabs you from behind, chances are they're going to try to pick you up and carry you away. They might try to wrap their arms around yours, trapping them at your sides," he said as he reached around her to clasp his hands together, again seeming to take care not to be too aggressive, and pulled her firmly against him.

Though it was far from an affectionate embrace, Sophie felt her eyes widen and her face heat at their closeness. The last time she had been in his arms was when they'd fled Nobarum, the port across the sea in Omer. Joel had just fallen, and she'd been trying to reach him when Khalil had picked her up, much the same way he was holding her now, and dragged her onto the ship while she fought uselessly against him. He'd been the smart one, focused on their escape, while she'd been reacting to her emotions. They'd barely gotten away. Now, there were no threats, no enemies, no impending doom to be thinking of. It was just the two of them. Alone.

Alarmed by the direction her mind had wandered, she inwardly chastised herself. This was a lesson, nothing more, and she needed to pay attention.

"They might also catch you around the waist," he said, releasing her arms and rejoining his hands around her abdomen, again pulling her back against himself. "If anyone does either of these, I want you to hook one of your feet around the outside and back of their leg. Go ahead and try it as I lift you off the ground."

He slowly began to pull her upward, and she did as he said, twining her ankle and foot around his calf. The upward motion stopped, and her other foot reconnected with the ground. He tensed his arms again to lift her, but her toes never left the grass this time.

"See? Now, what happens if you don't hook your foot around my leg?"

Khalil lifted her gently again, and this time she did nothing. Lifting her entirely off the ground, he turned and carried her a few feet away before setting her back down.

"Now that you know how not to get carried off, I want you to break free when I have my arms wrapped around you." He threaded his arms under hers and began to lift her off the ground again, but Sophie quickly caught the back of his leg with one of her own, and he set her back down.

"Good. Now, how do you escape?"

She tried again not to be distracted by his warmth against her back and strong arms around her. Right, break free. Unsure of what else to do, she gripped his clasped hands and tried to pry them apart.

"Yes, but put your thumbs behind my hands and try pressing down instead of out or apart."

She began to press down tentatively, and he urged in a

harder tone, "Like you mean it. Your survival may depend on it!"

At his words, the memory of the Spider sprang to her mind. When she'd been that vile man's prisoner, she had been helpless and had to rely entirely on others to save her. She had tried to resist, tried to escape, but it had been futile. She felt the familiar anger begin to burn in her chest. Sophie would never forget what he'd done to her.

She threw all her weight against his joined hands with a shout, and they broke easily apart. She stumbled away a few paces at the sudden lack of resistance before turning to face Khalil again, a small smile tugging at her lips.

As if he could see her reaction, the corners of his eyes wrinkled with mirth, and one corner of his mouth tilted upward. "How did that feel?"

"Great," she blurted out, surprised to find that she meant it. Her breath was coming fast, and her pulse thrummed loudly in her ears. She felt like she could run for miles without stopping. Some small rational part of her brain told her that this was a disproportionate response to the small thing she had just done, but she didn't care. She felt invigorated and powerful in a way that had nothing to do with magic.

Khalil grinned in earnest then. "Let's try one more thing."

This time, Khalil had her grab him from behind, assuring her that he would not let her get hurt. She did as he asked and wrapped her arms around his waist, clasping her hands together as he had done with her. Instead of breaking away, he grasped one of her arms with both hands and, with what seemed like no effort at all, popped her over his shoulder. Sophie shrieked as her feet flew up over her head, and her vision filled with a swirl of the sky, forest, and ground. Every muscle in her body tensed, anticipating the impact, but Khalil caught her inches before she would have landed flat on her back at his feet. Sometime during her tumble, she had grabbed ahold of his arms, and she stayed that way, blood pounding in her ears and gasping for air.

"What in the name of all the gods is going on?" cried a feminine voice.

As Khalil pulled Sophie back to her feet, she looked in the direction of the outraged shout. Eolisti stood half out of their tent, hair wild and clothes askew from slumber. A glint of morning light drew Sophie's eyes to the naked sword in the Anai's hand, and she noticed that Turin had also been drawn out of his tent. He, too, was armed, and there was an odd expression on his face as he surveyed their awkward pose.

As Sophie's eyes met the big knight's, he arched one eyebrow inquisitively. Realizing the question was still hanging in the air, Sophie cleared her throat and released her death grip on Khalil's arm, shuffling a step away from him. Her face felt like it was burning under the gazes of her companions. "Um, training? Khalil was showing me how to get away from an attacker."

She expected a sarcastic remark or retort, but Eolisti only rolled her eyes, yawned, and disappeared back into the tent. Turin let out a long breath as he visibly relaxed, his eyes closing while he ran a hand through his raven locks. Then, without further comment, he trudged out into the tree line.

Effectively alone again, Sophie peered hesitantly back at Khalil. She expected his mouth to be drawn in annoyance but was surprised to see him facing her calmly.

"Would you like to try it?" he asked as if they hadn't been interrupted.

She couldn't contain her grin. "Yes, please!"

BY THE TIME they were on the road again, Sophie was already exhausted. It had taken her more tries than she could count to throw Khalil successfully, and by the time she had, Eolisti had risen again and was asking Turin a string of questions about his qualifications to lead their group. The groggy knight occasionally looked like he might try to answer, but before he could, the Anai had already fired another question at him. It had taken Sophie not-so-subtly asking Eolisti if she had any game left for them to eat to divert her from her dogged interrogation.

For his part, Turin appeared more amused than annoyed at the Anai's somewhat hostile line of questioning and in much better spirits than he'd been in the previous day. He smiled easily and even seemed to approve of the training that Khalil had given Sophie, offering to show her the basics of using a sword if she ever wanted to learn.

Once they had eaten, everyone had worked together to pack up their camp in short order. Now, Sophie felt herself sagging in the saddle from the morning's exertion. At the same time, her lower half protested at being in said saddle again after the long ride the previous day. She had been so relieved that their time at sea was over that she'd forgotten the discomfort of traveling by horse. She vaguely remembered that, unlike being on a ship, riding grew more comfortable with time, but that was of limited use to her now. Knowing that dwelling on it wouldn't make the soreness any easier to bear, she forced herself to think of something else.

The climbing sun had chased most of the chill from the air, but now and then, Sophie thought she could see glimpses of snow-covered peaks far off to the north. She also noticed that the woods lining the road gradually shifted from trees still clinging to a few red and golden leaves to those covered in clusters of slender needles of varying lengths and shades of green. Academically, Sophie knew that there were plants that flourished all year long, even in colder months, but she had never seen any like this firsthand.

The thin blanket of snow they'd seen the previous day had melted, and the ground around them took on a muddy and damp look. The cold stung the tip of her nose and cheeks, but when she inhaled, the pleasant scent of those needled trees filled her senses. She tried to recall their name as she took in another deep breath. Pine trees. The wood was coveted for use in furniture or as building materials, and the resin could be used in potion making.

As Sophie let her mind wander, her eyes drifted to Turin, who was at the head of their group as he'd been the day before. He'd called himself a Knight of the Realm, but she wasn't sure what that meant. Oh, she had read about knights in her studies of the world, but they had always been described as solemn people clad head to toe in brilliant metal armor. The man before her was far from solemn, and while he did appear to be wearing armor, it resembled the leather that Eolisti wore more closely than the image she'd conjured in her imagination.

Turin glanced over his shoulder and met her eyes for a couple of heartbeats, and Sophie flushed as she realized she'd been caught staring. Before she looked away, an odd expression crossed the man's face. Discomfort? Irritation? Thankfully, by the time she glanced back up, he'd turned around. Her relief was short-lived, however. A moment later, Turin tugged his reins far to the side, wheeling his horse around to ride back toward her and Eolisti.

"Hey," Sophie said in a panic, turning toward Eolisti. The Anai looked at her and raised an eyebrow. "You— I mean— I like your hair."

"You like my hair?"

"Yes..." Sophie trailed off, realizing Turin had come around and was now riding on her opposite side.

"Ladies, am I interrupting?" the knight asked.

"No, we were just... no." *Really, Sophie? First hair, then this?* She wanted to bury herself in her cloak. Better that than face the look Turin was giving her.

"Yes, actually," Eolisti chimed in, tossing her auburn tresses over a shoulder for emphasis. "Sophie was just telling me how glorious my hair is."

Turin's eyes widened briefly, but with a deliberate blink, he shrugged off the Anai's words. "Good! Then, I think we should probably discuss our plans. I don't know exactly what you heard, but this isn't going to be easy."

Relieved that Turin was satisfied to let her awkwardness pass unremarked, Sophie happily turned her mind toward their objective. "What can you tell us about where we're going and this person we're supposed to rescue? All we heard is that we would need to sneak in somewhere to rescue one of those Nightingales."

He nodded along with her words. "We are heading to a place called Tempest Hall. It's an old castle on the border of Tanalin and Morigael. I don't know much about the place, but it's about a day's ride past where we would normally turn north to get to Morigael. I think it's the seat of one of the older noble houses of Tanalin, but I can't remember which one. There's a village nearby—Brumalar." Turin squinted into the distance and pursed his lips in thought before continuing. "There is usually a modest garrison there—anywhere from fifty to a hundred men at any given time, if I remember the latest reports correctly. Enough soldiers to put up a fight if the castle were ever under siege, but not so many that Morigael would need to worry about a concentration of forces so near the border."

"What about the Phoenix?" she asked.

"On that, I know even less. It's said that those more uniquely skilled among the Nightingales are named after birds, but I don't think I've ever met any of them. The Phoenix, in particular, has a reputation for being impossible to kill, but that could just be a rumor based on the mythical creature. Either way, I don't have the first idea of how we'll know who he is if we can even find him."

"Her," Sophie corrected the knight.

"What?" he asked with a start, focusing on Sophie again.

"Khalil said that the Phoenix is a 'her.'"

"Oh," Turin said, a look of contemplation crossing his face as he looked back to where Khalil still rode behind them. "I guess we know one thing about her then. Any other information you happen to have?"

Sophie opened her mouth to respond, but Khalil beat her to it.

"No."

That surprised Sophie. Khalil had told her that this was the person who had helped him out years ago. Sophie risked a peek over her shoulder. Khalil's expression was the same neutral mask he usually wore. He would know much more about this person than he was letting on, but maybe what he knew wouldn't help them on their mission. Khalil didn't like to talk about his past, and the Phoenix would have been a piece of that. "Didn't you say you, ah..." She glanced at Turin, who was listening intently. "You worked with her before, right?"

"Yes, but she goes by different names and, I assume, changes her appearance. Once I could've identified her gait, but she learned to disguise that, too, eventually."

The group fell into a thoughtful silence, made more pronounced by the sounds of the horses' hooves clopping along and the birds twittering in the forest. That was until Eolisti said what they were likely all thinking. "So, we're breaking into a place we know next to nothing about to rescue a person we won't be able to identify." When no one responded, she looked at Turin and asked, "Does your boss hate you or something?"

"Maybe," he answered with a chuckle. "More likely, I was the only person in the area they could reach, and they knew Khalil would be with me."

The conversation subsided after that, each contemplating the task ahead of them. Though Khalil still rode at the rear of their group, Turin continued to ride abreast of the women.

Sophie's thoughts drifted from the impossibility of their task to speculation on who the Phoenix was and what she was like. In her mind, she could picture a delicate, shadowy figure, cloaked much as Khalil usually was, poised and catlike in her movements. She knew she was most likely conjuring a feminine version of her trusted companion, but that didn't stop her from wondering about the mysterious woman.

Sometime later, Khalil's voice roused her from her contemplation.

"Riders ahead."

As Turin nudged his horse into a trot to retake the lead, Sophie peered ahead but could see only the forest and empty road. A few minutes later, she finally heard the rhythmic hoofbeats of other horses approaching. The sound was followed shortly by the appearance of a group of armored men rounding a bend in the road.

The approaching band of six or seven men was heavily armed and outfitted in various types of gleaming armor, many of them more closely resembling Sophie's concept of what a knight *should* wear. The most notable consistency in their appearance was the heraldry each man bore, some painted on shields or breastplates, others on full tabards. As they drew nearer, she could make out the golden figure of a bird of prey, wings outstretched on a field of purple.

"Leave this to me," Turin cast over his shoulder before turning again to face the oncoming coterie. When they were within speaking distance, he raised a hand in greeting and called, "Ho there, guardsmen!"

Though the armed men had been scrutinizing them as the two groups had approached one another, they had appeared prepared to ride on past Sophie and her friends. At Turin's words, however, a sharp-eyed man at the head of the soldiers raised a gauntleted fist, signaling his men to a halt. "State your business, traveler."

"We're just heading inland from Mattina," Turin said, his posture relaxed and demeanor jovial. "We saw signs of mountain trolls about half a day's ride back, though. Thought you might want to know about that."

The guard leader's eyebrows shot up and disappeared behind the brim of his helm at the mention of trolls, and by the time Turin had finished speaking, his expression had shifted from wariness to concern. "Odd. They don't usually venture this close to the main road. Are you sure it wasn't some other large beast?"

Some of the other soldiers had stiffened, their mounts

dancing about in response to added tension on their reins. Others began speaking in indistinct tones to each other, but Sophie heard the word "trolls" on more than one set of lips.

Turin tilted his head and shrugged. "Pretty sure. Anything we should keep an eye out for ahead?"

The guard's eyes drifted to the east as if his mind was still fixed on the prospect of trolls, but he answered, "Nothing of significance. A lot more people on the road farther west, though. Lord Castellus is hosting some big event at Tempest Hall soon, so many guests and common folk are heading in that direction—probably looking for work." The man's attention returned to Turin and the rest of their group, and he eyed each of them appraisingly. "Is that where you all are headed as well?"

Sophie felt herself squirm under the man's scrutiny. She smiled faintly with what she hoped was innocence and was relieved when his gaze moved on. She was glad Turin had offered to speak on their behalf but wondered if it had been a good idea to draw attention to themselves by stopping the patrol in the first place.

"Maybe," Turin answered as if he were considering the possibility. A few moments later, he inclined his head toward the guardsman. "Well, thank you for stopping, and keep an eye out for those trolls!"

With a smile and a small wave, Turin nudged his horse into a walk and started forward down the road. Sophie and Eolisti followed his lead, and Sophie didn't have to look back to know Khalil would be right behind them again. When she did chance a glance over her shoulder, Sophie saw the patrol moving away.

It could have been her imagination, but she thought she caught concerned expressions on a couple of the men's faces as she'd passed. She didn't know any of them, but she sincerely hoped they didn't run into any trolls. Something else nagged at her about the exchange, though she couldn't quite put her finger on it until the Anai spoke in a soft voice, meant only for Sophie to hear.

"So, now there's going to be some 'big event' in the same place this unknown bird person went missing." Eolisti's eyes narrowed as she shot a sidelong look at Sophie. "That's odd, right?"

Sophie nodded. On the one hand, it was possible that the Nightingale's disappearance and the gathering were coincidental. On the other, it also seemed plausible that the two things were related, but she couldn't begin to fathom how. There was simply too little information to go on at this point. She only hoped that they would learn more before they reached their destination.

CHAPTER
NINE

My name is Rhyn. I am from Morigael. I am the Phoenix.

Rhyn stared at the dark brocade canopy of the giant bed she lay in. The gold threads reflected the earliest rays of pre-dawn light that found their way through the heavily curtained windows. The only sound to be heard was her breathing.

She couldn't tell exactly how long she had been here but knew from these brief moments of lucidity between drug doses that it had been at least eight days. At least eight days that she could remember. Today was the ninth morning that she could recall.

Drowsily she flexed her right foot and felt the ring of hard metal around her ankle. As feeling began to trickle back into her body and her mind began to work again, she could sense the faint stir of energy in the thing that kept it locked tight around her leg. She reached under the covers to touch it, vainly trying to grasp it with her numb fingertips. It was probably foolish to expect a result different from what she'd gotten the last eight mornings, but she told herself that she had to keep looking for any weakness, any opportunity to escape.

Anklets such as this were more often used in the lands to the east. Even there, though, their use was relatively rare and, therefore, worn only by high-value slaves. Paired with a control ring, the anklet was used to incentivize perfect compliance with whatever command the person wearing the ring gave. She closed her eyes at the sudden memory of blinding pain that had made her wish she were dead. She would have done anything to make that pain stop if she could have.

Fortunately, or perhaps, unfortunately, none of Lord Castellus's people possessed the fine control over the anklet needed to use it as an effective means of interrogation. That hadn't stopped them from trying. She had the vaguest recollection from her first days in the castle of questions being shouted at her that she couldn't comprehend. The pain had been so intense that she hadn't been able to move, let alone speak.

The face of her father swam in her memories. He had been there, witnessing her weakness and doing nothing but observing, his eyes as cold as she remembered from years past. There had been another man there, but she couldn't recall what he looked like. He, too, had been a silent spectator to her suffering.

Later, there had been more questioning, and though there had been pain, it had been relatively tolerable. It had been the usual "Who sent you, who do you work for" routine one would expect. Unless she had lost the memory of it, she was confident she hadn't given up any information.

She knew that it was nothing special about her that let her withstand the questioning. It was far more likely a failing of the person asking the questions or the one controlling the anklet when they were different people. Or perhaps it was just that Tempest Hall rarely housed prisoners who had undergone training like hers, and they were unprepared to handle someone of her caliber. Whatever the case, the questioning stopped after some time. It was difficult to keep her sense of time straight, but she still remembered nine sunrises and prayed to the gods that there hadn't been more.

My name is Rhyn. I am from Morigael. I am the Phoenix.

After the questionings had ceased, she'd blissfully floated along on a cloud of sedatives. She had a vague awareness of the things happening around her, but no ability to grasp anything. But for some reason, it was not acceptable to her captors for her to be completely addled. Eventually, the drugs had been reduced to the point that she'd been able to nearly make her escape. Nearly.

She had awoken to find herself in this bedchamber, with a mousy little maid tending to her. Noting that they were alone in the room together, she'd decided to take a chance. The girl was preparing to change the bed linens and chattering about how pleased the lord was to have her safely home again. When she'd turned from her pile of sheets back to the bed, Rhyn had punched her squarely in the jaw, and the girl had crumpled to the floor in an unceremonious heap that would have been comical if not for her circumstance.

Thinking quickly, Rhyn stripped the maid of her outer garments and put them on herself. It was time to improvise and do what she did best. To keep from being recognized, she piled all the sheets and blankets she could into her arms until she could barely see over them. She'd made it almost to the kitchen before she'd been caught.

That was when she'd discovered another function of the slave anklet. Apparently, it conveyed an awareness of its location to the person who wore the control ring. At least, that was the only plausible explanation Rhyn could come up with.

After she'd been trundled back up the stairs to the room where the maid was just coming to, the physician had drugged her again, but this time under the watchful eye of Lord Castellus. Why he was keeping her alive she wasn't sure. She knew that the lord felt no affection toward her, though men like him believed people to be possessions to do with whatever they saw fit. He needed to be in control of her, and if he thought he could use her for any gain, he would do so. Even if he had not been pleased with the state she'd been left in at first, he certainly did not want her sober enough to escape.

Her memories faded again after that point.

Rhyn was unsure how much time had passed after that escape attempt, but she'd begun to find herself passively aware of things around her. The court physician had honed the dosage of the blue drug that was faintly magical to the point that it was enough to make her compliant, but not so much that she was catatonic. The result was that she found herself a prisoner of her own body, barely able to speak and requiring the constant attention of maids for the basic functions of living.

The only ray of hope that remained was that the potion did wear off after a few hours. As the effects began to wane, she found herself increasingly alert and clear-headed. She had acted hastily before—a mistake she wouldn't make again. This time, she played along, continuing to behave as though she was still stupefied. Doing so, she'd bought herself close to an hour three times a day when she was able to think, observe, and plan.

My name is Rhyn. I am from Morigael. I am the Phoenix.

That was when she'd started counting the days. Nine days. In that time, she'd begun to piece together the details of her situation. She'd overheard her maids gossiping about how exciting it was that the Lord's youngest daughter, kidnapped years ago and long thought dead, had finally been returned. They found it sad that she had been through such a terrible ordeal that she was now prone to fits of insanity if not kept properly medicated.

Other than the story being told about her sudden appearance, she gathered that Lord Castellus was, indeed, planning something, as the Nightingales had suspected. Nobles from across the land were being called to Tempest Hall for a feast, and the rumor was that Lord Castellus was planning to make a major announcement. Some of the maids speculated it had something to do with young Lord Gaius Castellus, but none of them had any idea what it could be. Rhyn had never personally met the boy—her brother—so she had no idea what to make of those particular whispers.

The other topic of chatter was about the various nobles that were arriving. Most of the names she knew, but none stood out to her as having any significance.

That changed when she heard that the Golistin family was in attendance.

The Golistins had been scandalously exiled from Morigael some twenty-odd years earlier for a failed coup attempt. Lord Golistin was the brother of the king of Morigael, and he had been discovered plotting with the Tanalin Empire to overthrow the king in exchange for being installed as the governor of what would once again become the Imperial Province of Morigael. After the failed attempt, word was that the disgraced family had somehow been able to exchange something of value to achieve their current standing in the Tanalin Empire, but she'd never heard exactly what that might have been.

A sound in the hallway pulled her attention from her thoughts. The growing whisper of footsteps resolved with a polite knock on the door before the latch lifted. It was one of the maids with her morning draught.

With an effort, Rhyn plastered a vacant expression on her face and continued to think. There were still too many things she didn't know or couldn't quite figure out, one of which was what had become of Winna. Had she succumbed to her injuries? Or had Castellus found another use for her? She was helpless to find out more unless the girl was brought up in her presence, so she mentally filed her apprentice away for the moment and forced herself to focus on a way out. Maybe then she could help Winna too.

The maid that entered was a portly older woman with blonde hair peeking from under her cap. She tottered a little as she curtsied and said, "Good morning, Lady Korynne." Recovering, she moved purposefully into the room and set a tray holding a pitcher, a cup, and a dark-blue vial on the bedside table before bustling over to throw curtains back from the room's windows. She chattered at Rhyn about the weather and other inane things, but Rhyn ignored her. She needed to focus while she still could!

Aside from her father promoting the fantastic story of her kidnapping and that she was a madwoman, Rhyn had no idea what he planned to do with her. Use her to gain sympathy? That wasn't really his style. Other men might see the advantage of feigned weakness, but Lord Castellus was not such a person. He was far too proud for anything of that sort. Perhaps he intended to frame a rival house as the party responsible for her abduction as a pretense for an attack.

The maid had already returned to Rhyn's bedside and was mixing the vial's contents with water in the cup. It took another mental effort to keep her stare passive and her neck and limbs limp as the woman slid a hand behind her head and lifted the cup to her lips. The concoction was vile, but somehow, she'd been able to keep her features relaxed as the liquid was gently poured into her mouth. After the last drop fell from the cup, the maid clucked, dabbed Rhyn's lips free of residual moisture with a small cloth and turned to arrange the tray again before carrying it away. Not much time now.

A thought struck her that almost made her break her calm facade. It was possible that Lord Castellus intended to marry her off in the interest of a political alliance. That was, after all, what daughters were for. Distasteful as the idea was to her, she'd be foolish to discount that option—both as Lord Castellus's plan and as an opportunity for escape. Marriage seemed unlikely, though, if he was claiming she was insane.

There was something else. Something she was missing. Something important. What was it? She tried to grasp at her thoughts, but everything seemed to grow foggy at the edges.

My... name...

CHAPTER

TEN

After a few days of riding, Sophie was utterly exhausted. In the mornings, she practiced physical combat with Khalil, and then after packing up their camp, rode until sunset with few breaks in between. Sleeping on the hard ground night after night did little to restore her energy, and she woke up tired and sore. Both Khalil and Turin assured her that the training would get easier as time passed, but Sophie wondered darkly if she would feel this way for the rest of her life.

The farther they rode northwest of Mattina, the colder it grew. The snow-covered mountains to their right grew more prominent, and frost coated the ground in the mornings. Snowfall happened more often, and by the second day, she was adding more layers to her clothing as the skies above them stayed consistently gray. The chill didn't seem to bother Turin or Khalil, but she noticed that Eolisti also started wearing heavier garments.

Khalil had begun riding ahead with Turin while Sophie and Eolisti followed. Eolisti didn't seem as eager to talk to Turin as she had the other people they'd met during their journey. Sophie smiled fondly at the memories of the Anai's rapid-fire questions when they first met. She didn't seem as suspicious of Turin as she'd been of Khalil when he'd first joined them, but she still seemed wary of him. Was Eolisti thinking of how easy it had been to believe that Joel was exactly as he'd presented himself? Was she hesitant to trust Turin because they had been betrayed in the past?

These last few days of traveling had made Sophie appreciate the knight. It wasn't just the added protection and knowledge of the area that he contributed to the group. There was a light-hearted optimism that almost radiated off him. He was interesting to talk to and was happy to discuss whatever she asked about at length. Sophie enjoyed listening to him talk about Morigael, and since she might be living there soon, paid close attention. She wanted to know what to expect when she finally reached her destination. He mostly talked about the food he longed for, but even that sounded much different from her old home.

They were still a few days' ride out from Tempest Hall and the town surrounding it. The countryside had shifted to yellows and browns, spotted with white patches of snowfall. Tall pine trees reached for the sky, and Sophie could see thousands of them forming a dense forest at the base of the mountains in the distance. She had been through the warm humidity of Zo'rahn and the dry heat of Omer, but the air here was clear and brisk. It was not as bitterly cold as in the mountains near Ta'Shela, though she had a feeling that the harsh winters in Tanalin weren't any more pleasant. Still, bundled up as she was, Sophie didn't mind the colder weather. It made her face tingle, and she had to cover her nose with a shawl every so often, but the crisp air kept her awake and alert on her horse.

As they crested a hill, Turin raised a hand for them to

stop. "There are a few wagons ahead of us," he said, squinting into the distance.

Eolisti pulled her horse up beside him. The Anai had demonstrated superior eyesight in the past and did not disappoint this time. "Two wagons," she confirmed. "Looks like five or six men and..." She trailed off, leaning forward in her saddle. "There are some more people on the ground. I think they might be tied up or something."

"It could be bandits," Khalil said as Sophie's eyes flicked over the plains, searching. She could see the wagons that Turin had noticed and the people moving around them in the distance. Given her experience with the Anai, she trusted Eolisti's assessment.

She and the Anai had come across bandits once before back in Zo'rahn. Sophie remembered the fear that had been coursing through her at the time. It hadn't been a pleasant experience. "We should help them," she said fervently, glancing at Turin.

He nodded at her. "We'll have the advantage coming down the hill." Tugging on the reins, he wheeled his horse around and thundered away.

They rode down the hill swiftly, and Turin, Khalil, and Eolisti all drew their swords while Sophie tried to focus her mind. It was difficult to do while bouncing around on the back of the animal, but she concentrated on the rhythm of the hoofbeats, and it gave her an idea. As they approached, she clapped her hands together, using the momentum of their ride and sending a thundering wave out in front of her companions. It washed over the bandits with a deafening CRACK, throwing them from their feet. Sophie winced as she saw the captives tossed aside as well. She would have to refine that spell.

As he reached the first wagon, Turin slid off his steed in

one smooth motion and brought his sword down on one of the fallen men. The bandit rolled out of the way, scrambling for his sword as Eolisti landed in front of him, kicking the blade away before jumping out of reach.

Turin's heavy booted foot connected with the man's stomach while he was distracted by the Anai. As the bandit fell onto his side, the knight rested the point of his sword on the man's throat. Even though Sophie saw Turin's lips move, she couldn't hear what he was saying as the clash of steel on steel pulled her attention away.

Eolisti was battling another man who seemed to have recovered quickly from being knocked prone. He brought his sword down on her, only to have the Anai deflect the blow and slip around behind him. She brought the hilt of her sword down savagely on the back of his head, and he crumpled bonelessly to the ground.

Khalil had similarly disarmed the last bandit. Dodging a sword swing with little more than a sidestep and lashing out, his fist connected with this opponent's stomach. The outlaw doubled over and retched before Khalil knocked the man out with the hilt of his sword in a similar motion to the one Eolisti had used.

As the fighting abruptly stopped, the only sounds were the nickering of the horses and Turin's voice as he said, "I suggest you hold still," to the still-conscious bandit. "Sophie, rope, please."

Sophie, who'd not participated in the battle aside from the initial burst of magic, shifted the reins, directing her horse toward Turin. She reached into a bag attached to her saddle and tossed him a length of coiled rope. The man on the ground looked up at her as Turin knelt to tie his hands behind his back. He wasn't in very good shape. His face and clothes were dirty, and his cheeks were hollow. Examining him more closely, Sophie saw that the tunic and breeches he wore were loose on him and the bones in his hands and arms stood out sharply against his skin. The look he gave her had no heat behind it. This man had the appearance of a person who had been beaten down and broken, and not by the recent fight. Sophie found herself feeling sorry for him. It was obvious that these people were suffering.

Turin finished and stood, staring down at the man he'd bound and gagged. While the downtrodden bandit had shown no aggression toward Sophie, when his eyes turned on the knight, anger sparked there. Turin frowned and shook his head, holding one hand out to help Sophie off her horse. "An unlucky day for you and your companions. I know times are hard, but you should stick to an honest living. Hurting others will gain you nothing in the end." Following Turin's lead, Eolisti and Khalil bound the other two bandits and dragged them over to the first one.

Sophie surveyed the robbers' victims, looking for injuries. While not an expert in healing magic by any means, she could heal some of the simpler wounds and sicknesses, things that were easy to identify and treat. Two women and three men were tied up by the wagons, and all of them watched her approach with wary expressions. She knelt to untie the gag on the closest one, a man looking to be in his late twenties.

"Are you all right? Is anyone hurt?" she asked as he gasped for air.

Before the man could speak, grass crunched behind Sophie. "Here, let me help," Eolisti said as she leaned down to untie him.

"Thank you, thank you!" the man cried. "We're a little roughed up, but they didn't hurt any of us badly." He looked around wildly at his companions. "We didn't see them coming. I never expected an attack in the middle of the day."

"Obviously," Eolisti snorted as the knot came loose. She moved on to the others. "Are there more people in the wagons?" she asked, looking around.

"No," the woman she released said, rubbing at her wrists. "It's just us out here. We're not bad with swords, but you—" She looked up at Eolisti with a reverent look in her eyes. "You were amazing."

A wide, self-satisfied grin spread across the Anai's face as she moved on to the next traveler.

As Sophie stepped back, Turin approached and helped the first young man to his feet. He stood a few inches shorter than the knight, who towered over the rest of them. "My name is Turin. Where are you headed? If it's in the same direction we are going, we can escort you to the next town."

"I'm Draxos," the man said, rubbing his wrists where there were angry marks from the rope. His skin was a dark brown, making the quickly forming bruises on his face and hands a garish purple. "We're heading west to Tempest Hall for the feast."

If Turin was surprised by Draxos' answer, he hid it well. He smiled at the other man and clapped him on the shoulder. "Azorah smiles on us, my friend. We're heading there as well."

Draxos returned Turin's smile. "We would be grateful if you and your companions accompanied us." He looked over at the blonde woman Eolisti had been talking to, and she nodded. "We don't have much money to spare, but we can share our food with you. This is my wife, Perella." Smiling, he took the woman's hand.

"Please, call me Peri," she said. "Thank you for saving

us." Peri's eyes followed Eolisti as she finished untying the others before returning to stand beside Turin.

Draxos turned to his other companions, introducing each one in turn. A tall man with short-cropped black hair was Troy, a young woman with mousy brown hair was Minette, and the older man with gray running through his coarse, dark hair and a scar over one eye was Lucky.

"Lucky?" Sophie asked. "Is that your real name?"

"It's short for Lucius," Lucky said in a deep, resonant baritone. "But that was my father's name, so they called me Lucky, and it stuck."

"This is Sophie and Eolisti," Turin said, gesturing first to Sophie and then to the Anai. "And the broody one over there is Khalil."

"Why do you have two wagons for just the five of you?" Khalil asked. He was standing a little way away from the rest of them. He'd collected their horses while Turin and Eolisti were helping the others. "You could all fit in one."

There were only two wagons but Khalil was right. Even factoring in provisions and other supplies, there would be no need for the extra.

"We're musicians," Lucky replied. "Our instruments can take up a lot of room. That one," he pointed at the wagon in the front, "is just what we need to perform."

The men and women brushed themselves off as they got to their feet. Sophie examined each in turn, checking for injuries, but there were only bruises and minor cuts, nothing that needed healing.

"Why did we all fall when you first rode in?" Draxos asked. "And what was that loud noise? It sounded like a cannon."

"Get your people ready to go," Turin said, ignoring the question. "We should get out of here before it gets too late."

Draxos frowned but didn't press. Eolisti helped Sophie back onto her horse as the travelers climbed into their wagons. "I guess your magic is still a secret," the Anai said in a whisper.

Sophie nodded, wondering why Turin hadn't told them. It wouldn't be dangerous to use spells here, as it had been back in Omer. She would have to ask him about it later.

"We'll leave them here," Turin said, climbing back onto his horse. He gestured to the bandits who still sat bound not far from them. "This is the main road for the area. It shouldn't be too long before a patrol finds them." He looked thoughtful for a moment, then, reaching into his saddle bag, threw one of the bandit's swords he'd confiscated earlier at the conscious one's feet, along with a small pack that Sophie knew contained provisions. The man glared up at Turin, but couldn't speak through the gag.

"You should be able to cut yourself free eventually," Turin said down to him. "Better than being eaten by trolls." He pulled on his reins, and the horse nickered softly. "Go home. This isn't worth your life." With that, he dug his heels into his mare's flanks, and the horse trotted to join the rest of them.

THEY RODE until just before sunset and set up camp not far from the road. The night was overcast and cold, so the musicians built a large campfire with the help of Turin and Eolisti. Sophie went to gather firewood with Peri and discovered why the woman had been so enamored with Eolisti.

"Anai are so wonderful and mysterious," she sighed, a bundle full of wood and kindling in her arms. "I've seen them in the capital, of course, but I've never seen one fight before! It was like watching a dance."

Sophie recalled having the same thoughts before. "Yes, it really is."

They brought a few armfuls of wood back. Before long, they had a roaring fire going. Peri set a pot over the fire, adding ingredients until steam rose from within and the air was filled with the smell of garlic and rosemary. Sophie settled down by the fire, stomach growling as she smelled the food. Trying to chase away the chill, she wrapped herself in a blanket and held her hands out to the flames.

The others unloaded wooden and leather cases, placing them on the ground near their seats around the fire. Draxos brought a stack of wooden bowls from one of the wagons and helped Peri serve the food.

"Here you are," he said genially, passing Sophie a wooden bowl filled to the brim with a steaming stew of carrots, potatoes, and little chunks of meat floating in a brown broth. "I didn't realize how desperate it would be out here." Draxos sat next to her on the grass. "We're from the capital, Dalophon, to the south. I heard there was a blight, but the emperor started pulling more supplies from the surrounding countryside, so we weren't hit very badly there."

"You're a long way from the capital," Khalil said, sitting on Sophie's other side.

Draxos smiled and took a bite of his food. "This is the first time I've come out this far, but Castellus is paying well, and we were the only troupe willing to make the journey. I can see now why others refused."

The stew wasn't bad. It had been a few days since Sophie had eaten a full meal like this and felt the warmth from the food and fire sinking deep within her. "So, this feast," she began between bites. She had to be careful not to let on what they were trying to do or that she didn't know anything about the feast he'd mentioned before. "It sounds like it's going to be pretty big."

"Are you guests? Your friend mentioned earlier that you were heading there as well." He glanced over at Turin, who was brushing down the horses.

Something in his tone told her that he knew they weren't guests. "No, we're... looking for work. Like you, we've also heard that the Castellus family pays well." She recalled the large gatherings and events the Vizier would host at his estate when she was an apprentice. They were grand affairs, offering guests the opportunity to indulge in food, drink, and entertainment. Her voice gained a touch more confidence as she continued. "Surely, an event like this will require more staff than is locally available."

Draxos seemed to relax a little at her words. "True enough." He set aside the half-eaten bowl of food and opened the wooden case next to him, drawing forth a beautiful, well-cared-for violin. He plucked a few strings on it and turned a knob at the top. "If you're looking for work, you could head to the castle with us. We'll be arriving the day before the feast, but I'm sure they will still need people to fill in. It'll probably be serving or something, but maybe you and your friends could get hired on as security." He took another bite before continuing. "I'd be happy to put in a good word for you."

Sophie thanked him and finished the stew. This could be their way into the feast. It would be much easier to get in and look around the castle as a servant than trying to sneak in.

Not long after dinner, all the musicians, except Lucky, retired to their wagon. It had been an exciting day for them, so Sophie understood their desire to get a good night's rest. Lucky went to stand watch, leaving the warmth of the fire and taking a book and a hooded lamp with him.

Once the others were out of earshot, Sophie, Eolisti, Khalil, and Turin sat around the dwindling campfire, and Sophie explained to them in a quiet whisper what Draxos had told her about finding work.

"Going in as servants," Turin mused. "Is that really the best way to infiltrate the castle? We would probably have to leave most of our weapons behind."

"Whatever we decide to do, we're not going to be able to get in there with all of our supplies," Khalil said. "Not when the castle is full of noblemen and their entourages. Security will be tight." He pressed his lips together thoughtfully. "Going in as servants is not a bad idea. We can still take whatever weapons we can hide under our clothing. It would allow us to see what we are up against, maybe even where they are holding the Phoenix."

Eolisti scowled. "I don't want to serve a bunch of humans, and I've done what other people have told me to do more than enough for one lifetime, thank you."

"We might have a problem with you being disguised as a servant anyway. There aren't many Anai who take employment with humans." Turin scratched his chin. He had a few days' worth of stubble growing in. "Though if we can convince the steward that you'll work hard, it may not be an issue. Surely, you can take orders from us humans for a day or two?" he said with a wink.

The Anai's scowl deepened. Sophie smiled to herself. She didn't think Eolisti would react well to Turin's suggestion, but she may not have a choice.

CHAPTER

ELEVEN

Brumalar was exactly how Sophie had imagined it, a collection of farms and houses, sparse at first but quickly growing more numerous as they approached. The large structure that was Tempest Hall loomed in the distance, a dark, foreboding mark in a field of white snow. It looked small from where they were, but she knew that was just their perspective of the town. She imagined it would be akin to a fortress once they were inside those walls.

"Sophie!" Minette called to her from the second wagon, waving the mage over. She was driving it while Lucky was napping in the back.

Sophie had gotten to know the musicians better as they'd traveled together the last week. Draxos was loud and boisterous, the obvious leader of the group, while Peri liked to laugh and chatted a lot with Eolisti, able to keep up with the Anai's rapid questioning of anyone she found interesting. Troy was also outgoing but seemed less confident than Draxos. Lucky and Minette were the quietest of the group, with Lucky proclaiming often that he was too old for this life on the road and lamenting that he hadn't retired years earlier. The way he said it made Sophie certain that it was all an act. She could tell by the way he carried himself when they made camp that he enjoyed spending his days outside.

The story that Turin suggested they use was that Sophie was from Omer and that the four of them had met at an inn there, deciding to travel to Tanalin in search of adventure and profit before they knew of the crisis here. Now, they were taking on any jobs they could to secure funds for their travels. The musicians seemed to take them at their word, but Sophie suspected that they didn't quite believe them.

Minette had approached Sophie when she was alone the second night they traveled together and asked her if she was a noble lady in disguise. The question had caught her off guard, and she had denied it in a fluster, but in the following days, she was extra careful around the brown-haired musician. Still, Minette had seemed to take a liking to her, and Sophie couldn't say that she disliked the conversation.

The mage pulled on the reins, directing her horse closer to Minette's wagon. "Is something the matter?"

The musician smiled at her. "No, but I noticed you looking around. You should know a little about the village and the keep since I'm guessing it's your first time here."

"Is it that obvious?" Sophie asked, feeling a blush on her cheeks.

Minette laughed. "With how you and your Anaiian friend are interested in every small detail of this land and its people, I doubt you've been in the country for very long." She was right of course, and the fact that Eolisti had dozens of questions for the troupe every night didn't help. "Lucky and I have been here once, before we joined up with the others. It was a few years ago, but I remember what it was like."

"Very well, what can you tell me about this place?"

Her eyes swept across the farms and buildings. "Brumalar isn't as bad as some of the other parts of Tanalin, but you should still be careful. I've heard that Lord Castellus does what he can for his tenants, but there's only so much food that can be brought so far out from a major city. You'll probably run into people like those bandits your friends fought off." Minette smiled at her. "But still, I hope to see you up at the castle. No point in you traveling all this way just to have to turn around. Serving the nobility isn't easy, there's a lot of bowing and saying m'lord and m'lady to every finely dressed person you meet, but the pay is good. Lord Castellus is known to provide a decent wage, even to temporary staff."

Sophie frowned as Minette talked. She made this "Lord Castellus" sound like a decent person, but if he was holding the Phoenix prisoner, that couldn't have been true. She was a Nightingale, so that meant Lord Castellus had drawn their attention, but something about this didn't add up. Why was the Phoenix here in the first place?

The Nightingales helped people, she was evidence of that, but was that all they did? Sophie had never thought to ask, being grateful that they were aiding her, but maybe she should talk with Khalil about it and get more information about this organization.

"Are you all right?" Minette asked. "You don't look pleased."

"It's nothing," Sophie said quickly. "My thoughts were wandering. Please, continue."

"Well, as I was saying, you should be careful in town. Stick with your friends. As skilled as they are, they'll be able to find some work up at the castle, even if it's mostly manual labor." She gave Sophie a sidelong glance. "I'm sure you can find a position as a maid."

The mage smiled. Minette was probably thinking that Sophie had never cleaned anything in her life, but the musician didn't know that she was a wizard. Back in Zo'rahn, she had gotten into her fair share of trouble, and punishments for apprentices usually involved scrubbing and laundering without the use of magic.

"I'm sure I'll manage," she said. "Do you know anything about Lord Castellus? I've heard his name before, but I don't know anything about him. It would be good if I knew a little more since we are seeking employment at the castle."

"Oh, you'll probably never see him. Servants don't usually interact with the nobility, and the lord of the castle won't converse with the temporary staff." Minette sighed and gazed at Tempest Hall in the distance, illuminated by the afternoon sunlight. "From what I've heard of him, he spends his time split between the keep here and his residence in the capital city. House Castellus is known as one of the more powerful families in the Empire, and the current head of that family is Lord Darian Castellus."

Minette scrunched up her nose as her brows furrowed. "There was something about him that was sad, but I just can't remember. Some of the ladies in Dalophon whispered about it."

"It was about his wife and daughter," called Lucky's voice from inside the wagon. He popped his head out the front next to where Minette was seated. For supposedly being asleep in the back of the wagon, he looked alert. "If you're going to tell the story, tell it right," he chided.

The brown-haired woman scowled down at him. "I don't remember the story. Why don't you tell it?"

"Let's see," Lucky began as he climbed into the seat next to Minette and gave Sophie a wink. "It was some time ago —eleven, maybe twelve years. Lord Castellus's wife fell ill while she was with child and died giving birth to the lord's heir. Right after her funeral, his youngest daughter went missing, and it was rumored that she was taken captive by another powerful house to keep Castellus in line. Such things were done in the past," he said to Sophie's outraged look. "Well, the girl never turned up, so she's probably dead. Losing his wife and daughter, one after the other, he was so heartbroken, he never remarried," he finished solemnly.

"You made that last part up," Minette scoffed.

Lucky shrugged. "It makes for a better story. The grief-stricken lord that cannot love again," he said dramatically.

Minette shook her head. "She needs *useful* information, Lucky."

The older man scratched his beard. "He's known for being strict but fair. He married his elder daughter off in a political alliance, but I can't remember what house it was to..."

His words trailed off as he focused on something in front of them. Sophie followed his gaze. There was a crowd gathering in a large area that must have been the town square. A tall man stood on a platform, reading from a scroll to the gathered people. She was too far to hear what he was saying, but Eolisti watched the man with rapt attention, a scowl marring her features.

Sophie gave Lucky and Minette a nod and directed her horse over to the Anai's.

"What is it?" she asked, leaning over in her saddle to speak quietly.

"I can't hear what he's saying, but it doesn't look good." They watched as a man was dragged onto the platform, his hands bound.

Pursing her lips, Sophie's eyes narrowed at the spectacle. She thought she knew what was happening. In Zo'rahn, public punishments were used on people who broke the Vizier's laws, both to administer justice and to shame the offender by ensuring that everyone knew of the person's crime and resulting punishment. Seeing the punishment imposed also served to discourage others from breaking the law. As she watched, the bound man was led over to a tall wooden post attached to the platform and tied there. Sophie averted her eyes, not wanting to see what came next.

"What's going to happen to him?" Eolisti asked as they rode closer. They caught up to Turin, who had stopped his horse and was waiting for them.

"A flogging, most likely," he answered instead of Sophie. Eolisti looked confused so he continued. "The person being punished is hit several times on his back with a whip or a cane. It's the usual punishment for thievery and other minor crimes."

The Anai looked aghast. "But that man looks like he's starving!" she said, pointing toward the platform. Sophie couldn't see as well as Eolisti, but she was right. Even from this distance, she could see that he was mostly skin and bones. "So, what? He steals some food and gets beaten for it?"

Turin didn't look happy about it either, but he just shrugged. By this point, Khalil had slowed to keep pace with them as well, riding on Sophie's other side.

"This is barbaric. The Anai wouldn't do something like this," Eolisti growled, glaring first at the knight, then at Sophie.

"We don't know that he's a thief, or if he is, what he stole," Turin said. "They can't afford to imprison him with the food shortage. What else could they do? He'll need time to heal, but he'll live." The knight sighed. He seemed uncomfortable with the situation, and Sophie had the impression he wanted to help, even though he was trying to soothe Eolisti.

"It's not much different in Zo'rahn," Sophie muttered.

Eolisti turned her glare on Khalil. "And you?"

"Where I come from, a thief would lose a hand," Khalil said, voice emotionless. "Or be put to death, if he robbed the wrong person."

"Eolisti, we agree with you," Turin cut in before she could go off on Khalil. "This isn't right, but we can't make a spectacle out of it, not so close to Tempest Hall. It would jeopardize the mission. Besides, they aren't doing anything wrong, according to their laws. There's no use getting worked up over something we can't do anything about."

She eyed him, her jaw tense, and her lips drew into a stubborn line. "Is it any different in Morigael?"

"The king wouldn't let it get to this point in Morigael," Turin replied with a sharp look in her direction.

Before Eolisti could argue further, Draxos' voice came from the head wagon.

"We'll be heading straight to the castle." A moment later, they could see his face as he looked back at them from the driver's seat. "Are you going to join us?"

"We'll catch up with you!" Turin called to Draxos as he slowed his horse to a stop again. "It'll just be a moment."

The musician waved at them as their wagons continued

down the road and toward the field that led up to Tempest Hall. The other three followed Turin's lead and allowed the wagons to get ahead.

"I'm going to head up to the castle and speak to the steward," Turin began once the musicians were far enough away that he would not be overheard. "Draxos said he would put in a good word for us and that will make getting into Tempest Hall much easier. With any luck, they are still hiring servants for whatever celebration the lord is planning." Turin leaned back in the saddle and surveyed the road that the musicians were traveling on. "I'll meet up with you at an inn called the Running Maiden this afternoon. Lucky recommended staying there. It's on the edge of town and closest to the castle." His eyes tracked back to the crowd gathered in the square, then to his companions.

"Stay out of trouble," he added, looking directly at Eolisti.

She pretended not to notice his look or comment, but when he turned his horse around and began to trot off, Eolisti stuck her tongue out at his back. Turning to Sophie, she said. "Let's explore the village. We have some time before that guy"—she frowned at Turin's retreating form—"comes back to spoil our fun."

Sophie nodded, flicking her reins, and directed her horse to follow Eolisti's. Khalil brought up the end of their small procession. He hadn't seemed bothered by the suggestion to look around. Back in Omer, he would have hurried her to their next destination to keep her out of sight, but here, there was no one looking for her and no need to hide. Not for the first time, she inwardly noted that the difference in the actions of their companion was like night and day. The mage smiled to herself.

The village here was in much better shape than what

they'd seen in Mattina. None of the buildings had their doors or windows boarded up, nor did the place look half abandoned. In fact, there were plenty of people on the roads. Men and women dressed in simple but warm-looking clothing made way for the travelers. Some waved at Sophie as they passed, but many more stared at Eolisti. Their stares varied from curious to wary and most hurried away as she approached.

Turin had been right. Eolisti stood out here. By the looks on their faces, these people did not trust the Anai.

As they approached a road with a row of shops, Sophie glanced down an alley, seeing small, glistening eyes and forlorn faces staring back at her.

They had the same look as the bandits that had attacked the musicians on the road, hollow cheeks from hunger and the look of those who had been beaten down by their circumstances. The children here were not so different from the ones she'd seen in Mattina. Hungry, dirty, and without much hope of surviving the winter.

The state of the people in Mattina had surprised her, but since then, she'd come to understand it was not uncommon all over Tanalin. But here, on the surface, this village appeared almost prosperous. The lord of the castle must want to ensure the truth remains hidden. To see their reality, one only need look into the eyes of these suffering children.

"A moment, please," Sophie said to Eolisti, then slid out of the saddle. She rummaged in her bag until she pulled out a small bundle tied in one of the rectangular pieces of cloth she'd used as a headscarf back when they'd been in the desert. Knowing that they were bound to run into more starving people on their journey, she had saved some of the travel rations that Turin had provided them.

It wasn't enough to feed everyone, but it was what she had.

Eolisti frowned but nodded when Sophie gazed up at her, and the mage approached the mouth of the alley. The small forms shrank back from her presence.

"It's all right," she called to them. "I'm not going to hurt you. Here." She held out the little package. "Please, take this." Sophie knew the small bits of food would not alleviate their suffering for long, but she couldn't stand by and do nothing. Turin didn't want anything to draw attention to their presence, but if this small thing caused them trouble, he was just going to have to deal with it.

The smallest figure moved out of the shadows, a little girl no older than ten with brown hair that was unkempt and dirty. She raised her arms, her little fingers brushing Sophie's as she took the bundle from her.

"Thank you, miss," the girl said in a soft voice. Sophie nodded as the girl placed the bundle on the ground and crouched next to it, untying it. Two other children emerged, another girl a few years older than the first and a boy that was even younger, both with the same brown hair and eyes. As the cloth came undone, all three sets of eyes widened at the slices of salted meat, bread, cheese, and dried fruit.

The sound of boots scraping on stone caught her attention, and Sophie looked over her shoulder. Eolisti had dismounted and approached, standing just a few feet behind Sophie. She watched the children, the same frown marring her delicate features. Khalil also approached, but he stood a little way off, holding the reins of their horses.

All three children eyed him suspiciously. The boy pointed, looking as though he were about to ask a question, but the younger girl pushed his hand back down and shook her head. "It's rude to point," she chided, but even as she said it, the girl ducked her head a little, trying to see under Khalil's hood.

"Do you live around here?" the Anai asked as the oldest one broke off a piece of bread and took a few hungry bites.

"A few streets down," she said after she swallowed. She blinked a few times and squinted up at Eolisti. "What's someone like you doing here?" Her tone wasn't exactly friendly.

"Whatever I want to do, that's what," Eolisti said, bristling.

"Where are your parents?" Sophie asked loudly before Eolisti could continue. "Surely, they don't want you wandering around town by yourselves." She was tempted to use magic to clean the younger girl's face. Dirt was smudged on her cheeks and forehead, and her clothes were little more than rags, not fit for the cold weather. The sun was out, and it wasn't as chilled as the previous days, but it would still be uncomfortable in the threadbare garments these children donned. Unable to do anything else, she settled for leaning over and wiping the girl's cheeks with the edge of her cloak. The child didn't seem to mind, continuing to chew on a sausage.

"Mum's working," the older girl said. "She cleans during the day. Our father died last year." She looked down at the piece of bread she was still clutching. "It's been hard since then."

Sophie straightened, and there was a tight feeling in her chest. She didn't know these children, but she felt sorry for them. "What are your names?"

"I am Aelia, miss," the oldest one said, then placed her hands on her sister's shoulders. "This is Maela, and my brother's name is Cam."

Eolisti focused on something in the alley behind them. "What are those for?"

Sophie's eyes slid past the children to where Eolisti's gaze had settled, and she spotted what the Anai had. On the ground in the alley was a set of dice, two wooden cups, and a length of twine fashioned in a small circle.

The girl smirked. "Erus-tali. It's a game of chance, though I doubt an Anai would know of it."

"That's easily fixed. Show me how to play."

"Why?" Aelia's eyes narrowed in suspicion.

"Because I want to play, obviously," Eolisti said, rolling her eyes. Then she glanced over at Khalil. "We have coin, don't we?"

His lips pressed into a thin line.

"Of course we do," Eolisti answered her own question as she flipped her long hair over her shoulder. "Let's play."

"I never agreed to teach you." Aelia crossed her arms over her chest petulantly. "What happens if I lose? I don't have money to pay you."

Eolisti seemed to be deep in thought for a moment before her lips spread into a wicked grin. "If I win, you have to tell me how great I am and how lucky you are to be in my presence. For five. Whole. Minutes." She punctuated each of the last three words. She turned on her heel and stepped toward the horses. "Coins, please." Eolisti held one hand out to Khalil, palm up. He hesitated for a few moments, then reached into a pocket and passed her a small leather pouch.

The girl grimaced, looking confused and a little angry. "That holds more than a few bits of copper."

"Sounds like you're afraid you might lose."

"Fine," Aelia growled, stomping back into the alley.

"Well?" she asked, turning back around and placing her hands on her hips. "Are we playing or not?"

Eolisti flashed Sophie a wide grin and followed. Cam and Maela gathered around their sister as she began explaining the rules of the game to Eolisti.

Sophie glanced at Khalil. Now that they were essentially alone and free to talk, perhaps it would be a good time to ask him the questions she had. She took a few steps back from the alley so they wouldn't be overheard.

"Khalil," she started, shuffling from one foot to the other. "Can I ask you about the Nightingales? There are some things I don't understand. Well, I don't really know much about them at all, and something about this rescue mission is bothering me."

He turned his hooded head toward her. As usual, she could only see the tip of his nose and mouth, and neither gave any indication of what he was thinking. It was maddening.

He seemed to think over her words, then nodded. "I'll answer if I can," he said. "What do you want to know?"

"What is it that the Nightingales do exactly?"

One side of Khalil's mouth tilted up in an amused smirk. "That's a far more complicated question than I was anticipating."

"W-well," she began, flustered by his response. "Since you work for them, I figured you would know a lot about them."

"I don't work for the Nightingales. I work with them."

"But working *with* them would mean you know much more about them than you let on back in Ta'Shela," Sophie pressed. "Who are they? What are they? Why are they helping people escape the east? Is that all they do?"

He pursed his lips. Khalil didn't look happy with this

line of questioning, and Sophie had the feeling that if she didn't convince him that revealing what he knew would help them, he wasn't going to tell her anything. She took a deep breath.

"Khalil, it might be important to know why the Phoenix has been imprisoned and what this Lord Castellus could seek to gain from keeping her. Would she be here freeing slaves or helping others that need to leave Tanalin, like how the Raven helped me?" The Raven had been another member of the Nightingales who had arranged Sophie's escape from Zo'rahn. "Or was she on another mission?" Sophie leaned forward a little, keeping her voice low so it wouldn't carry. "I want to help her, but if I don't have all the information, there is only limited aid I can give, or worse, it could get one of us hurt. Please, Khalil."

His frown deepened. Sophie waited for his response. She'd asked him uncomfortable questions before, but, at least this time, he didn't get up and leave her where she was. The silence grew strained, and Sophie shifted awkwardly. She was convinced that asking him was the right decision. They really did need all the information they could get about the Phoenix before they went into Tempest Hall. Eolisti had been right when she pointed out that they basically knew nothing, which would make their mission even more difficult than it was.

When he finally spoke, it was with a reluctant sigh. "I don't know who exactly they work for, but they are based in Morigael. From what I've heard and experienced, most of the Nightingales offer aid to those seeking refuge when they can, but most don't interact directly. They use intermediaries like the monks at Ta'Shela or the Anai of Elasariin."

"If they don't oversee those operations, that means they

have other responsibilities, and helping slaves like the Raven does is a... what? A secondary task?"

Khalil nodded, "Something like that. I don't know what they do," he said before she could ask the question. "I work for the church of Samar, and my interactions with the Nightingales are limited. I only know about the Phoenix because of my experience with her. The Phoenix gathers information about whatever area she's in or about anything her superiors want to know." He crossed his arms and frowned in thought. "She's very good at disguising herself and changes her accent and cadence. She can blend in seamlessly anywhere she goes. When we traveled together, she used a few different personas. I only worked with her when she was helping me get out of Alkhazai, but we cross paths every year or two."

Hearing him describe how elusive the Phoenix could be, her thoughts clicked into place. "The Phoenix is a spy," she said with certainty. "That's why she's imprisoned at Tempest Hall."

"I..." Khalil began, uncertainty lacing his voice. "I've never thought about it like that, but that does seem to fit."

Sophie spoke as her mind worked. "She was here observing Castellus and reporting back details about Tempest Hall, the feast that the lord is hosting, and probably about the presence of military forces so close to Morigael's border. If there are a lot of nobles heading out this way for the feast, there must be a considerable number of soldiers, maybe even more patrolling the roads like the group we saw."

Frustrated by his lack of response, she asked, "You've never asked her about what she does?" It seemed to Sophie like a huge oversight. From what she'd read, spies generally sought to undermine the enemies of the people they worked for, regardless of collateral damage. And, from what she'd seen of Tanalin, most of its people were struggling just to get by. "What if her actions hurt people who are innocent? People who need help like the villagers here."

His lips parted. Sophie wasn't sure if his reaction was out of surprise or distaste at her comment. Khalil was quiet again for a few moments before saying, "I trust her."

Sophie stared at him. She wanted to argue and point out how he should know more about the people he was working with, but stopped herself. Wasn't she doing the same thing? Trusting Khalil, Turin, and the musicians without knowing anything about them? Hells, she'd left her home with only the promise that there would be someone willing to help her at her destination. So far, it had all worked out, but did she really know what was waiting for her at the end of all this? Was it a life that she even wanted?

"Does that mean all of the Nightingales are spies?"

He frowned at that. "As I said, I'm not part of their organization, so I don't really know. I work for Samar and her temples."

"I know, but you've met some of them, haven't you?" she pressed. "I'm just trying to figure out what they are. Why did the Raven help me in Zo'rahn? If the Nightingales are all spies, do they want something from me?" As she said it, Sophie realized that question was what worried her the most. Did they think she held some useful information? She knew about the Vizier's artifacts, but those were across the sea and out of reach, weren't they? What if they wanted to use her as her old master had? Who would help her then?

"Sophie," Khalil said, his voice pulling her out of her downward-spiraling thoughts. His fingers brushed her arm, then he placed his hand on her shoulder and squeezed, trying to comfort her. "You can trust them. They do actually help people who need it." He smiled that lopsided grin that she knew well. "You're going to be all right."

Before she could say anything else, Eolisti bounded back toward them, and Khalil dropped his hand.

"Well, shall we?" she asked, a satisfied grin on her face. Sophie glanced back at the children. Aelia was counting coins in her palm. There were tears in her eyes.

"How much did you lose?" Khalil asked. He didn't sound upset. His tone was as emotionless as if he's just asked her about the weather.

"About twelve of the little copper coins and one of the silvery ones," she replied, tossing the small pouch of coins back at him. He caught it in his free hand. Eolisti took the reins of her horse from Khalil and climbed up into the saddle. "That should last them a few days, right?"

"More, if they are careful," he said, then turned to Sophie and helped her up before mounting his own horse.

Sophie gazed at the children. They were tying up the bundle of food she'd given them. They gave one last look back at the strange travelers and waved. Sophie waved back. "That was very kind of you."

"I don't know what you're talking about." Eolisti gave an indignant sniff. Blinking a few times, she said, "I was just unlucky today." After seeming to compose herself, she looked over at Sophie. With the distinct feeling she was being scrutinized by her Anaiian friend, she tried to smile.

"You're looking a little pale," Eolisti said with a pensive frown. "Do you need to rest?"

"Let's head over to the inn," Khalil said quickly, turning his horse northwest, toward Tempest Hall. The mage was relieved. She didn't want to talk about the Nightingales with her, at least, not yet. The Anai at Elasariin worked with them as well, and that meant Eolisti would not share her doubts.

As they made their way through the village in search of the Running Maiden, Sophie's thoughts still lingered on the conversation with Khalil. The Nightingales had done so much for her, but was there an ulterior motive? Or were Khalil's words true and she could trust them? He had seen more of them than she and had put his faith in them. The Phoenix had helped him, and he was confident that they would do the same for Sophie.

She hoped Khalil was right.

CHAPTER

TWELVE

"This is the plan," Turin began as he took a seat at the large, wooden table in the Running Maiden's dining area. It had been a few hours before he'd joined them at the inn. While they were waiting, they had already stabled their horses and purchased rooms. He had taken so long that Sophie had started to get worried, so she was relieved when he'd finally appeared.

"Tiberius, the castle steward, has agreed to set us up with work tonight at Tempest Hall. There's a pre-feast event happening." He glanced around the room to ensure no one was listening to them.

It was an hour or two before sunset, so the place was fairly empty. Two men, who had the appearance of regulars, were seated at the bar, engaged in conversation with the innkeeper and giving their group little attention.

Turin eyed them and lowered his voice. "Once we're inside, we need to gather as much information about the layout and defenses as we can—possible escape routes, where they keep prisoners, stuff like that." He set a bundle he'd been carrying on the table. "These are the uniforms the servants wear. Once we get inside, we'll need to talk to a woman named Dalia to get our assignments in the kitchen, but with all the extra people there, we'll be able to slip away at some point."

"I'll sneak down to the dungeons, but they might be keeping the Phoenix elsewhere," Khalil said. "Unless Lord Castellus is a fool, he'll know that someone might be sent to find her. I can check the usual places first so that we can rule them out."

Turin nodded. "All right. Sophie, you go with him. It would look suspicious if one of us, let alone a blind man, were caught wandering the corridors alone."

"Hold on," Eolisti interjected. "Why does Sophie have to go with him? Why can't you do it?" she asked, pointing at the knight.

"Eolisti—" Sophie began but was cut off by Turin.

"It's easier to explain a man and woman lurking around dark corridors alone. Which is why you and I will be sticking together."

The Anai's eyebrows knit together as she frowned. "I don't need your help," she growled. "I can take care of myself and gather the information that we need. Sophie should come with me, not with the guy most likely to walk into a wall."

"*You* need someone who knows how to act at court with you," Turin said hotly, pointing a finger at her. "You don't know what you're doing. Khalil and I do. It's as simple as that."

"*I* don't know what *I'm* doing?" Eolisti's face flushed as her voice rose. "Who was the one who was almost eviscerated by that troll? And who distracted it so that you could get away from it?"

Turin's ears reddened. "This is exactly why we should have left—"

"Enough!" Sophie said as she stood, hitting her palms on the tabletop. The conversation over at the bar had stopped, and she was sure the men there were listening to them. All this arguing was getting them nowhere and was causing a scene. They couldn't risk someone overhearing them and sending word to the castle.

She leaned over and spoke in a low hiss. "Eolisti, I'll be able to work my magic more easily if I go with Khalil. It's harder to keep it hidden if I'm out in the open." Eolisti crossed her arms over her chest but didn't say anything. "Turin," she continued, turning her glower on him, "Eolisti does not need a babysitter, but I'll concede you do know more about Tanalin etiquette than we do. Just please don't give her orders because it won't work." *Because Eolisti won't listen*, but she didn't say that part out loud. Sophie glanced over her shoulder, smiled at the men staring at them, and then sat back down. She could feel her face heating up from being the center of attention but tried to maintain a stern expression.

Sophie had only known Turin for a little over a week, but she'd realized early on that there was another side to his light-hearted nature. He was as headstrong as Eolisti was, if more polite about it. That meant a strong hand would be needed when dealing with *both* of them, and Khalil seemed to be fine with letting them bicker.

Turin and Eolisti stared at her with shocked looks on their faces, but Sophie managed not to back down. After a few moments, Eolisti averted her gaze, mumbling about how it wasn't her fault. Sophie allowed her expression to relax as Turin continued staring, and out of the corner of her eye, she caught the smug look on Khalil's face. It made her smile.

"Well," Turin began awkwardly after clearing his throat, "if that's settled, then we should make our way over to the castle soon. Whatever Lord Castellus has going on, it starts at sundown."

As Sophie and Eolisti departed to their room to change, the Anai mumbled, "Thanks for sticking up for me to Turin." She met Sophie's eyes and smiled before hurriedly turning away, a blush on her cheeks.

She had assumed that Eolisti hadn't paid attention to her words beyond the general admonishment it had been, but Sophie was pleased to have been proven wrong.

The road to the castle ran along the edge of the small village. Even in the distance, they could see the large structure towering over the surrounding walls. A small meadow separated the town from the walls, and the knee-high golden stalked plants swayed lazily in the breeze as they passed. Sophie had never seen a castle in person, but she had read books with drawings depicting them. Even the most detailed books she could have gotten her hands on would have failed to capture the majesty of the architecture she found herself staring up at.

Tempest Hall was multiple floors—Sophie counted six, based on the windows—and had towers that were taller still, reaching toward the sky. The square cut of the stone and the sharp, rectangular edges reminded her of the Ta'Shela monastery, but the castle was much, much bigger than that. Where the old monastery was like a sleeping giant of stone nestled in its fading former glory, Tempest Hall was bursting with life. Smoke rose from dozens of chimneys, and even from the outside, Sophie caught glimpses of activity through the windows.

"Halt," one of the armored men said as they approached the castle gates. There were two of them. Stepping forward, he raised a hand signaling them to stop. "State your business."

"Is there a problem?" Turin asked, slowing to a stop at the head of the group. "Tiberius told us to come for the event tonight. We are to help Dalia and—"

"Why is there an Anai with you?" the other one said, his voice gruff and distinctly unfriendly.

"So, what if I am?" Eolisti asked before Turin could answer the guard, crossing her arms over her chest and setting her jaw.

Turin gave her a warning look then turned back to the guards. "She's part of our group. I've already explained this to Tiberius." He smiled at them, trying to show that he wasn't a threat. The effect wasn't very convincing. Turin was taller and more muscular than the guards, a fact that was obvious even through his staff uniform.

"I'm not sure the lords and ladies in attendance will want to see another Anai here," the first guard said with a scoff. "We've already got one among the guests, so there's no more room for—"

"Felix! Marcos!" snapped a voice from behind the two men. "Why are you harassing my help?"

Both men straightened with a grimace, then parted and turned, coming face to face with a stern-looking woman with iron-gray hair and a sharp nose.

"We have to check everyone that comes into the castle," the first guard said in a petulant tone. "Lord Castellus's orders."

"So then why is it that you only have a problem with the Anai and not the others? Is she so threatening that you are turning away the help that Tiberius *just* hired? Are you going to find me new servants to take their place?" Dalia asked him. Sophie watched as the man, unable to offer an answer that would satisfy the woman, visibly deflated under Dalia's glare. The other guard started to speak, but she turned her gaze on him and he fell silent.

"Now you listen to me," Dalia began, her voice deadly low. "I don't care what she is or where she came from. If she'll work, she'll do. Do you have a problem with that? Or should we get the lord involved?"

With a huff, she turned away from the stunned guards and motioned for the group to follow her." Sophie and Eolisti exchanged an amused smile as they followed Dalia into Tempest Hall. The mage's levity was short-lived, however. If this was their new boss, they might be in trouble.

In sharp contrast to the early winter chill outside, the kitchen was pleasantly warm, with the smell of warm cinnamon, sugar, and butter permeating the large room. Against one wall that was blackened by soot was the oven. A long table sat in the middle of the room, one side used for preparation and the other to neatly place the food ready to be served. Men and women bustled about, some bringing in trays for cleaning and leaving with new ones piled high with a variety of smoked meats, while others were pulling bread and sweet buns out of ovens or standing over the stoves, cooking in sizzling pans, or stirring pots. In the corner, two young women sat beside a large wooden tub, scrubbing the dirty trays in soapy water.

The sight of so much food was surprising, considering the famine they'd witnessed or heard of in the rest of the country, and even the state of the village. Sophie immediately thought of the children she'd met earlier that day, excited to be eating the scraps she'd saved. With an effort, she pushed away the anger and disgust that was rising within her. Those feelings would not help them find the Phoenix.

"Who's in charge of him?" Dalia asked, pointing at Khalil. Instead of wearing his cloak with the hood pulled low, Khalil had tied a piece of black cloth around his eyes as a blindfold. The result was that he looked far less intimidating than he usually did.

"I am," Sophie said, glancing at Turin for confirmation. He gave her the tiniest of nods.

"Well then, you two pick up those trays"—she directed Turin and Eolisti to the platters full of single servings of sliced meats and cheeses—"and take them out to the great hall. There are already quite a few guests there. Lord Castellus won't make his entrance until later, but he wants his guests well-fed in the meantime. Carry them around and offer the food to the lords and ladies. Once it's all gone, bring the trays back and grab more. Don't stop until the lord makes his announcement."

Dalia turned her eyes on Sophie and Khalil and sighed. She sounded tired. "I don't want him spilling anything on a guest. Gods know these people have dueled each other for less." She continued to look him up and down. "He looks strong, at least. The two of you will fetch wine and grain from the reserve cellar and bring it back here." She pointed to a door. "Just go through there and to the end of the hall. You'll find a large door that leads down to a storeroom. The reserve cellar is down there." Dalia turned her back on them, seeming to dismiss their presence as she focused her attention on her other charges and their various tasks around the kitchen.

Turin gave Sophie a sharp nod and picked up a tray before leaning close. "We'll meet you back here if we find anything," he said softly. Then, handing another tray to the Anai, he headed over to the entry that led into the main part of the castle.

Eolisti hesitated for a moment, frowning. Sophie knew that the Anai didn't like this plan, but there was no turning back now. Sophie gave her a reassuring smile and took Khalil's arm in hers, pretending to guide him over to the door Dalia had indicated. She opened the door for him and followed him into a long corridor.

As the door closed, the sounds from the kitchen seemed to fade away, leaving only a muffled clanging of pots and pans behind them. The corridor was lit with oil lamps hanging from sconces that illuminated tapestries hanging on the walls. Colorful threads were woven into images of men and women in various activities—holding hands, riding horseback, attending feasts, and in general, being merry. Those depictions didn't fit with the atmosphere that lingered in the keep.

Standing there in the servants' corridor, Sophie could almost feel the weight of this place. The kitchen had been bustling with activity, but once the door was closed, the gray stone and musty passageways put her nerves on edge. Sophie focused her mind and reached out with her senses, using her magic to feel the energy around them. It felt... oppressive. She shivered and let go of Khalil's arm, following him swiftly to the end of the corridor.

As Dalia had described, they reached the large, banded-iron door that led down to the storeroom at the end of the corridor, but Khalil ignored it and instead turned down another passage. If they were quick, they could find the dungeons *and* fetch the wine before anyone got suspicious. Dalia had assumed that Khalil's blindness would be a hindrance, and they could use that to their advantage.

They went down two more passageways, moving quickly and silently. Right before they were about to turn another corner, Khalil held out his hand to stop her, then pulled her into a small nook next to one of the tapestries. A few heartbeats later, Sophie heard boots scuffing on the stone floor. She remembered what Turin had said about a man and woman together being easier to explain and suddenly realized what he'd been referring to. If they acted like a couple who had run off in between errands to find a dark corner, they would seem less suspicious. They would get in trouble if caught, but with any luck, no one would think any more of their actions.

She leaned in close to Khalil. Without needing to be told, he wrapped his arms around her while she laid her head on his chest in the way a lover might, breathing in the smell of oiled leather and clean linens. Sophie's heart pounded in her ears as the footsteps grew closer.

Risking a glance, she spotted a man of middling years walking toward them, wearing a fine brocade doublet and wool breeches. He had an angular face with the shadow of a beard, dark hair cropped close to his head, and piercing blue eyes reflecting the flickering light of the oil lamps. He must be a nobleman, judging by his expensive clothing and the way he held himself.

Something about him stirred her instincts, so she reached out with her senses, using her magic to feel for any auras around him. She brushed against an energy that made her pull back quickly, hoping that he hadn't noticed her prodding at him, because what she felt had been unmistakable.

This person could use magic, and he had used it recently.

Had he felt hers too? If he'd been using his senses in the

same way Sophie had been, he could have felt her magic touch his. Had she already alerted him to her presence, the presence of another wizard?

Her breathing grew more rapid as the sound of his boots on the stone slowed. Sophie felt Khalil squeeze her tightly, and she realized that she was shaking. Attempting to quell the fear that threatened to rise in her throat, Sophie tried to still her mind. She would need the focus to throw up a shield around them if he attacked. It wouldn't be the most efficient spell, as tightly wound up as she was, but it would buy them enough time to get away.

"What are you two doing?" came the cold voice of the wizard from behind them.

Sophie tore herself away from Khalil, and her eyes met the man's cold, blue orbs for just a second before looking away from him. The man hadn't startled her, and she knew he'd seen her looking at him, so Sophie acted embarrassed. She'd found this was the best way to get out of harsh punishment when she'd been caught doing something she shouldn't have back home. Lowering her eyes to a gold button near the waist of his doublet, she bowed her head. She didn't have to fake the blush that had blossomed across her cheeks. "Apologies, my lord."

Following her lead, Khalil took a shuffling step away and bowed his head as well.

"We were looking for—"

"You didn't seem to be *looking* for anything," he growled, cutting her off. She glanced up at him, catching the scowl spreading across his features before averting her eyes again. "You're lucky I don't have time to deal with you. Get back to work and don't let me catch you loitering around these halls again."

"Yes, my lord," Sophie and Khalil murmured together. He didn't move, but Sophie didn't dare raise her gaze.

After an agonizing second, he turned away from them and continued to wherever he'd been going.

"Are you all right?" Khalil whispered once the sound of the other man's footfalls had died away.

Sophie turned to him, rubbing her arms with her hands to try and calm her nerves. That had been a close call. Even if he'd believed that they were lovers trying to find a quiet corner to be alone, they were far from the kitchen and where they should have been. There was a chance he would have them thrown out or inform Lord Castellus of workers slinking around the castle. Thankfully, she'd held back from casting in the village, or he could have sensed any lingering magic on her.

"That man," she began, ignoring Khalil's original question. She was still trembling. "I think he's a wizard." Gathering her courage, she leaned out from the nook and looked down the hall. The other mage was nowhere to be seen.

Khalil's mouth twitched as he processed her words. "Let's find the dungeons, quickly," he said, taking her hand and pulling her along.

They continued searching the passageways, going up a flight of servants' stairs to the second floor, avoiding the entrance hall. Every so often, Khalil would pause by a door, and Sophie knew he was using his almost supernatural hearing to listen for any movement behind them. A few times, he even pushed one open—after Sophie reached out with her magic to make sure they were not spelled—but they had no luck finding where the castle prisoners were kept.

They were running out of time. With the state of chaos

the kitchen had been in, they hoped Dalia hadn't yet taken notice of how long they'd been gone.

The two met only a few more people roaming the halls. Sticking to the same plan as before, when Khalil heard someone approach, he would pull her into an alcove and they would hold each other close. A small group of three maids giggled as they passed, one saying softly, "Make sure you still get your work done." Sophie pulled away after the maids had left, knowing that she must have been blushing up to her ears. Khalil seemed as relaxed as he always was, and they continued their methodical search without a word.

What Sophie found surprising was how few people they ran into. Everyone must have been in the great hall tending to the guests, but it was strange that there weren't even guards patrolling the hallways.

Just as Sophie was about to suggest that they turn back and go fetch the wine, Khalil held a hand up for her to stop. They were back on the first floor on the other end of the castle, and he stood in front of another large, banded-iron door that stood out from the other wooden doors around them. Since the doorway to the cellar had a similar entry, that might mean this one also led down into another part of the castle. Sophie felt her stomach leap. Could this be where they were keeping the Phoenix?

Sophie felt for any trace of magic around them. This time, she did feel the workings of a spell on the door, a spell that would alert the caster if it were to be opened or the lock tampered with.

"There's something here," she mumbled, still focused on the door, examining the lock to see how the spell worked. She could quickly disarm it, but that would have the same effect as just opening the door. It wasn't a strong spell though, and Sophie thought she could suppress it for a short time without triggering it. It should hold long enough for them to slip through the door. There was one problem with that plan. If the person who cast the spell came and checked on the door, they would be able to tell that it had been tampered with, even if her personal magical signature faded from the working after an hour or two.

"It's an alarm spell," she said. "I can suppress it for a little while, but they might know it was tampered with if they check."

Khalil was silent for a moment, then said, "They'll have no way of knowing it was you." He frowned. "I think we need to risk it. It will be worth it if we can get the Phoenix out before this event begins."

"All right," Sophie said, then reached out her hands, placing them on the cool metal of the door. She envisioned her magic encircling that of the other wizard's in a paper-thin wrapping, one that would dissolve in a few minutes and leave little trace behind. As she sighed, she released a small bit of energy, just enough to power her own spell. Then, with her spell securely in place, she expended another small burst to move the mechanisms in the lock. There was a muffled *CLACK*, and the bolt released from its catch.

As the door creaked open, it revealed a set of stone stairs leading deeper into the castle. Torches hung on the walls here as opposed to the oil lamps in the more accessible areas of the castle, and there were high, grated windows. Together, they provided enough illumination for Sophie to see that the stairs curved around a corner. A foul odor wafted out from below, smelling of decay and human excrement. Khalil held the door open as she stepped inside and closed it behind them as he followed her in.

Sophie let out a slow breath, releasing the magic she'd been using to suppress the spell on the door. The other wizard's trap became active again, and when she used her senses to try to find her own lingering energy, she could barely sense it. "There, I'll have to do that again before we leave," she said to Khalil. He turned from the door and silently led the way down the steps.

The stairs wound downward another twenty feet before opening into a large room with a high ceiling. Cells with iron bars stood side by side in a long row on the opposite wall. All of them were empty except for one. As they approached, Sophie could see that the cell furthest from the door held what looked like a bundle of rags in one shadowy corner.

Quiet as they were, their footsteps echoed in the enclosed stone room. Sophie winced at every sound, looking over her shoulder back at the staircase, her mind treating her to an image of guards rushing after them, blades drawn. The odor drew her attention back to the furthest cell. It was much stronger here than it had been at the top of the stairs. The smell coming from the cell made Sophie's stomach turn, and she covered her nose and mouth with her hands.

Khalil leaned in close to the bars. The bundle of rags moved as he did, and Sophie caught the flash of a glistening eye that reflected the torchlight. Then, in a low voice that was barely audible, he whispered, "A sparrow cries in the night."

"And the Nightingale answers the call," rasped a hoarse voice from within the cell. The rags moved, and the battered face of a young woman appeared. Her left eye was swollen shut, and dried blood crusted around her nose and mouth. When she moved, dragging herself closer to the bars, Sophie saw that her arms were covered in cuts that oozed thick, greenish pus. The flesh around the wounds was red and inflamed, giving a mottled look to her skin. Considering how filthy it was here, it wasn't surprising that the wounds were infected.

Sophie glanced at Khalil. His lips were pressed in a thin line, and his brows were furrowed. "Is she the Phoenix?" she asked.

"No," he said immediately, his voice filled with certainty, "but she knows the correct passphrase. She must be associated with the Nightingales."

"The Phoenix," the young woman said, her voice strained. "Was taken captive by Lord Castellus. She's his daughter."

"*What?*" Khalil asked, voice harsh with disbelief.

"Her true name is Lady Korynne Castellus." The woman lay on the floor of the cell just out of reach, breathing hard. She seemed to have expended the last of her energy moving toward them, barely able to lift her head enough to look at them. "My name is Winna. I am her apprentice. I was caught and used by Lord Castellus to lure his daughter here." She paused, searching Khalil's face. "You... Are you Khalil Maszir?" When Khalil nodded, she continued. "She's told me about you. Have you come for us?"

Khalil nodded again. "Where is she?" he asked as he reached for the lock on the cell.

Sophie grabbed his hand to stop him. "Don't touch it!" she hissed on instinct. There had been no guards watching over the dungeon, which had been odd enough. The only explanation Sophie could think of was that the lord of the castle had thought no one could get in here without him knowing. Since the door above them was bespelled, this one might be as well.

When she reached out her senses again, she did, indeed, detect a spell, and one of much stronger magic than on the dungeon door above. This trap was not as benign as the one she'd seen at the top of the stairs. "If you get anywhere near that lock, the spell there will trigger an alarm and give you a nasty shock, enough to knock you out." She bit her bottom lip, thinking. "I don't think I can suppress this one. I'd have to disarm it, and then they'd know exactly what my magic feels like and would be able to track us down. *Magic used can be traced.*" Sophie repeated the words spoken to her so long ago by an old friend.

Winna stayed focused on Khalil. "The Phoenix is more important than I am, but I don't know where they are keeping her. They're controlling her somehow, and the mage has bragged about how compliant she is. The lord is bound to use her eventually." She took a few gasping, shallow breaths before continuing. "I'd like to last until you get her out, but I don't think I have very long."

From the look of her, Sophie knew she was right. "We can't leave you like this," she reasoned, kneeling on the hard stone floor. Winna's eye tracked her for the first time.

"You must," Winna groaned. "If they discover that I am missing, they won't let anyone get close to the Phoenix, and any rescue attempt will have to be done by force." She coughed, and blood spattered the floor. "The Emissary would rather just write her off as a loss than go to war over her."

Sophie heard a low growling sound before realizing it was coming from her own throat and stopped it immediately. Winna was dying. If she stayed like this, she would be dead within a few days, at the most. Even if she had the skills to close all her wounds and knit her broken bones back together, the amount of magic she would need to use would undoubtedly leave a mark that the court wizard could follow. But maybe something simpler would be overlooked. If she could help her without alerting Lord Castellus to their presence, Sophie didn't care what Winna said. She would do it.

Wracking her brain, her eyes scanned over Winna's prone form and examined her wounds from a few feet away. If she cleared the infection, there was a good chance her body would recover on its own. Sophie pressed up against the bars, stretching out her arm into the cell. "Take my hand," she said to Winna. "I can at least help you survive a little longer."

Winna eyed the outstretched limb suspiciously but, after only a moment's hesitation, took Sophie's hand. The poor woman's skin felt like it was on fire.

Sophie closed her eyes, exhaling as she concentrated on what she'd seen of the woman's injuries. She fixed the image of the infected wounds in her mind and, through their contact, used a spell to help heal Winna. While Sophie could not use her magic to heal her completely, she could help speed along the process of the body's own natural healing and pick out any flaws before they could take hold. Winna's hands grew even hotter as the magic entered her body, and she gasped.

As Sophie's eyes snapped open, Winna's wounds expelled the infected tissue and dirt like water flowing from a bucket until the fluid ran clear. The mage let go of her hand and touched the ragged blanket, pushing out more of her will. The filth on the ground sizzled and, within seconds, had faded away into nothingness. The dark stains on the rags covering the young woman evaporated. The chamber pot in the corner rattled as Sophie's magic rippled over it, leaving it clean and empty. The spell's effects dissipated, and while the dungeon still smelled foul, Winna's cell was much cleaner than it had been a moment ago.

"There," Sophie said as Winna stared up at her, the one visible eye wide. "You'll probably feel a little tired, but your infection is gone. I don't dare try to close your wounds, but this will give you a chance to heal on your own." She silently prayed that she had not overdone it with her magic, but even so, she didn't regret the decision.

"You're a wizard?" Winna asked, her voice much stronger than it had been seconds ago. Without waiting for an answer, she closed her eyes, and a tear slid down her cheek. "A wizard... I didn't have any hope that we would make it out of here alive, but now Khalil's here, and he brought you to help." Winna sat up and smiled, her teeth stained pink with the blood she'd coughed up earlier. Her movements seemed less painful than before Sophie had cast her spell. "Please, make sure she gets out, even if you have to leave me behind."

"We are not going to leave you behind," Khalil said firmly. "Once we get the Phoenix, we'll come back for you." He reached into a pocket and pulled out one of the sweet rolls that had been cooling in the kitchen. He tossed it to her through the bars. "It's not much, but we'll come back with more if we can."

Sophie blinked. When had he taken that?

Winna just nodded a silent "thank you" as they left and made their way back up the stairs. Sophie looked over her shoulder before stepping out of sight. Winna was curled on her side eating the sweet roll, crying silently to herself. "Hang on just a little longer," Sophie whispered and followed Khalil back to the iron door at the top of the stairs.

CHAPTER

THIRTEEN

Eolisti stared after Sophie and Khalil as they disappeared through the door that would lead them to the reserve cellar. She blinked at the tray in her hands until Dalia shouted. Eolisti jumped and glanced at the woman, but she was gesturing wildly with the towel in her hand, scolding a harried-looking young woman who was stirring a pot that was smoking. Motion from the double doors leading out of the kitchen and toward the great hall caught her eye, and she spotted Turin holding a door open with a shoulder, waving her over with one hand while he balanced his tray in the other.

A cacophony of falling pots rang out behind her, and she mentally shook herself and headed out of the kitchen. Something about this place made her feel insignificant. It was large and grand in a way that her people would never even attempt to build. She was but one person out of hundreds in a structure made of lifeless stone. It was just like humans to build something that would be a blemish on the landscape for hundreds of years to come. That thought brought another frown to her face. Catching her expression,

Turin flashed that stupid "I'm enjoying your discomfort" grin as she passed him. Unwilling to let him think he'd somehow won this round, she tossed her head, raised her chin, and stomped down the short hallway toward the sound of music and laughter, which she presumed was their destination.

The air on her face was noticeably cooler away from the humid kitchen. Like that room, the walls here were made entirely of uniformly cut stones stacked in an intricate pattern. She thought she could almost make out some great, repeating design, but even with her sharp eyes, the dim light and passage of time this castle had seen since it was built made it impossible to tell. A glance at the arched ceiling revealed that it, too, was made of cut stone with thick beams of wood supporting it at regular intervals. Remembering that the outside had appeared to be made of the same material, Eolisti felt a sudden sense of panic as she pictured herself buried under a giant pile of rocks the size of the building.

The scuff of Turin's boots behind her reminded her where she was, and, with a deep breath, she forced that lump of fear back down her throat. She remembered that the great monastery at Ta'Shela had probably been made of stone as well. The walls there had been washed white where there weren't murals, though, and even at night, the whole place had seemed to her like it was illuminated with a soft yellow light. In contrast, the dark gray stones of this castle appeared to drink the light instead of reflecting it, and there was a subtle smell of dampness that lingered in the air.

The faint echo of a man's guffaw and exaggerated clapping drew her attention as each step brought her closer to the great hall. Whispers of strange music mingled with an indistinct din of what she assumed were the chattering voices of the party guests. Ahead of her, one of two enormous and ornately carved double doors swung open, pouring a burst of sound and warm light into the bleak corridor as a cluster of servants escaped with their empty trays.

The last man through noticed Eolisti and Turin's approach and paused with a heel behind the door to let them enter. His slender build and gaunt face reminded Eolisti of the children from the village, but he smiled pleasantly when she met his eyes. She returned his smile with one of her own, then automatically dropped her eyes for a moment before looking back up at him as she approached.

A pang of homesickness slithered through her gut. How many times had she done that bashful little dance with Myron, an apprentice to one of the High Councilors back home? She would act demure and interested in him, and he would pursue her in kind. It had always been a ploy to get her way, and they both had known that, but the familiarity was at once comforting and melancholy.

The stirrings of a new song spilling from the open door roused her from her reverie, and she realized that the expression of the servant holding the door for her had changed from friendly to annoyed. With a tilt of her chin and a toss of her head, she flounced through the open door as much as one could while carrying a tray burdened with little plates piled with food. This was no time for thoughts of Elasariin, not when she was here, out in the wild world, finally *living*. She had taken no more than a couple of steps before slowing to a standstill, gazing around the room in awe.

The door she had just stepped through opened into the great hall from the far end, closest to the courtyard and kitchen. Before her lay dozens of trestle tables with people of all sorts milling about, talking, drinking, laughing, and generally enjoying the party. Nearest to her were humans dressed much like some of the others she'd seen in the village. Their adornment came from their genuinely merry expressions and the joy that emanated from them in a palpable wave.

Beyond those nearest her stood even more tables spaced farther apart and running the length of the room, where men and women of all varieties either sat or stood speaking with one another in a much more orderly manner. Their clothing was opulent in fashions Eolisti had never seen in her life. The women wore their hair in designs ranging from complicated braids and coils piled high atop their heads to halos of tight, curly hair. Dresses of equally intricate patterns of glistening fabric reflected every source of light in the room. In contrast, the hair of most of the men appeared slightly damp and gleamed in the soft illumination emanating from above, but they were clothed in obviously fine tunics. Some of those garments descended to their ankles where sandaled feet could be seen, and some of them were of the shorter length she was accustomed to seeing that ended above trousers or leggings that plunged into tall boots.

At the far end of the room stood a raised platform with yet another long table. Nine chairs were arranged to look out over the hall, the tabletop level with the heads of the seated guests. Only the chair in the center was occupied. The man who sat in it looked to be later in his years, his golden hair so light it shone white in the ambient light. On his brow rested a thin band of metal that Eolisti thought looked a lot like silver, but she couldn't be sure from such a distance. That brow was furrowed as the man reclined ever so slightly in his chair, his assessing gaze casting out over the feast from behind a raised goblet.

A chill ran down Eolisti's spine for no apparent reason. All in the room appeared to be enjoying themselves, except for the moderately dressed people closest to her. It was as if everyone was waiting, evaluating those around them, seeking an advantage, a weakness, and none as overtly as the lone human at the far end of the hall.

A breeze tickled the back of her neck as it swept through the still-open door behind her to stir among the lights and decorations hanging from the ceiling above. Softly glowing glass orbs containing flames that she recognized as magical constructs hung all about the room, with transparent colored stones dangling from those containers and long strips of shimmering cloth strung all around them. Combined with the grand music coming from the far corner of the room—from the very musicians they'd traveled here with, nonetheless—it gave the entire setting a delicate ambiance of merriment with undertones of danger, and Eolisti found herself fascinated.

Behind her, Turin cleared his throat and nudged her with the edge of his tray, bringing her back to herself and the reason she was here. *Right, act servanty*. With another quick glance around, Eolisti noticed that all the other people carrying trays were weaving among the fancier people, stopping periodically when someone caught their attention with raised fingers or eye contact. She frowned briefly at the tables directly in front of her before deciding to make her way around them toward the center of the hall.

Moving deeper into the room, Eolisti could see that another set of ornately carved double doors stood open to a high-ceilinged room beyond, and party-goers mingled there as well. To the side of the open doors stood a funny-looking man holding a long wooden staff in one hand. He stood stiff-backed and stared sightlessly at the wall opposite him. Eolisti glanced in the same direction for a few seconds but couldn't tell what the man was looking at. *Weird.*

Now that she was among the oddly dressed people in the middle of the room, she began looking at their faces more closely. Most were intent on their conversations and ignored her completely, but a couple saw her tray and raised a finger in her direction. Following the lead of the other servers, she approached and let people select their plates before continuing to make her way through the hall.

Eolisti maneuvered across the room, hoping to get a different perspective on the spectacle before her. As she neared the wall, a familiar melodious laugh reached her ears through the din. A flash of white-gold hair caught her eye, and her stomach jumped up into her throat as she pressed through the crowd with more purpose, completely forgetting that Turin was trying to stay close.

As Eolisti deftly avoided a small group of women wafting themselves with feather fans, she found who she was looking for. There, seated with his back to the wall and a polite smile lingering on his lips, was none other than Elindiir, the Anai who had sailed with them from Omer. He was wearing fine clothes like the people around him, but unlike the poofy shirts and tight pants of his peers, the cut and style seemed to naturally flow down his body, allowing his movements to be smooth and graceful without hindrance. The off-white cloth seemed to shimmer in the magical light, giving him the slightest of an otherworldly appearance.

Feeling her gaze, he glanced up to coolly meet her eyes

before recognition registered there, and a genuine smile blossomed over his face.

"Elindiir!" Eolisti felt her face flush with excitement as she grinned in return and made her way to his side, ignoring the gasps from the women with the fans at her sudden outburst. She opened her mouth and was about to ask what he was doing here when the sound of wood striking stone rang out across the room.

A loud voice near the door that the elegant guests had been filtering in and out of cried out, "Lord Alexi Lucius Golistin and Lady Kristanya Golistin, and their sons, Alexi and Yuri Golistin!"

As one, the guests who had been standing and conversing paused and turned to peer toward the open door. Curious at what had captured their attention, Eolisti bobbed about on tiptoe until she finally caught a glimpse of a tall man and a woman with shiny black hair making their way toward the high table where the lone man sat. Trailing them were two other men, one who appeared to be not much older than Turin and another who might have been a few years older still. Both men shared the same stature, jet-black hair, light eyes, and square jaws, but there, the similarities ended. The older of the two had creases around his eyes and mouth, the kind that came from frequent smiling and laughter, and he wore a pleasant expression as he made eye contact with a few other guests. The younger man strode along with a confident air, but the eyes he kept locked on the far end of the room were sharp and calculating.

Though the noise in the room had diminished as the four entered, the other guests began resuming their conversations in conspiratorial whispers after the entourage had passed. By now, Eolisti was starting to feel like all these people were only doing things for the benefit of those around them, so she dismissed the disruption and turned her attention back to Elindiir. The other Anai, however, was looking intently over Eolisti's shoulder. Eolisti followed his gaze to where Turin stood staring at the new entrants slack-jawed, his eyes wide and face white as a sheet.

CHAPTER

FOURTEEN

I t had been years since Turin had thought about his parents. Back then, he'd gone by another name altogether. Turin Lightbringer was as much his true name as that other one was, except that he didn't have to be ashamed of using it. Seeing the family that had abandoned him here, of all places, did not bode well for their mission. It brought back memories that he'd worked long and hard to bury.

THUNDER SHOOK the stone walls of the west tower, making the glass windowpanes rattle in their frames. Storms were always bad in this part of the castle, as lightning would strike the top of the tower and make the stone shudder, but this one was especially violent.

Dimitri had just been awakened by another flash of light and deafening clap of thunder, wide-eyed with his heart pounding. He rolled over in his bed, pulling the blanket up to his nose. Between lightning flashes, the room

160

was pitch black in the moonless night, and he could barely make out the shape of the other bed across the room, identical to his own.

"Yuri?" he whispered, but there was no movement. "Yuri?" he called again, louder. His voice sounded a little panicked, but he wasn't scared. It was just another storm, and such a thing wouldn't scare him. Only *girls* were afraid of storms.

He waited for a response, but none came. Dimitri's older brother was not a sound sleeper, and even if he were, no one would be able to sleep through this. He threw the blanket off and climbed out of bed. The stone floor was covered with soft, plush rugs, but being out from the warmth of his bed still made him shiver. Dimitri spread his hands out in front of him so as not to run into anything in the dark and walked forward in a straight line to where he knew his brother slept.

"Yuri?" he said again as his hand touched the other boy's blanket.

Lightning flashed outside, illuminating the room for a fraction of a second and showing Dimitri an empty bed. There was no doubt that the other boy had been there at some point during the night, given the wrinkled sheets and discarded blanket, but he was no longer.

The room fell back into darkness, but Dimitri remained where he stood, staring at where the flash had burned an imprint of the empty bed into his mind. Yuri had gone to bed at the same time as he had that night. Where had he gone?

Dimitri turned toward where he knew the door was and stumbled over something, probably the toy cart he'd left out. Falling to one knee, a painful jolt went up his leg. With a sharp exhale, he sat back on the floor and rubbed the spot. It throbbed, and he was sure there would be a bruise in the morning. It was tempting to go back to bed and wait for his brother to return, but he didn't think he would be able to sleep with the storm raging outside their windows. Thunder rumbled through the tower, and Dimitri jumped again. Heart pounding in his ears, he crawled quickly over to the door and leaped to his feet, grabbing the handle.

The door was heavy, and he had to lean back on his heels, using all his strength to pull it open. The creak of the rusty hinges was drowned out by the beating of the rain on the windows. Dim light flooded the room from the hall outside, casting long shadows across the floor behind him.

Dimitri poked his head out into the corridor. A single oil lamp hung on the wall, its glow illuminating the stairway. He waited and listened, but no noise drifted up to him over the storm. It must have been the middle of the night. The castle was usually still full of life far past his bedtime, which hardly seemed fair. He wanted to be allowed to stay up with his older brothers and cousins, doing whatever it was the adults did when the children went to sleep. Slowly and quietly, he left his room and descended the stairs from the top of the tower, tiptoeing across the cool stone in nothing but his nightgown.

The next landing was only twenty or so steps down, but Dimitri's breathing came fast as if he'd run a mile. He felt the distant clap of thunder through the stone on his bare feet again, moments before the sound reached his ears. Finally reaching the landing, he peeked around the corner to see if anyone was there. With the light from the lamp on this level, he could see about ten steps down until the staircase rounded another corner.

The door on this landing was identical to his own. Dimitri leaned on it and pushed. It wasn't locked. It opened a crack, and he peered inside, a thin band of light breaking the darkness. "Alexi," Dimitri whispered. "Are you awake?"

Alexi was the eldest of the three boys. He was seven years older than Dimitri, and their uncle said he was almost a man. Dimitri doubted that. Alexi had changed over the last few years, but he still did all the same things as before, except that he had started spending time with girls.

Dimitri grimaced at the thought and pushed the door open wide. Strange as he found his brother's behavior of late, Alexi always knew what was going on in the castle. He would know where to find Yuri.

"Alexi!" he called out, forgetting to keep his voice down. Realizing his brother wasn't there, Dimitri stepped into the room and looked around.

Alexi's room was bigger than his, even though he didn't have to share it, and he knew it was decorated with vibrantly colored rugs and paintings. Flora, their nurse, said it was elegant and sophisticated with that dreamy look that girls got when they had no idea what they were talking about. Who cared about sophistication? Alexi's room didn't have nearly as many toys as his and Yuri's room.

On the other hand, Alexi was allowed to practice with a real sword. Dimitri would have traded all his toys if it meant he got to use a real sword.

Stepping toward his oldest brother's bed, which was also much bigger than his, he was able to see in the dim light that the tidy sheets were still tucked in, and his blanket hadn't been touched. Alexi hadn't been to bed at all. Dimitri bit his lower lip, thinking.

He left Alexi's room, not bothering to close the door, and ran down the next flight of stairs. His stomach was in knots, and a cold sweat broke out on the back of his neck.

Something was wrong. He needed to find his brothers. They would know what to do, but where were they?

Dimitri came to the bottom of the stairs and stopped dead in his tracks. He had forgotten to look around the corner, but it didn't matter. The hall that connected the west tower to the rest of the castle stood empty. He looked around, blinking a few times before a chill ran down his spine. There should have been a guard there. There was always at least *one* guard there. What was going on?!

Panicked, he took off running down the hall, feet slapping hard on the stone floor. Dimitri didn't even notice the chill anymore. He wanted to call out for someone, anyone, but his voice caught in his throat. What if the castle had been attacked? Where were his brothers? Where were his mother and father?

The lamps in the hall cast deep, menacing shadows all around Dimitri as he ran. His imagination showed him images of unknown assailants waiting to grab him. His uncle had taken them through countless security measures to prepare for the day when the castle might be attacked, and in his mind, he could see phantasmal, black-armored men leering at him from the darkness, waiting for him to slow, waiting for him to stumble. He didn't give them the chance and dashed past quickly. If he was fast enough, they wouldn't be able to catch him. Doors flashed by him, his parents' rooms, but as he neared the end of the west hall, Dimitri froze mid-stride and almost fell, waving his arms to regain his balance.

Two dark shapes hunched together at the end of the hall.

He suddenly felt vulnerable in his nightgown and bare feet. He didn't even have a weapon. He could run back to his room and lock himself in, but what would he do then?

None of his toys would do him any good against a real sword, and the tower was too high up on the mountain to climb down from. Besides, with the storm, he would probably be struck by lightning or slip and fall in the rain. Maybe he could run back to Alexi's room and find his sword. He had watched his brother training with the knights. They had even let him fight against his brother with one of the wooden swords they had for the squires. He would just have to fight off the attackers and save his family.

One of the shapes stirred, and he swallowed hard. They'd noticed him. This would be his only chance. He needed to move before they came after him. Dimitri knew he could outrun any adult. He'd always been able to get away from the guards easily enough. He just needed to buy himself enough time to—

One of the figures leaned forward, a light from one of the lamps illuminating his face, revealing a young man with a kind face and smooth black hair that fell to his shoulders. Dressed in breeches and a dark tunic, his eyes met Dimitri's.

The tension in Dimitri's shoulders eased, and he found himself grinning in relief.

Alexi Golistin smiled at him and pressed a finger to his lips. His skin looked ghostly white in the light, and there was something about his body language that told Dimitri his brother was nervous, something he had rarely seen in the older boy. As he trotted closer, the other figure became clear as well. A boy a few years older than Dimitri with the same raven-black hair they all shared stood there staring at him, tightly controlled anger on his face. Yuri usually looked like he had tasted something foul. It was the reason people in the castle didn't give him as much attention as they did to Alexi, but tonight, the expression was especially grim. It reminded him of the look their father often wore.

The two boys were crouched on the floor outside a door that stood slightly ajar. Creeping over, Dimitri crouched down with them, trying to see through the small crack. "Wha—"

Yuri lunged forward, covering Dimitri's mouth with his hand and giving him a withering look. Alexi smiled and pressed a finger to his lips again. Up close, Dimitri could see that the smile was strained. His oldest brother's eyes were wide, and he really did look pale. It hadn't been just the lighting. Yuri's hand over his mouth was clammy, and he was trembling. Dimitri just stared at them, shocked. What he thought was anger from a distance was something else entirely. Fear. The unsettled feeling in his stomach rose again. Something was horribly wrong.

"You're lucky you're not in shackles," said a low voice from inside the room. Dimitri flinched at the words. He knew that voice. It belonged to Cenric, one of the men who worked for his uncle. All three boys pressed as close as they could to the crack in the door.

The room was large, big enough to swallow his and Alexi's bedrooms together. There were a few plush chairs near a fireplace and a lamp on a low table next to one of them, allowing him to see what was happening inside. Dimitri had been in this room before, the walls covered in maps and books on the tables. This was where his father would meet with all manner of people to discuss business, though he had no idea what business that was.

A man's face came into view, and Dimitri could barely make out the sharp features of Cenric's face, but he knew who it was without a doubt. The man was dressed in riding leathers and a half cape, as he had been earlier that evening. His muddy-brown hair fell into his eyes, and he glared at another man opposite him, whose back was to the boys, with a calm, detached expression.

The other man scoffed. "Thank Samar for my brother's naivety."

Dimitri's eyes widened, and his mouth fell open. That was his father's voice.

Cenric's eyes narrowed dangerously. "You had best watch your tongue when you speak of the king. His Grace is the only reason you are not headed to the executioner's block."

His father's shoulders tensed, but he said nothing. Cenric said no more, instead just maintaining his hard stare. Dimitri could imagine his father's face scowling back at Cenric. Father always scowled.

The silence seemed to stretch on for an eternity, and Dimitri became aware of how his muscles ached from holding his crouched position.

Then, just when he felt he could keep still no longer, a woman's voice in the room said, "What does he intend to do with us?" That was his mother's voice.

Cenric turned his head slightly and focused on a point beyond Dimitri's view. "His Majesty and the High Council have come to an agreement." He reached into his vest, pulled out an envelope, and tore it open. Pieces of red wax fell to the floor as Cenric unfolded a sheet of parchment. "Prince Alexi Lucius Golistin," he read, "for the crime of the attempted murder of His Majesty, King Markos Caelius Golistin, you are hereby exiled from the kingdom of Morigael, never to return on pain of death."

His parents didn't speak. Dimitri felt like he had been slapped in the face. Murder? Exile? He knew that the words meant they wouldn't be able to live here anymore. They wouldn't be able to play with their cousins, visit their uncle, or chase the girls around the castle with whatever crawling insect Dimitri had found. He'd never be able to be a squire like his cousin or become a knight. The future that had been so clear earlier that day was crumbling before his very eyes.

He looked at his brothers. Alexi peered at their father's back, his lips pressed into a hard, thin line. His expression was unreadable. Yuri stared into the room with eyes unfocused, slack-jawed, and wide-eyed.

Cenric folded the paper back up. Seeming satisfied with the reaction from the Golistins, he let the words hang in the air for a few moments before continuing. "However, His Majesty and the High Council have allowed your relocation to a country of your choosing. Land and housing will be purchased for you by the crown. Staff will be procured, and their wages paid in full for a year. You will also be given one hundred thousand gold lions for your living expenses and allowed to take any items you wish from your private rooms. The Archmage has already contacted the heads of suitable countries, and there are a few that have already offered to grant you a minor lordship should you make their lands your new home."

Dimitri's father said nothing as Cenric listed the terms of the exile. He had never seen that before. His father always had something to say. Was he shocked like the rest of them, or was he angry?

"One last condition," Cenric said, and his mouth twisted in distaste. "One of your sons must stay in Morigael to be a ward of His Majesty. The king will see to his education and well-being, and he will continue to hold his status and rights as a prince of Morigael. All communication with his birth parents will be severed, and you are to never attempt to reestablish contact. He will also be removed from the line of succession. The Council has granted you the choice of which child will stay." For the briefest of seconds, Cenric's eyes slid to the crack in the door, looking right at them. Dimitri's heart jumped into his throat, and he almost bolted, but when he blinked, Cenric was staring at his father again, showing no sign that he had seen the boys. Had he imagined it?

"You have a few days to get ready and make your choice. You'll be confined to your rooms under guard during this time, of course. You and the Lady Kristanya. Your children will be able to continue their training and studies, but they will be under escort. If you need more time to decide—"

"Dimitri," his father said, interrupting Cenric. "Dimitri will stay."

TURIN CLOSED his eyes and pushed the bitter memory away. For a time after his parents left, he had thought that stormy night in the west wing of the palace had been the worst night of his life, but he was wrong. He was not that boy anymore and hadn't been for twenty years. During that time, he'd realized that being left behind was the best thing that had ever happened to him. He was a knight, respected by his peers and loved by his cousins and his aunt and uncle, the king and queen. If he'd left with his family when they had been exiled, he would have grown up to be just like his brothers, following his father around like an obedient dog.

Still, a voice in the back of his mind whispered words he'd told himself then. *You're a terrible child. Who would want you?* It was an old pain that he thought he'd worked through, but seeing his parents dug up the feelings of insecurity he'd lived with throughout his childhood. He felt the doubt gnawing at his chest and wanted nothing more than to turn and bolt from the great hall.

"What's wrong with you?" Eolisti asked, breaking through his thoughts. The Anai was peering up at him, her eyes scanning his face. "You look pale." When he didn't respond she instead glanced at Elindiir. "Who are the Golistins?"

"They are a minor noble family here in Tanalin," Elindiir replied while Turin collected himself, not daring to look at the corner where his old family had seated themselves. "It's said they came over from Morigael a decade or two ago and quickly made allies in the emperor's court. It's rumored that Lord Golistin is related to King Markos of Morigael, but it's unknown why they relocated here."

"He's the king's brother," Turin said softly.

Elindiir looked at him sharply. The Anai's eyes traveled over his face, then looked over to where Lord Golistin was seated, drinking from a wine goblet. A small, knowing smile tugged at his lips. "Ah, I see."

"Golistin!" A sharp voice cut through their conversation.

A large man with a shiny, bald pate and a graying beard marched toward Lord Golistin and his family. Alexi and the younger Yuri stood, the men blocking this newcomer from reaching their father, but the man just jabbed one plump finger at Yuri.

"You!" the older man raged, his face going as red as the silk doublet he was wearing. "You dare show your face after what you did to my daughter?!"

Initially befuddled by the man's anger, Yuri's look of

confusion cleared and was replaced by a smirk when the noble mentioned a daughter. His eyes slid to see Alexi's stony expression—almost as if his brother had expected this of him—and his own fell into a pleasant mask before his gaze returned to the irate man. "I'm afraid I don't know what you're talking about," he said in a relaxed drawl that Turin had never heard before. "Lord Sentius, isn't it? Please, have a seat, and we can discuss this miscommunication." He gestured to the chair next to him.

If it was possible, Lord Sentius's face turned an even deeper shade of scarlet. "There is no *miscommunication*! Whatever business your family of traitors has with Lord Castellus, it ends here." Then, quicker than Turin expected from a man like that, Lord Sentius pulled a dagger out of his sleeve and plunged it toward Yuri's chest.

CHAPTER

FIFTEEN

As Lord Sentius attempted to murder the second son of Lord Golistin, several things happened at once. Drawing a longsword from his belt with a smooth, practiced motion, Yuri took a step to his left, moving out of the way of the dagger. Alexi grabbed the lord's wrist, using his momentum to pull him off balance and bring him to the ground. "Get ahold of yourself, Lord Sentius!" Alexi commanded, holding the portly man down.

Turin started to move forward, but Elindiir placed a hand on his arm. "This is for the nobility to resolve," the Anai said sternly. "Do not intervene."

Eolisti frowned at Elindiir. Turin set his jaw but didn't move toward the altercation. The older Anai raised one eyebrow and his eyes flicked to the other end of the great hall. Following his gaze, Turin spotted a man who could only be another lord silently watching what was happening. This man, seated at the head table, wore gold silks fit for royalty and held himself as if he owned the place.

"Let him up, Alexi." The words drew Turin's attention

172

back to the scuffle. "If he wishes to fight me, I will gladly oblige him."

There was no way that this old lord would be a match for a much younger and most assuredly more skilled swordsman. Turin's face grew hot as his temper rose. Yuri had to know that he would easily be able to cut this man down. He didn't like the malicious look in his brother's eyes. The boy Turin knew before had a mean streak but had never been cruel. *That was twenty years ago*, he reminded himself as his hands clenched into fists, knuckles white on the handles of the service platter he still carried. If he threw the dish at Yuri's head, that would certainly stop him from killing that man.

"Peace," Elindiir murmured under his breath, seeming to sense what was going through Turin's mind.

Alexi's head snapped up to look at his younger brother. "No, Yuri. Enough is enough." With a knee on Lord Sentius's back, he held the man down until he stopped struggling. Once the noble lord fell still, Alexi kicked the dagger away and pulled the older man to his feet. "Lord Sentius," he began earnestly, his tone leaving no room for argument, "I think it would be best if you excused yourself from this event. I apologize if you or your family feels slighted by my brother's actions." Lord Sentius's face was glowing an angry red again. Alexi leaned toward the lord and said something intended for his ears only.

Whatever Alexi had said to him, Lord Sentius seemed to calm somewhat, and he nodded. The two of them turned toward the door, and the guests parted for them as they made their way out of the great hall.

Through all this, Turin's father, Lord Golistin, never made a move. Now, his cold, dark eyes followed Alexi as he escorted Lord Sentius out of the great hall. Turin saw his father's lips move, and Yuri leaned close to speak quietly with him as an awkward chatter started up again around them.

Turin glanced over to the dais at the front of the room, but Lord Castellus had disappeared. Had he lost face for such a scene breaking out under his roof? Had he gone to offer his apologies to Lord Sentius? Somehow, Turin didn't think so. The lord of Tempest Hall didn't seem like the type to apologize for anything.

Tanalin politics were all pleasantries on the surface, but from his experience, everyone held a knife just out of view. He hadn't spent much time navigating the courts here, but the official courtesies weren't that different from those in Morigael, the border of which was only a few days' ride north of here. That was no surprise. Morigael had once been a territory of the Tanalin Empire until it had broken away about a hundred years ago in a brutal civil war. Even now, Tanalinian customs were similar enough for him to know how to act, but the subtle differences still managed to trip him up now and then.

The rumbling of the crowd descended back into quiet chatter. No one dared approach Lord Golistin or his son, and most stole only covert glances at the family, whispering under their breath only loudly enough for their neighbors to hear.

"So," Elindiir began, his melodic voice drawing Turin's attention. The Anai seemed to be mostly talking to Eolisti, but he glanced at Turin as he spoke. "You still haven't told me why you are here. Weren't you heading north? I seem to remember your hooded friend being very adamant about that the last time I saw you."

Eolisti grinned and leaned close to the other Anai conspiratorially. "We're on a mission!" she said, voice laced with excitement. "Oh, don't worry," she added, seeing the look on Turin's face. "Elindiir's a friend."

Turin opened his mouth, an angry retort on his lips, when Elindiir placed a hand on his shoulder and nodded toward the dais.

Lord Castellus had entered the great hall again and stood surveying his guests. The room quieted under his gaze. They seemed to know he wanted to speak to them.

"Thank you all for coming," he began once the chatter waned. "I have a very special announcement to make tonight, but first, allow me to introduce my daughter," he said with a smile that didn't quite touch his eyes. Turning, he gestured with one hand, and out of the archway near the dais, a young woman emerged from the shadows.

She was beautiful, with elegant features and posture as straight as an arrow. Her long, blonde hair cascaded down her shoulders in thick waves, shining in the soft yellow light radiating from the magical bobbles hanging from the ceiling. The skirt of her deep-green gown trailed behind her, making her movement appear fluid and even more graceful. The woman looked to be in her mid-twenties, and her lithe form and flawless skin drew every eye in the room. She wore a look of serene disinterest as she approached Lord Castellus, stepping up onto the dais to join him.

As this new woman turned her hazel eyes toward those watching, Turin's breath caught in his throat. He knew that face.

Lord Castellus took his daughter's hand and turned back to the gathered crowd. "It has been over twelve long years since my precious Korynne went missing, taken by those who wished to hold sway over house Castellus. Her disappearance left my family broken, and losing a child is a wound so deep that there were times I wasn't sure I could endure it." He turned his head to the woman next to him and smiled. She didn't react to his words. "But it is my pleasure to inform all of you, my friends and allies, that she is finally home and safe with us." He raised the arm that held Korynne's hand as all the lords and ladies applauded. Turin felt his own hands clench into fists.

The lord waited a few moments for the noise to die down again before continuing. "As you all know, you are here for a feast, but it is actually a wedding." There was a collective gasp that Castellus nodded at, as if he'd been expecting it. "Originally, this celebration would have been for my niece, Atria." He gestured to a young woman wearing a red ball gown in the front row. "But with her blessing, there has been a change of plans. It gives me great pleasure to announce the joining of house Castellus and house Golistin."

Every head turned to the corner that Lord Golistin and his family occupied. A wide grin spread on Yuri's pompous face as the lord stood and nodded at Lord Castellus. Turin had the sudden urge to go over there and punch him.

"Lord Golistin's second son, Yuri, and my daughter Korynne will wed in three days." As if on cue, a servant discreetly approached the dais and held out a tray to the lord on which there was only one goblet. He took it and raised it high, and the other nobles mimicked him. "A toast to the happy union of our children and the uniting of our two houses." He smiled at his guests and took a long drink from the goblet.

Korynne just stood there, still and silent, her eyes unfocused as everyone around her drank and applauded merrily. It was almost as if she didn't care about what Lord Castellus was saying. *But that's not quite it*, Turin amended in his mind. *It's like she's not even here at all.* Something was not right with that expression.

Lord Castellus gestured, and a woman dressed in the house uniform stepped onto the dais and helped the lady step down and exit back through the archway. "Tonight, we will celebrate the upcoming wedding. Please enjoy our hospitality." The lord stepped off the dais and began mingling with his guests, a pleasant look on his face as the nobles closest to him rushed to offer their congratulations.

Turin watched Lady Korynne's retreating form. He knew this woman by another name. She would not have been silent as others spoke about her, and she certainly wouldn't have allowed herself to be married off without a fight. What was she even doing here? Was she really Lord Castellus's daughter, or was this some sort of ruse? Did the Phoenix have something to do with this?

Turin glanced over at Yuri and his father.

Yuri looked like a cat who had just caught a mouse and swallowed it whole. He was reveling at being the center of attention, his lips set in a smug grin while his father shook hands with another lord who'd come up to speak to them. Turin felt his face growing hot again. His brother had just been attacked by another lord for an offense that he suspected he was guilty of, and now he was going to be married to Lady Korynne. He'd been looking at her like she was a prize he'd won. Turin may not have seen Yuri in the past twenty years, but he knew plenty of men just like him.

Elindiir stepped into Turin's view. "You need to calm down." The statement was made with a smile, but his eyes were blazing. The Anai's words made him notice that a few of the people around them were staring at him. Belatedly, he realized his hands were shaking, and his jaw ached from how hard he'd been clenching his teeth. He must have looked frightful for the Anaiian ambassador to step in.

Turin took a deep breath and schooled his expression. He smiled back stiffly at Elindiir, and the Anai nodded.

"Let's get out of here," Eolisti murmured as she tugged on Turin's sleeve. She turned to the table and slid the rest of the food off her tray next to an abandoned goblet. "My tray is empty."

They made their way across the great hall, leaving the Anaiian ambassador and weaving through the other guests who were intent on becoming inebriated with drink. A few men even tried to chat up Eolisti, but her scowl had them directing their attention elsewhere.

Turin tried to focus his attention on anything other than what had just happened. He wasn't an amateur, and he knew getting distracted during a mission was dangerously careless, but the shock of seeing *her* had awoken something he thought he'd buried. Before he could dwell long on those thoughts, there was a sharp prod in his side.

Eolisti had elbowed him, and when Turin saw who was only a few feet in front of him, he felt the bottom drop out of his stomach. Alexi, stood near the door that led to the kitchen, speaking quietly with a woman in a servant's uniform. Eolisti and Turin rushed past the pair, and Turin risked a glance back at his eldest brother.

Alexi Golistin's gaze slid over them, meeting Turin's eyes for the briefest moment before the knight looked away, concentrating on where they were going. The other man didn't say anything to them as he and Eolisti passed, and they were able to make their way quickly down the hall.

The kitchen was still as busy as when they'd first arrived at Tempest Hall. Eolisti set their trays down in a pile of other empty ones and picked up a platter piled high with colorful, exotic fruits, shoving it into Turin's hands. "Pull yourself together," she whispered, glancing over at Dalia and her assistants. "We still have several hours here, and if you don't stop reacting to every other word that's said, you're going to get us caught."

As Turin was about to speak, a door to their left opened. Sophie and Khalil entered, carrying burlap sacks of what he assumed was grain. Sophie's eyes met his, and she motioned them over. Setting down their trays again, Eolisti and Turin followed them to the corner where they stacked the sacks they'd brought up from the reserve cellar.

"We found the dungeons, but the Phoenix isn't there." Sophie glanced around the kitchen nervously. Turin didn't think that anything else could surprise him after seeing his family, but the young wizard's next words proved him wrong. "We'll talk more back at the inn, but Lady Korynne Castellus is the Phoenix."

SIXTEEN

Sophie wiped the sweat off her forehead with the back of her sleeve. She and Khalil had been bringing up barrels and sacks from the reserve cellar all night, and now that the guests had been fed and the evening was winding down, they were finally allowed a chance to rest. Sophie sat on a crate out in the courtyard, just outside the door to the kitchen. She took a sip of water from the tin cup in her hands and leaned back against the wall. The night was so cold that she could see frost on the ground, but the cool air felt good on her skin after the stifling heat of the kitchen.

She couldn't get the look on Turin's face out of her mind. When she'd told him that Lord Castellus's daughter was the Phoenix, he'd looked stricken. Did he know her after all, but by another name?

Khalil had also seemed shocked to learn of her identity. His and Turin's reactions caused the feeling of unease that she'd had earlier that day to grow. It was painfully obvious to her that they were missing vital information about the Nightingales.

The door next to her opened, bathing Sophie in a wave of warm air as Khalil stepped outside. He handed her a pastry with a sticky, white glaze and sat on the crate next to her. She watched as he bit into a steaming roll of his own, her mind wandering. Would it be easier to get the Phoenix out of the castle now that they generally knew where she was being held? It had been simple enough to break into the dungeons, but getting into the upper living quarters without being seen...Well, there were just so many people here.

"Everything all right?" Khalil asked, breaking into her thoughts.

"Oh, yes. I was just thinking about... what we have to do." No one was around, but it didn't seem like a good idea to talk about sneaking into the castle for a rescue mission while they were sitting outside. "It's not going to be easy, and I'm not sure how much help I'm going to be without being able to use my... skills." She took a bite of the pastry. It was still warm and sweet, filled with a fruit she'd never had before but liked its taste. It was tart and refreshing, a kind of citrus that was a light-yellow color.

Khalil was quiet for a moment as Sophie chewed. "That man you saw earlier, you said he was a wizard."

"Yes," she said between bites.

"We don't know how they are keeping the Phoenix from taking Winna and leaving, but if she is truly getting married, they must be controlling her somehow. You may be more useful than you think." He finished off the rest of his own roll, chewing thoughtfully.

The servants coming in and out of the great hall had been chatting all night about Lord Castellus's announcement that his daughter would be married to the son of Lord Golistin. It appeared to be a political marriage that had been intended for Castellus's niece, but once his daughter had "returned," they had switched brides. She could see the reasoning. A direct descendant of the lord would provide a stronger familial bond than another relative. They hadn't gotten a chance to talk at length with Turin and Eolisti, but Sophie thought she grasped the crucial details.

She leaned in close to Khalil, speaking in a low whisper. "You think she's being controlled by magic?" Her stomach turned at the thought, remembering the pain she'd endured when being forced to obey the Spider. He had been cruel, and anyone who employed magic in such a perverse way would be the same.

The door to the kitchen banged open again before Khalil could respond, startling Sophie and making her almost drop her food.

Turin strode outside, followed closely by Eolisti. Judging by the scowl on his face and the set of his jaw, he was in a towering temper. Eolisti, for her part, looked both amused and annoyed.

"There you are!" Turin said as he spotted them. "We've been looking all over for the two of you!"

Eolisti rolled her eyes and made a face behind Turin's back.

"We just finished working a few minutes ago," Sophie said coolly. She didn't know why the knight was so upset, but she wouldn't let him vent his frustrations on her. "Are you two finished in the great hall?"

The Anai answered before Turin could. "Yeah, for tonight anyway." Eolisti yawned and stretched. "Who knew talking to humans could be so exhausting?" She looked at the door back into Tempest Hall, and a mischievous grin spread across her face.

"Guess who's here?" She was practically vibrating with excitement, but Sophie just raised her eyebrows. Anyone interesting could have drawn this reaction out of Eolisti. "It's Elindiir!"

Sophie felt her mouth form an 'o' shape. "Why?" she asked, recovering quickly. She hadn't expected to see the other Anai again so soon.

"He's an ambassador. I remember asking him about all the places he'd traveled. But he'd kind of droned on about going around doing social engagements for Nemethy or something like that, and I wasn't really listening," Eolisti said nonchalantly, but that last statement didn't surprise the mage. "Why he's here isn't important," the Anai continued. "The fact that he's at the castle means we have someone on the inside, right? It could be useful."

"Perhaps," Turin said with a grumble. What was wrong with him? Did something happen while they were in the great hall?

"Of course it is!" Eolisti glared at him. "Maybe I should stay here." Eolisti said hopefully to Sophie. "I could stay with Elindiir and check out the upper floors. I already stick out, but if I made myself out as a guest, we could get some more information."

"Out of the question," Turin said flatly, returning the Anai's glare. Eolisti stuck her tongue out at him.

"Nice to see that you two are getting along," Sophie said, licking the frosting off her fingers. "He's probably right, though. We don't want to drag Elindiir into this if we can avoid it. As you said, you stick out too much. Because you're so beautiful, obviously," she added with a grin, holding out the remainder of the sweet bun.

Eolisti rolled her eyes but leaned in for a bite. "Hey,

these are pretty good! I guess these Tanalinians can cook." She took the pastry out of Sophie's hand, tore it in half, and gave her back the larger piece. "I'm starving. Did the kitchen give you any more food?"

"No, just this." Sophie eyed Turin. "Are you okay?"

The larger man sighed. "Yes, I'm fine. It's just..." He looked around the courtyard. "We should get back to the inn. There are some details we need to go over, and we can't do that here."

Sophie glanced at Khalil. He was frowning slightly, but he didn't argue with Turin. She stuffed the rest of the pastry in her mouth, slid off the crate, and wiped her hands on the apron Dalia had given her. They followed Turin out the castle gate, passing guards that seemed less diligent compared to those who had been there earlier. They didn't give the group a second look and wished them a disinterested goodnight. Sophie supposed they were watching for threats coming into the castle, not leaving.

The walk back to the inn was chilly now that the sun had set, and a breeze blew through the valley, picking up the loose deposits of snow still on the ground and sending it fluttering around their feet. Sophie glanced up at Aeris, one of Lanis's two moons. It was low in the western sky, meaning Thaera, its smaller twin, would rise in the east soon. For now, the snow glittered in the bluish light Aeris cast upon the land.

The castle wasn't too far from the inn and the rest of the town, and the four of them made good time, walking with little chatter. All of them seemed to be lost in thought over the task still ahead of them. Sophie felt a weight settle on her shoulders, and she couldn't shake the feeling that they were in over their heads.

As Turin opened the heavy door of the tavern, a cacophony of sounds hit them like an avalanche. The inn was packed. Every table was full of people who had come for work at the keep. The castle would house the visiting nobles, but the extra workers would have to find other places to stay.

Stepping into the inn was like stepping back into the kitchen at the castle. The air was hot from the roaring fire in the hearth, and that heat was only amplified by the number of bodies crowding around every table. The raucous laughter and shouting voices rang throughout the tavern. The portly innkeeper was behind the bar, furiously alternating between cleaning tankards and filling them with foamy, golden liquid while harried men and women dashed around with bowls of steaming food and drink for the patrons. It seemed as if the entire town had come to this one inn.

Turin looked back over his shoulder, eyebrows raised, then tilted his head toward the stairs that led to the second floor and up to their rooms. Sophie and Eolisti nodded, following the knight, with Khalil trailing behind them.

He led the way to the room that had been assigned to the two women. It was simple, with two single beds and a table for two against one wall. Khalil disappeared for a few moments, then came back in, holding two more chairs, presumably from the room he and Turin were sharing.

Almost as soon as the door swung closed, Turin started in on them. "What did you find out?"

As Sophie gathered her thoughts, Eolisti let out a soft snort. "Why are you in a rush? We've been working all day, and I'm starving. At least give us a chance to rest before you start interrogating us."

The larger man glared at Eolisti again.

"It's all right," Sophie said as Eolisti's eyes narrowed at Turin. It was best to cut them off before they could start arguing. "We were able to search part of the first floor in between fetching items from the reserve cellar." She glanced over at Khalil, who gave no indication that he was going to speak. "We found the dungeon, but the Phoenix isn't being kept there, just her associate, and she's in bad condition."

"That's all you found?" Turin asked, frustration clear in his tone.

"It's not like you were much help," the Anai snapped. "We weren't even there ten minutes before you started acting like you'd lost your mind. What happened, hmm? Did you lose your nerve?" She smiled conspiratorially. "Or maybe you were quite taken with Lady Korynne. You couldn't seem to keep your eyes off her."

Sophie rubbed her temples with her fingers. All the bickering got on her nerves, no matter how much she tried to ignore it. "The woman in the dungeon was not the Phoenix," she continued, speaking over Turin's indignation. "She said her name was Winna, and she seems to be associated with the Nightingales. It was Winna who told us that the Phoenix is Lord Castellus's daughter, Korynne."

"Impossible," Turin said, and he sounded angry. "The woman that Lord Castellus is claiming to be his daughter can't be the Phoenix." He crossed his arms over his chest in a huff, and it reminded Sophie of a petulant child. "I recognized her. She goes by the name of Rhyn and is the Lord High Commander's niece. He's not related to that puffed-up toad, and neither is she!" He averted his eyes, and Sophie saw a slight redness in his cheeks. He was completely in denial, refusing to see what was in front of him.

There was a history here between Turin and the woman he'd seen, Sophie was sure of it. Lovers or friends, he was incensed at the very idea of this woman being related to Castellus, but that didn't change the fact that they had identified her as the Phoenix. She wanted to know more about their relationship but now wasn't the right time. He needed to see reason, and with Eolisti provoking him, that just made it even more difficult.

"If it's been a while since you've seen her," Sophie began again gently, "she could have changed. Anyone can become something else if they're pushed. Believe me, I speak from experience."

Turin eyed her and opened his mouth like he was going to argue, but Khalil cut him off.

"The woman you knew as Rhyn is the Phoenix," Khalil said, sounding certain. "I've worked with her before. She uses a lot of different names, and that is one I've heard her call herself in the past."

"Well, apparently she's getting married," Eolisti said, watching Turin's shocked expression. "And she didn't look very upset about it either. That Yuri guy looked like a right clotpole, though. That's the noble lordling Castellus said she was marrying," Eolisti added, seeing Sophie's questioning look. Then she leaned back in her chair. "Now that I think about it, the lady didn't seem to care at all. She looked barely awake, like she was in a trance."

"Yes, it was strange." Turin seemed to come back to himself at the Anai's words. "The Rhyn I knew would never have stood by while her fate was determined by others." He glanced over at Sophie. "Nobody changes *that* much."

Khalil nodded in agreement. "They are controlling her

somehow." He turned toward Sophie. "Probably with magic."

Sophie grimaced. When she'd been held captive by the Spider a few months ago, he'd forced her to comply with his wishes by using a magical artifact her people called a slave anklet. After a command was issued by the person wearing a ring that was magically linked to the anklet, the artifact caused debilitating pain to the wearer unless they obeyed. If the wearer tried to resist or tamper with the magic the anklet was imbued with, the pain could be so great as to easily cause unconsciousness. They were formidable tools. Sophie did not doubt that one could be obtained by someone with Lord Castellus's wealth and power, but those artifacts weren't something that would make their victims submit so peacefully. That is, not unless they'd broken her will—or mind—in the process.

"We need to find out more," Sophie muttered aloud. "She could be under a spell, or poisoned, or any number of other things. The lord could be threatening her with Winna's life, or she may not even know of her companion's condition." Sophie looked up at the others. They all wore grim expressions. "How long do we have?"

"Three days," Turin said. "By Tanalin custom, there are three days of feasting before the wedding, and tonight was the first of those. Lord Castellus may be in a rush to complete his plans, but I don't think he'd snub tradition. Not with so many other nobles here."

"So, we have two more days to figure out what we're going to do?" Eolisti piped in with a groan. "Great, two more days of serving humans."

"Three more days if we include the wedding day, but that may be too late," Sophie added.

A muscle in Turin's jaw twitched. "We should get her out now," he growled through clenched teeth.

"We don't even know where she's being held," Khalil replied, sounding annoyed with their companion. "We'll find out all we can in the next two days and then escape with her the night before the wedding. No one will know until long after we're gone."

Turin frowned but didn't say anything.

"I think our first priority should be finding her room on the upper floors." Sophie chewed on her bottom lip in thought. She'd never done anything like this before. She'd spent the last few months running away from her old life. She didn't know how to break someone out of a castle fortress and sneak her out under the noses of the guards, but no one stopped her from speaking. On the contrary, everyone seemed to be listening. "Most of the staff ignored Khalil and me as we wandered around, probably because of all the extra people here, but it might be suspicious if we were caught searching the upper floors. They're probably still guarded." Sophie looked at Khalil, who had one elbow on the table. "Maybe we can find an opening in their rotation?"

"Perhaps we should report earlier tomorrow," Eolisti suggested. "It would give us more time to check out the castle."

Right, and that had nothing to do with her wanting to see Elindiir.

Eolisti rubbed her arms with her hands and puffed out a long breath. "Why is it freezing in here too?! This stupid country is too cold. At least Zo'rahn was warm!" She stood and stretched. "I'm going to go thaw by the fire."

Turin gaped at Eolisti as she left abruptly. "But we haven't even decided on a plan yet!"

Sophie shook her head, exasperated by Eolisti's and Turin's attitudes and more than a little tired from the day's work. "She's not going to listen, and she has a point. We should probably all get some food and rest." She placed a hand gently on Turin's arm. "Don't let it get to you. For the most part, Eolisti may act immature, but she's been invaluable to me and is quite capable. She knows what she's doing."

Turin looked over at Khalil, who still didn't speak. "I can't believe I'm saying this, but if he trusts her, that has to be good enough for me. If he thought she would endanger what we are doing here, he wouldn't have allowed her to come along." The knight stood as well. "But if I have to choose between her and the Phoenix, I'll choose my mission over the Anai."

Turin mumbled something that Sophie didn't catch, then left the room, leaving her alone with Khalil. She eyed him, looking for any sign of emotion, but he was as stoic as ever.

"How are you feeling?" Sophie asked him. "The Phoenix is your friend too, right? This is a lot to take in."

The way Khalil's head tilted to one side reminded Sophie of a bird, and she covered her mouth with her hand to keep in the laugh that threatened to burst from her lips. *Focus, Sophie!* This was a serious conversation.

"We've gotten out of worse situations," he said with a smirk, giving her the impression he knew that she was amused. "Though, when I'm summoned, usually the target has already escaped captivity. I don't have much experience breaking someone out of a fortress like Tempest Hall."

When Sophie and Khalil met, she had already escaped from her home and had eluded the pursuit by her master's people for two weeks. She smiled a little, letting her mind drift back to that night.

Sophie had been wandering around the mountain-top monastery of Ta'Shela in the middle of the night and had stumbled upon a small prayer chapel. Khalil had been kneeling at the foot of Samar's statue and had volunteered to guide Sophie back to her room when she'd gotten lost in the winding corridors. At first, Sophie had been scared of him, but he had quickly proven himself to be a trusted ally and friend. He was so different from anyone she'd ever met before, and that was aside from his strange abilities.

"There is something I'm curious about," Sophie began, remembering something she'd felt when they'd first met, "but we don't have to talk about it now. It's been a long day." Even as she said it, she noticed the stiffness and exhaustion in her arms and shoulders. Back in Zo'rahn, the majority of her work had been studying. Magic could be physically draining, but it wasn't the same as lifting heavy crates and sacks all day. She tried stretching her arms over her head and sucked in a sharp breath. "Ow, I'm going to be so sore tomorrow."

Khalil held out a hand. "Let me help."

After a moment's hesitation, Sophie laid her hand in his, and he turned her palm to face up. Khalil slid his fingers up her forearm and leaned forward, reaching out his other hand to massage the muscles in her upper arm. "You'll still feel sore in the morning, but it won't be as bad."

"Thank you," she sighed, letting his fingers chase away some of her tension. It felt good, and she had to bite her bottom lip to keep from letting out a groan.

"What is it you want to know?"

"Ah, it's a bit of a personal question," Sophie said, suddenly embarrassed. "I realize we've only known each other for a few months, so if it's too personal, I apologize." She paused, but Khalil didn't say anything. Did that mean it was safe for her to continue?

"So…" she began again. It was difficult to get her thoughts together while he was this close to her, touching her. Giving up, she sighed. "This is going to sound foolish, but I've always assumed that you were blind because, well…" She gestured at his face but realized it was futile. He couldn't see her gesture, and she wanted to have at least a little tact.

"My eyes?" Khalil asked, an amused smile playing at the side of his mouth. Was he enjoying her struggle?

Sophie let out another sigh and made a frustrated noise. "How is it that you always know where you're going?" she blurted out. "And how do you fight so well? Even if you trained with the monks at Ta'Shela for years, you shouldn't be able to do any of that. Not that I'm complaining," she added hastily. There was a heat rising up her neck that made her uncomfortable. "I sensed something the first time I saw you. It was unlike anything I'd ever seen or read about before. It was like when I sense magic, but different." She let out a soft laugh. It sounded ridiculous, even to her. "Do you know what I'm talking about?"

Khalil's fingers stayed in constant motion as she spoke. After a few moments, he released her and held out a hand for her other arm. Sophie flexed her fingers. It didn't feel as tight as before, so she shifted in her seat and extended her other arm for him.

"I don't know what you sensed, but I don't believe my condition is natural," he said, his voice carrying no heat. Sophie was relieved. When she'd asked him personal questions before, he'd gotten upset. "My senses are much sharper than when I could see, and I'm able to focus on my hearing more, which allows me to function better than I would otherwise." He paused then, and Sophie could see his brows furrow in thought. "I'm not sure how to put this, but I can also feel where things are around me. Not by touching, but... I just know. It's very difficult to explain."

"I can use magic to sense energy. Is it something like that?"

"Yes, and no." He resumed massaging her arm. "As I said, it's difficult to explain. It's more of *knowing* that something is there even if it can't be seen. It's a sensation that I feel in my bones, not necessarily any kind of external force."

Sophie nodded. She thought that she understood what he was saying. The way he described it, it almost sounded like an enhanced intuition rather than anything he actively controlled. Maybe his blindness was a curse. There had been books on curses in the Vizier's personal library. A powerful one could have this kind of effect. If she could figure out what it was, maybe she could help him.

The door swung open with a deafening *BANG*, making Sophie jump so quickly that she almost fell out of her chair. Khalil caught her shoulder before she toppled over.

"Am I interrupting?" Eolisti stood in the doorway, framed by the light in the hall. Her eyes narrowed in suspicion.

"No, of course not," Sophie said, her face feeling warm. "We were just talking."

"Uh-huh," the Anai's tone was full of skepticism. "Well, the innkeeper said he was going to run out of food soon, so if you want some, you should hurry it up." With that, she closed the door again.

A ringing silence was left behind. It wasn't hard to see why Eolisti would have thought that they were doing something other than talking. If she allowed herself to think about it, the way Khalil had been touching her had been rather... intimate.

Sophie was about to suggest that they head down for food when she caught the look on Khalil's face. His brows were furrowed in deep concentration, and the muscles in his jaw flexed as he clenched his teeth. She wanted to ask him what was wrong, but by some instinct, she knew she should wait for him to speak first.

"This is all too dangerous," he said finally. "I'm sorry." It looked like the words pained him. "We shouldn't be here. By now, we'd be in Morigael, and you'd be safe. We wouldn't be doing this."

His words surprised Sophie. They were already here, and he was having misgivings now? "But the Phoenix is your friend. You can't just leave her here, Khalil."

He folded his arms across his chest. Whatever had brought this on, he was visibly upset. "I know. She needs my help. If it wasn't for that, this mission would be done, and I could go on to help others. It shouldn't be this complicated."

There was a tense feeling in Sophie's stomach. She knew that his mission was to deliver her safely to Morigael, and while she knew his responsibility for her would end once they arrived, the thought of him leaving her there made her feel like she was falling off a cliff. She took a deep breath to steady her words. "I know I'm a burden to you— No, Khalil, let me finish," Sophie said when Khalil began to interrupt her. "I'm a burden. I know that. Everyone who has helped me has suffered for it. You want to complete your mission and get me out of your hair. There will always be more people for you to help, and you want to get back to that as soon as possible."

"Sophie, that's not what I'm saying."

"It's okay. Though I feel we've become... friends, I know this is just another mission for you. I..." Sophie cleared her throat. There was a tightness in her chest that confused her. "Thank you for helping me. There is no need for you to apologize. I chose to come here and do this." She sighed heavily. "We really should get going before there is no food left for us."

Without waiting for Khalil to respond, Sophie stood and hurried out of the room, silently wiping away a tear.

CHAPTER
SEVENTEEN

The morning was gray and overcast as Sophie and the others made their way back to the castle. Despite Khalil's ministrations the previous night, her arms were still sore, but she suspected they felt better than they would have otherwise. At least she was able to move them around without too much stiffness. When they arrived at the gates, there were only a few people around, and the two guards seemed to be almost asleep on their feet. Neither of them questioned Eolisti this time, only waving them through with a yawn.

It wasn't just the guards. Everyone they saw seemed to be moving more slowly.

"The castle staff probably found it hard to sleep," Turin muttered, then glanced over at Sophie. "Feasting goes on well into the early hours, so the people who live within the walls likely had no peace and quiet."

Sophie nodded. It was lucky they were staying at an inn far enough from Tempest Hall that they didn't have to worry about the revelry spilling over into their rest.

Though, the crowd at the inn the night before had been rowdy all on their own.

"Thank the gods," Dalia exclaimed when they reached the kitchen. She was standing on a footstool, leaning over a cauldron of thick, bubbling liquid. Wisps of gray hair fell out of her bun, floating around her face and sticking to her skin where a sheen of sweat glistened in the sunlight drifting in through the window. Her apron was stained, and there were deep bags under her eyes. She looked like she could fall asleep where she stood.

"You two," she pointed a wooden spoon at Turin and Eolisti, "go help pick up the dishes in the courtyard. We need it all back here and washed for the feast today, and my girls are dead on their feet."

Eolisti gave Sophie an exasperated look, then followed Turin out the servants' door.

Dalia turned her gaze on Sophie and Khalil. "As for you two, Anya needs some extra hands tidying up the guest rooms where the visiting lords and ladies are staying." She frowned and gave the pot she was leaning over a few more quick stirs. "She's in the great hall, I think. They are getting ready for today's feasting, cleaning up from last night and setting up the new decorations. You can't miss her. She's the one who'll be looming over everyone else." Dalia muttered something under her breath, then turned back to what she was doing. "Once she's done with you, come back here. There is still a lot to do before we'll be ready for tonight."

Sophie glanced at Khalil, whose expression remained neutral. She took his arm and led him out of the kitchen.

They found Anya in the great hall, just as Dalia had said. Other men and women wearing the house uniform scrambled around, setting out exotic fruits in shades of red and purple on the tables, lighting candles, or scrubbing the floors and furniture.

Anya was a tall, lean woman with dark brown hair pulled into a tight bun, and a hawkish nose. There was not a wrinkle in her dress or a hair out of place. She looked like a person who would settle for nothing less than perfection. By her demeanor, it was obvious that this woman was the head maid and took her job very seriously. Her pale-blue eyes scanned the room, watching the staff for signs of anything that would displease her before her stern gaze settled on Sophie and Khalil.

Sophie hurried up to the woman, unnerved by her scrutinizing eye. It was almost like she was an apprentice again, being watched carefully as she performed a spell for the first time. "Miss Anya," she began with a bow of her head and as much politeness as she could muster. "Miss Dalia sent us to assist you in taking care of the noble lords and ladies."

Anya looked down her nose at her, and Sophie's anxiety tripled. She tried to look innocent and helpful under that penetrating gaze.

"Very well," she said, apparently approving of whatever she had been looking for. "Head through that door"—she pointed to a small door painted the same color as the wall —"and then up the stairway at the end of the passage. The entire second floor is guest suites. You'll need to empty and clean the basins so we can refill them with fresh water, and empty the chamber pots." The head maid eyed Khalil and his blindfold. "Is he going to be a problem? I don't want him offending any of the lords or ladies."

"No, miss, he will not be a problem."

"He'd better not be. Just pick up a bucket and rag on your way out." Anya turned away, dismissing them as her attention focused on a small girl in a maid's uniform. She couldn't have been older than fourteen. "No, no! You have it backward, Prina."

Picking up an unattended bucket and rag, Sophie pulled Khalil toward the door that Anya had pointed out. If the woman hadn't told her where it was, Sophie would have never noticed it. It was made to look like just another panel on the wall and was in the corner so as not to be seen. This must have been one of the ways that servants moved around the castle without running afoul of the nobility.

As they approached, the guard that was leaning on the wall near the servants' door shifted, his eyes assessing them. Sophie's heart pounded in her ears. She'd hoped the cleaning assignment would allow them to explore other bedrooms, possibly finding where the Phoenix was being held. Even though Anya had just directed them to use that door, she was sure the guard would stop them, and they had to ensure nothing brought undue attention to them. If she used magic to subdue him, surely, it would alert the court mage to their presence, and they'd have to make their escape sooner than planned. If Khalil knocked him out, it would be the same. There were so many people here that someone would see it.

Breathing in deeply through her nose, she reminded herself that they were working here and that there was no reason for the guard to find them suspicious, but she couldn't shake the feeling.

She needn't have worried. The man dressed in the shade of brilliant blue of house Castellus barely gave them a second glance as they passed and never moved from his position against the wall.

"Relax," Khalil whispered once they reached the

second-floor landing. "We're supposed to be here, remember?"

"Yes," Sophie said, scanning the corridor before them. They'd emerged from a small stairwell that was obviously for servants into a large hallway with a plush, red carpet. Fresh-cut flowers rested in ornate vases between each of the white-washed doors lining the walls. Instead of oil lamps and torches like the floor below, Sophie was surprised to see mage lamps hanging in the sconces on the walls. A tiny, golden flame danced in the center of the paned glass of the lamps, their flickering radiance giving off a soft illumination that mimicked a late afternoon glow.

She stared around in amazement. If the castle only housed one wizard, then the lord must have purchased these at an exorbitant cost. Was he just leaving them around to show off to guests?

"Do you think the Phoenix is on this floor?" she asked distractedly, glancing back at him.

Khalil was silent for a moment, his head tilted slightly to the left. "No," he said finally. "Castellus wouldn't want the slightest chance of a guest finding her. There should be another stairway somewhere that goes directly up to the chambers of the Castellus family. If it were me, I'd keep her in a tower. It's the hardest position to get to and the easiest to defend."

Sophie nodded. "All right. Let's take a look around then. Maybe there's another servants' staircase we can use."

There was no one else in the hallway, but it was likely they were not alone on the floor. Guests could have slept in, and, after the late-night festivities, a lot of them probably had. But there could also be other maids assigned to cleaning as they were, so they moved quietly. Khalil paused every few steps, listening intently for sounds within the rooms in front of them. He would nod to Sophie before they moved on to show that he thought it was safe to continue.

It was slow going, but there were many interesting things for Sophie to look at. On each door was stenciled a different image in red paint. One door they paused in front of had a rose painted on it, while the one across the hall had a willow tree. In addition to the flowers and mage lamps, which were spaced at every other door, paintings of forests hung on the walls between rooms. Adding those to the plush carpet beneath their feet, it seemed the lord had gone to a lot of trouble to make this floor visually pleasing to his guests.

Sophie also noticed that this part of the castle was very warm. Not as warm as the kitchen, but warm enough to make someone forget the winter outside.

There was a loud *click*, and a door right behind them opened.

A tall, lean man exited the room, a sour expression on his face. He was older, in his fifties if Sophie had to guess, with his golden hair so light it almost appeared white and a neatly trimmed beard on his strong jaw. A cape made of a brown and gray pelt sat upon his shoulders, and the clothing he wore beneath was of rich, blue velvet.

She knew instantly who this was. There was a portrait of his likeness hanging in the great hall. Sophie threw a panicked glance over at Khalil, who, to her surprise, was bowing deeply, his right foot back a step.

At that moment, Lord Castellus noticed them and turned in their direction.

Thinking fast, Sophie curtsied in the same way that she'd seen the other maids do and murmured, "My lord."

Lord Castellus beckoned her forward, his cold blue eyes examining her from head to toe. "I don't recall seeing you before," he said, his voice deep and resonant. "What's your name?"

Her stomach clenched as she stepped closer to him, but to her credit, she didn't cringe away. "Sophie, my lord. I've been hired as extra help for the wedding. Miss Dalia has me working in the kitchen and assisting Miss Anya." She kept her eyes on the ground as Castellus walked around her in a slow circle. His gaze had a weight to it, like he was examining a prized horse. She almost expected him to pry her mouth open to inspect her teeth, which would somehow have been less unnerving. Sophie hated having him at her back, but a maid would be used to this. She couldn't give herself away.

He paused next to her and leaned in. "What accent is that? Where are you from, girl?"

Panic threatened to buckle Sophie's knees. "Omer, my lord," she managed to say in a steady voice, "but I've been living in Tanalin for some time." Sophie dared not look him in the eye. She felt sure that he would be able to see the lie on her face. "It's my pleasure to serve house Castellus."

Out of the corner of her eye, she saw Castellus reach out toward her.

"My lord!" came an echoing voice from down the hall, making Sophie start. A harried-looking maid of middling years scurried up to them.

Castellus took a step back, and Sophie risked a glance at him while his attention was elsewhere. He was closer to her than she thought he'd been. The lord folded his hands behind his back in a relaxed manner. What had he been about to do?

The glint of light on metal caught Sophie's eye, and before it was hidden, she spotted an ancient ring with a large garnet on the middle finger of his right hand.

"I apologize, my lord," the woman puffed out as she reached them. "I'm having trouble with Lady Korynne." The maid glanced at Sophie, and it was then that she noticed the bright blue liquid staining the woman's apron. A sickly-sweet scent filled the passageway, coming from whatever that substance was.

Sophie's eyes narrowed. She knew a potion when she saw one.

While Lord Castellus was distracted, Sophie reached out with her senses. The blue liquid had a faint energy, but she immediately felt an aura coming from the ring the lord was wearing. It was similar to one that she'd felt before.

Castellus sighed heavily. "Very well. Lead the way, Marilla."

As the lord and the maid—Marilla—departed, Sophie glanced over at Khalil. His mouth was pressed into a hard line, and his hands were balled into fists.

"Are you all right?" he asked her once they were alone again.

"Yes," she said, letting out a relieved breath. "But I think I know how they are controlling the Phoenix. Do you still have that slave anklet the Spider used on me?"

"Why do we have to do this?" Eolisti sighed as she picked up yet another dirty plate and placed it on her tray. This reminded her all too much of Elasariin, the Anaiian city she'd grown up in, and how she'd been sent to do manual labor when she'd misbehaved. Which was often.

"At least we aren't scrubbing the privies," Turin said, infuriatingly cheerful and nodding politely as people passed by. His tray was full of dishes. He had been in a suspiciously good mood all morning, which was surprising since he'd been moping around the night before.

Eolisti picked up an empty goblet, eyes scanning the courtyard. There were fewer than a dozen guests up and about. Most of them were standing in groups, talking, as staff wove around them, picking up the evidence of a night full of revelry. When she and Turin arrived, the place had been a mess. These humans were just as filthy as her people after the summer solstice, leaving a huge mess for her to clean up.

Most of the nobles ignored the staff, not even sparing a glance toward their comings and goings as they tidied up around the guests. They were all dressed in layers of furs and coats as a few flurries of snow floated down from the sky.

A foppish-looking nobleman had spotted Eolisti and started to approach, but after catching sight of the glare on her face, he quickly turned around and found someone else to talk to. Human events were so dull. All they did was eat, chat, and drink. Where was the dancing, and more importantly, the fighting?

She was surprised Elindiir wasn't bored to death. But then again, he must have been used to this, being an ambassador and all.

A tall, regal-looking woman emerged from one of the archways leading back into the castle proper. She was dressed in a long, burgundy gown and wearing a coat of black fur. It took Eolisti a moment to remember where she'd seen the woman before, and she finally did when she spotted the man following close behind. She recognized the face of the vile lordling, Yuri Golistin. The woman had been standing next to Lord Golistin the previous day, which meant that this was Lady Golistin.

As the lady stepped into view of the others in the court-yard, the men closest to her bowed.

"Lady Kristanya," boomed an older gentleman who bounced over to her, taking her hand in his and bringing it up to his lips. She smiled at him, but the expression didn't touch her eyes. Those eyes were so devoid of emotion that they made Eolisti shiver. The lord spoke a few quiet words to her, then placed a hand on Yuri's shoulder, grinning. He must have been congratulating the groom-to-be on his upcoming nuptials.

Eolisti frowned. If that woman she'd seen the day before really was the Phoenix, why was she going along with this wedding in the first place? And was she really the lord's daughter? She was supposed to be some highly trained spy or something. So, was she pretending to do what her supposed father was telling her to do, or was she being forced?

"Stop staring," Turin whispered right next to her ear, causing her to jump.

She glared at Turin. "Don't do that!" she hissed, then rubbed her ear.

"You shouldn't stare at the nobles. They don't like it."

"So?"

"So," he said in a falsely patient way that made Eolisti smile, "we don't want them to pay any more attention to us than necessary."

"I hate to break it to you," she said, eyebrows raised, "but I always draw attention." She glanced over her shoulder to confirm what she'd suspected. The groom was eyeing her. She smiled at him in a way she'd seen Sophie do before, hoping it came off as shy. "See?"

Turin groaned under his breath as Yuri broke away from the others and started heading their way. "You just can't help yourself, can you?" he asked out of the side of his mouth, bowing to the approaching man.

"Not even in the slightest," she replied as she lowered her head, not bothering to attempt that clumsy half-kneeling thing the women did here. Hopefully, he wouldn't notice.

"We're all going to die," Turin muttered, and her grin widened.

The lordling stopped a few feet away from her, and Eolisti could feel his eyes on her. It made her skin crawl.

"An Anai," he murmured to himself. Then louder said, "I didn't realize house Castellus had a good enough relationship with your people that they would send one of you to serve him." He stepped closer and leaned toward her. With the strong smell of rosemary emanating from the lordling, Eolisti had to force herself not to take a step back. "Perhaps you would be willing to be my attendant," Yuri said with a leer.

Eolisti bristled at that. As if she would willingly serve some Tanalinian lord. She knew what he was implying and glanced around, wondering if anyone would notice if she hit him.

Turin stepped up behind her and answered before she could say something that she'd probably get in trouble for. "The house of Castellus is noble and great, m'lord," he said with an accent that made his voice sound nasally. "It's an honor to serve him."

Eyes widening, the lordling seemed intimidated by Turin's size and took a startled step back. Eolisti tried not to smile. She guessed she could forgive the knight for stepping in, just this once.

The young lord seemed to forget all about Eolisti and focused on her companion. "Why don't you go off and mind your own business, *boy*?" All the friendly pretenses had dropped, and Yuri openly scowled at Turin.

"Forgive me, m'lord, but I am tasked with keeping an eye on this one and assisting her when necessary," he replied, a note of defiance in his voice.

Great. As much as she wanted to show this "lord" that she was not someone to be trifled with, if the stupid knight fought with the gods-blasted groom, they would surely be thrown out.

The lordling continued to scowl up at Turin, who, for his part, glared back defiantly.

"Yuri," called another nobleman, striding up to them. The newcomer was the other Golistin son, Eolisti thought, and he looked to be the older of the two. "Having another drink?" he asked jovially, but something about his expression set Eolisti on edge. His name was Alexi, like his father, right? With the sharp look in his eyes, she knew there was something more to this lord than just a pretty face.

The younger man ignored his brother.

"You look familiar," Yuri said to Turin, his eyes narrowed. He made a show of looking Turin up and down. "You may be dressed like a servant, but you don't carry yourself like one. Who are you?"

"Leave him be, Yuri," Alexi sighed. "Stop trying to pick fights with everyone you see. Wasn't one enough?" He put an arm around his younger brother's shoulders. "Come on, you're getting married in two days! Let's have some wine." Alexi gave Turin and Eolisti a sharp look and gestured with one hand behind Yuri's back.

The older Golistin brother was giving them a chance to escape, and she and Turin quickly hurried away as Yuri muttered, "I suppose."

"Let's get out of here before my mother—er, their mother—sees us."

Her gaze snapped to his face. And then she knew what had been bothering her so much about the older Golistin brother. She saw the resemblance. How hadn't she realized it before?

"Your *what* now?" Eolisti asked with false cheer, smiling as they passed another group of staff. "Forgive me, but I could have sworn you said *my mother*. As in Lady Golistin is *your mother!*" She hissed the last part, causing the knight to look around nervously. "Isn't that something you should have mentioned before?"

"It's not like I knew she would be here," he whispered back guiltily. There was no use in denying it. Now that she'd seen all three of them up close, it was obvious that they were related. And if she saw it, that meant that anyone else could too. Except for Yuri, who seemed too caught up in his own life to notice anything else.

They stopped in the corner of the courtyard, on the opposite side from where the nobles were gathered. "Do the others know?"

"No one knows except for the Lord High Commander and a few others back home."

"Well, you need to tell Sophie and Khalil. We're all out here risking our lives, and our biggest risk is *you.*" There was the thrill of vindictive satisfaction saying that, since he hadn't wanted her or Sophie to come in the first place, but the feeling quickly passed. This unfortunate coincidence could get them thrown in the dungeon, or worse.

She leaned in close to ask, "When was the last time you saw them? Could they have recognized you?" She looked back to where the two Golistin brothers were standing together. Yuri had seemed to forget all about them and was drinking deeply from his goblet.

Another nobleman in a dark-gray surcoat joined them, letting out a barking laugh that echoed across the open space and slapping the would-be groom on the back with a pudgy hand. Eolisti felt her lip curl. The expression on the younger lord's face was one of quiet satisfaction. He seemed to love the attention.

"It's nothing. Don't worry about him," Turin said, following her gaze. "I'm the youngest of the three, but Yuri was never the brightest child. I doubt much has changed in the last twenty years."

"You'd better hope not. Otherwise, we all are going to die." She watched as the eldest brother broke away from the growing group of raucous noblemen and made his way toward one of the alcoves. "Do you think he was trying to keep his brother out of trouble?"

Turin was silent for so long that Eolisti tore her eyes away from the curtain the lord had disappeared behind. The expression on her companion's face gave her pause. "I thought knights were supposed to be prepared for anything. What is it with you and your family?"

"It's.... It's just been so long. I never thought I'd see them again." He looked at her, and she saw the same angular features, inky black hair, and green eyes that all three men shared. "We didn't exactly part under the best circumstances."

Eolisti looked down at the empty tray she was still holding, remembering her own departure from her mother. Ever since she'd been a little girl, her mother had been the only family she had—at least the only family she remembered—and she'd left her with only a note of farewell. She had not been the Vendarii chosen to escort Sophie to the monastery. She had whisked the young mage away while no one was paying attention. How was her mother doing? She was on the High Council back in Elasariin, but she still could have gotten in trouble because of Eolisti's actions. She'd just wanted to get out of there so badly! Now, she was across an entire sea from her home, and for the first time since she'd left, Eolisti felt guilty. "Were you at least able to say goodbye?" she asked Turin.

The question seemed to take him by surprise, and he looked at her in a way he never had before.

"Yes," he said after a moment.

"Don't look so torn up then," Eolisti said, smacking his back in annoyance. "Some people don't get that chance." Pushing aside thoughts of home, she led the way back toward the door to the kitchen, picking up a few more plates along the way. Best to stay out of sight for now. There would always be more to do later.

A shadow moved under the awning to their left, and Eolisti reached for her sword before realizing she wasn't wearing one. Damn these disguises.

She was about to drop her tray and grab the closest sharp, pointy object when their pursuer stepped out into the daylight. The man's deep, green eyes flicked first to her, then to Turin.

Alexi Golistin, long lost brother of her petulant companion, flashed a strained smile and beckoned them to follow him. Eolisti and Turin exchanged a look. Turin compressed his lips into a thin line, looking almost like Khalil. Eolisti shrugged. If the man made trouble for them, she could always just hit him on the head hard enough that he'd forget they existed.

Once they were out of sight, Alexi turned toward them,

directing his words at Turin. "You need to be more careful. If I recognized you, someone else surely will."

"I don't know what you mean, my lord," Turin responded, his voice flat and dispassionate. Eolisti noted that despite their constant bickering with each other, the knight was skilled at controlling his emotions when it mattered. She was only a little impressed. Barely. Not enough to even register, really.

"It's the eyes, I think," Alexi continued as if Turin hadn't spoken. "The shape and color aren't common here, and you look to be around the right age." His head tilted to one side, and his lips burst into a radiant smile. Eolisti could see his eyes shining in the torchlight. "I never thought I'd see you again, Dimitri."

Before either Eolisti or Turin could stop him, the lord pulled her companion into an embrace.

Eolisti had had enough. "What in the hells do you think you're doing?!" she growled at Alexi, prying the men apart. "Do you want to get us killed? What would one of those lords say if they saw you?"

Alexi took a deep breath and pulled back. "Forgive me, but I've missed you."

Turin seemed at a loss for words, staring at the older man.

"Maybe you can help us then," Eolisti said into the silence. What was wrong with Turin? They still had a job to do. Where was that control that he'd had moments before? "We need to talk to Lady Korynne. Do you know what room she's being kept in?"

He looked surprised. "I don't think that's possible."

"Why? Is she heavily guarded? Is she impossible to get to?" That seemed to snap Turin out of his daze, and he focused on Eolisti's words.

"We must speak to her," he said imploringly. "Please, it is urgent."

"You don't understand. It's not just that she's under guard day and night. I don't think she is in control of her mind," Alexi said seriously. "The Lord Castellus has only let us see her one time away from the crowd of other nobles, and she was mostly unresponsive. I'm unsure if Yuri cares since he's more interested in the connections this will give him. Castellus is an old house and a well-respected rival to even the emperor. Marrying into this family will allow my father to wield some real power at court with a formal tie to house Castellus."

"He's still playing the same old games, then," Turin glowered, dropping any pretense. "Nothing has changed."

Alexi grimaced. "I wish I could deny it. It's been like this since we left Morigael. Mother and Father have been clawing at any power that they can get. They almost disowned me when I eloped. Otherwise, it would be me getting married to Lord Castellus's daughter instead of Yuri."

"That's great and all, but how does this help us?" Eolisti cut in before Turin could ask another question that they didn't have time for.

"Right. Well, I think that Lady Korynne is being poisoned."

EIGHTEEN

"Are you sure we can trust this lord—what was his name?" Sophie asked. She was sitting on one of the barrels outside the kitchen door.

"Alexi Golistin," Eolisti told her again. Was she not paying attention? "He seems sincere, but who knows? Turin hasn't seen him in years, or so he says."

"It seems like something out of a storybook, doesn't it? If Turin's father is a brother to the king in Morigael, that makes him a..." She seemed to be searching for the right word.

"A prince," Eolisti filled in, wrinkling her nose in disgust.

"Right, a prince." Sophie seemed to mull that over. "He does seem kind of princely, doesn't he?"

"Oh please," she began, giving Sophie a level look, "don't tell me you're falling for *that*. You could do so much better."

Sophie burst out laughing. "Of course not. I'm just saying that it's interesting. I've never met a prince before, not that my *vasalii*"—that was what the head of a Zo'rahni house was called—"ever brought visiting dignitaries home, but I've read about them."

Before Eolisti could say anything else, the door to the kitchen opened, and the aforementioned *prince* stepped out, Khalil right behind him with quite a scowl on his face. "What's wrong with you? Walk into a wall?" she asked.

Turin gave her a flat look and answered for Khalil. "No, but now he knows that my family is here."

"I'd like to point out that you didn't want us here in the first place, and now you're the one causing trouble," she said.

The knighted prince sighed, his breath puffing out in a misty cloud. "Yes," he said with a grimace. "You've said as much." Sophie covered her mouth with one hand, but he seemed to have guessed what they had been discussing. "I see you've already told her."

Eolisti shrugged. "Was it supposed to be a secret? Honestly, our biggest concern should be keeping the lord-prince-thingy from telling anyone about us."

"He won't," Turin replied automatically, sounding supremely confident.

"How do you know?" Khalil growled. "It's been so long since you've seen him. He could be a completely different person than what you remember."

"I just know," Turin replied tersely, and Eolisti could see a muscle twitch in his jaw. "You'll have to trust me."

Oh no, Khalil did *not* like that answer. His lips pressed together again in that infuriating expression he always had when talking to her. At least it was being directed at someone else this time. Maybe he would hit the knight, and they would knock each other out. Eolisti tried to keep the grin off her face.

"Have you seen Elindiir today?" Sophie asked, a little louder than necessary.

Eolisti glanced over at her. Sophie was pointedly not looking at the others. It was obvious she wanted to change the subject.

Well, as fun as this was, it wouldn't hurt to help her out.

"No," Eolisti said, stretching her arms over her head. It was starting to get late, and she had been working all day. "He wasn't around while the humans gorged themselves on wine and venison." That drew Turin's glare from Khalil. "What? It's true. Where's the dancing? Where're the games?" She stood from the crate she was sitting on, took a few practiced steps, and twirled to the muffled music she could hear from inside the castle.

Sophie grinned and jumped from her perch. "In Zo'rahn, it's about time for Shar'Nalan—the winter festival. We eat and drink, too, but there is much more activity in our celebrations."

She closed her eyes, bobbed her head like she was counting beats, then moved in a way that seemed to flow with the rhythm of the music, her arms as much a part of the dance as her legs.

Eolisti watched her until she recognized the pattern in the dance and joined in, mimicking Sophie's steps. She found that it was easy to follow along. Zo'rahni dancing and Anaiian dancing were very similar. Sophie flashed her a grin and took Eolisti's hand in hers as they twirled around the courtyard. Some of the other staff stopped what they were doing and watched, seemingly mesmerized by the two women.

It was silly, the two of them dancing in the courtyard while the people around them watched, but it felt good to be doing something just for fun. They'd both been under a lot of pressure the past few months trying to get Sophie to safety, and they'd had more than their fair share of close calls. So, it was nice to forget about their problems, even for a short time.

A few minutes later, Sophie and Eolisti fell back onto the crates, both out of breath and laughing.

Turin was scowling at them, but Eolisti could tell by how the sides of his mouth turned up that he was trying not to smile. "Are you two finished?"

"Yeah, unless you'd like a go," Eolisti said as Sophie giggled. "I could show you a thing or two, *m'lord*." She added extra nasal to her voice on the last word. Sophie covered her mouth again, and even Khalil cracked a smile at that.

"And give you a chance to step on my feet? No way." He winked at her. Like her stepping on his toes would do anything to him. Turin had to weigh at least twice as much as she did, given all that knightly muscle. She stuck her tongue out at him, and he laughed.

"We should get going." Khalil had moved to stand next to where Sophie was still seated. That made Eolisti frown. It was *her* job to protect Sophie. Vendarii literally meant protector, and Sophie was her charge, but she had to admit he had proven himself to be a passable fighter.

"Right," Turin said, turning toward the front gate. "We'll have another long day tomorrow."

Only when they had left the castle walls and were alone on their walk back to the inn did Turin elaborate. "We have to make our move tomorrow night."

"Not the day of the wedding?" Sophie asked, looking at him sharply. "I thought we were waiting until then to get the Phoenix out?"

Turin glanced over at Khalil. "We think that the lord

will most likely be expecting something on the day of the wedding. There's no reason to think that he knows anyone is here to rescue the Phoenix, but he's not a complete fool. He'll be ready for anything out of the ordinary."

Eolisti glowered at the knight. So, the men were discussing plans without her and Sophie, were they? "I'm assuming you have a plan then," she said somewhat sourly.

"Tomorrow morning, I'm going to take our supplies and horses out of town and into the forests back the way we came," Khalil answered. "We should be able to use one of the carriages in the stables, and we can hide the Phoenix and Winna in the back. Turin can act as the driver and get us through the gates. Once we get away from the castle, we'll head straight to the mountain pass that leads into Morigael. There's an outpost not too far into the pass. If we can get there, it's unlikely that Castellus will pursue us."

Turin picked up where Khalil left off. "Sophie, you'll need to find the Phoenix and try to break whatever spell she's under. I want us to get out of there after tomorrow's feast, once everyone is good and drunk." Looking down at the ground as he walked, he put his hands in his pockets. His expression was worried. Eolisti didn't blame him. Their plan was flimsy at best.

"Alexi said that she was being poisoned," Eolisti added. "We need to find out what she's being poisoned with."

"Did he say anything else about it?" Sophie asked, looking toward the approaching village. Lights twinkled in the windows and Eolisti prayed a warm fire awaited them at the inn.

She thought hard to remember what precisely the lordling had told them. "He said she wasn't in control of her own mind and that she was unresponsive when he'd seen her."

Sophie puffed out her cheeks and let out a long breath, thinking. "That doesn't narrow it down much. There are plenty of substances that can make a person malleable to suggestions, though most of them have bad side effects."

"You know about poisons?" Turin asked sharply. His tone was almost accusatory.

"I am a wizard." Sophie sounded offended. "Part of that requires the study of *potions*. We have to know what plants and mixtures help and harm a person so that we can use them in whatever way we see fit." She threw Turin a glare. "I'm not some sort of assassin."

"What Sophie means is that it's not her fault if you've never picked up a book," Eolisti added. She enjoyed poking fun at the knight.

Moonlight glistened in Turin's hair as he ran a hand through it in frustration. "Perhaps we can get a sample of it," he began, ignoring Eolisti's comments. "Would you be able to counteract it?"

Sophie scrunched up her brows as she thought. "There was a potion spilled on the apron of one of the maids, and if I had to guess, that is what they are using to subdue her. If it hasn't killed her yet, it's something that isn't toxic in small doses."

"Damn," the knight muttered. "I wish we'd known about this earlier."

"Just one more thing to do," Eolisti said with a shrug. "Then we can finally get out of this place."

It was Turin's turn to tease her. "Is all this serving of lords and ladies too much for you? Are you getting tired?"

Eolisti turned her nose up at him. "The only thing I'm tired of is your ugly face."

That got the knight good and riled up, so much so that they bickered the rest of the way back to the inn.

By the time they got there, Turin and Eolisti had settled down. Khalil followed the women to their room, instructing them to pack up all their belongings tonight so that he could retrieve them in the morning, which was annoying. Like they needed him to point that out.

He bid them rest well, and Sophie lingered at the door, whispering to him. Eolisti tried to ignore them but caught Sophie's worried tone and noticed her placing a hand on his arm as she leaned in a little closer to say something. Khalil listened intently before nodding once. The whole interaction got on Eolisti's nerves. Khalil wasn't as annoying as the big, tall oaf, but his face wasn't even nice to look at. What did Sophie see in him anyway?

Before he left, Khalil handed a small object to Sophie. The candlelight glittered off something metal.

"What is that?" Eolisti asked once the door was firmly closed.

"Do you remember what the Spider used to make me follow his orders?" She held up a thick, bronze band. It was a piece of clunky jewelry with a barely visible seam and a few spots of rust that marred its surface. Eolisti had seen it before.

The bottom dropped out of her stomach. "Why do you still have that thing?!" she hissed. It was the slave anklet the Spider had used to control Sophie. When Eolisti and the others had finally found them, the Spider had been using the magical device to torture the young wizard.

"I saw Lord Castellus wearing a ring like this." She held up the ring that was used as a control device for the anklet. "So he's probably using one of these artifacts to control the Phoenix."

"And?" Eolisti asked impatiently.

"And," Sophie responded calmly, approaching their

small pile of supplies next to her bed. "If I can steal his ring or figure out how to disrupt the magic that controls the anklet, then he wouldn't be able to give her commands. She'll be free to escape with us, and we won't have to worry about him forcing her to come back or hurting her with it."

Eolisti scratched a spot where her servant's uniform had been itching all day. "What would happen if she was still under the anklet's magic when we left? Could he order her to come back?"

The mage frowned. "I'm not sure what the range of these is. The Spider had me right by his side while I was wearing this one. It could be a few hundred feet, a few miles, or—" She swallowed, and the color drained from her face. "There could be no limitations."

Eolisti stepped forward and placed a hand on Sophie's shoulder, trying to comfort her. "Don't worry about that. You'll find a way to get it off her, and we'll finally be back on the road tomorrow." She gave an exaggerated yawn as she changed out of the uniform and pulled on the oversized tunic she usually slept in. "Once this detour is over, we can get you somewhere safe."

"There are a few steps before we get to that part," Sophie said with a sigh. "And that's if everything goes smoothly. Who knows what will happen tomorrow?"

"It would be easier to take her in the middle of the night," Eolisti suggested, and she glanced at her sword resting against the wall. It would be so much easier if they could get the Phoenix out of the castle while everyone was asleep. There would be no more serving humans, and they could leave this stupid country. "We could dress up as nobles and sneak around the castle. There's no way the guards know the faces of all the guests."

Sophie laughed. "I think you'd be noticeable since, you

know—" She put her hands up to her ears, using her fingers to make them look longer. "And that would get Elindiir in trouble, wouldn't it? He's the only other Anai here."

Eolisti felt her cheeks heat up. "Well, you and Turin could probably get away with looking like nobles. Khalil doesn't exactly blend in with his blindfold." She tilted her head to one side in thought. "You and the knight could be a distraction while he and I sneak around."

"The feast is more of a distraction than we could be. Dalia told me that the feast the night before the wedding is the biggest one yet. The bride and groom will disappear right after the wedding in the morning, so this feast is the height of the festivities." She smiled to herself. "If it weren't for the bride being coerced into this wedding against her will, it could be a lot of fun."

"Are you really enjoying this?" Eolisti asked, incredulous.

It was Sophie's turn to blush. "O-of course not. We're here to save the Phoenix." She turned her back to Eolisti, pulling the black dress she wore over her head and changing into something lighter and better for sleeping in.

Teasing Sophie more was tempting, but it wouldn't help either of their nerves. Eolisti couldn't shake the feeling that their plan left too many things to chance. It just didn't sit right with her.

"Maybe I should go back to the castle," Eolisti mused. "Elindiir is there, and he could help us out. The more we know about the castle and what we have to overcome tomorrow, the better off we'll be."

"Don't do anything rash, Eolisti. There's a plan in place already."

"It's Turin's plan, and not much of one," Eolisti growled. "You find the Phoenix, and we all miraculously break her out after the feast? A child could have come up with that." She folded her arms across her chest and glowered. "I don't like this. He's putting you in danger. I'm surprised Khalil is okay with this."

"Khalil will be with me tomorrow, so that's probably why he didn't argue. We can move around more freely than the two of you can." Sophie laid out her clothes for the following morning on the room's small table, then tied up her bag. After a moment's hesitation, she set the slave anklet and ring on top of the clothes. "I'll admit, it's less preparation than I'd prefer, but we are on a very tight schedule with the wedding being the day after tomorrow."

"See?! Even you think this is stupid!"

Sophie held up a hand. "Let me finish, Eolisti. It's not much of a plan, but it's what we have to work with. If we can just get the Phoenix out of the castle and get to the horses, we should be able to outrun anyone the lord sends after us." She fiddled with the edge of her sleeve. "If I can incapacitate the mage before we go, they'll have an even harder time following us."

"How do you expect to do that?" Eolisti scowled. "We don't even know what he's capable of."

"I don't know. He's probably pretty strong since he's the court wizard, but I should be able to at least match him." Sophie blew out the candle on the table, and the room was plunged into darkness. "I'll have to figure out something."

"I still don't like this," Eolisti grumbled.

Sophie sighed. "I know, but that can't be helped. I'm going to bed. There's going to be so much to do tomorrow. You should get some rest too, Eolisti." The floorboards creaked as Sophie shuffled over to her bed and lay down. Even with the candles extinguished, a little light streamed in from the window, and Eolisti could still see the mage's eyes watching her in the dark.

This didn't sit well with Eolisti. They didn't know where the Phoenix was being held or what defenses were guarding her. If she could just talk to Elindiir... He had undoubtedly seen more of the castle than they had and could point them in the right direction. He had access to the upper floors since he was a guest, and maybe he would even know when the lady was the least guarded.

With Sophie's eyes on her, she didn't dare let her thoughts show. Eolisti stepped over to her own bed and climbed in, settling herself on the mattress and closing her eyes. "Don't worry," she murmured, knowing the mage still had eyes on her. "Everything will be fine."

Eolisti waited until she could hear Sophie's steady breathing to make her move. The Anai slid out of bed quietly and tiptoed over to her pack. She had grown up sneaking around with a mother who had eyes—and ears—like a hawk. That meant Eolisti was able to dress and leave the room without making a sound. She threw one last guilty glance over at Sophie, still fast asleep, red hair in a neat braid that curled behind her.

It will be all right, Eolisti told herself as she closed the door behind her. *I'll be back before she even wakes up.*

Putting on her heavy riding cloak, Eolisti crept down the stairs. It would be just her luck that Khalil or Turin would hear her, and then she'd never hear the end of it. She needn't have worried. Even though the inn's crowd had thinned, there were still plenty of patrons making enough noise to mask the sound of her passage. Additionally, since most were distracted by food and drink, she slipped outside unnoticed.

Eolisti shivered as she wrapped the edges of the cloak around her. She'd almost left it behind since it was too nice for a servant to wear, but the chill air made her think that she'd freeze to death without it. No identifying symbol was stitched into the cloth, and the darkness would disguise its fine make to any casual observer.

The walk back to the castle felt even longer alone, and there was nothing to distract Eolisti from the cold. There was no one else on the road, most of the extra help hired for the wedding having gone back to their accommodations by now. Eolisti pulled her cloak in closer. She wasn't used to cold like this. When it snowed back home, it was a light thing that didn't stick and barely penetrated the forest canopy. White flakes dusted the leaves and fell like gentle rain on the treetop houses of the Anaiian city, a welcome break from the warm and humid temperatures Zo'rahn had the rest of the year. Here, she had heard that the snow could be several feet deep and would soak into a person's boots. Eolisti frowned at the thought of walking around with cold, wet feet. Nope, she didn't like that at all.

By now, the guards recognized the only Anai working for them and didn't bother trying to stop her from entering the castle grounds. Music still floated out from the great hall, echoing through the courtyard like a quiet lullaby. Men and women sat on barrels and crates outside the servants' entrance, just like Eolisti and Sophie had done earlier, having a little party of their own. A flask was passed around while they ate more of those fruit-filled pastries she'd tried before. Even though it was freezing outside, the only evidence that it bothered them was their red cheeks and noses. Other than that, the workers gave no indication of discomfort and laughed among themselves.

Eolisti looked around the courtyard, searching for a familiar face. Even though she worked at the castle all day, none of the humans, aside from Dalia and Eolisti's travel companions, spoke to her. Most either stared at her or ignored her presence altogether. Eolisti felt a scowl spreading across her face. These humans were all so incredibly boring. All they did was work.

And on top of that, she hadn't seen Elindiir all day. What if he was already sleeping? What if she'd missed her chance to find out what he knew?

"Fancy seeing you here," said a voice Eolisti recognized.

Under one of the awnings was the musician with the scar over his eye, Lucky. She grinned and strode toward him. It was good to see someone she knew.

"Done prancing around for the lords, then?" she asked with a wink.

"That's rich coming from you, the Anai who's stooped to picking up after some lofty human nobles." He chuckled when she grimaced. When he smiled, the lines at the corners of his eyes crinkled. "Don't talk if you can't take it in return."

Eolisti's eyes narrowed, but that only made Lucky's smile wider.

"Where are your friends?" he asked, looking around. "They don't like to party late?"

"No, they're all back at the inn. Big day tomorrow and all that."

He shrugged and took a long drink. "Their loss."

Eolisti grinned. "Where can I get some of that?"

"Not from me. I snuck this off some nobleman's table as I was passing by. It's pretty good, though."

"Isn't that stealing?"

"Nah, we're the entertainment. We're expected to mingle with the guests a little, so what's one drink? It's not like the lord I swiped it from will miss it. The last I saw, he was fast asleep in his chair." Lucky took another long drink. "The rest of the troupe is still performing inside, but I'm old and have to rest often." He winked at her.

"Right," she began, "and it has nothing to do with that mug you're nursing."

"Nothing at all," he agreed. "Give it a few more hours, and everyone will be passed out. Most of the nobility can't drink much anyway and don't want to embarrass themselves. There are a couple who can hold their own, but they are more worried about playing cards or womanizing to care if there is still music playing." He shrugged. "None of my business, really. I just play my fiddle and keep my head down."

Eolisti gave the musician a sidelong glance. His weathered face was cast deep in shadow, but with her sharp vision, she could tell that his cheeks had the glow of someone who'd had a little too much to drink himself. Maybe enough drink to talk about what he'd seen of the castle's occupants. "The bride was beautiful, don't you think?" she asked casually.

"Aye. She was a vision. The groom is a lucky man. Not a nice fellow, but he's a lord. Most of them have their heads so far up their—"

"Have you seen her since that first day?" Eolisti cut in. She already knew the groom was an ass and didn't need Lucky to point that out. "You'd think she'd be joining in on the festivities before her own wedding."

Lucky frowned in thought. "No, I haven't seen her. It is

odd, but the lord doesn't seem fussed about her one bit, which I guess is even odder..."

Damn, he didn't seem to know anything about the Phoenix. "Have you seen another Anai about?" Eolisti asked Lucky, her eyes following a group of partygoers as they left the entrance hall, seeming to move their festivities into the courtyard. They were staggering and laughing merrily.

"That fellow with the long hair? I haven't seen him for a few hours. Is he a friend of yours?"

"Yeah," Eolisti shivered and inched toward the doors to the entrance hall. The sky above them was clear, and both Aeris and Thera were out, casting the courtyard in pale, bluish light. "He's a guest, though. I had no idea he was going to be here."

Lucky nodded absently. "I saw him wandering the halls around sunset, looking at the paintings and the tapestries. He didn't seem too interested in the feast, but I'm sure Anaiian celebrations look much different, eh?"

"Less consumption of roasted meats, that's for sure."

The musician laughed. The other staff members looked over in their direction. Eolisti waved at them, but they just stared at her. Rude.

The doors to the entrance hall opened, and one of the other musicians poked her head out. Her dull, brown hair was pulled back into a loose tail, and she looked much neater than Eolisti had seen her the few days they traveled together. Minette looked around and spotted Lucky, frowning. "You should come back soon. Troy and Peri need a break, and the lords and ladies should be settling down shortly."

The old fiddler muttered something that Eolisti missed. A flash of golden blond over Minette's shoulder had caught her eye.

Bounding over to the door, Eolisti pulled it the rest of the way open to a surprised Minette. With the interior double doors wide open, she looked around at the guests that were still in the great hall. The rest of the musicians were playing their instruments off to one side of the dais. They looked tired. A few nobles were drinking alone, and there was a group playing a game of cards at the back of the large room, but there was no sign of the sunny-haired Elindiir.

"Eolisti!" Minette squeaked in surprise. "What are you doing?"

She bit her bottom lip, thinking. "Looking for someone. Have you seen the ambassador for Nemethy recently?"

"Oh, that Anai lord?" She looked over her shoulder. "He was just here a moment ago. Perhaps he retired to his room." Minette blinked a couple of times, then looked Eolisti up and down. She pointed to the stairs at the end of the entrance hall. "That way goes to where the guests are staying. You don't look like one of the staff right now, so the guards might think you're with him if you tell them so." She gave Eolisti a knowing smile, then turned from her and hissed, "Come on, Lucky!"

"All right, all right," the older man said with a sigh. He squeezed past the Anai. "Keep yourself out of trouble," he said with a wink.

Eolisti grinned back at him. "I always do." That made him chuckle.

The guards didn't even try to question Eolisti. The one standing at the bottom of the grand staircase took one look at her ears, and his expression glazed over again. Security really was terrible here. She and the others shouldn't have any trouble getting the Phoenix to safety.

Eolisti took the opportunity to look around while she

climbed the stairs. Unlike the plain and practical servants' areas, the entrance hall was decorated in lavish blue and green carpets covering the cold stone floors. Fresh bouquets of white and blue roses lined the banisters, and paintings of the current and previous lords hung in ornate frames on the walls. Golden flames glittered from small glass globes suspended from the ceiling by fine silver chains. Eolisti recognized these as a version of a mage lamp, much like the one Sophie carried.

The guard shifted in his armor below her, and Eolisti quickly hurried up the stairs and through the large archway that led to the second-floor rooms, cursing herself for getting distracted.

After turning a corner to her left, she was out of view of the guard and able to look around freely. The second floor was lined with doors, each sporting a different symbol painted on it in red, and there were no guards in sight. This passage was not as ornately decorated as the main entry, but it was still grander than anything she'd ever seen.

The Anaiian city of Elasariin was built a hundred feet in the air on the branches of millennia-old trees. There, everything was sturdy but simple. Tempest Hall was like a polished marble statue, beautiful and sleek. But for all its elegance, the castle felt like a rock with no soul. Where were the children running around? Where was the happiness of a building in which a family dwelled? The cold facade of Tempest Hall put Eolisti on edge and made her miss her home—more than she would ever admit.

She stopped in the middle of the hall and listened. Her hearing might not have been as good as that blind man's, but it was better than most human hearing. The soft sounds of steady breathing filled her ears. It seemed that many of the guests on this floor were already asleep.

Someone was humming in a room a few doors down and to her left, and she thought she knew that voice. Eolisti crept along the hall, trying not to wake any of the slumbering occupants, until she stood in front of a door that had a willow tree painted on it. With only a moment's pause, she raised her hand and knocked lightly, softly enough not to disturb any of the humans, but loudly enough to be heard by someone with hearing as good as hers.

The familiar voice murmured, "Come in."

Eolisti swallowed hard and wiped her sweaty palms on her tunic. Well, it was too late to back down now.

She pushed the door open to reveal a large room that was sectioned into a sleeping area and a sitting area, with a wooden folding screen separating the two. A crackling and popping fire in the small hearth helped chase away the winter cold. Red and yellow curtains lined the walls, covering the stone and giving the room a warm appearance.

Elindiir was standing near the fire, his hands outstretched as if trying to absorb the heat radiating off the flames. The light from the mage lamps hanging from the ceiling caught on his golden hair, making it glitter in a way that took her breath away.

Eolisti shook her head slightly, chasing away thoughts of touching those golden strands. There would be plenty of time to get distracted once they were all safely away from this castle.

"I've never liked the cold," the ambassador said, his back still to Eolisti. "But, sometimes, my duties require me to be put in uncomfortable positions. If I had it my way, I'd never come near this place again."

"I prefer the summers of Zo'rahn to this," Eolisti replied, closing the door behind her before moving toward the fire herself. Once she was a few feet away, the other Anai finally turned toward her.

"What is it that brings you to my room in the middle of the night?" If he was insinuating something improper, he hid it well. The flickering fire bathed one side of his face in golden light while the other was cast deeply into shadow. His expression was the calm and serene mask that she was used to seeing in the presence of others. Eolisti didn't think anything she could say would phase him.

It was hard to ignore how good he looked in his fine clothing. None of the Anai from where she'd grown up looked this good.

Eolisti cleared her throat. "Ambassador," she began loftily. "I never thought you would be so forward. Are you accusing me of attempting to find you in your bed?" She tried to keep the smile off her face, but it was hard.

"I would never dream of it," he replied, not missing a beat. "But as much as I adore your presence, I assume you must have had a reason for coming to find me. Is this about the mission that you and your friends are on? What exactly is it that you're doing?"

Eolisti pursed her lips. She wanted to tell him, but the big dumb knight would probably just complain. Then again, he didn't have to know. Elindiir was her friend, and he would help them if he could, of that she was sure. "Lady Korynne is being held against her will by Lord Castellus. We're here to help her escape from this castle."

The Anai's pale golden eyebrows shot up. "You're saying that Lord Castellus has kidnapped his own daughter and is forcing her into this marriage with the Golistins?" He let out a long breath through his nose when she nodded. "That is a serious accusation. Do you have proof?"

"They are holding her associate, a young woman by the

name of Winna, in the dungeon. She was severely injured when Sophie found her." She could tell him of the Lord High Commander that had sent Turin, but that might be going too far. "Maybe you could give me some information or help us get the lady out of here..." Eolisti trailed off. As she spoke, Elindiir's surprised expression had slowly fallen back into its neutral mask, albeit one that was a few degrees colder than what he'd shown her before.

"I cannot act on this without proof," he said flatly, glancing around with just his eyes. They were still alone in the room, but Eolisti got the feeling that that didn't mean they weren't being watched. "As detestable a man as Lord Castellus is, I am an ambassador for Nemethy, and I can't be seen starting an incident with a Tanalinian lord. A prisoner's testimony isn't going to be enough. By Tanalin law, the lord of the castle has done nothing wrong in that regard, but his daughter is another matter. As a noble lady, she has rights. If you can get the lady out of whatever spell she's under, she'll be able to testify to the lord's actions. Then, and only then, can I offer you aid."

Eolisti frowned at that. "And if we can't?"

"My hands are tied," he said simply. "But you and your friends are quite capable of finding trouble." He grinned, making his eyes twinkle in the firelight. "I'm sure you'll manage."

So, Elindiir was saying that he would only support them if they could break the Phoenix out first. Eolisti didn't see how that made a difference if he would still help them in the end, but Elindiir was playing a political game that was admittedly beyond her. Being on the High Council back in Elasariin, her mother would have understood his motivations, but Eolisti didn't have a knack for politics. It all seemed so incredibly boring.

"Fine," she managed, trying to sort through her feelings. "But you'd better be there when we succeed."

When they had first met, Eolisti had been infatuated with him—as a good time and a handsome face. Now, she saw him in a different light. There was an intellect and cunning behind those blue eyes that she'd never noticed before. They may have met in that bar across the sea by chance, but she couldn't help but feel that his actions after that had been a calculated move. She tried to shake the feeling off but was unsuccessful.

"When we met, did you know what I was doing, that I was a Vendarii? Did you know about Sophie?" *Did my mom send you?* was what she wanted to ask but couldn't bring herself to say it.

Elindiir regained the surprised look. "If you're asking if I sought you out, then no. When I met you, I could tell that you weren't from either court." He meant the Anaiian courts of Nemethy to the west and Drushald in the east. "That could only mean you were from the old city in the great forest. As for your friend, I had no idea what she could do until she defended the ship." Eolisti's expression made him chuckle. "I swear to you, I am no spy for whoever you have in mind.

"As ambassador, my role is quite simple. I mostly attend social functions for the courts. Many of the higher human noble houses in Morigael and Tanalin invite the Anai to large celebrations as a courtesy. I am one of those sent to represent our people out of politeness. It just so happened that I was in Drushald when I was summoned back to Nemethy. Once we arrived at Mattina, there was a message waiting for me to attend this event."

Eolisti had heard the name Drushald before. It was the Anaiian court to the south of her home. He must have gone back and forth between the continents regularly if he traveled between the courts in the east and west.

"So you've never met my mom?"

He blinked those large blue eyes. "Who is your mother?"

Instead of answering, she waved the question away. If he recognized her mother's name, Eolisti didn't want his attitude toward her to change. There was a good chance he *had* heard of Vyraeli since she was on Elasariin's High Council. "No one." She looked around at the mostly empty room to avoid his piercing gaze. This was not how she'd envisioned this conversation going.

"I guess I should go back," she grumbled. "There's nothing I can do here."

The ambassador nodded, striding over to the door and opening it for her. "Let me escort you part of the way. I've promised Lord Dracus a game of cards, and if I miss it, he'll be writing me about it for a year."

Dejected, Eolisti stepped back into the corridor. She'd come all the way back here for nothing. She didn't have any of the proof that Elindiir needed, and by the time they got it, they would be halfway to Morigael. Hopefully. And he was going to a stupid card game, so she couldn't even spend time with him.

Alone. In his room. It seemed criminal that he would choose the company of some stuffy old human over her.

Eolisti felt so put out that when Elindiir leaned close to her and whispered, it made her jump. "What I can tell you is that there are a lot of passageways hidden in the walls that allow Lord Castellus and his family to move around the castle freely and swiftly. He resides on the top floor, but there is a way that he can get down to the guest quarters quickly. That passage"—his eyes flicked to a nondescript door at the end of the hall—"is guarded at the top level, but not here in the guest quarters. While this one is open, the ones on the upper floors are probably locked, but..." Elindiir flashed her a wicked grin. "It wouldn't be hard to pick if one were so inclined. I'm assuming Lady Korynne is residing on the uppermost level."

It was hard for Eolisti to keep a straight face. She wanted to hug him. "You've been doing some of your own investigating, I see."

"Lord Castellus isn't exactly a friend to the Anai, and, to be honest, something about this whole affair seemed off even before you arrived. I can't make the first move, but the High Council can hardly take umbrage with me for defending myself or helping an innocent woman who was being wrongfully imprisoned."

"But you need proof."

Elindiir allowed a small smile to play on his lips. "As honest as I'm sure you and your friends are, I can't just take your word on it."

Eolisti rubbed her temples with her fingers. "And what would this proof look like?" she groaned.

The ambassador shrugged one shoulder nonchalantly. "That's for you to figure out." His eyes focused past her, and his lips stretched into what seemed a forced smile. "Now, if you'll excuse me."

Elindiir gave Eolisti a shallow bow as one of the other doors along the hall opened. A skinny, older man with brown and gray-flecked hair stepped into their view. His fine brocade doublet in a rich red gave him away as a visiting lord. The man looked around and spotted Elindiir.

"Ambassador!" he said in a deep, booming voice. "Are you ready to join me for that game you promised?"

"Just for a few rounds, I'm afraid, Lord Dracus. It's getting quite late."

Eolisti turned from them in a huff, trying to rein in her feelings. She had to admit that the information he'd just shared would be very useful, but she'd assumed Elindiir would be of greater help, and his refusal to aid them without proof stung. His words had been reasonable, but was he really willing to let Lord Castellus get away with this just because he hadn't seen anything that would justify action? It didn't sit right with her, and that was when she made her decision. She would find the proof he needed. Tonight.

While Elindiir led the lord back toward the stairs, Eolisti made it look like she was going back into the ambassador's room. Once they turned the corner, she hurried back down the hall to the door painted the same color as the wall around it. Perhaps tonight would not be a total waste after all.

NINETEEN

The door was unlocked, just as Elindiir said it would be. Eolisti glanced over her shoulder, but she was still alone in the hallway, for now. There was no telling when a guard would pass through, or a drunken guest would stumble to their room. Without another moment's hesitation, she pulled the door open and slipped through it.

Behind the wall was a short corridor of bare stone walls, ending at the foot of a narrow stairway that led up, curving and disappearing from sight. This area looked as old as the castle itself and, unlike the rest of the building, she doubted it had been updated over the years. The stone steps were worn down in the middle from years of use, and the space had the smell of stale air. Light flickered from somewhere beyond the first turn, and she imagined torches in sconces on the walls as she had seen in other servants' areas in the castle. Why spend the money to make it look nice if none of the fancy people would see it?

A human might have a hard time seeing in the dimness, but Eolisti's eyesight was fantastic, and she was easily able to pick her way up the stairs. She wasn't as heavily armed as she would like to have been, but while she'd had to leave her sword and shield behind, she had a dagger hidden under her shirt. It would have to do. If she landed in a situation where she needed a weapon, maybe she could steal one from a guard. As far as Eolisti could tell, most of them weren't in top fighting shape. They probably didn't even know where the pointy end went.

Eolisti crept along, stopping to listen every few steps. On the third landing, there were muffled voices from beyond a door much like the one she'd entered from, but the speakers were too far from where she was for her to hear them properly.

The stairs ended on the fifth landing up from where she'd started. This must be at the top of the castle, she reasoned, where Lord Castellus and his family resided.

Before touching the door, she remembered Elindiir's comment that the entrance might be guarded on this floor. Eolisti backed away from it as quietly as possible and descended the stairs back down to the previous landing. With any luck, there would be no guards here and she could get up to the top floor using the main stairs. She said a quick prayer to Azorah and pushed on the door.

Locked.

She let out the breath she'd been holding since descending from the floor above. Right, Elindiir had mentioned something about picking locks. Where she'd come from, people rarely locked doors, so she didn't know how to pick a lock. If this door was like the others she'd seen in the castle, it had a latch in the jamb. Eolisti pulled out her dagger and wedged it carefully into the space between the door and the wall, guessing where the mechanism would be. She had to push it to get the blade in there, but the weapon was good Anaiian steel, so she was confident it wouldn't break.

With a quick exhale, she pulled the dagger up as hard as she could. There was a muffled *Snap!* as the metal latch broke.

Hopefully, there was no one close enough to hear that. Eolisti pressed her ear to the opening, listening hard for any sounds. After a full minute of silence, she allowed herself a wide grin. *Ha! That blind guy never got this far.* If she'd been the one sneaking around the castle with Sophie, they'd already have the Phoenix and be long gone by now. They didn't need that big clumsy knight either.

The door slowly swung open as Eolisti put weight on it, opening into another hallway. This corridor looked a lot like the one on the second floor, only it was much less lavishly decorated and held only four doors. More mage lamps were hanging from sconces on the walls, casting the dark-red carpet in a soft golden glow. It seemed to her like a waste to have the mage lamps going at all hours—did the magic in them go out? She would have to ask Sophie. But Eolisti reminded herself that this castle was probably bigger than her city. She wouldn't have been surprised if everyone in Brumalar could fit in here with room to spare.

Eolisti put her dagger back and pushed the door closed behind her, but it swung open a few inches when she let go. She spotted the jagged metal where she'd broken the latch. Oh well, there was nothing that she could do about that right now. If Sophie were here, maybe she could have fixed the door, but with any luck, the little wizard would be fast asleep for a few more hours still.

There were no sounds to be heard from the rooms as Eolisti passed them. Given the hour, the resident family should have been asleep, preparing for the big day tomorrow. Eolisti briefly wondered what could be beyond these doors. Would she find servants' quarters or perhaps the bedrooms of extended family? Or maybe they would just be empty. It was unfathomable to her what so many rooms in one building could be used for. What would happen if the castle came under attack? They could not flee up into the trees like the Anai of her homeland could, but maybe that's what the high walls and many storage rooms were for. If the castle came under attack, they could defend from within and wait out their assailants.

Where were the stairs up, though? That roughly built servants' entrance couldn't be the only access for this floor. Maybe she could—

"What are you doing?"

The voice made Eolisti jump and almost lose her balance. Falling into a fighting stance, she whirled around to face her attacker, only to come face to face with a human boy who came no higher than her shoulder. Dressed in a long garment that fell to his knees, he had a mop of curly blond hair and eyes the color of summer skies.

The boy was watching her curiously, his brows furrowed, and his arms crossed over his chest. Eolisti wasn't the best judge of the ages of human children, but he couldn't have reached puberty yet.

She looked around the hall. There was no one behind him. It seemed this boy had been wandering the halls by himself. He must have come out of one of those rooms. As soon as she thought it, she spotted the door closest to the secret staircase she'd come through standing slightly ajar.

Eolisti relaxed, taking a few deep breaths to calm her speeding heart. It was just a kid, nothing to worry about, right?

"I asked what you are doing," the boy repeated, giving

the impression that he was looking down his nose at her, which was impressive as he was almost a foot shorter than she was. He glared at her, not breaking eye contact. "You're not supposed to be up here. None of the guests have access to this floor. Who let you up? Was it one of the guards? I'll have to tell my father about this."

He reminded her of one of the kids back in her village, and she felt her lip curl up in a sneer. "Shouldn't you be in bed? Might you have a wet nurse looking for you?"

The boy's eyes widened, and his mouth fell open in shock, as though he'd never heard someone talk back to him in this way. The expression would have been comical if something hadn't been bothering Eolisti about the boy. This floor should have been empty, except for...

It was then that she noticed the gold pendant around his neck, and, looking more closely, his clothing was made from finely embroidered silk. He must have been the son of a lord. No, not just a lord, but Lord Castellus. The upper floors were where the lord of the castle's family lived. *Shit.*

"I just got lost," she said, waving one hand dismissively and relaxing her stance. The excuse sounded lame, even to her ears. Should she bow? Was she supposed to bow to a child? "I was just trying to find..." Eolisti trailed off, getting an idea. It was risky, but it might just work and leave them with less work to do tomorrow.

"You know," she began, smoothing her features and summoning the sweetest smile she could, "I was just looking for the room of Lord Castellus's daughter. I wanted to congratulate her." Eolisti glanced around, then leaned in conspiratorially. "Just between you and me, she looked a little nervous. I think seeing a friendly face will greatly help her tomorrow."

"Lady Korynne?" he asked, and his eyes brightened

when he said the name. "She's my sister!" His chest swelled with pride at that declaration. "Are you a friend of hers? Have you come to see her get married?"

Eolisti's smile widened, and she hoped to all the gods that it looked genuine. "Something like that. I wanted to wish her the best with her new husband. Could you take me to her?"

He pushed his curls out of his eyes with one hand and frowned, his bottom lip sticking out in a pout. "Father won't let me see her. He says she's been frail since she returned home." One foot digging into the carpet, he glanced up at her. "But I know where her room is. Maybe you can ask her to let me visit her? I'd really like to talk to her." The boy started walking past her, and Eolisti turned to follow him.

"My name is Gaius. Gaius Castellus," he said, looking over his shoulder at her.

"Eolisti," she replied.

"I didn't know she knew people like you," he said, then quickly added, "an Anai, I mean. Father said she'd been taken prisoner in Morigael. Are you from Morigael then? Do you know how she escaped? Did you help her?" Gaius asked questions so fast that Eolisti didn't have time to answer any of them. It was a good thing, too, since she hadn't made up a believable story to tell this kid.

"I can't remember her," Gaius continued without pause. "She was taken right after I was born. Our mother died in childbirth," he said, and his voice was somber. "Father says the loss was too much for my sister, and she left the castle grounds after the funeral to go into the town. That's where she was kidnapped."

"Did he now?" Eolisti wondered if that was true. If Lord Castellus was her father, why would he be poisoning his own daughter to make her marry some lord who obviously cared nothing for her? Maybe Korynne was like Sophie, who had left her home because she feared what those who had control over her would do. But unlike Sophie, Korynne was just a nobleman's daughter.

But maybe leaving her home out of grief was not so far-fetched. She found it easy to imagine the pain that the Phoenix must have felt at the loss of her mother. Eolisti had been too young to remember when her father died, but if something happened to her mother, she would be lost. Even though they fought and squabbled over the smallest of things, she loved her mother, and it hurt to think of how she'd left Elasariin without a word to her, just a hurriedly scribbled note left on her bed.

If her mother had died, Eolisti would have left home too. Especially with a father like Lord Castellus.

"I don't want to disturb her if she's not feeling well, but I was hoping she'd want to meet me. Father says I need to be patient, but if she's getting married and leaving, I might never see her again," the young boy's voice cut into Eolisti's thoughts. The disappointment and pain in his voice gave Eolisti a bad taste in her mouth. He was so eager to meet his sister that Eolisti felt sorry for Gaius. If she succeeded tonight, he would probably never see Lady Korynne again.

Eolisti bit back what she wanted to say and, instead, said through gritted teeth, "She's probably so happy to be home she's not paying attention."

Gaius nodded, but he didn't seem convinced, still frowning as he opened a door at the end of the hall.

Within, there was a small room that housed a fireplace, table, and chairs. The fire was down to embers and looked like it hadn't been stoked in hours. Nothing adorned the walls, but there was a staircase across from the door that led up. The only comfort was a rug hiding most of the stone floor. There wasn't room for much else.

"There are usually guards here," Gaius explained. "But father wants them watching over the guests, so they're not here as much."

Thank the gods for that, Eolisti thought to herself. Guards would only complicate things. She didn't want to cause an incident with this kid. He seemed innocent enough.

"These are the stairs that lead to the west tower," he said, pointing. "Father said I'm not allowed to go up there, and my sister has never called for me, so I guess she really doesn't want to see me." He crossed his arms over his chest and looked away from the stairs, his bottom lip sticking out.

It was hard not to smile. It was lucky that she'd ended up on this floor. The one above it wouldn't have led her here.

"Tell you what, if you keep my visit a secret from your father, I'll tell your sister that you miss her and really want to see her." Eolisti winked at him. It was an empty promise, but maybe she could get the Phoenix to write him a letter. It wasn't too late for her to get to know her brother.

Eolisti had placed one foot on the staircase when she caught the sound of running footsteps. The Anai whipped around just in time to see a guard dressed in the blue and silver of the Castellus house trot through the doorway.

"Young master, we have been searching for you! Your father—" He skidded to a halt upon seeing Eolisti and the boy together.

By the time Eolisti thought to reach for her dagger, the man was already shouting "INTRUDER!" for everyone in the castle to hear.

"No, wait!" Gaius threw up his hands to try to stop the guard.

The boy bought her a few seconds to think. Eolisti glanced up the stairs. If she went up to the tower, she'd be trapped with no real weapons. *Damn.* Eolisti hopped off the stairs, grabbed one of the wooden chairs, and threw it at the guard.

She lunged forward past the boy, her fist connecting with the guard's jaw. While he was recoiling, she pulled the sword from its scabbard at his waist. There was yelling somewhere back down the corridor. Eolisti dodged as the man she was fighting tried to grab her. This guard treated her like some little girl who couldn't hurt him. His mistake.

Eolisti rolled to the side, then used the flat of the stolen weapon to smack him on the back of the head. She didn't want to kill him, but he was making so much noise. Her strike just seemed to make him angry. He finally put his hands up in a defensive position and squared his shoulders.

The Anai rolled her eyes. If she wanted to kill him, she would have already done it. Eolisti raised the sword like she was going to take a swing at him, and when he ducked behind his arms, she turned and bolted down the hall.

It took him a moment to notice she was gone. "Hey!" he shouted after her, but Eolisti was much faster than some middle-aged human.

She risked a glance behind her and spotted Gaius standing in the light of the hall, a confused look on his face as the house guard chased after her.

There was a pang of guilt in her stomach, but this was no time to be worried about the kid. She was the one in real trouble.

A door to her left flew open, and two more guards came rushing into the corridor right behind her. One of them tried to snatch at her cloak, but she pulled it out of reach at the last second. If she could make it to the servants' stairs and back to the second floor, maybe there would be enough confusion with the guests to allow her to escape. If she could just get out of the castle, she could tell the others where the Phoenix was imprisoned.

She threw open the door to the stairs and ran down them as fast as she could, taking them two at a time and trying not to lose her footing on the warped stones. When she finally reached the bottom, Eolisti dashed down the hall, her pursuers on her heels. She risked a glance over her shoulder and saw four men wearing blue and silver tabards chasing her. They weren't as fast as she was in the long stretch of the corridor, and she started pulling away from them. If she could get down the grand staircase, she could slip into the kitchen and lose them there.

A door in front of her suddenly swung open. Eolisti was too close to dodge, so with one swift move, she kicked the door closed again, drawing a pained yelp from the person inside.

The distraction was all the guards needed to catch up. Something heavy hit her back, and the next thing she knew, she was tumbling forward. Eolisti took the fall gracefully, using the momentum to roll back up into a fighting position, facing her attackers.

As one of the men reached for her, she swung the sword she'd taken from the guard, but it was much heavier than her own, and the blow missed wildly. Taking advantage of her momentary loss of control, the guard in front of her brought a club rushing at her head. There was a bright flash of light and the feeling of something heavy crushing her to the ground, then all sensation faded into nothingness.

Eolisti awoke to a searing pain in her skull. With a groan, she rolled over as her stomach threatened to expel everything she'd eaten in the last month. Clenching her teeth, she fought down the nausea. Her cheek rested on cold stone, which meant she was still in the castle.

After all of that, she hadn't been able to escape.

Muscles ached as Eolisti tried to move. The guards hadn't been gentle when they'd pinned her to the ground. She was sure she'd have bruises in the morning.

Wherever they had taken her smelled absolutely foul. Looking around, Eolisti got to her hands and knees. A few flickering torches on the walls illuminated the wide, open room. Iron bars surrounded her, dividing one side of the room into small, sectioned-off areas. This must have been what the others had called the dungeon.

Ignoring the twinge in her stomach, she staggered to her feet and tried to open the door of her cage, but it was locked. Her first instinct was to go for her dagger, but when she reached for it, there was nothing there. The guards must have taken it while she'd been unconscious.

It was then Eolisti noticed that she was not alone. There was a woman lying on the floor of the cell next to her, and in the corner by the stairs out of this foul hell, a man sat in a wooden chair, hands folded in his lap. Eolisti hadn't seen him before, and she was pretty sure she'd seen all the lords and ladies over the past few days. This man had dark hair and an angular face. Blue eyes watched her as she pulled away from the cage door. He was dressed well, much better than all the servants and almost as nicely as the guests, but the hardness in his face was something she would have remembered. Out of pure stubbornness, Eolisti crossed her arms and returned his scowl.

He didn't say anything as they stared each other down. She wanted to ask him who he was and why she was here, but Eolisti had the feeling that he wouldn't have answered her anyway. With all her aches and pains, all she wanted to do at the moment was sit down, but she would not allow herself to be beaten by this unknown man. Maybe, just maybe, she had been too hasty and should have stayed back at the inn.

After the longest minute of her life, there was the sound of a door opening from above. A few moments later, Lord Castellus descended the stairs and, to her surprise, was followed by none other than Elindiir.

She almost spoke then, but when Castellus's eyes met hers, a chill went down her spine that made the remark wither and die before it could even reach her throat. That gaze could freeze fire.

The man who had been sitting in the chair stood and bowed low to the lord of the castle as the latter stepped into the dungeon.

"Ambassador," Castellus began, directing his attention at Elindiir. "This is my court mage, Lucan."

Elindiir nodded to the man. Eolisti waited for him to look at her, but he seemed to be ignoring that she was even there. She kept staring at him. Why was he with Castellus? Wasn't he there to help her?

Lucan returned the nod, then began questioning the Anaiian ambassador. "Do you know this woman, Ambassador?" the court mage asked, his tone accusatory.

It was only then that Elindiir looked down his nose at Eolisti, and the coolness of his following words shocked her. "Not well. We met on the way here, and I was surprised to see her working for Lord Castellus. Normally, Anai wouldn't stoop so low as to serve a human." Those handsome lips curled into a sneer.

His words stung, and she gritted her teeth. What had happened to the kind man that she'd met in Omer? Had Elindiir been looking down on her this entire time for traveling with humans? No... They'd been together for months. She would have known if he'd been lying to her. Was he saying this for the lord's benefit?

"I admit that I didn't think much of it when I saw her with the serving staff, Ambassador. I never thought one of your people would be a spy." The lord's voice was calm and disinterested, but even Eolisti could hear the subtle insinuation as his eyes drifted from her to Elindiir.

The ambassador seemed unperturbed by this. "The woman can make her own choices, my lord, but rest assured, there will be the severest punishment for this embarrassment." Elindiir took a deep breath, let it out slowly through his nose, then gave the lord of the castle his full attention again. "I apologize, my lord, but as an ambassador for the Anaiian people, I must insist that you release her into my custody, unharmed, to face judgment by her own people—after the wedding, of course."

Lord Castellus gave Elindiir a hard look, but he didn't argue. If he was feeling any indignation at the other man's insistence, it didn't show on his face. The silence stretched out for a few moments before he spoke. "Of course, Ambassador, but I must know what kind of threat she brings into my home."

"By all means," Elindiir said with a slight bow of his head. "I only require that she be kept in one piece and that no permanent damage is done." He turned cold eyes on her. "We will, of course, compensate you for your inconvenience as her actions are an embarrassment to all Anai."

The lord turned to the other human. "Lucan, question her," he ordered his mage, seemingly satisfied with Elindiir's terms. "I have too much riding on this to let anyone interfere. Find out who she is working with and what their purpose here is."

"With pleasure, my lord," the mage said, watching Eolisti with a wicked gleam in his eyes.

She stuck her tongue out at him, because she could.

Castellus gave her one last contemptuous glare, then ascended the stone steps out of the dungeon, his personal guards in tow.

Elindiir also turned to leave, but before he could, Eolisti threw herself at the bars, careless of the cold stare of the court mage.

"Why?" she asked, blinking away tears as she clutched at the cool metal beneath her fingers. "Why are you doing this to me?"

The ambassador paused, looking back at her over his shoulder. He was silent for a moment, seeming to mull over his reply. All the warmth he'd displayed before was gone, and his expression was unrecognizable.

"I told you before, didn't I?" he asked. "You shouldn't trust so easily." He shifted his focus to Lucan and frowned, his eyes narrowing slightly at the human mage. "No permanent damage," he repeated and left the dungeon, leaving just Eolisti, the sleeping woman, and the court wizard.

As the door above them thudded shut, Eolisti sank to her knees. She'd trusted Elindiir. She'd thought he was a good man and an ally. Even worse, she *liked* him, and she'd thought he'd felt the same. True, he'd saved her from death by this man's hands, but for what? To take her prisoner and present her to the other Anai as a criminal? Eolisti would rather die than be shipped back to her mother in irons.

The wizard approached her cell and knelt by the bars, making it so that he was at eye level with her. "You're here for Lady Korynne. Any fool could see that, but you couldn't have infiltrated this castle alone. Who was helping you?" He smiled, and the look on his smug face made Eolisti's blood boil. "One of the maids, maybe? Or the kitchen staff? If you tell me who they are, you'll be able to sit quietly in this cell until the ambassador takes you back to Nemethy with him."

Eolisti laughed, and it sounded bitter to her ears. If she couldn't get out of this, then she would damn well make sure no one suspected the others. She tried hard to remember what Turin had said to her throughout their journey. Maybe there was some detail she could use to convince this man she was working alone, but it was diffi-cult to concentrate. She'd just been betrayed by Elindiir, and it made her want to stab someone. Someone like this callous bastard in front of her.

Eolisti thought of the look in Elindiir's eyes and tried to mimic his contempt. "I wasn't working with anyone. Why would I need any help from a human?"

The wizard clenched his jaw, having the same look that some of the High Council members got when they'd been forced to talk to her. She wasn't very popular back home. "If you're alone, then it's strange that you wouldn't have used magic to escape from the castle. You could have easily over-powered the guards. They aren't trained to fight a mage. That's what I'm here for."

Eolisti licked her lips, trying to play it cool. Had Sophie used magic in the castle? That would be the only reason he'd brought it up, right? "I dabble in it from time to time, not enough to fight anyone off with it. So what?" she said as flippantly as she could manage.

"Someone suppressed my alarm on this dungeon two days ago!" he shouted, losing all semblance of control. "Then that same person healed her!" Lucan pointed to the iron bars next to her own, where the sleeping young woman was, curled in on herself atop a pile of rags. "You want me to believe that someone who just *dabbles* in the art can bring someone back from the brink of death and cast a suppression spell so subtle that I almost missed it?"

Even in the dim light, Eolisti could see that the woman next to her, who must have been Winna, was bruised and bloodied, but she did look a little better than how Sophie had described her. If the woman had been much worse than she was now, she would have died. Eolisti didn't doubt Lucan's words. Once, when they had fought a Soulless, Eolisti had been injured, and Sophie had healed her wound. It was an amazing and frightening power, but her friend was an amazing and frightening wizard.

Eolisti steeled herself. She would not let this man have Sophie.

Meeting the wizard's eyes, she smiled widely. "It's not like it was hard. Maybe you're just not that good."

Lucan clenched his teeth, and pain flooded Eolisti's body. It washed over her like a wave, starting at her toes and reaching up to every part of her. She gasped and fell back from the bars. It was almost as if ten thousand needles had pierced every inch of her skin. She tried to think through the burning agony flooding her senses. Back in Elasariin, she had been trained to resist pain like this, but it had been so sudden and with no apparent source.

The court mage stared at her intently as it began to fade, and Eolisti knew where the pain had come from. He must have been waiting to use that spell until she mouthed off to him. *Bastard.*

"If you don't want that to happen again, you should just answer my questions plainly," he growled. Lucan grabbed the chair he'd been using earlier and dragged it over to her cell. He sat in it and crossed his arms. "Now tell me, who were you working with? Just describe them to me, and we'll pull them from the staff." He tilted his head to one side and grinned. "Or maybe you really were working with that ambassador. He was very quick to give you up, you know. And how convenient that our laws would force us to let you go with him back to your people. Maybe this was all planned."

"I told you," she said, able to make her breathing steady. She stood and straightened to her full height, unwilling to let him see how much his spell hurt her. "I wasn't working with anyone. The ambassador clearly doesn't want anything to do with me, and why would I ever work with humans?" She repeated something she'd heard one of the High Council members say. "Humans are all weak and deceitful. Why would I trust any of you?"

If the insult affected Lucan, he showed no sign of it. "So why would you help a human, then? You were looking for Lady Korynne's room, were you not?"

Eolisti felt the heat creeping up her neck as her temper rose. "How could I not? You would imprison and poison your own lady, force her to marry some lordling, and for what? Political power?" She spat onto the stone floor of her cell. "It's disgusting. My people would never do that to one of their own." Her hands clenched and unclenched. She wished she had her sword so that she could cut that slimy look off Lucan's face.

"And what's the point of this deception? Once she's

married, she'll eventually regain her senses. There must be laws here against imprisoning and poisoning people, let alone a citizen of another country." Eolisti clenched her fists again. "Why would you risk a war over something like this?"

Lucan said nothing, just staring at the Anai with a blank expression, which pissed her off.

"Hello? Did you suddenly go deaf?"

"Isn't it obvious?" The voice didn't come from the wizard, but from the woman in the cell next to her. The pile of rags moved, and Eolisti saw the glint of dark eyes reflecting the torchlight. She thought the young woman had been sleeping before or maybe passed out, but Winna looked up at Eolisti as she pulled herself into a sitting position on the ground. By the way she moved, slowly and carefully, Eolisti could tell the woman was in pain. She had cuts and bruises, but she appeared to be healing.

"In Tanalin, marriages go through a bonding ceremony that ties their families together in the eyes of the law, no matter if something happens to the bride or groom. Even though Lord Castellus lives in this remote part of the Empire for part of the year, he is still the head of a powerful noble family. A marriage between the Castellus and Golistin families would make the Golistins' noble status legitimate." She glanced up at Lucan, but his focus was still on Eolisti. "You see, since they came here from another country, the Golistins have standing only in name. No other nobles take them seriously, but with the backing of house Castellus, not even the emperor would question their status."

Winna grabbed the bars of her cell closest to Eolisti and shakily pulled herself to her feet. "They don't plan on keeping the Phoenix alive after all of this," she growled, her voice full of contempt. "They'll kill her after the emperor verifies the marriage bond."

Lucan suddenly stood from his seat, knocking back the chair and bringing one hand down in a slashing motion in front of him. Winna was thrown backward as if hit by an invisible hand, colliding with the wall and sinking to the ground again. A cut on her arm reopened, and blood trickled from the wound and pooled in the crook of her arm.

"Hey!" Eolisti shouted, lunging at the bars and trying to swing her fists through them, but the wizard was too far away for her to reach.

Those cold eyes turned back to her. She felt pressure against her temples, and blackness began to close in at the edges of her vision.

You will tell me who you are working for. His voice rang in her ears even though his lips never moved.

Eolisti stumbled back. She would never give him Sophie.

"Go to hell," she said through clenched teeth as the pressure increased.

The wizard grinned at Eolisti as pain radiated through her again, pain like nothing she'd ever felt before. It burned as though she'd been thrust into a raging fire. Then all she could hear were her screams echoing off the stone.

TWENTY

Sophie didn't give much thought to Eolisti's absence. The Anai often awoke earlier than she did and would keep herself busy while Sophie slept. Perhaps she had already gone to find something to eat.

The mage blearily looked around, rubbing her eyes against the sunlight pouring in through the window. There wasn't a cloud in sight.

A light rapping at her door had woken her, and Sophie stumbled over and opened it to find Khalil, already dressed in his Tempest Hall staff uniform, blindfold and all. Today, he had his dark-brown hair pulled back from his face with a leather cord. It was nice to see his features plainly, without being obscured by hair or clothing. His high cheekbones and strong jawline were pleasing to look at. While usually clean-shaven, Sophie noticed stubble for the first time. She smiled to herself, thankful that he couldn't see how closely she watched him.

"Are you packed?" he asked, sounding far more alert than Sophie felt.

Right, he wanted to take her bag. "Let me change first,"

she said stifling a yawn. It would have been awkward to have him stand out in the hallway, so she invited him inside. It wasn't as if he could see her dress anyway.

Even so, he turned his back to her while she hurriedly pulled on the black dress and set her hair up in a neat bun. She carefully placed the slave anklet in her pocket but hesitated before tying up the bag. Sophie had a few pouches with items that she used to help her cast spells. Those might come in handy today. She knew they weren't really necessary to work her magic, but any number of things could go wrong, and she wanted to be prepared, especially with another wizard in the castle.

But as much as she wanted to be ready for any obstacle, she decided it would look suspicious to show up at the castle with her pockets laden with magical reagents. Maybe the guards wouldn't think anything of it, but on the off chance the wizard took note of them again, he would know exactly what the items in her possession were for.

Sophie went to tie up Eolisti's bag as well, but paused. There was a small pile of discarded clothing next to it. It was the Anai's staff uniform.

Her gaze tracked back over to Khalil waiting patiently next to the door. "Do you know where Eolisti is? She left her uniform here, and her cloak is gone."

Khalil shook his head. "She isn't downstairs."

Sophie bit her bottom lip. This had a familiar ring to it. Eolisti had run off while they were back in Nobarum before they'd boarded the *Westwind*, but she'd returned later that night—perhaps drunker than she should have been, but in one piece. It was possible she had done the same last night, finding some bar to enjoy herself at, but Sophie had a bad feeling. Eolisti knew how important today was. She wouldn't blow that off. "She was here when I went to sleep, but gone when I awoke. I didn't even realize she left."

Stepping forward, Khalil picked up Sophie's and Eolisti's bags. "It's not your fault, Sophie. None of us can control that Anai." He didn't sound angry, but Sophie could tell by the set of his mouth that he was annoyed.

"I'm sure she wouldn't do anything to put us at risk of discovery," Sophie added quickly, wanting to defend her friend. "She probably just went to see Elindiir like the last time." Even as she spoke, she didn't feel very confident about it. Eolisti should be here.

Khalil didn't say anything else, but his jaw clicked as he clenched it. A second before he would have reached the door, he dropped the bags and threw it open. In a blur of motion, Khalil grabbed a man standing on the other side by the collar of his shirt and slammed him against the wall. Sophie jumped back out of the way, not having heard the newcomer approach, and her companion pulled a dagger out of his belt and pressed it against Lucky the musician's throat.

"Khalil!" Sophie gasped.

"Please don't hurt me," Lucky rasped, his eyes wide. "I just need to speak to you about your Anaiian friend."

"What do you know about her? Where is she?" Khalil growled, not letting the older man go.

"The other Anai— He found me out in the courtyard and asked me to come and find you," Lucky said, his wide eyes darting to Sophie, then back to Khalil. "He said Lord Castellus caught your friend in the upper levels of the castle last night, and she's being held in the dungeon—questioned by the wizard."

There was a sound of heavy footsteps in the hall before

Turin appeared behind Khalil and Lucky. He stopped in his tracks at the scene before him.

"What in the hells is going on here?" Turin asked, looking from Khalil to the musician and back again. He wore his weapons, though his sword was still sheathed.

"Get in here and close the door," the blind man said flatly.

Turin looked like he wanted to argue, but let out a long breath, then squeezed past Khalil into the room, closing and locking the door.

Once they had a degree of privacy from the rest of the inn, Khalil finally let go of the musician and took a step back. Lucky slumped against the wall, hands groping at his neck. There was a thin red line against his dark skin from Khalil's dagger. He stared up at both men as if he'd never seen them before.

"T-they didn't question any of the other staff, so I don't think they know who you are, but I can't be sure. The other Anai seemed to think that she wouldn't have told them anything." Lucky straightened and wiped his brow with a handkerchief that he hurriedly stuffed back into his pocket. "I need to get back before the others notice I'm gone. They're still sleeping. We played so late last night." He let out a nervous chuckle as his eyes flicked between the three of them.

"All right, Lucky," Turin said, brows furrowed in concern. The white-knuckled grip on the hilt of his sword betrayed his true emotions. "Thank you for telling us. We'll do what we can to have her released."

"That's none of my business." Lucky swallowed hard. "The Anaiian ambassador just told me to come and apprise you of the situation. I only agreed because I like Eolisti, and

I don't want her to get into trouble, that's all," he muttered quickly, inching toward the door.

Nobody stopped him, so with one last nervous glance around at them, he dipped his head in farewell and scurried out of the room.

It was quiet for a moment as Sophie slid into one of the chairs at the small table, her two companions still looming over her. She put her head in her hands. Eolisti had been captured and was being held in the castle dungeon? She waited for one of the others to speak. Surely, one of them would have a plan to rescue her. There had to be a way to help her. It felt like the moments of calm before a strike of lightning.

Khalil sucked in a breath through clenched teeth, but Turin struck first. "She's ruined everything." His voice was tight with anger. "They are going to know we are coming now. We'll have to abandon the mission."

"What about the Phoenix?" Khalil snapped. "You want to just leave her here?"

"I can't believe this," Turin growled, ignoring the other man's question. He started pacing back and forth, then turned a scowl on Sophie. "How could you not notice that she was gone?"

Sophie was taken aback by the accusation in his voice. Did he think she could have somehow stopped Eolisti from going back to the castle? "S-she must have left after I fell asleep." She turned her gaze to Khalil. "How are we going to get her out? If she's being questioned by that wizard, who knows what he's going to do to her—what he's already done? If Elindiir sent Lucky to tell us what happened, he must think we can do something."

"Or it was a warning that our cover was blown and not to come back." Turin had stopped pacing and was glaring down at her. She could tell by the way the muscles around his mouth twitched that the knight was holding back when he spoke. "She got herself into this mess and jeopardized all of us. What happens if she tells them who we are and why we're here?"

"Eolisti won't tell them anything," Sophie said, feeling a flush creep up her neck. "You don't know her as I do."

"I know her well enough to know that she's trouble! We should just leave her to face the consequences of her actions," he growled. "If she doesn't tell them anything, she'll make for a good distraction while we get the Phoenix out of there."

Sophie didn't remember getting to her feet, but she leaned over the table, palms down on the wood. Rage boiled inside her chest, and she unleashed that anger on Turin. When she spoke, she didn't recognize the deadly, flat voice that left her lips. "I will tear that castle apart stone by stone if I have to, but I am not leaving her behind."

Sophie and Turin glared at each other, his dark-green eyes meeting her gray. She wanted him to see her fury at his words, wanted him to see her resolve. She would not abandon Eolisti. The Anai had been by her side since the beginning of her journey, and she was Sophie's friend. The scent of burning wood filled her nose, but she ignored it, keeping her eyes on Turin.

The knight looked away first, glancing down between them. His eyes widened. "You're burning the table," he said in a concerned voice.

After a glance down, she quickly pulled her hands away, leaving the charred imprints of her palms on the polished oak. With a deep, steadying breath, she glared back up at Turin, idly rubbing her hands together to get rid of some of the soot. "I won't leave her," she repeated, her voice low and firm.

Turin's eyes flicked to the burn spots and then back to her face before he ran a hand through his black hair. When he spoke, his voice was calmer than it had been moments before. "It's not going to be that easy, Sophie. We can't just walk into the dungeon. They'll be expecting someone to come for her."

"I'll find her," Khalil said, making Sophie jump. All her focus had been on the knight. She'd forgotten that he was still there. "If they think she's a spy, they should be keeping her with Winna. I can get them both out while the two of you rescue the Phoenix."

Turin sighed, turning his back to them. "And how are you supposed to do that? The castle is going to be heavily guarded, Khalil. Even if Eolisti has somehow convinced them that she was operating alone, they would be fools not to tighten up security around both the dungeon and the Phoenix."

Khalil didn't seem bothered by Turin's words. "I've gotten out of worse situations." He tilted his head toward Sophie, and she saw the barest hint of a smirk on his lips. "A distraction would be helpful."

She blinked once, then grinned. "I think I can come up with something."

"Am I the only one who feels like we're in over our heads?" Turin groaned, folding his arms across his chest, reminding Sophie of a pouting child. "It's one thing after another. Something is always changing with this job, and I don't like it. It's too risky."

"Sometimes, you have to be flexible," Khalil said, and Sophie caught a hint of irritation in his voice. "Every assignment has its challenges."

Looking at the two men, there was a stark difference between them that Sophie could see clearly now. Though Turin's outlook on the world seemed always positive and full of compassion, his approach to the mission—and maybe life—was more straightforward than Khalil's, who seemed to live in a realm of grays. The knight was so thrown off by the unexpected change to their plans that he considered abandoning it, but Khalil just saw it as another obstacle to overcome. He was like water flowing in a river, able to wind and move with every bump and bend, while Turin was a stone wall, sturdy and strong but nearly impossible to move.

To her eye, Khalil was just as upset as Turin at what the Anai had done, but rather than brooding over what they could not change, he channeled that energy into creating a solution. The monks at Ta'Shela trusted Khalil with the special assignments they had, and Sophie could see why. Even with a blow such as this, he was calm and already thinking up a new plan.

Sophie reached out and gripped his hand, grateful to have someone like him on her side. "Thank you."

He squeezed her fingers and then stepped over to where he'd dropped their bags. "I still need to move these to where we can easily get them after we escape the castle." He turned toward Turin. "There's no use making whatever face you are giving me. Our mission hasn't changed."

Turin was, in fact, making a face like something he'd eaten hadn't agreed with him. Khalil picked up their effects and then held out his hand to the knight. "Sword," he said simply. Turin stared at him for a long moment, then reluctantly undid his baldric and placed it in his hand. Khalil moved to the door, where he paused and turned his head slightly back to face them.

Sophie had the feeling that he didn't want to leave while the tension lingered between her and Turin. "Go," she said. "We need to be ready."

He nodded once and exited the room, closing the door behind him with a click and leaving her and the knight alone together. Turin stared broodily out the window, and it wasn't hard to see that he was avoiding her gaze. They hadn't known each other that long, so the silence was awkward.

Though much had happened, it had only been two weeks since they'd met on the docks in Mattina. He'd treated her and Eolisti like children since they'd first met. As soon as he'd discovered that she was a wizard, his attitude toward her had changed, but apparently, that respect did not yet extend to Eolisti—especially now. Sophie had a suspicion that part of the reason Eolisti went out on her own was to prove herself useful to Turin and Khalil. It was reckless and had backfired, but she knew the Anai was only trying to help.

Sophie wasn't sure what to say to ease his fears, but she tried anyway. "It will all work out, Turin. Khalil is one of the most skilled men I've ever met. If he says that he can get Winna and Eolisti out of the dungeon, then he will do it." She stepped around the table to stand next to him. He was a good head and a half taller than she was, so she had to look up to him.

The knight didn't respond to her. He stared out the window at the field that sat between the village of Brumalar and Tempest Hall.

"Turin," Sophie said and waited until his gaze shifted to her to continue. The anger lingered in his eyes, but there was also weariness and fear that she hadn't picked up on before. "It will be all right." She smiled in a way she hoped was reassuring. "I'm not going to make excuses for Eolisti, but she's with us. She and Khalil helped me get out of Zo'rahn, and we will all get the Phoenix to safety."

Sophie could almost hear him grinding his teeth. He was so focused on everything that could go wrong today. What he needed was a distraction.

Something he'd said the first night they'd arrived at Tempest Hall stuck out in her mind. He'd talked like he'd known the woman who had been presented as Lady Korynne. "Before, you told us that the person we now know is the Phoenix was the niece of the Lord High Commander," she began. "You called her Rhyn. Does that mean you know her well?"

A flood of conflicting emotions crossed Turin's face. There was shock at the question, anger—though at the inquiry or some memory, Sophie was not sure—fondness, and then embarrassment. She gave him a few moments to collect his thoughts before leaning on the windowsill and raising an eyebrow.

Turin managed a smile. It was strained, but it was there. "It's a long story. Are you sure you want to hear it?"

"Absolutely," she replied and meant it. Distraction aside, she was curious about the personal interest the knight had taken once he discovered the Phoenix's identity. The look in his eyes told her that there was history between Turin, the abandoned prince, and "Lady Korynne."

He chuckled at the look on her face. "All right, all right. Well, it's been a long time since I've seen her. We were both teenagers. During the winter about twelve years ago, she stumbled into Griffin's Bluff—it's a fortress in the mountains north of here—alone and half-frozen. The Lord High Commander recognized her immediately, and the maids nursed her back to health. When she could talk, she told us her caravan had been attacked by bandits and that she was the only survivor, but"—he chuckled softly—"she was a bad liar back then. I figured she had run away from her family and, being a noble's daughter, hadn't known what it would take to cross the mountains. Honestly, I thought she was a boy at first. She was so skinny, and she'd cut her hair off."

"She did that in the middle of winter?" Sophie asked, aghast. She'd crossed through the mountains back in Omer at the end of autumn, which had been miserable. She couldn't imagine doing it in deep winter, and alone, no less. But when she thought about it, that was what they would be doing if all went well at the castle. It was nearing the end of winter now, but its bite was still as sharp as ever.

"I never said she was the smartest person, at least not when we were teenagers. It's fine if you have the supplies, but she had nothing." His hands fiddled with his belt, at the spot where his sword normally hung. Sophie knew Eolisti hated going to the castle unarmed, and it seemed Turin felt the same. "Anyway, we fought a lot at first. She was quite clever and willing to do whatever it took to get what she wanted. I was still adjusting to my training, and we argued all the time. We were always in each other's face since I squired directly under the Commander. She became his ward, so we had lessons, ate, and did chores together most days. A year or so after she'd arrived at Griffin's Bluff, the arguing turned into..." The big man's cheeks turned pink. He seemed to be at a loss for words.

"Turin, I'm not a child," Sophie said with a knowing smile. "I understand."

He nodded, his face still red. "Well, we did that for a while, and then she left while I stayed to finish my training. I thought she was going to the capital to join high society, but it seems that wasn't the case." The glower came back at his words, and the muscles in his face twitched as he clenched his jaw.

"She must have had a reason for the choices she made, Turin," Sophie said as gently as she could. "As you said, it was a long time ago that you two were together. You haven't seen her in, what, ten years? A lot can change in that amount of time. Before you get too angry, you should talk to her. Judging by how her supposed father is treating her, I'm guessing her childhood was not a good one, and that kind of thing can change a person—often for the worse."

He let out a long sigh, stretched his neck, and then leaned one shoulder against the window frame. The corner of his mouth twitched as he eyed her. "I'm not sure you're qualified to give me relationship advice. How old are you? Fifteen?"

"Eighteen," she said with a sniff, "but I'll be nineteen in a few weeks."

"Gods give me strength," Turin muttered and shook his head. "Eighteen? And I thought Khalil was too young to be doing this." He pinched the bridge of his nose with his thumb and forefinger.

"You're not that much older than we are," Sophie grumbled. She kept herself from balling her hands into fists, but only just.

"Yes," Turin countered with another sigh, crossing his arms over his chest again. "I am. And speaking of relationships, what about you and Khalil?"

The question took Sophie aback. Had Turin seen her looking at Khalil? "What about us?"

Turin snorted. "He follows you around like some lost

pup. He always knows where you are, or at least, where you should be."

"He's only doing that because he was hired to get me out of Zo'rahn." She answered coolly, her eyes narrowed.

"I don't know if you've noticed, but you're out of Zo'rahn, and he's still zealously protecting you. I know he wants to get you to Morigael—he has an obligation to do that—but I've seen him work before. He doesn't hold hands with the other people he helps."

Her face was uncomfortably warm. "He was just comforting me, that's all." She tried to look indifferent to his comment, but Turin's widening grin told her it wasn't convincing. She remembered how Khalil being close in the narrow halls and alcoves of the castle had made her heart race. She tried to push the memory away.

"Khalil has told me before that I remind him of his past self," she finally managed. It had been on a cool desert night back in Omer, an ocean away, when he had told her that. Like her, he had a special gift and had allowed others to abuse it. Back in her homeland, Sophie had found out in the worst way possible that she'd had the ability to control an artifact that everyone had thought just a broken or useless bauble. She had been faced with the same choice as Khalil, and, instead of staying, had chosen to give up everything she had, everything she was, and flee. "He sees himself in me, and that is the affection you think you see, Turin."

"You're wrong. I see it when you look at him too."

A knot formed in her stomach at his words. She'd been hurt before by people she'd trusted over and over again. It made her think of the long nights back in her homeland, working late, and having to endure sweet lies whispered in her ear behind closed doors. Khalil wouldn't hurt her, but then she'd thought the same thing about her Vasalii who'd used her, her father who'd given her to the wizards, and Joel, her "friend" who'd sold her to the Spider. She looked away from Turin and out the window at the cloudless sky, taking a few deep breaths to calm her pounding heart. "I don't know if I'm ready for what you're implying. I'm not sure I'll ever be ready."

He reached out, intending to place a hand on her shoulder. "Sophie, I didn't mean to—"

"Please," she interrupted, taking a step away so that she was out of his reach. "Don't. It's okay. I consider Khalil a friend, and..." She didn't finish. All she could do was shrug. "We'll see."

Sophie glanced at the door. Khalil would be back soon, and they needed to be ready. "I'm hungry," she lied. "We should get something to eat. It's going to be a long day."

TWENTY-ONE

Everything seemed normal as Sophie, Khalil, and Turin passed through the gate and entered the castle grounds. Despite Lucky's report that no one was looking for them, Sophie had still half expected to be stopped by the guards. However, the ones at the gate didn't seem to be paying much attention to those who came and went.

Many more people were within the castle grounds than she had seen on any previous day, standing in small clusters in the courtyard. In addition to the groups of nobles, Sophie thought she recognized a few of the people she'd seen in the tavern over the last few nights. They weren't dressed in the staff uniform.

"What's going on? Are the villagers guests too?" she asked Turin as they made their way through the courtyard. Now that she thought about it, she had seen some villagers the previous day, but there were dozens more than she remembered.

"The wedding may be tomorrow morning, but tonight is the biggest celebration," he said as he smiled and waved at some of the other staff. "It's traditional for the hosting lord to allow those he governs to attend the final feast before the bride and groom are wed, as a display of generosity. The day of the wedding is supposed to be for the couple to begin their honeymoon and is reserved for family."

Sophie frowned. That was not how things were done where she was from, but each country had its own traditions, she supposed.

"It's much different from the east," Khalil said as if he was reading her mind. He'd taken her arm as soon as they'd left the inn. People avoided looking at them because his blindness made them uncomfortable, and the guards practically looked through him. That realization bolstered her spirits. If Khalil was able to move around the castle without anyone noticing him, maybe they could actually pull this off.

"More people will make it easier for us," Turin said in a low voice as he took the lead. He was so large that people naturally moved out of his way. "There will be a lot of unfamiliar faces within the castle walls today. The guards will be watching newcomers instead of paying any attention to the staff."

"Right." Sophie went over the plan in her mind one more time. "I'll find out where they are keeping Lady Korynne, get the ring from Lord Castellus, and make a distraction," she recited.

"It will be easier for you to get close to him than either of us," Turin reminded her, speaking out the side of his mouth as he nodded to some of the other people working across the courtyard.

"Be careful, though," Khalil whispered. He hadn't liked this part of the plan but had agreed, if reluctantly. With

Eolisti gone, cornering the lord was entirely up to her. He'd be more likely to let a young woman get close to him than her masculine companions.

Sophie remembered Turin's comments about her and Khalil. Was her friend worried that she would be in danger or that she wouldn't be able to accomplish her tasks? Sneaking around the castle would be far more dangerous than getting in the same vicinity as Castellus. Was his concern something more?

She caught Turin stealing a smug glance at them and felt her cheeks burn. It was his fault she was questioning Khalil's actions. She pursed her lips annoyed. "I can handle it," she replied tersely.

When they reached the kitchen, they were greeted by utter chaos.

"Thank the gods!" Dalia said when she spotted them. Staff darted from place to place around her, and the matron had a dark stain on her white apron. "I need about a dozen more pairs of hands, but you three will do. Here." She picked up a basket of potatoes and thrust it into Turin's arms. "These needed to be peeled an hour ago." Dalia pointed to a basin full of soapy water and a mountain of dishes. "Those need to be washed from breakfast. The whole village will be here today, and half of the temporary staff didn't show up this morning!" The gray-haired woman wiped her forehead before planting both hands on her hips, a scowl on her face. "They're probably out there joining the party. We'll see if they get a single coin after this!" She grunted and turned away to check on one of the pots, its contents spitting angrily as it boiled over.

Sophie and Turin exchanged a look. The knight shrugged and took a seat on a stool, picking up a knife from a small table nearby. Khalil knelt next to the foamy basin and began rolling up his sleeves.

Sophie was about to join him when a door to the inner castle flew open with a *BAM!*

The mage jumped, and Dalia whipped around to see what fresh hell was disturbing her kitchen, eyes full of rage. The cook's brows furrowed as her eyes fell on the woman who rushed through the door.

"Great," Dalia muttered as the new woman cast her eyes around the kitchen. "What does she want now?"

The woman, who looked very familiar to Sophie, spotted Dalia and rushed over to her, clutching a small drawstring bag in her hands. "Can you spare one of your girls to help me? Cassandra has fallen ill, and Anya has already set the others about their tasks." The woman sounded desperate. "Everything must be perfect today! If I have to ask her for help again..." The woman trailed off, looking terrified.

"No, no, it's better for all of us if the harpy isn't bothered with something like this." Dalia sighed and looked around the kitchen. All her people were already working furiously on various roasts, soups, and confections that were to be served at the celebration. The matron didn't look like she wanted to let any of them stop what they were doing.

Then her eyes fell on Sophie, and her dark eyebrows rose. "You. Girl."

"Sophie, ma'am," Sophie responded. As busy as everyone was, she couldn't blame Dalia for forgetting her name.

"Yes, yes," the woman replied dismissively. "Sophie, you can assist Marilla with Lady Korynne. Your friend can wash dishes. Surely, he can handle that on his own until you return."

Sophie nodded and took a step toward the maid.

"Come on, then." Marilla quickly exited the room, leaving Sophie to jog after her.

They exited into the same hallway that led to the reserve cellar. "Of all the times to overindulge! Has that girl taken leave of her senses? She'll be lucky if Anya doesn't sack her after this," the older woman muttered as she walked. "Keep up, girl! We need to reach the tower before the guests begin stirring. Otherwise, we'll be bowing every few steps and will never get anything done."

They hurried to the second floor, into another servants' stairway, then down another hall and through a door leading to yet another staircase that wound its way up a tower. It was dizzying trying to keep track of it all. Marilla kept talking about how much there was to do, but Sophie was barely listening. Her heart pounded in her ears as the two women ascended to a place that could only be where the Phoenix was being held hostage. She couldn't believe her luck. Sophie had needed to find out where she was being kept, and the opportunity had quite literally found her.

"—just be careful, dear," Marilla said as she pulled a ring of keys out of her apron and examined them. "The lady is in a strange place right now. The lord has assured us that the Golistins will get her to a proper healer once they get back to the capital—one that can work on the mind, you know. Ah, here it is." She put one thick iron key into the lock, turned it, and pushed the door open.

Sophie winced as sunlight poured into the room beyond from large windows cut directly into the stone walls. Paintings of flowers and trees were placed evenly along pale-blue walls. There was a large folding screen in the corner with more flowers painted on it, which must have hidden a tub for bathing. The rug was a vibrant grass green. Paired with the walls and flowers, it brought to mind a spring meadow, which was probably the intended effect. The only thing that detracted from the cheery atmosphere was the stale-smelling air and the iron bars that had been installed over the windows, preventing them from being opened.

For such a large room, there were only a few pieces of furniture—a small settee, a chest of drawers, and a bed. There were no personal effects, not even a book or a pair of gloves. It may not have been as filthy as the dungeon, but this tower was its own kind of prison.

Lady Korynne Castellus lay in the middle of the four-poster bed, her golden hair fanned out around her. A lace nightgown covered her lithe figure, and from the lack of wrinkles in the material, Sophie guessed that she'd hardly moved the entire night. Her eyes were open, and she stared straight ahead, up at the canopy. She looked like a doll—perfectly positioned, delicate, and lifeless.

The woman didn't react as Sophie and the other maid approached.

"Help her out of bed," Marilla instructed as she set the bag she'd been carrying on the dresser. "We need to get her cleaned up and ready."

As Sophie helped the lady swing her legs off the bed to sit up, she smoothed out the bottom of her nightgown. While she knelt, her hand brushed against exactly what she knew would be there. A thick metal band encircled Korynne's ankle. To Sophie's touch, the item practically vibrated with energy, but to someone who could not use magic, it would look and feel like a piece of clunky jewelry. Just as she'd suspected, Lord Castellus had placed a slave anklet on his daughter, and the ring she saw him wearing was surely what controlled it.

She reached out with her senses, brushing up against the magic of the anklet. There, she met resistance. Sophie had braced herself for pain, but since she was not the one imprisoned by it, none came. She pressed harder against the device with her will, but the magic would not budge. Maybe she could break through its protective enchantments with time, but they had precious little of that. She would need the ring to get it off.

"She's already been bathed, girl. We just need to give the lady her medicine and get her dressed for the feast." Marilla sighed. "I told the lord that she wasn't ready for this. Better to get married quietly and have the Golistins take her to a healer, but he insisted. The family wants to make a show of it and pretend nothing is wrong. Well, if this is what it takes to get the lady some help, then she can endure it for one more day, I suppose."

The maid was talking about Korynne like the lady couldn't hear them, which Sophie suspected was at least partially incorrect. When she'd first noticed the potion spilled on Marilla the day before—which she now realized was where she remembered the older woman from—she'd been thinking about what kind of mixture it could be. If the potion had damaged the lady's mind, it would have been evident to anyone looking at her. She apparently couldn't speak or move much on her own, but she could stand in place and walk at least a few steps. After all, Turin and Eolisti had seen her on display that first day. Therefore, the concoction had to be something that only made the lady compliant with some restrictions to her motor functions. There were plenty of magical recipes that could accomplish such results, but few that could be turned into a potion and bottled. Most of the recipes Sophie knew produced only temporary effects. If a dose was missed, with any luck Korynne would start to regain her senses and control. Assuming Sophie could get the anklet off her, of course.

Her own horrible experience with an anklet flashed through her mind. She remembered her limbs moving against her will, even though her mind railed against the anklet's control. The pain had been crippling, and even though she had been desperate to resist, she'd done whatever the Spider commanded. The harder she'd resisted, the more agonizing the pain had grown until it felt like every inch of her had simultaneously been set on fire and was being ripped apart. She could almost see the cruel hunter's face twisted in sick pleasure as he watched her scream.

"...are you listening?"

Sophie started. Her breath came hard, and her fingers were still on the slave anklet. She pulled her hand away and straightened from where she'd been kneeling. "I'm sorry, I was just trying to get the wrinkles out of her gown."

"Don't be silly! We'll be changing her into something more appropriate. You're obviously not from around here." Marilla laughed softly to herself. "Wearing a nightgown to a feast, honestly." As she talked, she started opening drawers in the dresser. "Now, where did they put it?"

Sophie couldn't just leave Korynne like this, hopelessly awaiting her fate as her captor slowly poisoned her. She had to give her some hope, some indication that there were people here to help her.

She leaned in close to the lady, pretending to busy herself with tidying her hair. If she could understand what they were saying, perhaps Sophie could let her know that Khalil and Turin were here. What was it that Khalil had said to Winna?

"A sparrow cries in the night," she whispered into Korynne's ear as Marilla fussed and laid out the lady's gown on the bed.

The eyes that had been unfocused a moment ago snapped to Sophie. The Phoenix grabbed her sleeve, her grip surprisingly strong for someone who was so heavily drugged.

Sophie stared back into those hazel eyes, trying to convey that, yes, there was the hope of rescue. She could see something stirring in the woman's face. Against all odds, Korynne was fighting the control of the potion and the slave anklet.

"Ah, there it is! The lady's medicine. It's so kind of Lucan to make this for her every day. He's not a healer, but he's been keeping the lady stable these last few weeks. Here, hold this," Marilla said handing Sophie a small glass bottle with a cork in it. Inside was a bright blue liquid. "We'll need to give her this medicine before we dress her. The poor dear had a fit and spilled it all over herself last time, and the lord will not be pleased if she ruins another dress." Marilla turned back to the dresser and opened the bottom drawer.

Sophie had only a few seconds to act, and she would not allow this woman to be poisoned further.

While Marilla's back was turned, Sophie quickly focused her mind, using her power to force the potion to change. The color reminded her of picking blueberries in the summer in Zo'rahn, and she concentrated on the flavor. She could almost taste it on her tongue when she let the magic flow through her, turning the liquid in the glass vial into harmless blueberry juice. The bottle warmed in her hand as the viscous liquid inside swirled. She could sense the other wizard's power inside resisting, but potions were a diluted form of magic, and his enchantments were washed away under Sophie's fresh spell.

By the time Marilla had turned back around, the only evidence of the change was a slight change in color, from the vibrant sickly blue to one darker and richer.

Sophie smiled at the woman, concealing the change with her hands as she uncorked the bottle.

Korynne stared blankly again as the liquid hit her lips. No doubt she tasted the difference right away, but she kept her eyes vacant and willingly drank as the maid watched them like a hawk.

"Well, she seems calm this morning, thank the gods. We need to have her presentable since she'll be at the feast today. I can't imagine why the young lord wants a bride like this, but I suppose marriages between nobles for more political reasons than for love." Marilla sighed heavily again. "Hopefully, they have a skilled physician in their manor that can continue treating her. Maybe she'll be able to recover eventually. I'm not sure a healer will be enough."

As she helped the Phoenix out of her nightgown, Sophie nodded along with Marilla's words. The lady placed a hand on Sophie's shoulder to steady herself, which was more movement than she'd seen from her this entire time. Marilla didn't seem to notice.

Together, they dressed Korynne in skirts, lace, and ribbon, with Marilla showing her how to properly outfit a Tanalin lady as they went. It would be a useless skill after today, but she listened as Marilla talked about high society and what it must be like in the capital. The woman was a little envious that their lady would be leaving soon to go on a grand journey and live a life of luxury with the country's elite, once she was cured of her affliction, of course. Sophie smiled and nodded. There was no doubt in her mind that if

Korynne did marry Yuri and left Tempest Hall with him, whatever remained of her life would not be the rosy picture Marilla had painted.

Sophie laced up the lady's corset as Marilla fussed with her skirts. She'd never worn things like this herself, but it wasn't hard to figure out. She tied it tightly, though not as tightly as Marilla thought she should and had to do it again. Forget trying to rescue her. If she stayed in that contraption for too long, the Phoenix would suffocate.

Once they were finished, the maid took a step back and surveyed their work. "Lovely," she said, beaming. "Perfect for a bride. Oh, how I wish she was in the right state of mind to enjoy her own wedding celebration."

She will be soon, Sophie thought to herself. While she had been doing her makeup, she'd seen a degree of intelligence seep into Lady Korynne's eyes, and she was grateful that the woman had had enough presence of mind to continue playing along.

"There are a few more things we need to get ready, and you'll have a big job to do today, so I need to go over that with you." Marilla smoothed her hair back. "I've got a million other things to do, and the lord prefers pretty young women to serve him anyway, so you're going to have to learn quickly."

Sophie looked up sharply. "Excuse me? Serve Lord Castellus?" Did she dare hope that she would be close enough to the lord to get that ring off his finger?

"Yes, yes," Marilla said, her voice impatient. "Did you think that this was all we were doing?" She shook her head and gathered up the empty potion bottle and the lady's nightgown. "The lord favored Cassandra, lovely girl that she is." Marilla paused, examining Sophie from head to toe. "Hmm, you're a bit thin, dear, but you'll have to do. Oh, don't look like that. It's not what you're thinking. Now come on. We've still got a lot to get done before the feast." She started heading toward the door. "We'll come back for the lady closer to the start of the feast. She'll be fine by herself for a few hours."

Korynne was, in fact, sitting on the bed again and staring serenely forward. When Marilla huffed and turned away, the lady's eyes found Sophie's. Her intense stare was unnerving. Her face showed no emotion, and Sophie hoped she understood that she was here to help.

She had no choice but to follow the maid as she left the tower room. But she glanced back at the Phoenix, who never took her eyes off her as Marilla shut the door behind them.

TWENTY-TWO

"I'm far too old to be doing this," Turin muttered. "I'm not a squire anymore." He set down the potato he'd just finished peeling and sighed. His hands felt like they had a fine layer of dirt on his fingers from the potato skins. Turin glanced over at Khalil. The other man seemed focused on what he was doing, scrubbing away at the plates in the washbasin.

Covertly, the knight looked over at Dalia. She worked furiously, going back and forth between adding spices to a large pot on the wood-fire stove and basting a large roast boar in the stone oven. Three other women were working on various tasks—one rolling dough, another chopping vegetables, and the last filling decanters with wine from a large barrel. Other servants filtered in and out of the kitchen, picking up serving trays and goblets and depositing used dishes into the pile that Khalil was cleaning. None of them were paying attention to him.

Turin scooted his stool closer to Khalil and leaned over. "We can't just sit here all night," he said in a low tone. "Do you think Sophie has found out where Rhyn is being held?"

Khalil didn't say anything. The blindfold hid his eyes, but it didn't matter. No expression at all crossed the younger man's face. Turin was beginning to doubt that Khalil heard him when he whispered, "Sophie will come through. Just have faith."

Turin frowned. The Khalil he knew didn't trust easily, but it seemed that the little wizard had somehow gotten through his defenses. Sophie was wrong about him, Turin was sure of it. Helping her wasn't just another job to Khalil. Turin suspected the other man's feelings were far more complicated than even he was willing to admit.

While the knight wanted to point all this out to Khalil, now was not the time.

"Fine," he allowed, "but we need to get out of here to do our part."

Khalil's mouth pressed into a tense line, and Turin wanted to slap him. That was the face he always made when he was annoyed, and it frustrated the knight. This wasn't Turin's first time doing this. Well, it was his first time going in disguise to rescue someone from a fortress, but he'd done plenty of escort missions. Granted, sneaking around was what Khalil was good at, but that didn't mean that Turin wasn't capable as well.

"Sometimes, you have to think of a solution yourself," Khalil said, his voice flat and emotionless. He put the towel he was using down and stood. Dalia looked at him, proving herself more observant than Turin had originally assumed. "Is there something you need?"

"The privy," Khalil said flatly and reached out a hand, taking a few unsteady steps until his fingers connected with a wall. He seemed clumsy and ill-footed. Turin almost asked if he was drunk, but he bit his tongue at the last moment. He was so used to the capable man Khalil was, at times, Turin forgot that to those that didn't know him, he was just another blind man. Now, he was downplaying his capability for the benefit of everyone around them. Khalil moved with care, feeling his way over to the door that led deeper into the castle and pulling it open slowly.

Dalia dismissed him with a snort, shaking her head and going back to what she was doing. She muttered something to herself that Turin couldn't hear over all the other noise.

Khalil turned his head back toward Turin before disappearing into the corridor beyond, the door swinging shut behind him.

Great. Now he had to figure his own way out of here.

While Turin was trying to think of an excuse to get out from under Dalia's watchful eye, the cook and her helpers pulled the roast boar out of the oven and began carving it into smaller pieces. "Hurry it up," she snapped. "The lord will have already been seated by now, and you know he doesn't like to wait."

Sensing an opportunity, Turin jumped up. "I can take it out to the great hall, miss. There aren't many potatoes left, and that looks heavy."

Dalia pursed her lips in a way that reminded him very much of Khalil, looking at him like he was a child who had spoken out of turn. Turin shrunk in on himself a little but managed to keep the pleasant smile on his face. The head cook reminded him of the seneschal back at Griffin's Bluff. She was formidable as well.

The woman narrowed her eyes at Turin, then, after a few moments, sighed and said, "Very well. I can't spare anyone anyway. Are you sure you can lift it yourself?"

In answer, Turin lifted the platter the roast was resting on with one hand. It weighed more than he expected, and his muscles strained to keep it aloft, but he thought he hid it well.

Dalia raised her eyebrows at his display. She seemed impressed, and Turin allowed himself a broader grin. He couldn't help it.

She returned the smile. It made her look younger. "All right, all right. You don't need to show off to this old woman." She pointed to a pile of folded clothing in the corner of the room. "Change your shirt first. You're covered in sweat and dirt."

At her words, Turin looked down at himself. His tunic was indeed covered in water, sweat stains, and potato starch. With a nod, he shuffled over to the pile and fished out a clean tunic that looked to be about the right size and pulled off the dirty one. There was suddenly the feeling of eyes on him, and Turin glanced over his shoulder.

Every person in the kitchen was staring at him, even Dalia. At first, he didn't know what they were looking at, then it struck him. They were watching *him*. Turin was a knight in his late twenties and in peak physical condition. He was used to being around others like him, but even so, he knew he was handsome. Sometimes, he forgot how other people reacted to that. Feeling his face flush, he turned away from them and yanked the clean tunic over his head.

By the time Turin turned back around, all the cooks had gone back to their tasks, but he caught them giving him covert glances as he passed. He lifted the roast with both hands this time as Dalia placed the final touches on it, brushing it with butter and placing a few herbs for garnish. It smelled heavenly, and he could feel his mouth watering.

"Take this out into the great hall," she said, taking a step back and looking at the platter. She nodded in satisfaction. "The lord will be seated at the head table along with his family and the Golistins."

He took a deep, steadying breath before leaving the kitchen. There was no turning back now.

Turin's hands were steady, but he couldn't ignore the sick feeling in his stomach. It wasn't the mission that had him so on edge. Coming face to face with his family after so long had not been something the knight ever thought he'd have to do, but they were here now. If he had to go through with it to save Rhyn, then that was what he would do. He prayed to Samar that they wouldn't recognize him.

The great hall was grandly decorated, with blue and silver banners lining the walls and jewels hanging from the chandeliers. People rushed past him as he entered, servants dressed in dark-blue velvet carrying empty pitchers and trays. The villagers at the back of the room talked and drank, the women throwing glances at the head table with dreamy expressions on their faces and whispering behind their hands, while the men ate and laughed. A few of them looked at the roast with open hunger, but no one spoke to him. They seemed to know where he was going and did nothing to hinder his progress.

The noble guests showed him even less attention. They didn't so much as glance his way as they sipped from silver goblets. He was a servant and beneath their notice. High-born ladies spoke to each other, some with their mouths hidden by fans. Others looked pointedly at the villagers with scowls on their precisely painted faces, but none said anything loudly enough for him to hear over the din of voices and music.

Turin spotted the musicians with whom they had arrived in a corner near the head table. Minette and Troy played away on harp and lute while the others were nowhere to be seen. The two performers were focused on what they were doing and didn't seem aware of what was happening around them. With everything that could have gone wrong, they had been very lucky so far, and meeting the troupe on the road had been part of that. There was a part of him that felt guilty since the musicians had vouched for Turin and the others, but he wouldn't let that get in the way of what needed to be done.

Even though he'd been expecting it, it was a shock to his stomach when he finally turned his eyes on his family. As expected, they were seated at the head table no more than twenty feet in front of him.

Alexi looked stunned as he spotted Turin and quickly grabbed his goblet to cover his expression from their mother, with whom he'd been speaking a moment before. *What in the hells am I doing?* Turin berated himself as he approached. It had been stupid for him to volunteer for this. He'd been so desperate to get out of the kitchen that he hadn't thought this through. Of all the idiotic ideas he'd ever had, this was by far the worst.

Lady Golistin, sensing her eldest son's distress, followed his gaze. She looked much as she had when Turin was a child, if perhaps a little harsher in her features. She was still haughty in demeanor, but she also looked wiser and sharper than she had in the past. Having to make her way in life without the help of her husband's family must have been a difficult transition for her. Her bright green eyes followed Turin, and he prayed that she assumed Alexi was just hungry and took no more meaning from his expression.

Nearly as disturbing as the sight of his family, Rhyn sat at the head table with Lord Castellus on her right and Yuri on her left. She looked like she had on the day of the first feast—beautiful in her long stunning gown that was a delicate shade of green, her blonde hair styled impeccably, and hazel eyes with a distant look that made it seem as if she was far away from everything happening around her. He tried not to stare, but her gaze was unsettling. It was as if she was looking through him as he approached their table, his hands laden with the roast boar.

To Turin's relief, Yuri wasn't paying attention to him, instead speaking quietly to a red-haired woman who was filling his goblet. The woman looked up, and Turin started, faltering in his step before catching himself.

Sophie spared him only a momentary glance before turning back to his brother, smiling at whatever he was saying. She moved to pull away from him, but Yuri caught her arm.

His brother leered, and his mouth moved, but the room was too loud, and Turin was too far away to hear what was said. Rhyn didn't seem to notice that Yuri was speaking at all and continued to stare ahead, but he thought he saw her eyes narrow when he stepped into her line of sight.

Turin could hardly believe it. They'd needed to find Rhyn and figure out a way to get close to her, and now Sophie was in the perfect position to not only help her but also to take the ring from Lord Castellus once an opportunity arose. He hoped Khalil was having as much luck with the dungeon.

He risked a glance at his father, Lord Golistin. What Turin remembered of his father was a man in his middling years, still strong of frame and handsome like his sons. Now, twenty years later, his father looked even sterner than he had before, and there were far more lines on his face than Turin remembered. He wore fine clothes similar to how the nobles in Morigael dressed and was still what some would consider a good-looking man even in his advancing age, but he was thinner, and the similarities to his brother, the king of Morigael, were much more pronounced than they had been before. In fact, Turin could almost have mistaken him for the king himself at first glance. They were only a few years apart, but after childhood, such a small age gap hardly mattered.

The biggest difference between the two men had always been in their eyes. His uncle's were full of life and laughter, while his father's were cold and calculating.

As if he could hear Turin's thoughts, Lord Golistin looked up from his goblet, and their eyes met for just a moment before Turin looked away, heart pounding. He could feel the man's eyes on him as he approached.

When Turin reached the table, he set the boar down harder than he'd intended to, rattling the plates and goblets on the table. He bowed deeply. "Congratulations, my lord and lady," he said through clenched teeth.

If he wasn't doing a good job of hiding his disgust, Yuri didn't notice. He waved Turin off, his focus still on Sophie. She seemed to be listening to him intently as he spoke, and she smiled at him, her eyes focused on the table. To Turin's eyes, she looked like she was playing the pompous oaf while he flirted shamelessly in front of all these people.

Anger over his brother's behavior drowned out his fear of discovery. Turin may have been four years younger than Yuri, but he had undergone intensive training to become a knight. There was no doubt in his mind that he could overpower his brother in an even contest. He briefly imagined reaching across the table and dragging the idiot away kicking and screaming. It would be so satisfying… and insanely stupid. They'd already had one person thrown in the dungeon. Best not to make it two.

With an effort, he ripped himself away from the head table.

Now that he was in motion, every muscle in his body wanted him to leave the great hall as fast as he could, but he kept himself steady as he bowed to the nobles sitting at the head table and backed away. Once he was far enough to politely turn his back on them, he hurried to the doors that led back out into the corridor, ignoring another servant who tried to hand him a pair of empty pitchers. There was no one in the hallway. Most of the food had already been brought out while he'd been carrying the roast, and the other servants would be busy pouring drinks for the guests. He wouldn't be alone for long, but he only needed a few moments.

Turin leaned an arm against the wall, giving himself a chance to breathe. Thoughts swam around in his mind, and it was an effort just to try to get any of them to come through clearly. He chastised himself again, repeating in his mind that of all the stupid ideas he'd ever had, that was by far the dumbest. From afar, Turin might look like any other servant, but put him next to his brothers, and the resemblance would have been clear to anyone paying attention. His only saving grace was that there was little chance of anyone putting together a disowned prince from two decades ago and a random servant in a foreign country.

No one recognized him—not his parents and definitely not Yuri. He should have been relieved, but one fact surfaced that he couldn't shake. Alexi had. He had known who Turin was.

But how had he done that? It didn't make any sense. Turin had been a child the last time they'd seen each other, but, somehow, his brother had known his face immediately. He hadn't even asked if the servant standing in front of him was his brother or not. Alexi had been sure of it from the start. Why hadn't he considered that earlier? Turin had been so focused on the mission and then distracted by what Eolisti had done that he was missing obvious truths.

"Dimitri!"

On a reflex he didn't know he had anymore, Turin looked over his shoulder, back at the entrance to the great hall. His eyes fell upon his mother, holding her skirts and breathing as hard as if she'd been running. She looked regal even when out of breath, the pink spots on her cheeks the only cracks in the facade.

Turin's brain screamed at him to get out of there, but his legs wouldn't move. He stared at her as she smoothed out her skirts, regaining her composure with every step she took toward him.

Finally, he found his voice. "Is there something you need, my lady?" He tried to sound calm as he turned to her. "I would be happy to fetch some more drinks for you and the lords."

She stopped in front of him, reaching out a hand to cup his face. It took all his willpower not to back away from her.

"Dimitri," she said with more tenderness than he'd ever heard from her before. "Don't play games with me. I know it's you. Do you think I would not recognize my own son?" Her thumb brushed over his cheek. "You may have been only a child when you were taken away from me, but I would know your face anywhere." Tears formed in her eyes, and her mouth twitched.

All the emotions he thought he'd buried years ago came surging back up, and just like that, he was eight again, watching his parents decide his fate through a crack in the door. He had been so devastated when they had said his name. His parents had offered him up as a hostage without a second thought. The son they didn't want.

No, he thought, *that part of your life is over. Uncle Markos loves and trusts you, and this woman betrayed him.*

Turin took a deep breath through his nose and reached up, gently removing Lady Kristanya's hand from his face. "I'm sorry, my lady, but I think you have mistaken me for someone else."

She pursed her lips, her eyes narrowing and the emotion vanishing from her face. The lady took a step back from him, looking him up and down. "You've grown up well," she said, her voice tight. He'd upset her, and when she was upset, she got angry. That was the mother he remembered. "The reports don't do you justice."

"Reports?" Turin asked despite himself. "What reports?"

"Are you really so naive? Of course, your father and I have been keeping track of your progress." She snorted derisively. "You seem to have fallen for your uncle's lies more readily than I would have hoped."

Heat crept up Turin's neck, and he set his jaw. "His lies?" he said, all pretenses forgotten. "You and father tried to *murder* him!" he hissed. "The only lies here are yours, Mother. What did you expect would happen? That he would laugh it off, and everyone would forget about it?"

Her cheeks flushed. "We were doing what was best for the kingdom! Markos is a weak fool. Your father would have served the kingdom much more ably." Her hands balled into fists. "We were so close, but now look at us. Cast out of our home and betrayed by our own son."

"Betrayed? That's rich coming from you."

Her eyes widened in shock and anger. "How dare you speak to me that way! You have no idea what we have endured to get here. The embarrassment of crawling to Tanalinian noble houses to beg for favors. Rebuilding our wealth and making deals with the common folk."

Turin laughed bitterly. "Embarrassment?"

"You will not—"

"I am not an obedient child anymore, *my lady*." He said the title like an insult. "I am a knight and beholden only to Markos Caelius Golistin, the rightful king of Morigael." He stood straight and tall like a true knight, towering over the woman before him by more than a foot. She seemed small compared to his memories of her.

His proclamation rang out over his mother's stunned silence. The words drove a wedge between them as surely as if he'd drawn his sword on the lady.

Despite the tense silence, Turin wanted to laugh. He'd dreamed of meeting his parents again and what he'd say to them. But now that it was happening, he could not have chosen his words more perfectly.

The lady had started trembling. With vindictive pleasure, he realized he'd hurt her, much as she'd hurt him all those years ago. Now she had some idea of how he'd felt when she and his father abandoned him.

He had little time to gloat, however. With a quick motion and a flash of steel, Lady Kristanya lunged forward, pressing a knife to his throat, and driving him back against the wall.

His head swam as she pressed the blade hard against his skin.

"You will not ruin this day for Yuri," his mother said, her voice a deadly hiss. "We've worked too hard for this." Her eyes showed no remorse, and Turin knew that she held no love for him anymore, if she ever had. "I have only two sons now."

TWENTY-THREE

"You'll be serving the lady personally today," Anya said as they walked down the grand staircase. "You will stand against the wall between Lady Korynne and Lord Castellus. Usually, Cassandra would be doing this, but, well," she sighed. "Just try not to spill anything on the lord, and you should be fine." Marilla had Sophie change into a dark-blue dress before going back to get Korynne. The maid said that all the servants attending the head table would be wearing this color and that it would help her blend in. The velvet was hot, and it showed too much of her bosom for Sophie's taste, but it wasn't nearly as revealing as some of the dresses she'd seen on the noblewomen.

"Shame we can't do anything about that hair," Marilla added as an afterthought. "Covering it is out of the question. Oh well, just don't do anything to make yourself stick out more. We wouldn't want you taking attention away from our beautiful bride."

Korynne's grip was firm on her arm as the mage escorted her to the great hall, but she still gazed blankly ahead. Sophie didn't know what had been in that potion, but it might take some time for the effects to wear off. Or maybe she was pretending that nothing was amiss. If she was acting, she was doing it flawlessly. She walked steadily enough, and Sophie hoped that meant the Phoenix would be able to assist them when the time came to make their escape.

Marilla paused before they reached the large oak doors. "This is as far as I go. Just remember what I said, and you'll be fine. Pick up a pitcher from the table after the lady is seated. *Discreetly*," she emphasized, then smiled at Sophie. "Good luck."

Sophie nodded, swallowing hard as her heart beat loudly in her chest. This was it. They would have no better chance to get Korynne out of the castle. She wasn't in her tower. She wasn't guarded. If the previous two days were any indication, everyone would be good and drunk before moonrise. It would have to happen by the end of this feast.

As they entered the great hall, the hum of noise that Sophie heard from beyond the doors died out, and all heads turned to look at Korynne in her gown of green and gold silk. All the guests stood from their seats. Even Lord Castellus got to his feet, watching his daughter and Sophie approach with his cold blue eyes. The silence only intensified the thumping of Sophie's heart. She couldn't keep the blush off her face as she averted her eyes from the noblemen and women, guiding the lady to the head table and helping her take the seat between her father and her fiancé.

People crowded the hall, filling the tables. Sophie thought at least a hundred, many more than she'd seen around the castle until now. The men and women were all dressed in fine silk, lace, and velvet, with feathers in their caps and jewels in their hair. Sophie spotted Elindiir, his doublet and half cape less ostentatious than those of the other men around him, but still elegant, nonetheless. The villagers who had made the journey to the castle were seated closest to the main exit near the back of the hall. There were dozens of them, packed tightly at tables clustered closely together, but the people didn't seem to mind. Most of them were smiling ear to ear, also dressed in their best. Even though their clothing wasn't as fine as the nobles in front of them, Sophie could tell there was no less care taken. As they watched the bride enter, she could almost feel their joy, and their gazes were much warmer than those at the head table.

Once the bride was settled, the guests seated themselves again, but the chatter did not resume. Instead, their gazes shifted to Lord Castellus, who was still standing. As Sophie stepped back to take her place against the wall, he began to speak in a loud, booming voice that echoed across the hall.

"Tonight is the night that we have all been waiting for. In the morning, house Castellus and house Golistin will be bonded together, and our family, with our home being so far in the north, will have new allies in the capital. It is with great honor that I give my blessing on this marriage to the bride and groom and welcome Yuri Golistin into our family." All the guests around them raised their goblets, and there were even shouts of "Hear! Hear!" from the tables where the villagers were seated.

"Please, be merry tonight and have a drink to honor my daughter, Korynne Castellus, and her soon-to-be husband, Yuri Golistin."

Cheers erupted from the mouths of all the guests. As if on cue, servants in outfits the same color as Sophie's dress burst from the entryways, carrying platters of food and drink. They swept through the room in a flurry, depositing the food on the tables and pouring drinks for the nobles. As soon as the wine filled their goblets, guests would raise them to the bride and groom, happening in ripples throughout the room as drinks were filled and consumed. Laughter and chatter filled the room again, and Sophie almost forgot why she was there. All these people seemed so happy, and that made her both sad and angry. It was all a lie.

As soon as the pitchers of wine were set at the head table, the other two women attending the Castellus and Golistin families stepped forward to pour drinks for the lords and ladies. Following their lead, Sophie jumped forward, being extra careful not to let her shaking hands spill a drop.

Music began, and Sophie spotted Minette and Troy playing a soft, happy melody on their instruments. It didn't drown out the noise in the great hall, which was substantial now that everyone had food and drink, but rather seemed to complement it. Sophie had never been to a Western wedding before, and, though less festive, it didn't seem all that different from social gatherings back home.

The bride and groom were seated next to each other, with Lord Castellus to the right of the Phoenix and the Golistins on the other side of Yuri. The nobility were seated near the bride and groom, with the long tables forming a large empty area in the middle of the room.

The commoners in attendance were seated far away from the nobles. The two groups didn't intermix at all, each seemingly trying to ignore the other. Sophie had the impression that the villagers knew they were only invited to attend the feast out of long-standing tradition, but that didn't seem to bother any of them in the least.

She did exactly what Marilla had instructed her to do. Sophie held a pitcher filled with wine and stood a few steps behind where the bride and groom were seated, waiting for either of them to signal that they needed assistance. There was another woman on the other side of Lord Castellus, so she wasn't assigned to him as the maid had indicated, but she was to keep his goblet full, nonetheless.

The atmosphere around the head table, if not joyous like the rest of the room, was at least relaxed. Lord and Lady Golistin seemed content in how the celebration was progressing and murmured between themselves and their sons. Occasionally, Sophie caught a smile or a laugh. The only one who seemed tense was the oldest son, the one Turin had called Alexi. His movements weren't as smooth as the others, and the smile he wore as he spoke to his mother looked strained. He was older than Turin by a few years, but his inky black hair, green eyes, and dignified demeanor reminded her so much of the knight that she couldn't help but stare. Good thing he had his back to her.

On the Castellus side of the table were the lord and a young boy that could only be his son. He seemed cheerful compared to the lord of the castle, who showed little emotion as he sipped his wine. The young boy was full of energy, blatantly pointing at people seated at the other tables and asking his father loudly who they were. He seemed genuinely excited to be here. Sophie hadn't witnessed the other two feasts, so she guessed that he hadn't been allowed to those since he was asking so many questions.

It was hard to see the lord's hands from this angle, and Sophie prayed to the gods that he still wore the ring. She assumed he would want to keep control of his daughter, but Castellus might have given the ring to Yuri Golistin already. If she focused on the wrong man, it would be disastrous. She had to make sure that the groom didn't have it.

Yuri raised his right hand, flicking his wrist forward in a beckoning motion. It took Sophie longer than it should have to realize that was her cue. All she could see were the backs of heads and chairs, so it was hard to tell when the people sitting at the head table needed anything. Stepping forward, she held up the pitcher to fill his goblet, mumbling a soft "excuse me" as she leaned in between Yuri and his father.

The elder Golistin ignored her, but the groom's eyes focused on her.

Yuri reached out as she pulled back, taking her hand in his and holding her there. "You're pretty for a servant," he said with a mischievous grin.

She choked back her disgust at his advance. "You are much too kind, my lord," she replied, flicking her eyes down in what would have seemed a submissive gesture, but she was checking his hands. Part of her was still shocked at his brazenness. Was he really doing this in front of his father and the woman he was supposed to be marrying? Surely, most of the people here didn't know that the lady was being controlled and would think ill of the groom flirting with a woman at least ten years his junior the night before his wedding.

He ran his fingers over her knuckles, turning toward her and leaning an elbow on the table. The smile on his face made Sophie want to strike him, but she instead looked at his other hand, searching for the garnet ring.

Sophie glanced up and, to her surprise, spotted Turin approaching the head table with a platter laden with a roast boar for the nobles. He looked nervous, his gaze sweeping the room before him. They made eye contact, but she didn't dare give any indication that she knew him, not with Lord Castellus so close to her. If she were being honest, she felt relieved seeing the knight. If anything went wrong, he'd be there to help.

"Don't worry about her," Yuri said, misinterpreting her gaze. He'd assumed she was looking at Korynne. "She doesn't care if I have a little fun."

"Yuri," came a sharp voice from Sophie's left, and she froze. She'd never heard Lord Golistin speak, and while his voice wasn't as cold as Lord Castellus's, it still sent a chill down her spine.

"Let her go and pay attention to the woman you're betrothed to."

Yuri frowned but did as his father commanded and released her. Judging by how long his eyes lingered, he was reluctant to do so, but he seemed unwilling to disobey his father. Sophie smiled at Lord Golistin and filled his goblet as well, then took a step back from the table.

At least one thing was certain. She hadn't seen any rings on Yuri's fingers, which meant it was still with Lord Castellus.

A clattering drew Sophie's attention as she settled back into her position on the wall. She peered past Lord Castellus's head to see Turin, backing away from the table as he'd set down the roast, a fierce look on his face.

Panicking, Sophie tried to catch his attention, but he didn't have eyes for her. What was he doing? If anyone else saw that look, it was sure to cause trouble.

Luckily, he didn't linger. Turin bowed to the lords and ladies and disappeared back into the crowd. Sophie closed her eyes in relief. Lady Kristanya excused herself after Turin was no longer in sight, but no one said anything about his strange behavior, so she doubted any of the nobles seated at the head table had noticed him. At least he would be close by when she made her move. With the Phoenix here, all she needed to do was get the ring, but how was she supposed to take it from Lord Castellus in front of all these people? She hadn't seen the court wizard yet today, but he could be anywhere, watching his lord from the shadows and waiting for any sign of a threat. Perhaps she should wait for him to use the privy and ambush him there, but for all she knew, one of the guards posted around the room would accompany him.

What was it that Marilla had said? Lord Castellus liked young women to serve him? Well, she'd said "pretty young women," then called Sophie too thin and said she would "have to do." Sophie chewed on her lower lip. If she could get him to talk to her, maybe she'd be able to see if he was wearing that ring. And if not, she would just have to come up with something before the feast was over.

Sophie pulled a few strands of hair out of her bun and then tugged at the already low-cut dress. Finished adjusting her appearance, she watched the servant who was supposed to be attending to the rest of the Castellus family out of the corner of her eye. The young woman with brown hair wasn't paying attention to Lord Castellus, instead chatting animatedly with the boy seated next to him.

Now was her chance. If she could master complicated spells and turn a poisoned potion into a harmless juice, she could do this. Sophie took a deep breath, then stepped forward. She leaned over the table farther than was necessary to fill Lord Castellus's goblet, purposefully brushing against his arm. Sophie gasped in surprise and hoped it was convincing. "I'm sorry, my lord," she simpered as he looked up at her.

He watched her as she went to fill Korynne's goblet. She knew that it would still be full, but it was reasonable to think that a new servant wouldn't know that.

"That's unnecessary," he said, placing a hand on hers and stopping her from pouring. "My daughter doesn't drink very much."

"Oh, I'm sorry, my lord," she giggled nervously. "I didn't know that. I suppose all this wine will be for you then."

His hand remained on hers. "You're the girl from Omer, yes? Forgive me, I can't recall your name."

"Sophie, my lord," she said, looking down at the table. "I do not expect you to remember me, of course. My lord is a very busy man, and I'm just a servant." His hand moved to brush her cheek and tuck those loose strands of hair behind her ear, then he placed his fingers on her chin, turning her head to bring her gaze back to him. His other hand was on the table in front of him but facing in such a way that she couldn't see what the rings he wore looked like.

"Sophie," he repeated her name as his eyes roved over her face. Sophie felt her shoulders tense. She should have come up with a false name to use.

"Where is Cassandra?" the lord asked, pulling his hand back. "Normally, she would be attending me during the feast."

"I'm afraid she's fallen ill, my lord," she answered, remembering Marilla's complaints of the maid drinking too much. "But she'll be back on her feet soon. No need to worry."

Castellus turned in his seat to better look at her and picked up his goblet with the hand Sophie had been trying to examine. "She should take her time to recover. I do hope you'll take up a permanent position in my household once the wedding has passed."

She smiled and hoped it looked genuine. "Thank you, my lord. It would be my pleasure to continue serving you."

He seemed satisfied with that answer, raising his goblet to his lips, and there it was—a weathered ring with a large garnet in its center. She didn't dare reach out with her magic to verify it, not with the court wizard potentially lurking just out of sight, but she was confident it was the same ring that she'd seen before. Now, she just needed to get it from him.

Just as that thought crossed her mind, a man stepped up to the lord's other side. It was the tall man with the angular face and dark hair she'd seen before, and Sophie was immediately grateful that she hadn't tried to use magic. This man was the court wizard.

Their eyes met for a second before Sophie looked away, her fingers squeezing the pitcher she was still holding.

"Excuse me, my lord. I'm sorry to disturb you."

Castellus didn't even spare the wizard a glance. His gaze dipped lower, and she felt heat rise to her cheeks. "What is it, Lucan?"

The court wizard leaned in and whispered something that Sophie couldn't hear.

The expression on the lord's face quickly turned to annoyance. He turned away from Sophie, dismissing her with a wave of his hand. "Where were they found?" he asked as she backed away.

"Near the library, my lord."

"Show me." Lord Castellus got to his feet. "I'll be back in a little while," he said to the boy seated next to him. "Watch over your sister for me."

"Yes, Father," the young lord replied, eyeing Lady Korynne and scooting his chair closer to her. He said something to the lady, but Sophie didn't hear it. All of her attention was focused on Castellus.

Her thoughts raced, and she watched the lord follow the wizard out of the great hall through one of the side doors. She had to have the ring to get the slave anklet off Korynne, and she didn't know when there would be another chance to get it. Sophie looked frantically around the room, searching for Turin, but she couldn't see him.

She cursed under her breath. Of all the times for him to disappear, now was the worst. If she was going to act, it needed to be now. She would just have to trust that Turin would know what to do.

Sophie braced herself, then purposefully spilled the contents of the half-full pitcher of wine down the front of her dress, trying to make it look like an accident. The liquid was cold as it soaked into her clothes, and she let out an involuntary gasp.

Both Yuri and his father glanced over their shoulders at her. She must have looked silly, standing there shivering with wine spilled down her dress.

"F-forgive me for my clumsiness, my lords." She bowed to both of them. "I will return momentarily," Sophie said before rushing to the servants' entrance at the back of the hall, the one she knew led to the second floor. It wasn't guarded during the feast, and she was able to slip out of the great hall with no one paying her any mind.

As soon as she closed the door behind her, she set the pitcher down and ran up the stairs, bursting into the second-floor hall. She needed to find Lord Castellus. This was the only chance they were going to get.

TWENTY-FOUR

The farther from the great hall Khalil moved, the fewer people there were. Even most of the servants were clustered around the ongoing feast, and he could walk the halls of the castle without being stopped and questioned. He was grateful for the distraction and disarray the feast caused. It made his part in this much easier.

The guards were another story. There were surprisingly few of them near the feast keeping watch over the guests, and those ignored him readily enough, but as he went deeper into Tempest Hall, the number of patrols increased steadily in frequency. A few muttered words about needing a privy satisfied the first ones he met, but that excuse would grow less believable the closer he got to the dungeon.

Khalil stood in one of the small alcoves, not unlike the one he and Sophie had shared on their first day here, letting the shadows hide him from the notice of patrolling guards. They sauntered about the corridors, their relaxed steps telling him that they expected no trouble this evening. The intruder had been caught, and now the wedding was proceeding as planned. Their lord was happy. The Anai must have convinced them that she was working alone. At least she could do one thing right.

As soon as the pair of guards passed, Khalil moved, darting from his hiding spot on feet that made no sound on the stone. It had taken him years of training to perfect that, but it had been more than worth it. He moved like a shadow, using the noise of the guards scuffing boots to tell him where they were.

He turned a corner and stopped to listen. The men gave no indication that they'd seen or heard him. There were two more pairs of feet moving in the next corridor, walking away from him. He crept forward, using not just his hearing, but *knowing* that there were fifty paces more to the next turn and three doors in the hall before him and to his right. Flat things were hanging on the walls that he guessed were some sort of paintings or tapestries, and he could almost feel the warmth of the four lamps in their sconces. He didn't know how he knew these things, but he'd learned to trust his instincts a long time ago.

Khalil crept forward, pausing every twenty steps, listening to the sounds that echoed off the stone. The guards in the next hallway had stopped and were chatting casually, armor creaking as they shifted weight from foot to foot.

"...was hoping we would get to have some of that food that they were cooking in the kitchen."

"That's for the guests, not for the likes of us," said a deeper, gruffer voice. "Don't worry. Dalia will have set something aside for us. She always does."

"Sure," the other mumbled. "She always saves us the scraps." They continued talking quietly, remarking on some of the guests they'd seen, while the whiney one complained about how unfair it was for the villagers to attend the feast while they still had to work.

The guards had stopped in the middle of the hall, and there was no way for Khalil to get around them without being seen. He could wait for them to move, but the other patrol behind him would eventually come back this way. He couldn't wait all night. The longer he stayed in one place, the higher the chance he'd be caught.

Khalil took a deep breath through his nose, then stumbled forward, holding on to the wall. He was making so much noise that it was amazing the two guards didn't take note of him until he was almost upon them.

"Where do you think you're going?" the gruff man said. "You're not supposed to be here." His voice echoed off the stone as he spoke loudly to Khalil. His belt creaked as he shifted his weight, getting ready to use force.

"I'm sorry, sir, but I'm lost. I went looking for a privy a while ago, but this castle has so many turns and corridors." Khalil groped at the walls, taking another shuffling step forward as he spoke.

Only then did the guard seem to notice Khalil's blindfold. "Ah, well," the man's posture immediately relaxed, but his voice still sounded suspicious. "You shouldn't be over here. Who is supposed to be watching you?"

"Give him a break, Leo," the other man said. His voice was higher and gave Khalil the impression that he was younger than the other. "He's one of those newly hired servants. The lord hired a few dozen of them to help with the wedding."

"I don't care who he is or that he's blind," the other guard said firmly. "There are lots of others patrolling these halls. How did you get here? Why weren't you stopped?"

The man named Leo wasn't going to let him go. Khalil was sure the other patrols were far enough away that they wouldn't hear an altercation, provided he acted quickly. He was close to them now. "There were no other guards that I ran into. Please, if you can, tell me how to get back to the kitchen. Dalia is probably wondering where I am."

"You're not going anywhere." He turned to the other guard. "Alert the wizard," Leo said. "Get him down here. He wanted to know if we saw anything suspicious."

While the man in charge was distracted, Khalil moved in a flash, lunging forward and seizing the sword hilt at the younger guard's belt, pulling it free. He crouched as the guard swore, and swept the unsuspecting man's legs from under him. The young man toppled to the ground, helmet hitting the stone with a loud *Clang!*

As the other guard took in a breath to sound the alarm, Khalil popped back up and thrust a fist hard into his stomach. The man stumbled back, gasping. Khalil used the moment to kick the one on the ground, being careful to hit hard enough to knock him out, but not so hard that it killed him.

Leo caught his balance. Still gasping from Khalil's gut punch, he fumbled for the sword at his belt. Khalil stepped forward, striking with the flat of his stolen blade and connecting with the man's neck, but it wasn't a solid blow, and the old guard managed to pull his weapon free.

He thrust his sword at Khalil, but the former assassin sidestepped it, then trapped the guard's outstretched arm under his own and twisted sharply. There was a popping sound as the limb was pulled out of its socket. Khalil used the momentum to shove the guard to the ground, pushing his face into the stone to muffle the pained screams.

Khalil pulled Leo's helmet off and brought the hilt of his sword down sharply on the back of the man's head, silencing him. As the hallway fell silent once again, he listened for the sound of anyone approaching, but all he heard was the distant sound of slow and steady boots on stone. Once he was certain that no other guards had heard them, Khalil checked to make sure that Leo was still breathing. He was, and for that, Khalil said a mental prayer of thanks to Samar. These men were just doing their jobs and may not know of their lord's schemes. They shouldn't have to lose their lives for that.

His instincts told him there was a door up the corridor to his right, and he quickly threw the old guard over one shoulder and carried him down the hall. There were no sounds from inside the room, so he carefully opened the door.

Khalil inhaled deeply. Parchment, ink, and leather. Lots of it. This room was filled with books. He could almost see the room in his mind's eye. There was a desk in the far corner and tufted armchairs closer to him, so he placed the guard on the floor behind the chairs that did turn out to be there and hoped it was enough cover to hide the man if someone were to casually open the door. He went back and repeated the process with the younger guard, who he confirmed was also merely unconscious.

Once the guards were out of the corridor, Khalil moved swiftly, still carrying the stolen sword and helmet. There was no telling when those men would wake up and raise the alarm. They were now on a time limit. He could only trust that Sophie and Turin were doing their parts.

Turin would be all right on his own, but Sophie didn't have the experience he and the knight did. He didn't doubt she could find both Rhyn and the ring, capable as she was.

She was his responsibility and he cared what happened to her. If she was caught...

Now was not the time to dwell on what could happen. He needed to focus on his task and have faith that the others would do theirs.

Back in the hallway, Khalil made another turn before he heard the next pair of feet, and he knew this one was guarding the dungeon. Like the others, his movements were lazy and relaxed, thinking that nothing would go wrong tonight. Khalil squeezed the helmet that he held. There were only a few torches in his corridor, so it would be difficult for others to see clearly. That was no problem for him, and it would help hide him from the guard's eyes. Thinking quickly, Khalil used the shadows to cover his movements and threw the helmet as hard as he could down the corridor.

"What in the hells..." the guard muttered under his breath and shuffled down toward where the helmet had landed.

By the time he'd reached it, Khalil had slipped up behind him and swung his stolen sword, hitting the man squarely on his unprotected jaw.

The guard let out a strangled cry and stumbled sideways, spitting out something wet onto the floor, but Khalil brought the hilt of his sword down hard on the back of the man's neck.

The guard crumpled in a heap, and Khalil caught the man's head before it hit the ground. He searched his pockets until he found a ring with six iron keys. There was a magical lock on the door, but without Sophie, the best he could hope for was that the key would bypass it and not alert the court wizard that there was another intruder.

Eolisti sat in the corner of her cell, her back against the wall. All she wanted in the world was to curl up into a ball and go to sleep, but she forced herself to stay awake. The feast was likely in full swing by now, and her companions would be moving around the castle. She had to stay alert to help them in any way she could, though, she didn't know how much help she could be from the dungeon. She tried not to move too much, still aching from the wizard's questioning. He'd used his magic to cause pain, and the guards had kept her awake all night, delivering their own form of torture by making an unholy amount of noise, banging on her bars every time she was about to drift off. It was her own fault. She was stuck here because of her own stupid mistakes.

Maybe she should have been grateful to Elindiir for requesting that she not be severely harmed, but she was too busy being angry at him for betraying her in the first place. She was sure that he could have said something to convince Lord Castellus that the whole incident had been a misunderstanding, but he had let her stay in the clutches of the nobleman and his court mage.

That wizard was a sadist. If the ambassador hadn't said anything, she'd probably be missing fingers and toes by now, if not dead. But no matter what the creep did to her, she wouldn't give up Sophie and the others.

A sound made her look up at the staircase. There was the creak of hinges as the door above opened and closed. Were the guards back to taunt her more? Or was it Lucan, here to ask her again who she was working with?

She gritted her teeth, steeling herself for another round

of torture from that damned wizard. If she got the chance to kill him, she would take it, even if it meant her death.

To her surprise, a familiar shadow moved down the stairs, pausing to listen every few steps, reminding her of a large cat stalking its prey. The moonlight drifting in through the high windows made a hatched pattern on his face, his usual hooded cloak traded in for the blindfold he'd been wearing the past few days. Khalil reached the bottom of the stairs, and Eolisti snapped her jaw closed, causing his head to swivel in her direction.

"What are you doing here?" her mouth said before running it past her brain. It was a stupid question. There was only one possible reason for his presence in this filthy place.

Apparently, Khalil didn't think her question warranted a response. Without a word, he stepped over to her cell and started trying different keys from an iron keyring in the lock.

Great. Now she was the one that needed rescuing from *him*. She would have preferred if Turin had been the one to pull her out of this place. At least the knight would have gotten it over with and berated her while he worked to free her. Instead, it was Khalil with his disapproving frowns and silences.

The lock clicked open, and he pulled on the bars. Eolisti got to her feet a little more slowly than she would have liked and winced at the twinges of pain radiating from her arms and legs, but she was steady on her feet. Khalil stood there for a moment, and just when Eolisti thought he would say something to her, he turned away.

She couldn't take it anymore.

"What's wrong with you?!" she demanded, her hands balling into fists as she stalked forward. "Aren't you mad?

Why aren't you saying anything?" He didn't even seem to be listening to her. "I know it was stupid to come back here last night, but I thought I could make this easier if I found out where the Phoenix was. And I did find out! *And* I almost got away," she reasoned to his back. She couldn't stop the words from pouring out of her mouth. "If you're here, it's not like the plan was messed up, right? I didn't mess up the mission. We can still do this. *It isn't my fault!*"

Khalil whipped back around, his jaw clenched and muscles tense. Her words had finally gotten under his skin. For once, she was grateful she couldn't see his eyes. "Stop thinking about yourself! We are all here risking our lives for this mission! You claim to care about Sophie, but have you considered what your actions have done to her? What you could have caused?"

Eolisti's mouth fell open in indignation, but Khalil continued before she could respond.

"Do you know what would happen if she was caught?" It was a question, but he didn't give her time to respond. Khalil took a step closer to her, and this was the first time she'd considered how much bigger than her he was. "She would be tortured until they discovered her identity. Then her master would come for her. He would drag her back to Zo'rahn and keep her under lock and key, ensuring she would never see sunlight again. He would use her for her abilities, which I might remind you, access an artifact so powerful it can kill in moments." Every word was a blow, and the tightly controlled fury in his voice made her want to shrink away from him. "If *that* is indeed all it does, it will be a mercy, because whatever it does will be solely for that man's benefit. Gods help us all.

"And if he ever figured out how to use it without her, she would be tried for treason and executed. So, I ask you, do you understand what you have done?" Khalil asked the last in almost a whisper.

It would have been better if he'd hit her. Eolisti blinked rapidly, trying to make the tears that had filled her eyes go away. Her stomach clenched with guilt. If Sophie was caught because of her, she would never forgive herself. "If I messed up so badly, why didn't you just leave?"

"I don't like your attitude, but I will not leave you behind." He turned away from her again and started trying the keys in the lock on Winna's cell. "We are your friends. *I* am your friend. Stop making this mission harder than it needs to be." The lock clicked, and the catch on the door released.

Winna tried to sit up but winced and leaned back against the bars again. She had said nothing during their conversation, but she glanced between the blind man and Eolisti.

Eolisti wiped her eyes on her sleeve, rushed past Khalil, and knelt to help the other woman. She managed to get Winna over her shoulder and stood, carrying the injured spy as she silently vowed that she would make this up to Sophie and ensure they all got out of here alive. She had always been suspicious of Khalil, but even so, he was here for her now, risking his life to rescue her from this dungeon.

Guilt knotted in her stomach again, but she pushed it away. Now was not the time. "Let's get out of here. Where are the others?"

CHAPTER

TWENTY-FIVE

Sophie rushed down the corridor, passing nobles whose colorful clothing flashed by without her registering who they were while she searched the decorated halls of the second floor. A few exclaimed in startled outrage. She never paused to bow or curtsey to them in her haste, but most of them were too drunk for the lack of decorum to register. There was only one lord that she was looking for. There was no time for any of the others.

Where was Lord Castellus? The court mage had said that something had happened at the library. Sophie had no idea where the library was in this castle, but it had to be on the second floor somewhere.

She dashed down a passage to the left, moving farther away from the great hall. They hadn't come across a library when she and Khalil had been exploring the castle, but they hadn't been looking for it. They could have passed by without realizing it.

Sophie slowed to turn a corner and caught a flash of a blue and silver brocade doublet coming around from the other side right before she collided with its owner.

The man she ran into stumbled back as Sophie tumbled to the ground, throwing her hands out to avoid hitting her head on the stone. Pain raced up her thigh as her right knee hit the ground, and she winced as she looked up at who she'd run into. "I'm sorry! I wasn't watching where I was..."

She trailed off as Lord Castellus straightened himself. She glanced around, but that wizard was nowhere in sight. He was alone. Whatever he had left the feast to take care of, he must have already seen to it and was making his way back to the great hall. His eyebrows rose as he looked down at her, and Sophie immediately ducked her head. "F-forgive me, my lord. I should have paid more attention to where I was going." Trying to ignore the pain in her knee, she braced herself for the lord's ire.

"Are you all right?" Lord Castellus held out a hand to her, and after only a moment's hesitation, she took it. He clasped her wrist and pulled her to her feet. Castellus looked more surprised than annoyed.

"Yes," she said breathlessly, her run through the castle and subsequent fall finally catching up with her.

Lord Castellus looked her up and down once, not letting go of her wrist. When he spoke, she could smell the drink on his breath. "Are you lost?"

Sophie tried to curtsey, but it was difficult to do with one hand trapped as it was. Her eyes flicked to the ring on the hand that was holding her arm. She could feel the magic in it as it touched her skin. It set her on edge, but she stammered out, "N-no, my lord, I was just going to fetch a new uniform." She gestured down to herself with her free hand.

He glanced down at her dress again, this time registering the dark stain on the front. An expression passed over his face that she didn't recognize, but it made her stomach clench. "I see. Why don't we get you some new clothes then? Come with me," he said and pulled her along, not giving her a choice in the matter. He led her back the way he'd come, not toward the kitchen or the great hall.

Think, Sophie, think! Now that he was here in front of her, she wracked her brain, trying to figure out how to get that ring off his finger without him noticing. She could use a spell, but the court wizard had to have some way to track the lord if magic was used on him. That's what she would have done, at least. It was too much of a risk to try it. She looked around desperately as they walked, trying to formulate some semblance of a plan. This corridor looked familiar, but most of the castle looked the same. Maybe she could knock him out with one of those lamps on the wall.

Before she could decide, Lord Castellus stopped in front of a heavy-looking door. He pulled it open, then, with a tug at her wrist, shoved her inside ahead of him.

In the dim light, it appeared to be a storage room with barrels and shelves grouped at the back, then the door thudded shut, and it all went dark. A lamp on the wall sputtered to life, revealing Castellus closer to her than he had been moments before.

Sophie took a startled step back, knocking over a pile of folded linens as the lord of the castle advanced on her. "I think I can find my way from here," she said, startled at the intensity with which he was gazing at her. Sophie backed even farther away from him until she hit the wall.

Lord Castellus pounced, pinning Sophie against the stone with his body. One arm wrapped around her waist and pulled her hips against his.

"My lord, what are you—?!" Sophie gasped as his lips found hers, and she tasted spiced wine and garlic as his other hand ran down her side. She tried to push him away, but he was much bigger than she, and she wasn't as strong as Eolisti or Turin. He didn't budge an inch. Castellus grabbed at her dress, pulling the skirt up until his hand touched her bare thigh, and she flinched, trying even harder to push him away but with minimal success.

She felt his smile against her lips, then his mouth moved to her neck, and panic settled in. Gasping for air, her brain raced, going back to her training in Zo'rahn. Magic was her most potent weapon, so she did the only thing she could think of. She focused her thoughts and called forth a mental image of a drunkard passed out on the street, and used that to direct her spell. Though she recoiled inwardly, she leaned in and whispered, "Sleep, Lord Castellus..." into his ear. Even a word as simple as "sleep" would immediately bring the thought of slumber to the target's mind, making it that much easier for Castellus to succumb to her spell.

The effect was immediate. One moment, he was reaching under her dress, and the next, the older man slumped against her, his grip slackening. On reflex, Sophie tried to catch him before he fell to the ground, but he was heavy, and she was not very strong. They both slowly slid down the wall, Sophie struggling not to be pinned under the slumbering man. She grunted in exertion as she rolled him off her, then sat on the ground for a moment, trying to catch her breath. What in the hells had just happened? Had the lord of Tempest Hall really just attacked her?

Glancing down at Lord Castellus, her face flushed in anger. How dare he?! Is this why he liked to be attended by "pretty young women"? Any other servant would have found themselves at his mercy.

Sophie scrubbed her lips with her sleeve as she got to her knees. She could still taste the drink that had been on his tongue, and the mere thought of it made her stomach turn. Energy danced on her fingertips. He deserved more than a dreamless slumber. She could make it so he would never be able to drag any woman off ever again.

It took a few deep breaths to calm her mind. She wanted to *hurt* him, but she could not let her emotions get the better of her, not now when they were so close to their goal. Castellus was the lord here, and someone would come looking for him soon. She needed to get the ring and leave before she was caught. It took a few more seconds than it should have for Sophie to keep herself from placing a curse on the bastard, but she was finally able to put her anger aside.

Untangling his right arm, she gently pulled the jewel-adorned ring from his finger. The clunky old ring slid right off, giving her little resistance. Examining it closely, Sophie reached out with her senses and immediately felt the same energy as before pulsing from it.

Khalil had instructed her on how to activate it back at the inn before they'd left for the castle. When Sophie placed it on her middle finger, she was surprised that it fit perfectly, even though Lord Castellus's hands were much bigger than hers. She tried it on a different finger and felt the metal shrink to accommodate the difference. Fascinating.

Now was not the time to get caught up in interesting magical properties.

Sophie focused on the ring and brought the image of Korynne to her mind. Then she touched the ring to her forehead and spoke the words in her head, *I am her master now.* The energy of the item focused into a single line, pulling something on the other end, like the fishing lines the sailors use on the *Westwind*. There was an awareness that hadn't been there moments before, and Sophie thought she knew what the item was doing. The magic it possessed allowed her to sense where the linked anklet was and the general state of the person who wore it. It wasn't that her mind was now linked to Korynne's, but she could sense the fear in the woman as if she were watching someone's shadow through a curtain.

Sophie's mouth twisted in disgust. The woman's own father could feel his daughter's pain this whole time and had still gone on with this charade. Where was the respected nobleman that the villagers had spoken of? How could someone like that treat his own family this way?

"You can't hurt her anymore," she said and briefly considered cursing him again but reasoned that would only cause more trouble for them. She didn't know what laws were in place here for wizards, but back in Zo'rahn, there were harsh consequences for those who lashed out with unsanctioned magic, ranked wizard or not. The last thing they needed was the entire country of Tanalin looking for her because she'd killed or injured some high noble. Even if she really wanted to.

"His loss of face will have to be punishment enough," she muttered to herself as she got to her feet. "Time to get out of here." Hopefully, Khalil had gotten to Eolisti and Winna by now. She needed to get as far from Lord Castellus as she could. Her spell would only last a few minutes.

Sophie picked her way carefully over the linens and cleaning items that had fallen during the struggle, glancing back over her shoulder one last time before leaving. Castellus was sleeping peacefully on the ground, curled around a bucket of clean rags. Maybe the wine would keep him asleep even after her magic wore off, but she couldn't count on it. She had to hurry.

The corridor was empty as she closed the storage door behind her. Good. That meant that no one had seen them.

Just as she was about to turn back toward the great hall, the hairs on the back of her neck stood up. Her skin tingled as she spun around and came face to face with Lucan, the court wizard, materializing before her out of thin air.

Sophie jumped back, almost falling again, but, this time, managed to catch her balance. The wizard's small, piercing eyes looked even more ominous up close, with his focus solely on her. Longing to turn and run from that gaze, she instead forced herself to take a deep breath and school her expression into one of bewilderment. Why would he be sneaking up on a servant, using an invisibility spell no less? Sophie had only sensed his magic at the last moment, so her surprise had been genuine. She could only pray that he hadn't seen the lord push her into that storage room.

"Girl," he began, his voice sharp and cold. "What are you doing? Where is Lord Castellus?"

"I don't know—"

He sneered at her. "Don't you lie to me. I saw him go this way with you. Where is he?"

The panic that had settled in her stomach at seeing the wizard threatened to climb up her throat, but she forced herself to try to look embarrassed. "T-the lord was a bit drunk, you see," she began, her fingers working nervously on the hems of her sleeves. "He passed out right in front of me," which was true. "I think he just needs to sleep it off for a bit. I'm sure he'll be fine." Sophie laughed, but it sounded forced even to her own ears. She looked around. They were still alone in the hallway.

"Well, I should get back to the feast." She turned her back on him, trying her best not to drop all pretense and flee as fast as she could. "I'm sure the Golistins are wondering what's taking me so long."

Before she could take more than a step, Lucan snatched at her arm, making him the third person to grab her wrist today.

His cold gaze choked her protest before it could leave her throat. "Tell me, if what you say is true, why do you have the lord's ring?" He took a menacing step toward her, as he pulled her closer. "And why do I smell magic on you?"

Without thinking, Sophie twisted her wrist and yanked her arm away horizontally, breaking his grip in a move she'd practiced with Khalil. Then she focused her energy and released a concentrated blast of air at his chest with her other palm, sending the court wizard staggering backward and away from her. The shock on his face told her that he hadn't been expecting that, but Sophie didn't stick around to see what he would do.

She turned and ran.

TWENTY-SIX

Lady Kristanya pressed the blade of the dagger harder against Turin's throat, preventing him from moving without cutting himself. "Don't make me do this, Dimitri." Her hand was steady, and her voice told him that she would not hesitate to kill him if he tried to escape. "Let this wedding happen and go back to Morigael."

"Just what are you going to do to Lady Korynne once Yuri marries her?" he asked while desperately trying to think of a way to get out of this situation. It wouldn't be difficult to overpower her, but this was his mother. He couldn't use the force he would with any other combatant. "You can't keep her drugged forever. Someone is eventually going to notice and report this to the emperor."

She sneered. "Is that why you're here? To rescue the princess like a good little knight? I thought Markos might have sent you to stop us from securing an alliance with Castellus, but I guess that's just a happy coincidence for him. Or maybe he thought he'd kill two birds with one stone. Get the girl and diminish our standing here. Force us to continue begging for scraps from these wretched Tanalin lords. I was a princess before Markos took that away!"

Turin balled his fists. "The king doesn't care if you amass more power here! Is that what all this is about? Trying to regain your old status?" Even as he spoke, he searched for any escape, any wavering from the woman before him. He had to get away and help Rhyn and Sophie. They might need him, and he was stuck out here, being threatened by his own *mother*.

Suddenly, there was a rumbling noise, and the stones of Tempest Hall shook. Lady Kristanya, for all her focus, lost her balance for a split second, and Turin took the chance to knock her hand away. There was a hot pain in a thin line on his neck, but he didn't think the cut was deep. The dagger skittered across the stones and away from them, out of reach.

She let out a howl of rage and leaped at him, clawing at his eyes with her nails. Turin grabbed her wrists, keeping her hands away from his face. He could hear shouting coming from the great hall, and he prayed that no one could hear them over whatever commotion was happening. His eyes darted around the corridor, looking for something, anything that could help him, but this was a servant hall and, thus, free of adornments. The last thing he wanted was to hurt her, but he would if he had to. Almost two decades since he'd seen his mother, and at their first meeting, she was trying to kill him?! Turin thought he had outgrown the ability to be wounded by her actions, but he'd been wrong.

Turin dragged Lady Kristanya away from the entrance to the great hall and pinned her against a wall closer to the kitchen. He grimaced at what had to be done while she struggled against him, crying out in the effort of it. The knight slammed the woman against the stone behind her once, twice, until she went limp in his arms.

One hand kept her upright while the other fumbled at a door to his left. Finally getting it open while balancing his mother's unconscious form, Turin looked down at her. He had never seen her like this before. She had been a little distant when he was young, but she had still cared for him when he'd been sick and kissed his forehead before she'd tucked him into bed at night. He felt a pang in his chest. Where had that woman gone?

Turin unceremoniously shoved her inside the privy and slammed the door behind her. He brought a fist down hard on the knob, breaking it so that hopefully, it would not open from either side. It wouldn't hold the noblewoman for long, but he prayed he had bought enough time to get Rhyn away from his brother.

The dagger lay where his mother had dropped it, and Turin quickly retrieved it, tucking it in his belt before he made his way back to the great hall. With any luck, no one would come to check on her for a while. Once back with the rest of the guests, he could pick up a serving tray and blend in with the other servants. He would need to make his way back to the head table but would have to keep to the edge of the room. If his mother had recognized him, he feared his father and Yuri would as well. Perhaps they already had.

He slipped through the entrance, careful to make sure he was not seen, but he shouldn't have bothered. Everyone was too distracted to notice him.

The music had stopped, and a few guests had left their seats. Nobles and villagers alike talked loudly and looked around nervously, disturbed by the rumbling of the castle walls moments before.

Turin moved behind a group of villagers, eyeing the

head table through the chattering men and women. Yuri, Alexi, and his father were still in their seats, talking among themselves. Alexi looked anxious, but Yuri was as smug as ever, seeming not to care about the commotion going on around them, laughing as he said something to their father, who wore a serious look as he watched the reactions of the other noble lords and ladies. Rhyn was still seated, gazing forward, but Lord Castellus was gone, and so was Sophie. Her bright red hair would make her stand out even here, but he did not see her in the great hall at all.

Turin moved behind the next group of people, staying against the wall behind the seated guests and picking up a nearly empty platter that still held a few glossy pastries from a nearby table. He smiled at the noble guests and offered up his food, but they took no notice of him. There was no time to think about where the young wizard had gotten off to. She could take care of herself.

Just as he was about to move up to the long table again, Lord Golistin's gaze locked on him. As their eyes met, Turin was reminded of his father in his prime, teaching him fencing as a child, sunlight shining through his raven-black hair as the older Golistin walked his son through the same steps that his tutors had shown the boy. He'd been a good teacher, and they'd laughed together as he allowed Turin to best him. It was the fondest memory he had of his father.

Recognition flashed over his father's face as his gaze lingered. Turin willed his legs to move, but he was frozen in place by the overwhelming memory of happier times. Lord Golistin's face seemed to soften for just a moment before his expression hardened. His lips moved with words that Turin could not hear, but he could have sworn the word he spoke was "Dimitri." The knight forced himself forward, ripping his gaze from his father's and abandoning the platter of pastries and all sense of stealth. Weaving around servants and guests, he hurried toward the head table. Would he be able to get to Rhyn before his father dragged her away?

The next time he could see his father through the crowd, the older man's hand was on Yuri's arm, and he was speaking into the younger man's ear. Yuri frowned as his eyes scanned the crowd. Two guards were posted by the head table, and Lord Golistin motioned for one of them to come closer. *Shit.*

Turin quickened his pace to a run, but before he could gain more than a few steps, the doors to the great hall slammed open.

CHAPTER
TWENTY-SEVEN

The blast of brilliant blue energy missed Sophie's head by inches, shattering the stone behind her and sending shockwaves through the castle. The force of it made her stumble, but she managed to stay on her feet, running as fast as she could toward the great hall. The court wizard was on her heels, cursing when his attack missed. He may have had the upper hand at first, but Sophie was faster than he was.

Startled screams rang out ahead of her. A few of the guests that had been loitering in the halls looked around to see what the commotion was, shocked by the sudden shaking of stones. She dodged between them deftly, all semblance of propriety abandoned. There were a few more indignant gasps as she scurried past, but the ruse was over now. Sophie was no longer a servant employed by the lord of this castle.

She was a wizard and a damn good one.

Sophie created an invisible step in the air and used it to jump over a lady whose voluminous skirts blocked her way. Then she used more power to soften her landing, not breaking stride. Risking a glance over her shoulder, she caught a glimpse of Lucan far behind her, getting caught up in a sea of silk and jewels as guests demanded to know what was happening. She allowed herself a small triumphant smile. The court wizard wouldn't dare risk harm to the noble guests of his master. She didn't feel good about using them as a shield, but her priority was to get back to the others as quickly as possible.

A few of the nobles stared at her in slack-jawed amazement as she passed. Sophie ran down the main staircase and onto the ground floor, ignoring the shouts of the guards. One tried to grab her, but he was too slow. She headed to the double doors of the great hall, using another gust of wind to throw them open.

She burst into the room, looking around frantically. Many of the guests that had been seated stood, trying to get a good look at her over the heads of their peers. Yuri Golistin and Korynne were still at the head table. The lordling rose to his feet, staring at her with his mouth agape. The same expression was on the faces of the guards near the head table. Rhyn did not stand, but the dazed look in her eyes was gone. She seemed to know exactly where she was and what was happening around her. No one seemed to notice the shift in the bride's demeanor—not even the senior Lord Golistin, only a few feet away from the lady. No one was looking at Korynne Castellus.

Everyone was staring at Sophie.

"The feast is over!" she shouted to the stunned crowd. "You all need to leave!" She had a bad feeling that violence was imminent and the fewer people in proximity to that, the better. Sophie looked around. Turin was nowhere to be seen. Where could he be?

No one moved at her warning. It must have been quite a

sight—a servant throwing open the large double doors of the great hall with the strength of a giant and telling them all to leave. Sophie almost laughed at the absurdity of it. While her mind raced through her options, she finally spotted Turin out of the corner of her eye. He was moving swiftly toward the head table, weaving through the crowds of nobles who had jumped up from their seats when she'd rushed in. Their eyes met, and he nodded.

Right, he needed a distraction—*more* distraction.

Before she could think of anything specific, the tingling sensation of a spell being cast nearby washed over her, and instinctively she threw up a shield of air and invisible force behind her. There was a bright flash of light, and a few people cried out as a ball of red-hot fire hit her shield, flames dancing and threatening to envelop it before extinguishing.

Lucan stepped into the great hall, a look of murder on his face as his breath came hard. His dark hair was disheveled and was at odds with his pristine gray doublet. The villagers near him backed away, giving him room to approach. Sophie turned to face the wizard, putting the head table in her peripheral, but she couldn't see Rhyn or Turin past the guests who had risen to their feet. She prayed that no one would be paying attention to them.

The court wizard threw another bolt of fire at her, but her shield still held. Lucan scowled and waved his hand. The rug under her feet quivered. Sophie only had a moment's warning before it bucked, throwing her to the ground and sliding her forward toward the waiting wizard. She kicked at the rug as it tried to wrap around her and rolled off of it. Regaining her feet, she used her shield as a wall, shoving it at Lucan and pushing him away from her.

He struggled with the force of her shield, drawing sigils

in the air that she recognized as an attempt to ground out her magic. Sophie didn't give him time to finish them. She threw one arm into the air, enchanting a few of the strips of cloth hanging from the ceiling, then pointed at Lucan. They broke free of the string and crystals keeping them aloft and raced toward the struggling man, attempting to bind his hands and legs while he tried to tear apart Sophie's shield.

Lucan grunted in frustration, and Sophie felt it as he finally broke through her spell and called more fire to burn away the cloth that harried him. She watched him closely, hands out in front of her, preparing to cast again to counter whatever he did.

Despite their exchange, the older wizard took the time to straighten his clothes and hair. He faced her confidently, regaining his composure from their mad chase through the castle. "You're in way over your head, girl. You're strong, I'll give you that, but something tells me that you never finished your training, did you?"

"I'm strong enough to beat *you*," she taunted. She needed to keep the wizard's focus on her, and not what Turin was doing. If he could get Korynne out of here while everyone was distracted, they might still be able to pull this off. She licked her lips. What would Eolisti say in this situation?

"Lucan. That's your name, right? What's wrong? You can't handle one little untrained apprentice?"

Then, he did the one thing she hadn't expected. He grinned. "You can't even comprehend how much trouble you're in. Trying to kidnap a lady of noble birth in a country you don't even call your home? You'd be lucky to make it to the gallows." He crossed his arms, surveying her. "But there's more, isn't there? I heard the lord say you were from Omer." He tilted his head to one side in a quizzical manner before continuing. "But I don't think that's correct. Your accent is not quite right for you to be Omeran. No," he said with a grim smile, "I think you're from Zo'rahn."

The bottom dropped out of her stomach. How could he possibly have guessed that? Omer and Zo'rahn shared a border, and their people traded frequently, so they sounded very similar to someone foreign to that area. How could this wizard from across the sea know *exactly* what her people sounded like?

Lucan's grin widened at the look on her face. "I received a message from one of my contacts there. A young apprentice from the household of one of the Viziers went missing a few months ago." He took a step closer, and Sophie instinctively backed away. The people around them had fallen silent, watching the confrontation with terrified expressions.

"And we captured an Anai, who also spoke with an unfamiliar accent, trying to get to the princess. She'd claimed to be working alone, but the maids told me that she'd been seen dancing in the courtyard with a red-haired girl who had a similar accent, and I remembered there's a forest in Zo'rahn where Anai live, not Omer."

"You don't know what you're talking about," Sophie growled. She gathered power again, ready to throw up another shield. He kept approaching, and she continued backing away but was running out of room. She wasn't far from the villagers now. "I'm not who you think I am." She scanned the crowd again and, this time, found Turin. He had pulled Korynne away from the Golistins without them noticing and was heading toward the door at the back of the hall.

"Don't I? I'm sure your master would be interested to know where you are. Maybe he'd even come to fetch you himself. I'm sure the lord would be happy to sell you back to him." He held out his hands as if he was offering her some grand bargain. "You needn't wait for your Vendarii locked up in the dungeon. Just turn yourself over to me and tell me who you are working for. I promise I'll be gentle."

That almost made her laugh. "Like you were gentle with Winna?" When he didn't respond, she continued. "She looked to be at death's door before I healed her. I've seen your methods," she growled.

"How dare you judge me as you commit the same crimes?!" His grin had disappeared and was replaced with a glare. "Your reckless actions will—"

Another door behind her slammed open, cutting off whatever the wizard was saying. Thinking it to be the guards or some other assailant, Sophie whipped around to see Lady Golistin emerge into the great hall, her hair askew and her makeup smeared. Her eyes were wide, and she had a thunderous look as she glanced first at Sophie and Lucan, then behind the mages.

"Stop them!" the woman screamed, pointing directly at Turin and Korynne. All heads turned to the front of the room as Turin, now carrying Korynne, reached the door behind the dais.

As a guard lurched forward at Lady Golistin's words, Sophie thrust a hand toward her friends, using magic to create a buffer between the knight and the people around him. The nobles near the head table stumbled backward, looking around to see what had pushed them, and it looked as though the guard ran into an invisible wall. They wouldn't be able to approach Turin. The knight could make his escape, but that spell wouldn't hold if she had to keep fighting Lucan. She needed one more distraction. A big one.

While Lucan stared at Lady Golistin, Sophie raised her

palms toward the ceiling, calling for the memory of the storm from the other side of the Silver Sea. The spell had been cast by the ones pursuing her, and it had almost torn the *Westwind* apart. Lightning had struck the deck, setting it aflame, and had only been stopped because she'd gotten lucky and deflected a strike back at its caster.

A spell like this was dangerous. Sophie had never practiced it and had only seen it cast from afar, but it was effective, and she knew that she was strong enough to pull it off. Pouring power into conjuration, she swayed and stumbled as the spell took shape, and the ceiling above roiled with dark clouds. A wave of exhaustion rolled over her. This was taking more power than she'd expected.

Glass fell on shrieking nobles and villagers as the lamps and crystals above them shattered. The guests took shelter under tables as a violent wind kicked up, causing plates and goblets to fly in all directions. Lightning crackled and laced through the clouds while thunder rumbled through the room, echoing off the stone walls.

Lucan used his magic to divert some of the shattered glass from falling on the young Castellus boy, screaming for the guard nearest him to take the boy to safety, then whipped around to glare at Sophie, his eyes full of rage. Before he could utter another word, lightning from her spell struck down at him with a deafening crack, missing him by only a few feet. He threw himself back as Sophie grimaced, her control wavering as she fell to one knee—the same one she'd hurt colliding with Lord Castellus what felt like ages ago.

The other mage yelled something at her, but she couldn't make it out over the now raging squall. The confidence she'd had moments before dissolved. It had been foolish to try this, she berated herself. An unfamiliar and unpracticed spell was so dangerous. Slumping forward, Sophie stopped feeding energy into the working, but that didn't calm the storm. Lightning struck again, this time, hitting one of the tables to her left. It exploded into splinters and embers, causing the people taking shelter there to scream and run.

No, no, no! she thought desperately as she watched the spell she'd cast surge out of control. Sophie tried to stop it, to end the spell's effect, but it was like grasping at air. She would have to ground out the energy, as the other wizard had done to her shield, but she didn't have the fine control to dispel something like this.

Lucan dashed to where she was kneeling. She raised her hands, but before she could throw up another shield, he grabbed her and pulled her face close to his.

"Stop this!" he shouted. People screamed around them as the wind blew over chairs that the guests had occupied only moments before.

All she could do was shake her head. "You stupid whore!" he yelled with a look of pure loathing, pushing her to the ground.

The interaction jarred her from the horror of her handiwork, and she scrambled away. With a flick of her wrist, an overturned chair righted, and Sophie used it as a stepping stool to propel herself on top of the long table where the nobles had been seated earlier. The wizard had turned his attention away from her and was trying to dispel the storm still churning above their heads. The wind whipped at her hair and sent villagers and nobles alike running for cover.

When she reached the edge of the table, Sophie jumped, trying to land near the exit. She slipped, smacking her shoulder hard into the door frame as she dashed out of the great hall and slammed the door shut behind her. Pain surged down to her fingertips, but she ignored it.

"Turin!" she cried, looking around wildly. "Khalil!"

"Sophie!" Turin's voice came from her left. She turned and bolted in that direction.

She spotted them at the end of the long corridor. Turin had an arm around Korynne, helping her walk. The poison must have still been affecting her. Sophie ran up to them, almost collapsing to her knees before Turin caught her with his other arm.

"Whoa! Sophie are you all right?" he asked.

"Fine," she gasped, clutching to him for balance. "Just a little tired."

"That was amazing!" he said, staring at her in awe. "How did you think of that?"

"I lost control," Sophie answered with a cough. "People who had nothing to do with any of this could have gotten hurt." She took deep breaths, trying to calm her pounding heart and spinning head. "I shouldn't have tried that."

"Well, it was a great distraction." He grinned, steadying her on her feet. "Are you able to help Rhyn walk so that I can protect the two of you?"

"The mage seems like she can protect herself," Korynne said, and it was the first time Sophie had heard her speak. Her voice was deeper than expected, and she spoke softly. Korynne looked Turin up and down pointedly. "She can defend us much better than you can with just that little dagger. What are you going to do? Poke at them while they stab you to death?"

Turin rolled his eyes. "Just take her, will you?" he said to Sophie.

"Let me get that anklet off of you first." She showed

Korynne the ring she'd taken from Lord Castellus, then knelt and lifted the hem of the lady's dress.

"Those bastards didn't hurt you, did they?" Korynne asked as Sophie touched the ring to the anklet, willing it to come off.

The question brought back the memory of the storage closet, and Sophie had to concentrate on unclenching her hands. "No, I put him under a sleeping enchantment before he could do anything to me." There was a small *pop*, and the seam in the anklet opened. The connection that Sophie still felt to Korynne faded, and she took the anklet, stuffing it in her pocket. They could dispose of it properly later with the other one she carried.

Korynne let out a bone-deep sigh as she was freed of the anklet's power. She closed her eyes, sagging more heavily against Turin, and whispered, "Thank you."

Sophie put Korynne's arm over her shoulders. Her left one throbbed painfully. There would be a bruise there in the morning. If they made it that long. "Are you able to walk at all, Lady Korynne?"

Korynne made a face as if she'd eaten something rotten. "Please, call me Rhyn. Anyone who risks their own life to save mine has earned that right." She leaned on Sophie as they moved. "I can walk a little. Ever since you switched out the potion, I've been getting more and more control back, but I'm still a bit shaky on my own. It should be much better in a few more hours." She gave the mage a tired smile. "That was some quick thinking, turning the potion into juice. And that storm! Are you a new recruit?"

The two women, following closely behind Turin, moved swiftly away from the great hall. The way they'd come wasn't directly adjacent to the kitchen and servants' entrance, so they had to find another way.

"Since I don't know what I could possibly be recruited for, I'm going to guess no," Sophie said, drawing a laugh from Rhyn.

"I heard you shouting Khalil's name. Is he here with you?" she asked.

"Yes," Sophie said. "He went to the dungeon to help Winna and our other companion."

"I can't believe Turin and Khalil are working together," Rhyn muttered, a smirk on her face. "Khalil told me that he didn't like him very much."

Sophie allowed herself a grin. "They do tend to argue. Well, as much as Khalil bickers with anyone, that is."

"Less talking, more escaping," Turin said with annoyance, throwing a scathing look at them.

At the other end of the corridor behind them, the door to the great hall slammed open. Yuri Golistin stepped into the passageway, sword drawn and an enraged look on his face. "How dare you!" he snarled as he spotted them. "Korynne Castellus is mine!"

Turin cursed and placed himself between the women and their newest enemy. He took a defensive stance with the dagger, his knuckles white on the hilt. "Go," he said to Sophie. "Find the others. I'll take care of this."

Sophie chewed on her bottom lip. She didn't want to leave Turin with just the dagger to defend himself, but what else could they do?

"Go!" he urged earnestly, not taking his eyes off the other man.

Sophie began to move away, but was pulled back. Rhyn seemed to be rooted to the spot.

"I..." the blonde woman began, staring intently at the knight. Sophie tried to move her again, and that seemed to bring the woman back to her senses. Her lips moved, but no sound left her mouth. Turin glanced back at her, his green eyes reflecting the torchlight. The muscles in Rhyn's jaw twitched, and she finally said, "Don't die."

Rhyn nodded to Sophie, and they hurried around the corner and down the next corridor, leaving Turin to face his older brother on his own.

They hurried along the passages. Sophie didn't know the castle well, but Rhyn directed her to turn right or left whenever she was unsure. The shouting and frantic voices behind them grew more distant as the pair pushed on.

After only a few minutes, Sophie was out of breath. The dungeon must be close. She was pretty sure that it was at the end of this hallway. They passed a few closed doors, and she feared that at any moment, they would burst open to reveal the castle guards waiting to capture them. Before she could see the entrance to the dungeon, something ahead of them rattled.

Thinking quickly, Sophie used her magic to throw open a door to their right and ducked into it, praying she hadn't just thrust them back into the hands of Lord Castellus's men.

To her relief, the room was unoccupied. It was adorned with four small beds and heavy footlockers. It must have been sleeping quarters for the guards. Sophie leaned Rhyn against the wall and whispered, "I'm going to check the corridor."

Rhyn nodded, a grim look on her face.

The mage carefully opened the door just enough to peek out, looking down the hall and toward the entrance to the dungeon.

A tall figure emerged from the dark stairway behind it, followed shortly by two smaller figures which appeared to be leaning on one another. The three paused, talking among themselves. She squinted, having difficulty making the people out in the dim torchlight, but after a moment, she was certain the tall one was wearing a blindfold.

Sophie threw the door open and whispered loudly, "Khalil!"

His head snapped in her direction at the sound of his name. She stepped back inside and put an arm around Rhyn, then the two made their way to the other group, stopping in front of the door to the upper floors she and Khalil had used the day before.

"Are you hurt?" Khalil asked as soon as she was within a few steps. He reached out, and Sophie gripped his hand with her free one.

"No," she said, a little breathlessly. "We managed to get out all right, but Turin is still fighting back by the great hall."

"Turin has trained for this. His skills are far superior to anyone else here," he said in a reassuring tone. "Don't worry about him." Khalil's head turned toward Rhyn.

"Yes, I'm fine," the Nightingale said, intuiting the question. Her next words were delivered casually, but Sophie thought she detected the relief in them. "Winna, are you all right?"

As the Nightingale and her companion spoke in rushed whispers, Sophie's attention turned to Eolisti, who strangely had not uttered a single word. One hand was wrapped around Winna's waist while the other held a sword she must have taken from a guard. The Anai supported Winna much as Sophie did Rhyn, but wouldn't meet her eyes.

Sophie felt the fear that had gripped her heart since they'd learned of Eolisti's capture melt away. The Anai looked the worse for wear, battered and bruised as she was, but she was alive and appeared whole. What was important was that her friend was back with them. Physical wounds would heal.

"The fourth floor is mostly unoccupied," Eolisti said, finally looking up at them. Her eyes had purple bags under them. "I was up there last night. There is a servants' entrance there that will take us directly to the kitchen. It's better than wading through all the guards in the entrance hall."

Khalil nodded at the Anai. His fingers slipped out of Sophie's as he turned to open the door next to him, revealing the staircase beyond. Then he took Rhyn's other arm and helped Sophie carry her up the stairs.

CHAPTER

TWENTY-EIGHT

Turin faced his older brother, holding only the dagger he'd taken from their mother. Yuri stared at Turin with a look of both fury and disbelief. The young nobleman's fine clothes were disheveled, and his eyes were wide and wild. A longsword was clenched in his right hand, lamplight glinting off the naked steel. He looked far from the perfectly composed and smug groom of a few minutes ago.

The knight stood between Yuri and the retreating women. He would not let him pass, brother or not.

"It's over, Yuri," he said as his older brother approached. The dagger seemed inadequate compared to the blade the other man held, but Turin did not want a fight. If he could convince Yuri that there was no saving this wedding, perhaps he would give up. "Turn around and go back to the great hall. Lady Korynne does not want to marry you. She never did. There is nothing more you can do. Go back to your parents."

The young lord squared off against Turin, his sword by

his side. He glowered at his younger brother. "Don't you mean *our* parents, Dimitri?" he spat out.

Turin's eyes widened. Yuri had finally realized who he was. "You know, and you're still doing this? Why?"

"Why?" Yuri snarled. "Do you know how many times I heard that I was the one who should have been left behind? That Dimitri wouldn't have messed up the way I always did? Mother and Father have compared me to you for years, lamenting that the son they chose to stay with Uncle was flourishing while I was never good enough. I had to sit there and say nothing while they sang your praises. Squired to the Lord High Commander. A knight by his twentieth year. Meanwhile, all of *my* achievements were overlooked." Yuri had the face of a man desperate enough to do anything to prove himself.

"Yuri," Turin said, trying to reason with him. "I am not your enemy. Our mother and father used my name to bend you to their will, you know that. Hells, I wasn't even there, and *I* know that. What you're doing is wrong. This whole wedding is a sham. You can't possibly think that everything is as it seems."

Yuri barked out a harsh laugh. "I'll tell you what it seems like. It seems like I was finally going to be freed from the scrutiny and pressure of our parents, but here you are again to ruin everything! This is the last time you'll get in my way!" Yuri raised his sword, lunging forward and swinging wildly at Turin's head.

Expecting the attack, he ducked as the blade cut through the air where his head had been. Turin tried to grab Yuri's arm, but his brother snatched it back and out of reach, slashing downward in a backhand swing. Knowing he wouldn't be able to dodge in time, Turin turned to the right on reflex, thinking of allowing Yuri's blade to hit his pauldrons instead of biting into his face, but he wore no armor and was reminded of that fact as his brother's sword cut deeply into the muscle of his left shoulder. He grunted in pain, and his left arm from the elbow down tingled and went numb, blood soaking the sleeve of his tunic. He stumbled back.

Yuri followed Turin's steps, pressing his advantage. He swung the longsword at his brother's face again, landing a scratch on his cheek as Turin whipped his head back.

"What's wrong, little brother? I thought you were supposed to be a knight!" he taunted gleefully. "You can't even defend yourself!" He slashed again.

Turin sidestepped the blow and tried to punch Yuri's face with his right hand, still holding his mother's dagger, and the motion caused Yuri to take a backward step. This was much different from the bouts they'd had when they were children with wooden swords. Yuri was far more skilled than Turin had expected, but he shouldn't have been surprised. He needed to be more careful.

Yuri scowled at him. "You think you can beat me with a dagger?" He lunged forward, aiming low, but Turin was able to parry the strike.

"I don't want to hurt you!" Turin cried, trying to reason with him. *I can't die here*, he thought desperately. *The others are still in the castle!* He hunched his shoulders, holding his injured arm to his chest. If Yuri wasn't going to give up, he would have to stop him, even if that meant hurting him. He pushed Yuri's sword away with his superior strength and aimed the point of his dagger at his brother's sword arm, slashing through his clothing and biting into the flesh beneath.

Yuri cried out in pain, jumping away. With a curse, he switched the longsword to his off hand, his eyes blazing with rage. "You know nothing of what I had to go through! You know nothing of the pressure that has been placed on my shoulders! The Golistin reputation rests with me. I deserve this!"

He charged, trying to run Turin through with his blade, but his anger had overtaken him, and the thrust was sloppy, allowing Turin plenty of space to step out of the way. He stuck out his leg, tripping his brother. Yuri stumbled and turned, still trying to land a blow, but Turin grabbed his wrist and followed him down to the ground, dropping the dagger in the process.

Yuri struggled under the weight of his younger brother, kicking and punching as he struggled to get his sword hand free. Turin used his numb arm to block Yuri's blows and slammed the man's wrist against the stone over and over again, trying to get him to drop the weapon. Desperate, Yuri tried to headbutt him, but Turin took it on the chin where it would do little damage and focused on disarming his brother until he let go of the sword, his knuckles swollen and bloody.

As soon as the sword clattered to the ground, Turin released Yuri's wrist, then pulled back and punched him as hard as he could across the jaw. Yuri's head bounced off the stone, and he stopped flailing, his limbs going limp.

Turin sat back, panting. He rolled off his brother and lay on the floor, clutching his injured arm and attempting to examine it. The pain in his shoulder was excruciating, and though his fingers moved when he wanted them to, he could barely feel them. There was no way that he would be able to fight. He would have to get a healer to look at it later.

With a grunt, Turin got to his feet, picking up the fallen longsword and surveying it. It was an expensive piece adorned with jewels and a lion's head on the pommel, but the blade was as finely made as his own and would suit his needs until he could retrieve the rest of his weapons. He took one last guilty look at his brother, unconscious on the ground, and moved to follow after Sophie and Rhyn.

Behind him, the door to the great hall banged open again just as he rounded the corner at the opposite end of the corridor. Voices exclaimed in outrage as they found Yuri, and Turin picked up the pace, running down the corridor with all notion of stealth deserted.

As he neared the end of the hall, Turin heard shouting ahead of him. *Damn!* he thought, slowing to a stop and looking around frantically. Just as he was about to resign himself to another fight, he spotted a door to his right that stood ajar. A brief look revealed a staircase behind it leading to the upper floors. Not having any time to waste, he slipped through the door and raced up the stairs two at a time.

TWENTY-NINE

Sophie, Rhyn, Eolisti, Winna, and Khalil moved as quickly as they could down the fourth-floor corridor with Sophie helping Rhyn and Eolisti half-carrying Winna. Eolisti had been correct. There were very few rooms before them. With all the commotion on the first floor, it seemed that the guards had been summoned away, so they moved through the hall with no one to stop them, for now. Khalil was in the lead, followed by the Anai and Winna, while Sophie and Rhyn brought up the rear.

Halfway down the corridor, running footsteps echoed behind Sophie. Thinking it a pursuer, she released Rhyn and whipped around, drawing in power and holding up her hands, ready to defend them all.

"Whoa!" Turin said, stopping in his tracks and throwing up his right hand, letting the pommel of the longsword he was holding rest in the crook of his thumb and forefinger while the blade pointed at the floor, swinging back and forth loosely. His eyes widened at the spark of electricity at her fingertips.

"Turin!" she gasped, dropping her hands. Sophie was so

relieved to see him that she wanted to throw her arms around him, but as her eyes traveled down him, she took in his various injuries. There were angry red lines on his neck and cheek where he had been cut, and his shirt was soaked through with dark blood at his left shoulder. "You're bleeding!"

"Yes, but I'm alive, and I prefer to stay that way," he said with a grin.

"What happened with Yuri?" Sophie asked as she chewed on her bottom lip. There wasn't time to stop and heal him, though she didn't know how useful he would be in a fight with his arm in that state. After a moment, she put an arm around Rhyn's waist again and began to turn to follow the others, but she threw him a worried look. "Are you going to be all right?"

"Don't worry about me," he said and tried to shrug his injured shoulder. He drew in a sharp breath through his teeth and winced. "I'm fine."

"Liar," Sophie growled. Rhyn's movement pulled Sophie's attention to her. The woman had one arm over Sophie's shoulders but was staring at Turin, the muscles in her jaw tensing as she clenched her teeth. She was furious. Was it because Turin was injured?

Turin looked back behind them, at the door that led to the lower floors. "Let's worry about it after we get out of here. Castellus's guards will find us if we don't keep moving." The knight raised his voice as he spoke his next words. "I assume you have a new plan?" he directed at Khalil.

Khalil's head turned so that they could all see his expression. He looked annoyed and didn't answer the knight. Eolisti glanced back and rolled her eyes.

"I'll take that as a no, then," Turin said under his breath.

"Yuri shouldn't wake up for a while, but I left him mostly unhurt. He'll have quite a headache, but at least he's alive." He laughed bitterly. "He didn't hold back. I'm not surprised, but I had hoped that if I ever saw him again, it would have turned out... differently."

He surveyed the corridor as they walked. Sophie knew why. This floor was less ornately decorated than the first and second, but it had more signs of being lived in. It would be where the Castellus family lived most of the time. "Has anyone figured out how in the hells we are going to get out of here?" the knight asked more loudly this time.

"We could slip out of the kitchen," Eolisti suggested. "Sneak out with the carts or find a carriage, like the original plan."

"The kitchen will be guarded," Khalil said as they approached the end of the hall and the servants' stairway that Eolisti had told them about.

"Everything will be guarded, Khalil," Sophie said. "We need *something*, though."

Rhyn spoke next, and her voice sounded stronger than it had before. "There's a passage in the kitchen storeroom that leads out of the castle. It will be guarded," she conceded at the look Sophie gave her, "but since it goes under the castle walls, it's still the best way out."

Khalil sighed. "How many guards?" he ground out.

Rhyn thought about that for a moment. "Probably no more than ten, but I can't be certain. When I arrived, security was light. The storeroom isn't that big, but there's no telling what Castellus has planned."

"They have to know that we're coming by now," Turin said apprehensively. "They'll be waiting for us there."

"There's no other choice. We'll never make it through the gates," Khalil said, and no one could argue with him. He paused to listen at the door that was painted the same color as the wall surrounding it. After a moment, he nodded and pulled it open, being the first to step through.

The group descended the winding stairs. Khalil stopped to listen at each landing and, when satisfied, continued. None of them spoke, fearing that anything they said would carry through the passage and alert a guest or guard to their presence. Sophie tried to listen for anything when they stopped, but all she could hear was the pounding of her own heart in her ears. She couldn't shake the feeling that wound in her stomach. No one said it, but there was a good chance that they wouldn't be able to escape the castle.

At the bottom of the staircase, Khalil held a hand up to stop them. Voices drifted through the closed door as someone passed just in front of it.

"...as many men as possible to the gates," one man said as he passed within feet of them.

"Have you heard what's going on? There was some sort of storm in the great hall." Sophie felt her cheeks grow hot as the guard continued, the sound of their footsteps and voices growing distant. "It's a disaster. Some of the guests said there was a mage disguised as one of the servants."

"No wonder the lord is so furious..."

They walked too far for Sophie to hear them anymore. Khalil waited for another minute before nodding and beckoning the rest of them to get close.

He pushed the door open slowly. No shouts came from the corridor, and he stepped out, the rest of them following cautiously. There was no sign of the guards. Sophie helped Rhyn out into the corridor, and they all hurried in the direction of the kitchen.

"Hey! What are you doing?" came a voice from behind them.

Sophie looked behind her to see two men in light armor with the Castellus house colors and weapons running toward them.

Turin stepped between her and the guards. "Go! I'll meet you at the exit."

She hesitated for a moment before heeding his words and hurried to the kitchen doors with Rhyn, taking the lead in front of Eolisti and Winna. Khalil stayed behind with Turin, guarding their retreat. Panting from the exertion of dragging Rhyn along, Sophie pushed the door open.

The kitchen was mostly the same as it had been that morning. Hot air hit her in the face as she breathed in the smell of roasting garlic and baking bread. Various items were still on the stove, cooking. The large table in the middle of the room was laden with food prepared for the feast, waiting to be taken out to the guests.

The difference was that, though Dalia and her assistants were still there, they were huddled by the ovens, staring at Sophie and Rhyn. A guard was standing in the far corner, next to a door that led down to the storeroom.

He looked startled as they burst through the doors but quickly recovered. "Lady Korynne?" he asked, uncertain. Then his eyes fell on Sophie. "You!" he snapped, reaching for his sword.

Before Sophie could react, Rhyn spoke.

"The lord requires your presence out at the gates," she said, and her voice had a quality that made Sophie's skin tingle. She could feel the magic in Rhyn's words, and it surprised her. No one had mentioned that the Phoenix could use magic. It was a subtle spell, and not particularly strong, but Sophie could feel the intention behind it.

The man blinked for a moment, confused, then shook his head once and took a step forward. "My lady! Everyone is looking for you!" Noticing the others again, he went for the weapon at his side.

"Try it once more," Sophie said to Rhyn.

The Phoenix glanced at her but didn't hesitate.

"The lord requires your presence out at the gates," the two women said in unison, and Sophie added her magic to Rhyn's spell. She let the woman direct the enchantment, giving it the power it needed to take effect.

The guard's eyes glazed over, going unfocused for a moment. "The lord requires my presence at the gates," he repeated, then turned toward the side entrance and left the kitchen.

"Dalia." Rhyn directed her gaze to the head cook, who was still standing in the corner. She stared at them with her mouth hanging open while the other women who worked for her cowered. "It would be best if you were not here when the lord arrives."

Dalia started at the words but, after a moment, seemed to regain some of her former countenance. She looked around at her assistants. "Well? Don't just stand there. The guests must be hungry since the feast was disrupted. Grab those platters and take them to the second floor." Dalia picked up one as well, and, with only an uneasy glance at Sophie and Rhyn, she and her assistants brushed past, leaving the kitchen empty.

"What was that?" Eolisti asked, her eyebrows climbing up her forehead. "Why did that guard just leave?"

"Later," Sophie replied. "Let's get out of here first."

Once the servants were out of the way, Sophie and Rhyn hurried across the kitchen to the storeroom. Sophie used her magic to throw the door open and helped Rhyn navigate the stairs while Eolisti and Winna followed close behind them.

As they descended the twenty or so steps to the storeroom, Sophie noticed something amiss. Before they reached the bottom, she realized there was light ahead of them where there shouldn't be. Rhyn had said there could be more guards down here and that it was likely for this exit to be watched. They could very well be running into an ambush, but they had no choice but to move forward. She conjured her second shield of air and energy that day and raced for the bottom step.

As Rhyn had said, the storeroom was not large, nowhere near as big as the wine cellar that Sophie and Khalil had visited on their first day. It could have fit ten short rows of casks with space to walk around. This storeroom housed crates and barrels filled with root vegetables and salt. Dried herbs hung from the ceiling and rested in bundles on the shelves that lined the room. It smelled of damp earth and stone.

The middle of the room was cleared of obstructions to make room for the five guards waiting for them, weapons drawn and hiding in the shadows cast over them from the four support pillars.

From behind one of those pillars stepped Lucan, a scowl on his face and murder in his eyes. Even though Sophie had been expecting to see him again before the day was done, her breath still caught as she jerked to a halt a few steps from the bottom. His gaze met Sophie's, and his frown deepened. There would be no offer of surrender this time.

As she raised a hand to reinforce her shield, Lucan yelled, "They are trying to kidnap Lady Korynne! Stop them!"

Eolisti rushed past Sophie as her shield redoubled in front of her and Rhyn. "Hide!" the Anai hissed to Winna as she jumped down the last few steps. She stumbled and winced but regained her balance in a moment. Then she charged at the nearest guard, sword at the ready and a wild grin on her face. Steel rang on steel as the man blocked Eolisti's strike at the last second, surprised at her eagerness to fight.

The other men moved toward them, and Sophie felt pressure on her shield, though nothing physical had touched it. She sensed the magic sustaining the protective enchantment begin to fray and fracture. Lucan's lips moved and his hands traced sigils in the air as his power attacked her spell, attempting to unravel it.

Rhyn pulled herself from Sophie's grip and stumbled forward, around Sophie's shield. Sophie opened her mouth to stop her, but the Nightingale turned back and threw her a wink, cutting off Sophie's protest.

"Thank the gods you are here!" she cried with a relieved sob. "They were trying to take me!" The fear in her voice sounded convincing. The guards hesitated, letting the lady pass as she rushed to Lucan and into his arms, collapsing against him.

The wizard's eyes narrowed as he caught Rhyn. He knew full well that she was acting—he was the one who had been poisoning her—but he couldn't attack her in front of the men who were trying to save their lady. It was enough of a distraction to break Lucan's concentration, and the assault on Sophie's shield eased. The guards weren't paying attention to Sophie anymore, watching the exchange between Rhyn and Lucan.

That gave Sophie an idea. She took a deep breath, focusing on Rhyn and moving her now free arm in a large circle in front of her. In front of the guards, four illusory images of Rhyn materialized out of the air. They looked and sounded like the real Rhyn, asking the men in front of them for help. The guards looked stunned, and their weapons drooped in their hands.

"My lady, what is happening?" one asked while looking back between the illusion in front of him and the real Rhyn struggling with the court wizard.

The man struggling with Eolisti ignored the illusions, swiping at the Anai as she danced out of his reach. Another guard that wasn't close to Sophie's spell charged toward her, his sword blade flashing. It connected with her shield, bouncing off and causing the air in front of her to ripple. Sophie took a step back from him. Her shield felt weaker than it should have. She could still feel the edges of it fraying and knew she wouldn't be able to keep it up for long.

The deflection of the weapon surprised the guard, and the shock from hitting her shield caused him to lose his grip on the sword. It clattered to the ground, and Sophie retreated a few more steps up the stairs while he retrieved it.

"They aren't real, you fools!" Lucan shouted, pulling his arm out of Rhyn's grasp. "Attack the Anai and the girl!" He waved a hand and said an incantation that Sophie couldn't hear.

Power coursed through the air. Rhyn's wrists and ankles snapped together, and she toppled to the floor, the silks of her gown fanning out around her. Lucan sneered down at her and then dismissed her as unimportant. He met Sophie's eyes, and there was a sudden sharp pressure at her temples. The illusory Rhyns flickered and faded as the wizard tried to break through her spell. He couldn't dismiss them completely, but the damage he'd intended had been done. The men around him saw that they weren't real.

To her left, the man with whom Eolisti had locked blades shouted out in pain as the Anai drew her sword across his thigh, dropping him to one knee. He rolled away from her and tried to stand, but only succeeded in crouching, his wounded leg shaking beneath him.

As the guards moved into striking range of the two women, Sophie heard rapid footsteps behind her. Khalil dashed into the storeroom, lunging between Sophie's shield and the guard closing in on her, his short sword flashing. The tip of the weapon slid into the gap in the man's armor, between the chest piece and the spaulder, with precision accuracy, drawing a cry of pain from the guard and a trail of blood as he reeled back.

"Khalil!" Sophie gasped. He stepped in front of her just as her shield faded away. Over his shoulder, she saw Lucan reach down toward Rhyn. Unable to get to her in time, Sophie wove her hands over her chest and threw up another shield between the wizard and his target. The spell was weaker than it should have been. She had used so much magic already that she was quickly becoming exhausted, but even so, it was enough to stop Lucan from reaching Rhyn.

The wizard glared up at her, but then there was another person rushing past Sophie.

Turin leaped down the last few steps, tumbled past the man swinging his sword at Khalil, and came up with a stab aimed at the back of his leg. The wound caused the guard to falter, swinging wide. Turin then grabbed his sword arm awkwardly but managed to pull him off-balance, throwing him to the ground.

"Stay down!" Turin commanded as he kicked the man's sword away.

As the last glimmers of Sophie's illusion wasted away,

another guard charged them, raising his sword and shouting, "Kill the mage!"

He was aiming for Sophie, but Khalil's blade caught the strike, and he parried the blow. In her panic, Sophie tripped on the stair behind her and landed on the stone steps, quickly scooting back and up another few stairs from where Khalil and the guard fought.

Another guard came up on Khalil's right while he was distracted. Before he could throw the first guard off, the second thrust his blade at him. Sophie almost screamed as the steel tore through cloth and flesh at Khalil's side, leaving a deep gash. Blood soaked Khalil's tunic, and he grunted, taking a step back toward Sophie. Keeping his weapon raised, he braced himself for another attack.

The final guard that had been distracted by the images of Rhyn swung at Turin's back. The knight managed to spin around and bring his longsword up in time to block the blow, but the angle was off, and the guard's sword slid along the edge of Turin's, glanced off, and found the flesh of the knight's already injured shoulder. He hissed in pain and used his good shoulder and arm to push the man off him. Turin gritted his teeth and held up his longsword with his still-working arm, his skin pale and his face drawn. He moved to stand next to Khalil, keeping the guards away from Sophie.

The man engaged with Eolisti collapsed to the ground as she cut into his other calf. The Anai stepped on his dropped blade before he could retrieve it and raised her sword, bringing the weapon's hilt down hard on the man's skull until he stopped moving.

Sophie wrenched her eyes from Eolisti as Khalil took a defensive stance in front of her. He dodged a stab from the guard on his right and grabbed the man's wrist, using the seconds before his attacker could pull back to cut a deep gash into his forearm through his tunic. Khalil released him and lunged, pressing his advantage and forcing the man to defend himself from the quick and precise blows.

I have to do something! Sophie thought as she took in a deep breath. Focusing her mind, she pulled on the energy of those around her, using it to fuel her spell. Magic was life and right now, the storeroom was filled with adrenaline-fueled vigor. She reached between Khalil and Turin, touching the guard that stabbed Khalil. As soon as her fingers contacted his bracer, she funneled that power and shoved him away, the magic propelling him across the room, knocking over a couple of barrels and sending him crashing into the opposite wall in a heap.

As she drew her hand back, she touched Khalil's side, using her magic again. There was a sudden ache on her own side as she pulled some of the pain from him, taking it on herself and letting him focus. She wouldn't be able to heal him in the middle of a fight like this, but she could dull the pain and make it easier for him to move. He would still need tending to after this, but at least the spell would keep him on his feet long enough for them to escape.

The guard in front of Turin swung his sword, but the knight parried the blow and used the momentum to bash the man in the face with the flat of his blade, breaking his nose and rocking him back on his heels. Blood sprayed the knight, but he ignored it as he shoved the guard back while the other guard that he'd pushed to the ground previously scrambled away, trying to retrieve his weapon from where Turin had kicked it.

Eolisti lunged at the guard still engaged with Khalil. The man raised his sword to block her, but she danced around the weapon, getting behind him and stabbing up and under his armor with her own blade. There was little more than a gurgling gasp from the guard before he crumpled, a pool of dark liquid spreading beneath him.

Holding her side, Sophie looked around frantically for the wizard. Over Khalil's shoulder, she spotted Rhyn on the ground next to one of the pillars, struggling to pull her wrists and ankles apart, but there was no sign of Lucan. Berating herself for losing sight of him, she searched the storeroom over the heads of her companions and their opponents. He wouldn't have left the fight so soon, would he?

As if in answer to her thoughts, there was that same ripple of magic that Sophie had felt before outside the storage closet, and the court wizard appeared in the corner of the room to her right, dropping his invisibility spell. He smirked as he raised one hand and pointed at Sophie. He had a clear line to her.

Before she could throw up another shield, searing light streaked through the air, and lightning hit her squarely in the chest. She screamed in pain and fell to her knees as a wave of thunder and raw force radiated from the strike, sending Eolisti, Turin, and Khalil sprawling.

The pain was so intense that Sophie could barely think. Gritting her teeth, she tried to stand but only succeeded in slouching forward. Her muscles twitched from the electricity that had coursed through her, and her limbs wouldn't move when she told them to. One thought was able to pierce through the pain. The lightning wasn't as strong as the storm she'd conjured up in the great hall. If it had been, she would be dead.

With an effort, Sophie glanced around. Turin had been knocked into the closest supporting pillar, and he lay on the ground next to it, unmoving. Khalil and Eolisti were struggling to get to their hands and knees, both moving like they were in immense pain. Sophie could still feel the ache at her side from Khalil's injuries, but it was overshadowed by the feeling of fire under her skin. She couldn't see Rhyn, but she had to be here somewhere. Had she been knocked back by Lucan's spell as well?

Footsteps sounded on the stairs above, and she looked up in time to see Lord Castellus and three guards stepping out of the shadows of the small staircase. His perfect bearing was gone. The Tanalin lord wore an open scowl, and the clothing and hair that had been so neat earlier that evening were rumpled and messy. He had the appearance of a man desperately trying to regain control of the situation.

Sophie tried to move away, but her legs still wouldn't respond. The lord glared down at her, then nodded to his men. Two of them left his side, one moving to loom over Sophie and the other to stand between Castellus and the rest of her companions. All three men drew their swords.

Before Castellus could give the order to finish them off, Rhyn stepped out from behind the pillar furthest from the stairs. She leveled a crossbow that she must have pulled off one of the unconscious guards at her father. There was a shocked silence, then his eyes narrowed dangerously, and he scowled.

"Drop your weapon," he growled.

"Call off the guards," she replied, the crossbow not moving an inch.

"Do you take me for a fool? I have you right where I want you. You're in no position to make demands." He raised his arms to either side in invitation. "Go ahead, shoot. My wizard will ensure your bolt never reaches me, and then you will be at my mercy again."

Rhyn laughed. "Me at your mercy, *Father*? You seem to be losing your touch," She grinned at him. "Have you thought about what people will say about all this? If you can't even control your own daughter, how can you possibly be trusted with more important things? I wouldn't be surprised if the emperor hears about this fiasco."

"How dare you?!" he shouted at her, his face reddening. "You question me, your father and the lord of this castle?" His fists clenched at his sides and his expression twisted in rage and disgust. "You have no idea what it is like to be the head of this family! To ensure that our legacy survives this utter joke of an imperial lineage. I am living in reality, where at any time, the other houses could pounce on us at the slightest sign of weakness." Lord Castellus laughed, and it was not a pleasant sound. "You're living in a dream and need to wake up. You will never be anything other than what I have made you!"

While the lord was shouting at his daughter, the pain had faded enough for Sophie to focus her mind. Her muscles had stopped spasming, and she could even flex her fingers. She glanced around the storeroom carefully without turning her head, looking for anything that could help them. Her eyes settled on Turin, lying against one of the support pillars, his eyes closed and his breath coming hard. It was difficult to tell if he was still conscious, but his tunic was wet again with fresh blood. If he didn't receive healing soon, the injuries to his shoulder could cause permanent damage. That was if they even made it out of here alive.

Her eyes traveled up the pillar to where it connected to the ceiling. If they were destroyed, would the stone above them come crashing down?

She sucked in a deep breath through her nose and

turned slightly toward Rhyn, only an inch so as not to alert the guards or the raging lord who stood only a few feet away. Their eyes met, and Sophie winked at her, praying that she understood.

"But I can be generous," Lord Castellus was saying. Three of the guards that had been fighting with Sophie and her companions had regained their feet. They loomed over the others, blades ready if any of them tried to move. "If you return to me willingly and marry that Golistin boy, I'll consider allowing these *criminals* to live." He said the word "criminals" with a sneer. "There's no need to add their deaths to the damage that has already been done here today. If you do not do as I say, I will kill them all and take you back anyway."

Rhyn stared across the room at her father, her aim unwavering. Her face was flushed, and she was breathing heavily as if she too wanted to scream and shout, to berate the man who should have been her greatest champion, but had instead made her life a living hell. She said nothing to him, rejecting his offer as resoundingly as if she had screamed it.

After a few seconds of silence, Lord Castellus's scowl deepened even further. He signaled to his guards. They raised their swords to execute Sophie, Eolisti, Khalil, and Turin.

At the last moment, Rhyn moved the crossbow's aim from her father to the guard looming over Turin. She pulled the trigger, putting a bolt into the man's chest, then threw the crossbow at the guard over Sophie, landing a direct hit and causing him to stumble.

"Kill them all!" Castellus screamed as Sophie slung a wave of red-hot fire at the lord, then rolled out of the way of her stunned guard's sword.

Lucan blocked the strike from hitting Lord Castellus, but while he was distracted, Sophie slashed a hand through the air, using the rest of the energy she'd managed to gather. All four support pillars exploded under the pressure of her will, raining chunks of stone and dust down on them all. Sophie directed the stones away from her friends with a few well-placed shields, then threw a hand straight up, using her power to shake the castle above them as the ceiling began to crack. She jerked her arms down as if yanking on a rope, pulling at the stone above them with her magic.

The remaining guards jumped to defend their lord as Lucan dashed toward the stairs, bits of dust and rock raining down on him. He threw Sophie one final glare as she staggered over to Khalil, then he was preoccupied with blocking the falling stone and getting Lord Castellus out of the storeroom safely. She could hear the nobleman cursing and screaming as he left. His people followed—all the ones that were conscious, at least.

Khalil was already getting to his feet when Sophie reached him. "Help Winna!" he shouted over the noise, pointing to the woman cowering by a crate near the stairs. Eolisti was already helping the injured Nightingale to her feet as Sophie dashed over to assist. Eolisti grabbed one of Winna's arms then turned her back and grabbed the woman's same-side leg, hoisting her body up onto her shoulders.

"This way!" Rhyn beckoned from the opposite side of the room. There was a loud, ominous cracking in the ceiling above, and they ran to the door she stood next to.

Sophie used another burst of power to break the lock and fling the door open, and they sprinted into the dark tunnel and away from the storeroom, Eolisti carrying Winna and Khalil half-dragging Turin.

There was a deafening crash behind them, and the narrow tunnel filled with dust and dirt. Sophie stumbled forward and threw her hands out, coughing and unable to see. She touched the cool, damp rock and used it to keep herself upright while still hurrying forward. Her ears rang in the sudden silence after the crash, only the sound of their heavy breathing echoing in the shaft.

After a few more minutes of fumbling around in the pitch-blackness, they broke clear of the cloud of dust. Ahead of them, a small amount of light shone through the keyhole in another door. Sophie waved her hand again, breaking the last set of locks as her legs grew weak and a different quality of darkness threatened to overtake her. Rhyn threw the door open, and the last dregs of setting sunlight illuminated the stones of the tunnel around them. A cold breeze hit Sophie's face, and she felt herself smile. There was still much more work ahead of them, but one thing was clear—they had escaped Tempest Hall in one piece.

THIRTY

The last thing Sophie remembered of Tempest Hall was seeing the sunset-painted walls dissolve into blackness as they left the castle behind them. The memory of their escape through the fields surrounding the village was a blur. The next thing she knew, she was in a dimly lit barn, blinking her eyes open. Lady Korynne was waving a small vial of some foul-smelling substance under her nose and asking her what her name was. Her words sounded like they were coming from a great distance or through water. *Wasn't she supposed to be getting married?*

"Sophie. Sophie, dear, wake up. We're not safe yet."

Her head felt like it was about to explode, and the rest of her felt like she'd been turned inside out. Sleep... sleep would help. Sophie let her eyes fall closed again until there was a sharp pat on her cheek, not quite hard enough to hurt, but certainly hard enough to prevent her from retreating into oblivion.

"No, Sophie, you can't sleep. You're badly injured."

Sophie stared at the blonde woman, trying to make sense of her words. She knew what they all meant individually, but she couldn't make her brain comprehend their collective message. Was she injured? It was hard to think. She was supposed to be working at the castle. The wedding was today, wasn't it?

"Here, drink this. It will make you feel better," Lady Korynne said, raising another small bottle to Sophie's lips.

This one lacked the foul odor of the first bottle, but the taste was bitter on her tongue. She wanted to spit it out, but the stern expression on the face of the woman stopped her. When the last of the liquid was gone, Sophie coughed at the burning sensation in her throat. As her breath returned, she realized she could think clearly again. Her whole body hurt, but as she looked around, she understood where she was and what was happening.

Sophie sat on the cold ground, her back to a wooden wall. Lady Korynne—Rhyn, now dressed in a simple shirt and trousers covered with a rough cloak—had straightened to stand and was stashing the now empty bottle in a pack. Beyond her, Khalil and Eolisti were finishing loading up a packhorse next to four other saddled horses standing quietly in the dimness. The small, slumped figure of Winna was seated atop one, and Turin held the reins of the others in one hand. He sagged against the corner post of a stall, breathing heavily. The knight looked exhausted and still cradled his injured arm close. He'd changed out of the staff uniform and wore a clean linen tunic.

With a jolt, Sophie's eyes jerked back to Khalil. Remembering that he had been hurt badly as well, she forced herself unsteadily to her feet. Rhyn lunged forward to steady her, dropping the pack she'd been carrying.

It was good that she had because, for a moment, the barn swam drunkenly, and blackness threatened to overcome her again. She grasped the lady's arms, closed her eyes, and took a few deep breaths until the spinning sensation faded.

Opening her eyes, she croaked, "Khalil... Turin..." Swallowing with some difficulty, she added, "need to heal them."

Rhyn's brow furrowed with concern, and she looked at each of the injured men in turn. Neither of them looked capable of the long ride ahead. When their eyes met again, the concern in Rhyn's still lingered, but she nodded her head once in agreement.

It was the Nightingale's turn to help Sophie walk. She didn't have far to go, though, since Khalil had approached after hearing her words.

"Sophie, I'm fine. Save your strength," Khalil said, but he couldn't hide the grimace as he stepped closer.

She ignored his protest and stretched out one hand to gently rest over the wound on his side. He too had changed clothes, but she remembered where their enemy's blade had pierced through his side. The muscles tensed under her touch as she lifted his shirt to reveal a hastily applied, blood-soaked bandage. She stripped it away as gently as she could. When her fingers prodded at the skin near the wound, Khalil gasped sharply, his body betraying the lie he'd just told her. She'd had a front-row seat as he'd taken several grievous blows, first from the guards, then from Lucan, and those were just the ones she knew about. A detached part of her mind lamented that she wasn't cleaning the wounds before trying to seal them magically. She knew there was a greater chance the healing could go wrong this way, but there simply wasn't time.

Sophie closed her eyes and, with an effort, stretched out her senses to the life within Khalil and herself. She gritted her teeth and pushed herself further until she could feel the spark of everyone else in the barn and beyond, the even fainter glow of the trees and other plants outside, dormant though they were for their winter rest. The energy came to her call slowly but surely, and she focused her will on the sticky, drying blood that marked the hole in Khalil's side. It seemed an eternity, and she felt a cold sweat break out on her brow, but eventually, the skin heated under her palm, and the blood dried and flaked away. She opened her eyes and let her hand drop when Khalil released an involuntary sigh of relief.

"Thank you," he said softly.

A lump rose in Sophie's throat, threatening to choke her, and her vision blurred with tears. She'd been so scared when he was hurt, but he was going to be okay. *No, no time for this*, she scolded herself, and she swallowed the emotion down. "You're welcome," she whispered.

Rhyn's voice near her ear helped bring Sophie back to the moment. "Are you sure you have the strength to heal Turin too?"

Sophie realized that she had started to tremble at some point, but she straightened slightly, though it hurt to do so, determined to prove that she was capable of this.

"Yes," she replied, willing fortitude into her voice. She raised her free hand and beckoned, "Turin?"

The knight passed the reins to Eolisti, who was looking on with an expression of worry, even fear, on her face. It was unsettling to see the confident Anai looking so shaken. What *had* happened to her in the dungeon?

Sophie's inquiry would have to wait. Turin stood before her now, looking almost as bad as she felt. She could tell he had been hurt as badly as Khalil—perhaps worse—but the gash in his shoulder was still the most obvious and worri-some-looking laceration. Choosing that as her focus, she raised her hand, concentrating again on the tacky feeling of the cut.

The swirling motes of energy were still all around her, but they came even more slowly this time. She began to tremble again, and there was a ringing in her ears, but she directed her attention where her skin met Turin's. She felt the heat beneath her fingers again and strained to feed the healing process, but before she could be sure that it was done, her knees buckled, and the world melted away into nothing again.

SOPHIE DRIFTED in and out of consciousness over the next few days. The first time she remembered anything after the barn, the twin moons were high in the sky, and she found herself astride one of the horses, bundled in one of the sleeping blankets under her cloak. She sat in front of Eolisti, the Anai's body being the only thing keeping her from tumbling off as she frantically looked around to see where her other companions were.

Turin was riding in the lead as he had on the way to Tempest Hall, and Khalil once again brought up the rear, this time, leading the extra packhorse. Two other cloaked figures shared the mount in front of her and Eolisti—Winna and Rhyn.

Everyone was quiet, and they rode at a steady trot along the frozen road.

"We're all safe, Sophie," Eolisti's soothing voice whispered to her. "Go back to sleep. You need your rest. We'll handle it from here."

That was all the prompting she needed to retreat into unconsciousness once again.

The next time she woke, dawn was breaking through

the trees, and she was being handed down from the horse. Strong arms cradled her like a child and carried her to a waiting tent and bedroll, where she slept for what felt like only moments before she was shaken awake and coaxed to eat.

She felt a little more human after eating a bowl of hot soup, a little more in charge of her faculties, and she offered to do some healing again. Rhyn, however, reminded her that Lucan would know her magic now and may be able to track them. Sophie thought she should have known that, but was still too tired to do anything but accept the information with a weary nod.

The next few days passed in a similar fashion. Sophie nodded off while riding, only to wake when they stopped to rest or to eat, and neither of those for very long. She remembered little of those days, trusting her companions to continue their journey while she recovered.

Near sunset on the third or fourth day since they'd fled Tempest Hall, a new feature broke the landscape.

A small wooden fort with walls timbered from large trees came into view. From the watchtowers flew red banners with something white in the center. Though the need to close her eyes again pressed in upon her, Sophie kept staring at the emblems as they approached. Eventually, the shape resolved into the profile of a lion, its mane smoothed back from its face in a swirl.

Did that mean they were finally in Morigael? For a moment, Sophie thought that Griffin's Bluff was far less impressive than she'd imagined it, but then she remembered overhearing someone say they were heading for a small outpost on the way to the mountain fortress. Still, she felt a tension she had not known she was carrying leave her as they passed through an opening in the wall. Castellus's men wouldn't follow them here.

Their group drew to a halt inside the courtyard, and she watched Rhyn hand Winna down to Turin with practiced motions just before Eolisti did the same with her. As she felt surrounded by the safety of Khalil's arms once again, the weight of her fatigue pulled more insistently at her. This time, however, it was with a sense of peace that she surrendered to it.

A SOFT SNORE teased Sophie's mind back into awareness and she shifted, but that small motion was all it took for the sensation of pain pulsating from every muscle in her tired body to distract her from sleep. With a groan, she cracked one eyelid and found the source of the noise that had awoken her.

Eolisti lay inches away, one arm flung over her head, perfectly oblivious to her friend's suffering.

With a frustrated sigh, Sophie clamped her eyes tightly closed again before opening them fully. Though her sore limbs protested, she sat up enough to examine her surroundings. Aside from the bed she shared with the slumbering Anai, the small room was furnished with three others, all occupied. The room's only other feature, a low-burning, covered lamp hanging near the solitary door, shed enough light for her to make out the forms of Turin, Khalil, and Winna in each of the others. The two men occupied the beds closest to the door. They were all sleeping soundly, and she noted that Winna looked far better than when Sophie had first seen her. The woman she had met in the dungeon would have died there if she and her companions had not intervened.

As carefully and quietly as she could manage, Sophie extracted herself from under the rough woolen blanket to sit on the edge of the bed. Rubbing at her eyes, she wondered how long she had been asleep. There were no windows to hint at the time of day, and even though she had been unconscious for most of the journey here, she felt like this last stretch was the first time she had truly gotten any rest.

A look down at herself revealed that she was still dressed in her stained servant's garb from Tempest Hall, but her feet were encased in thick, warm stockings. Near where her toes touched the floorboards rested her now-worn traveling boots. Stiffly, she reached for them and pulled them on. She found a heavy winter cloak draped over the footboard and awkwardly fastened it around her shoulders. Though the motions hurt, the small amount of warmth they had generated in her muscles was a relief at the same time. A walk might help her clear her head and soothe her aches.

Turning toward the door, she crept forward as quietly as she could, lamenting that she hadn't thought to wait to put on her boots until *after* she was out of the room. There was no way she was going to try taking them off again now, though. Her hand connected with the metal of the latch, and she smiled at her success.

"Where are you going?" Khalil asked softly.

Despite her aches, Sophie jumped and clamped a hand over her mouth to restrain a startled squeak. Khalil was still lying on the bed with his eyes closed, but a knowing smirk touched his mouth. Was he *laughing* at her?

Sophie hoped he felt her glare. "I need some fresh air."

He moved to rise, but she crossed the distance between

them to place a hand firmly on his chest, pushing him back down.

"Rest. I'll be fine on my own here."

Khalil must have agreed with her assessment, for he just smiled and settled back on the bed again.

Though she had disturbed one of her companions, she still lifted the latch as silently as possible so as not to wake anyone else and exited the room. She closed the door behind her softly and found herself in a short hallway lined with a handful of doors. More hooded lamps flickered in sconces on the walls. No other sounds reached her ears, but she assumed there must be soldiers here somewhere. She tried a few of the doors until she found a washroom. Sophie used her magic to warm the water in the washbasin and cleaned herself up as best she could.

Once finished, she stepped back out into the hallway, looking around. At either end of the hall stood other doors, but daylight seeped underneath only one of them, making her choice easy.

When she stepped outside, the frigid air clutched at her throat and made her gasp momentarily at the drastic temperature change. Her breath fogged the air before her face until she got her breathing under control again, belatedly realizing she should close the door behind her to keep the bitter chill out. It had been cold at Tempest Hall, but she marveled that she hadn't taken note of it as they rode, exhausted as she'd been. Now the snow-capped mountains she had seen in the distance on the way from Mattina were poking up above the walls all around her.

Once she had regained her composure, Sophie was able to survey the interior of the small outpost. A backward glance revealed that the building she'd just exited was as small as it had seemed from the inside, with smoke curling lazily from a chimney. It had a wide clear walking area all around it, covered with overhanging eaves that sheltered firewood and some crates. There were a few men outside, soldiers that were moving barrels from a wagon into one of those eaves. They were bundled up in thick winter jackets, gloves, and wool hats all in red and white like the banners that fluttered lazily in the breeze. One nudged the man next to him and they both waved at her. Managing a smile, Sophie waved back.

As she turned away again, she saw that the gate they must have ridden through when they arrived stood opposite her, with a modest stable built into the wall to the left of the gate. A thin layer of snow coated the courtyard, though it was littered with footprints from the men living here. The entire outpost was set up in a triangular shape, with two guard towers set at either end of the side that held the fort's main exit. Wooden stairs led up to walkways that lined all the walls, and Sophie felt drawn in that direction.

Climbing the steps was difficult, but it gradually eased some flexibility back into her wooden extremities, so she took her time and pressed on. On her way up, she passed a guard who greeted her with a friendly smile and a nod. At the top, she stopped to marvel at the towering mountains again. Though they were blanketed in white, she could see now where the rock thrust forth from the earth to tower high enough that not even the trees dared scale them, and all that remained was a shimmering, glassy surface that gleamed in the late afternoon sunlight. Without the bitter wind, it was almost a pleasant experience.

As if summoned by her thoughts, another gust of wind from the south abruptly peeled back her cloak, seeking the tiny holes in the weave of her garments. Sophie closed her eyes against the bitter gale and blindly captured the hem of her outer garment, clutching it tightly around her as the wind died away to nothing again. Opening her eyes, she spotted Rhyn on the wall nearer to the southern tower.

The woman was also dressed in a long cloak, her hood thrown back to show her blonde hair escaping a braid where the wind had teased it. She was bent forward at the waist, leaning on the wall with both forearms. If the cold bothered her, Sophie couldn't tell.

Sophie's feet seemed to pull her in the direction of the lone Nightingale. As she drew nearer, fat snowflakes began to float down on the little fort. Though the sun was still visible in its eternal march toward the horizon, darker clouds drifted directly overhead. By the time she stopped next to Rhyn, the woman's shoulders were covered in a light dusting of the winter precipitation, and she had tilted her head up to let the flakes fall directly on her face. Sophie realized that this was probably the first time she'd caught a glimpse of the real person behind the masks of Lady Korynne and the Phoenix.

Sophie rested her arms on the wall as well, staring out at the frozen landscape that extended as far as the eyes could see. After several minutes of companionable silence, Rhyn opened her eyes and said, "You know, the first time I came through these mountains, I was even younger than you probably are now." She sighed heavily before continuing. "How little things change."

Curious but not wanting to pry too much, Sophie asked, "Was that when you met Turin?"

Rhyn snorted softly and glanced over at her, amusement dancing in her eyes. "Is *that* what he told you?"

Sophie felt herself blush a little, though she didn't know why. That *was* what he had told her, so she nodded.

Smiling, Rhyn simply returned to gazing out over the

treetops. "No, that's not when we first met, but I don't suppose he would remember."

Sophie waited, expecting Rhyn to explain further, but the silence went on long enough that Sophie began to get uncomfortable. She was about to excuse herself and leave the woman with her thoughts when the Nightingale finally spoke again.

"Running is the easy part, you know," she said sadly, and a touch of bitterness crept into her voice, "especially when you're running from people who were supposed to have loved and protected you. Learning how to be the person you want to be without letting that change you, that's the hard part."

Sophie did blush then. She knew Rhyn must be referring to herself, but her words hit way too close to Sophie's reality. She didn't know *who* she wanted to be, but she knew who she *didn't* want to be. She would *not* be a pawn or someone who hurt others for their own gain.

Rhyn's eyes drifted over to her again, and Sophie's thoughts must have been written all over her face, for the woman's tone softened. "It's not easy, but I believe it can be done. We just have to surround ourselves with people who do love us, who help us *be* better, and who see us as we truly are. They're the ones who matter. They're our true family."

As if to punctuate her words, a door below in the courtyard opened and closed. Rhyn stayed leaning on the wall but twisted to look over her shoulder, and Sophie turned to follow her gaze. Khalil was crossing the open area, his heavier winter cloak pulled close around his shoulders, hood once again obscuring his face. Sophie felt her lips curl up into a smile when she thought of how far they had come and how he had stood by her through it all. She wouldn't be standing where she was now, safe and on her way to a new life, without his, Eolisti's, and Turin's help.

"But maybe you've already figured that out," Rhyn added, meeting Sophie's eyes with a crooked grin. There was no judgment or mockery in the words. Just truth.

"Yes, I think I have," Sophie replied with a nod, though she wasn't entirely comfortable with the turn the conversation had taken. As much as she'd denied it, Turin had been right. Her feelings about Khalil were... complicated. Better to change the subject. "So, what will you do now?"

She suspected the woman knew she was deflecting, but Rhyn let it pass with a shake of her head, looking off to the south again, her expression sobering. "What I've always done—keep moving forward. There's always another mission, and I'm not dead yet, thanks to you and your friends."

Always another mission. Sophie wondered what Rhyn's life must be like, going from place to place, risking her life to complete whatever task she'd been assigned. She imagined it could be exhilarating, and Tempest Hall had been anything but dull, but it also seemed lonely. "What about the family *you've* chosen?"

With a sad sigh, Rhyn finally straightened and crossed her arms. "Sometimes, it's better to watch over them from a distance."

A creak of the walkway behind Sophie made the Nightingale look over sharply. Turning around, she spotted Khalil approaching, one arm peeking out from under his cloak, holding one of the scratchy wool blankets from the sleeping quarters. Sophie knew that he could move silently if he wished, so he must have been politely alerting them to his presence.

A hand on Sophie's shoulder brought her attention back

to Rhyn, whose intent gaze met her own. "Thank you, truly. I'm here because of you. No matter what happens or where we both end up, I will never forget what you did and what you risked for me."

Sophie began to duck her head in embarrassment, but Rhyn stooped until Sophie met her eyes again. With a firm nod, the woman who was the Phoenix squeezed Sophie's shoulder before she stepped away and walked toward the stairs. As she passed Khalil, she tapped a fist on his shoulder and said, "Don't do anything I wouldn't do."

His mouth twitched, and he murmured, "That's not very prohibitive."

Rhyn staggered and clutched one hand to her chest, throwing her head back as if she'd been shot. "Ouch," she said with a grin and turned one last time to wink at Sophie before she disappeared down the stairs.

Sophie chuckled under her breath at the interaction. It reminded her of how Khalil had been with Captain Alvar on their voyage from Omer. The two were friends, and she had caught them playing cards—quite a feat for a blind man— in the captain's quarters on more than one occasion. It was nice to see these glimpses of his less serious side.

The hooded face turned in her direction, and she realized he must have felt her stare. Sophie blushed and turned to watch the snowflakes drifting into the surrounding forest. "I thought you were going to rest," she said, rubbing one arm to generate warmth.

"I could hear you shivering from all the way back in the room."

She heard the smile in his voice and looked up in time to see it still curving his lips before he shook out the blanket and wrapped it around her shoulders. Once that was done, he stood next to her, facing the forest as if he, too, could see their surroundings outside the wall. Unlike with Rhyn's companionable silence, new worries nagged at Sophie, and she could not be content to stay quiet for long.

"So, what will happen to me when we get to Griffin's Bluff?" she asked, unable to keep her thoughts to herself.

"You'll rest," he said, tilting his head slightly and nodding with each point as if reciting a well-rehearsed list, "figure out what you want to do and where you want to settle. The Nightingales will help set you up somewhere safe."

Sophie was silent for a long moment as she felt a creeping fear start to grip her heart. The near future that Khalil described was nothing less than she'd expected, but she felt like there was something missing. She wasn't sure what she wanted, but she found herself hoping for more. Sophie didn't want to watch over her friends from a distance. She didn't want to be alone.

"Will you be leaving then?" she asked. *Leaving me?* The words were on the tip of her tongue, but she held them back.

It was Khalil's turn to pause. "I don't know," he finally answered. His expression softened. "Sophie, I know you're scared, but no matter what happens, you won't be alone."

She felt his compassion, but it was too close to pity and not the emotion she realized she hoped to sense in him. Unbidden, a single tear fell hot on her cheek, and she forced herself to keep her breathing steady so as not to betray her response. Khalil had helped her escape Zo'rahn and had quite literally saved her life on multiple occasions. She was safe, and they had succeeded in rescuing the Phoenix.

Forcing a smile, Sophie discreetly dabbed at her eyes with the corner of the blanket. He had already done so much for her. She couldn't ask anything else.

Staring out at the blurry landscape, movement on the nearby road caught her attention. Sophie blinked her eyes rapidly, thoughts of concealing her feelings momentarily forgotten, and she peered at the figure riding up the road from Tanalin.

"Is that..." she trailed off, unsure that her brain was correctly interpreting what her eyes were seeing, until a flash of gold caught the fading sunlight. "Elindiir?"

"So, after a sudden thunderstorm in the great hall, most of the guests ran for their rooms. Many wanted to leave altogether, but Lord Castellus had the place locked down," Elindiir recounted, unable to mask the excitement in his voice.

The whole group of travelers sat around a small table in the outpost's dining area, listening raptly as the Anaiian ambassador shared his perspective on the events at Tempest Hall. Even Eolisti, who had conspicuously positioned herself as far as possible from Elindiir, couldn't help casting glances in his direction as he told the story. A fire burned cheerily in the hearth, and Sophie had gladly taken one of the nearest seats after her walk on the chilly walls, which gave her the spot directly across from the man of the hour.

Elindiir explained that part of the castle had collapsed in on itself not long after the storm. He didn't think any of the attending nobles or servants had been hurt, but wasn't sure. The court wizard had come to his quarters and threatened to detain him, but he'd politely pointed out that they did not have the grounds to hold an ambassador, and attempting to do so would invite an international incident on top of whatever other drama they had already allowed to descend on the gathering.

"He didn't like that at all," Elindiir said with a smirk. "I thought he might try to keep me anyway, but Castellus intervened. How would it look if his court wizard was holding a foreign ambassador based on false accusations?"

Despite the threats and upheaval, the Anai had lingered an extra day to fulfill his obligations and attend the wedding. He recounted that Lord Castellus had told everyone that Lady Korynne had graciously stepped aside for her cousin, who was supposedly madly in love with Yuri Golistin. He said his thoughtful daughter—despite knowing it was not what her father wanted—convinced her cousin to take her place, to marry her true love.

The aforementioned "Lady Korynne" had just taken a sip of her drink as he told that part of the story, and choked, drawing chuckles from most of the others gathered, except Turin. The knight had been uncharacteristically silent and in a dark mood despite the levity around him. He rose from his seat across from Eolisti, abandoning his dinner to stand in front of the fire, leaning a forearm heavily on the mantelpiece as he stared into the flames.

Elindiir continued merrily as he explained how the nobleman had made up a story to explain away his daughter's disappearance the night of the final feast, and how worried he'd been that she'd fallen ill on such an important occasion.

"No one believed it, of course," the ambassador noted, "but what could they say in the man's own home?" He waved a hand dismissively and shook his head. "It will just be another piece of gossip at court."

"I'm sure he'll *love* that," Rhyn chimed in, her voice edged with sarcasm.

"Anyway," Elindiir concluded, his eyes still crinkled with mirth, "I'm heading to Griffin's Bluff next. There's a route to Nemethy near there, and I was eager to get out of Tanalin."

Though he spoke to all of them, his eyes lingered on Eolisti. For her part, the Anai was doing a relatively good job of pretending the ambassador didn't exist, but at the mention of Griffin's Bluff, Sophie saw her eyes fly up and meet those of the man she'd been so assiduously trying to avoid. Not for the first time, Sophie wondered what had passed between them back at Tempest Hall.

Rhyn, who had been sitting between Sophie and Winna, stood and raised her cup to Elindiir in a silent salute before downing its remaining contents. The ambassador lifted his cup in return before turning to Khalil, asking when they planned to be leaving for Griffin's Bluff. Khalil indicated that most of them were still "recovering from their travels" and would likely need to stay another night before moving on.

Meanwhile, Sophie's eyes were drawn back to the fireplace, where Rhyn had approached Turin, the two speaking animatedly in harsh whispers. No one else seemed to notice, but it was clear to her that they were arguing. Sophie felt a little guilty for witnessing even this much of their private conversation, so she tried to turn her focus back to Elindiir and Khalil, the ambassador congratulating them on such a spectacular escape. He was cut off midsentence as Turin's voice rang out across the small room.

"What do you mean, *tell you what*?!" Turin thundered. He was gripping his mug so hard that Sophie was surprised it didn't crack under the pressure. He glared down at the blonde woman. "You disappeared, and I didn't hear from you for years!"

All conversation around the table ceased, and every head in the room turned toward the Knight of the Realm and the Phoenix.

"That is *not* true! I wrote to you," Rhyn pointed out. She didn't seem to notice the attention. "You wrote back to me! Clearly, you received my letters."

"Once a year!" he countered. "And that only started *three years* after you'd been gone!" Turin ran one hand through his hair in frustration, looking as though he was trying to calm himself. That effort proved to be in vain. "You told me you moved to the countryside!"

"I did!" she exclaimed, but her anger dissolved quickly into sheepishness as she added, "for a while."

The glare was back. "You could have told me what you were doing!"

Though it had seemed like the Nightingale had been on the verge of conceding something, at Turin's words, her eyes grew heated again—this time, with a low and furious burn. "No, I *really* couldn't, and not that I need your approval, but would you really have just gone along with it?"

Ignoring the storm brewing in front of him, Turin railed on. "At least I would have known! Instead," he cried, pointing a finger in Rhyn's face, "you chose to *lie* to me for the past seven years!"

Not waiting for a response, the large man turned his back on her and marched out of the room, leaving everyone stunned in his wake. Almost as one, all eyes tracked back to Rhyn, who still stood in front of the hearth, mouth open and strangled sounds coming from her throat. At that moment, with the fire blazing behind the woman, Sophie couldn't help but picture her mythical namesake, a firebird poised to lay waste to any that stood in her path.

The Phoenix blinked hard once, her eyes darting to her seated companions before she clenched her teeth in a wordless shout and stomped after the knight. She slammed the door to the small room behind her but could be heard distinctly through the closed door.

"You don't get to call *me* a liar and walk away, *Your Highness!*"

A hush fell over the room as Rhyn's footsteps retreated. The only sounds were the crackling of the hearth and the creak of the bench as someone shifted uncomfortably.

Elindiir broke the silence first with a polite clearing of his throat. "So, Khalil, what are your plans after Griffin's Bluff?"

The blind man sighed, and his lips were drawn as he said, "I'll find out when I get there."

CHAPTER

THIRTY-ONE

The pass to Griffin's Bluff was covered with a fine dusting of snow as the group made their approach. The outpost had provided them with a safe place to take some much-needed rest, but they couldn't stay there forever. The soldiers there had given the group of seven more supplies and fresh horses, then sent them on their way. It had taken two more days of riding up into the mountains, but as the sun sank low on the horizon on the second day, the fortress and the little town surrounding it were finally in sight. Looking up at Griffin's Bluff, the stone fortress reminded Sophie of when she and Eolisti had first reached Ta'Shela, the mountainside monastery where Khalil had joined them. It too had loomed over a little valley with a village below, though this structure was easily ten times the size.

A lot had happened since Sophie had left her home all those months ago. Being so close to the end of their journey was a relief, but she was also anxious. The future before her was full of unknowns. She didn't want to say goodbye to

Eolisti or Khalil, but their obligation to her was complete once they stepped through those gates.

Technically, Eolisti's had ended back in Omer, but the Anai had insisted on accompanying her at least as far as Khalil did. Would other assignments be waiting for them? How long would it be before they left her to face her new life alone?

Golden sunlight caught Elindiir's hair, giving it a warm glow as he raised a hand to shield his eyes. Turin bounced along in front of them, his horse trotting toward the town while Rhyn and Winna's horse followed closely behind him. Sophie couldn't help but smile. She'd made some new friends since they had gotten off the *Westwind* in Mattina, and she didn't want to leave their company soon either. As she watched, Eolisti pulled her horse up beside Elindiir's, and the two of them rode next to each other, talking quietly. The second night they were at the outpost, Eolisti told Sophie what had transpired between her and Elindiir while she had been in the Tempest Hall dungeon.

It sounded to Sophie like Elindiir had only been trying to convince the wizard that he was not working with them and to spare Eolisti the more painful ways of extracting information from her. It was a necessary subterfuge, but it had hurt her friend all the same. Hearing someone she cared about talking about her like she was nothing had damaged Eolisti's perception of the other Anai, and now she was guarded around him. Sophie could understand that feeling of betrayal all too well. Eolisti had been giving Elindiir the cold shoulder at the outpost and on the first day of their ride through the mountains, but as the group neared their destination, she seemed willing to speak to him again.

After a while, Sophie let her eyes drift over to Turin, who was in the lead. The knight was riding along in silence, but he was in good cheer as he waved to a pair of young women they passed. They'd reached the cobbled road that led up to the fortress just before dusk, and while they were all tired and hungry, Turin insisted on pushing through to Griffin's Bluff.

"It's just ahead," he'd said. "There will be soft beds and hot meals waiting for us."

Some of the townspeople stopped and stared at them, but for the most part, they acted like this happened every day and went on with their lives. For all Sophie knew, a group of strangers riding into town was commonplace. The young women giggled and waved back at Turin, giving him covert glances as he rode by. He seemed comfortable in this environment, more so than Sophie had ever seen him. Griffin's Bluff was his home, and he was happy to be here.

Rhyn brought up the rear of the group behind Winna and hadn't said anything since coming in sight of Griffin's Bluff. Sophie didn't know the woman well enough to judge her silence but thought she seemed tense. Sophie didn't get the impression that she was exceptionally cheerful, but it felt odd that she was so quiet. After Rhyn had chased after Turin back at the outpost, Sophie was sure that they'd made up or at least come to some sort of agreement, judging by the state she'd found their sleeping quarters in later that evening.

Rhyn was probably feeling similar to how Sophie felt, anxious and afraid, like at any second, she could turn around and ride off in the opposite direction. Though hopeful, the thought of being alone again overshadowed any relief Sophie felt about her journey being over.

Khalil was also silent, but that was not out of the ordinary. The conversation they'd had at the outpost came to mind, and she tore her gaze from the man riding beside her. Trying to push the emotion that had welled up in her chest back down, Sophie stared ahead. This was Khalil's job. She shouldn't read anything more into it.

Even so, a part of her hoped he would stay with her, at least for a little while longer.

The gates to the fortress stood open in the waning light, banners of red and white waving lazily in the light breeze. Griffin's Bluff appeared to be even bigger than Tempest Hall, with walls surrounding the fortress at least thirty feet high and parapets lining the top. More structures made from the same gray stone could be seen over the walls, towers, and walkways dusted with snow. There were multiple archways to pass under as they rode up to the gates. Sophie could see small vertical slits in the stone, no doubt to shoot arrows into any invading army. It made her feel uneasy, but she tried to remind herself that these people had agreed to help her. She gripped the reins tightly in her hands and tried to look more confident than she felt.

As they entered the courtyard, a small group of men in shining silver armor walked up to meet them. At the front was an older man with white-blond hair and a long crimson cloak with gold embroidery. His armor gleamed, and he held himself as someone important, striding toward their group with purpose. The same profile of a lion that adorned the banners was etched into his breastplate.

Sophie felt her heart skip a beat. For just a moment, she thought she was looking at Rhyn's father, Lord Castellus, but as the man in the armor drew closer, she could see that he was taller and more muscular, with a slightly wider nose and a more prominent jawline. He waited patiently for

Turin and the rest of them to dismount, his eyes roving over them.

The resemblance to Castellus was so strong that this man could have only been the lord's brother and Rhyn's uncle. Which also meant this was the Lord High Commander.

"Lord High Commander," Turin said as he straightened his clothing, confirming Sophie's suspicion. "I didn't realize our arrival warranted a welcome from a man of your importance." Despite his words, Turin looked pleased.

A warm smile spread across the older man's face, seeming to chase away the chill in the air. "Of course I would come out to greet the ones who rescued my niece." They clasped forearms, and the older man looked over the rest of them. "You are all welcome here. I'll have food and rooms prepared…" He trailed off when his eyes fell on Sophie, and he frowned. "My lady, I—"

The doors of the main building opened, and four more knights exited, led by a man with sharp features and muddy-brown hair. They walked briskly toward the travelers, and the man in the lead stared directly at Sophie. She shivered, and it had nothing to do with the crisp mountain air. Whoever this person was, he seemed to have a lot of interest in her.

The Lord High Commander sighed as the new men approached, and he glanced back at Sophie again, the apologetic look on his face making her stomach tense. She had a feeling that she knew what was coming.

The man pulled up next to the Lord High Commander and finally looked away from the mage, instead offering Turin a small smile. Eolisti stepped toward Sophie and took her hand, interlacing their fingers and holding on tightly. She must have sensed it too.

"Lord Veryan," Turin said as he clasped the man's forearm in greeting. "It is good to see you, but I am confused as to why you're here." He looked around at the knights flanking the other man. "Is something wrong?"

"Dimitri," the man named Lord Veryan said with a nod. Then he waved to someone behind them. There was the clinking sound of chains straining as the gates closed, echoing off the stone walls with a ring of finality. He fixed Sophie with that detached stare again and said to the knights, "Take the Zo'rahni mage into custody."

As the men moved toward her, Sophie glanced around at the faces of her friends. Turin looked surprised, but he made no move to stop them. Khalil's lips were pressed into a thin line, but he also did not respond. Rhyn had the same detached stare as Lord Veryan, and Elindiir's and Winna's faces held almost no expression at all. Eolisti was the only one to react, snarling as the men came nearer.

"Get away from her!"

Sophie felt a great swell of affection for the Anai, but she knew that without the support of the others, this was a fight that she could not win. Sophie squeezed Eolisti's hand, then pulled away from her, stepping out to meet the knights. There was a sinking feeling in her stomach, but she told herself that there had to be a reason for this. These people were supposed to help her. After everything they'd been through, fighting now seemed pointless.

She stared down Lord Veryan in the way she'd seen the wizards of her family do. "Very well," she said with all the dignity she could muster, her heart pounding heavily in her chest.

"Sophie—"

"It's okay, Eolisti." Sophie tucked her hands into her cloak to hide how much they were trembling. "I'll be fine."

The knights led her to the main building. They didn't touch her but surrounded her in such a way that she was never out of arm's reach. Sophie glanced back at her friends as the large double doors closed behind her, wondering when she would see them again.

About the Authors

Accountant by day, writer by night, Vivian Bricker has been penning fantasy stories since she was old enough to pick up a book. She lives near Denver, Colorado, with her husband and three dogs: Hiro, Kalli, and Mira. Free time is hard to come by, but when she has a few extra hours, she likes to paint, practice archery, and run tabletop roleplaying games.

@VBrickerAuthor

Karen Nobles also lives near Denver with her husband and their giant rescue dogs, Stella and Hugo. In order to keep her babies in the luxury they deserve, Karen spends her weekdays chained to a desk writing contracts. In her free time, if she isn't writing, you're likely to find her training to kick ass at the local gym, exploring the wild mountain forests near her home, or dreaming up new adventures—for her characters and herself!

brickerandnobles.com

www.ingramcontent.com/pod-product-compliance
Lightning Source LLC
Chambersburg PA
CBHW020342010826
48973CB00005B/1244